THE CENTURION

"Old men ought to be explorers." At a time in life when his days often seem to be one long wait to die, retired sea captain Martinus Harinxma heeds the exhortation of T. S. Eliot. Gently prodded by his loving wife Sylvia, he takes up dowsing and, to his wonder, discovers he has a genuine gift. Soon he is following a trail of ancient ruins back in history to the darkly violent world of a fourth-century Roman centurion. As his own and the centurion's destinies mysteriously collide, Martinus confronts a nightmare that has dogged him for years. In the wellsprings of his subconscious — or is it a ghostly reincarnation? — there lies an explanation for his actions during a fateful World War II encounter when the ship he commanded and the U-boat attacking her both went down, causing huge loss of life.

De Hartog has explored man's mystical yearnings before, but never with such stark eloquence and power. *The Centurion* is a magical portrait of an aging man glimpsing the vast miracle and enigma of life.

"A spellbinding novel, a tour de force combination of mystical exploration and compelling narrative drive."
Publishers Weekly

"A magnificent storyteller. Like the ancient mariner, he holds you with his glittering eye and his stirring tales of wonder." *New York Times*

THE
CENTURION

Jan de Hartog

ROBERT HALE · LONDON

ISBN 0 7090 3967 0

Robert Hale Limited
Clerkenwell House
Clerkenwell Green
London EC1R 0HT

Printed in Great Britain by
St Edmundsbury Press Limited, Bury St Edmunds, Suffolk
Bound by WBC Bookbinders Limited

Author's Preface

When, after World War II, I became acquainted with peace-time Britain, one of the discoveries I made was that in England ghosts are members of the household.

Our neighbor in those days was the writer J. B. Priestley. J. B., as he was known, lived in an old manor house complete with ghost. I remember talking to his wife in her study; she was urging me to invest my earnings in the stock market. I was about to tell her that I did not have enough money to invest when her dog, a mongrel called Phaeton, leaped to his feet, back bristling, and growled as he followed with his eyes something which seemed to make its way from one end of the room to the other. Mrs. Priestley appeared to be irritated by the fact that I was paying more attention to her dog than to her; when I suggested that the dog must have seen something, she said, "Oh, it's the ghost. As I was saying . . ."

At one time their small son Tom, in his playpen in the garden, suddenly burst into howls; when asked what was the matter, he cried, "Tell that nasty old lady to go away!" There was no old lady; it was the ghost again. The five daughters of the family had, each in turn, been wakened in the middle of the night by a hand touching their faces. The housekeeper said she had seen dishes move on the counter all by themselves.

I took those stories with a grain of salt until one day J. B. told me they were going away for a week and asked if I would look after the coal-fired boiler of their central heating. I was happy to do so; twice a day I went next door to stoke the ancient monster in the basement. At that time a Dutch shipmate of mine called Willem was staying with us; one morning he walked over with me. While I was in the basement, Willem wandered about the house. When finally we left and he saw me double-lock the front door, he said, "Hey! What about the woman?"

"What woman?"

"The woman upstairs! The housekeeper or whatever. She's still in there."

I was sure she was away, but went back inside and called, "Miss Pudduck! Are you there? Hallo!" There was no response; the house was empty. "Where did you see her?" I asked.

"Up there, on the little landing at the end of the passage. A youngish woman, wearing a long dress. She crossed from one side to the other; when I said 'Good morning,' she nodded and smiled. Maybe she's in the attic."

I said, "Willem, the housekeeper is away this week. You've seen the ghost."

He would not believe it. He had been a radio officer on oceangoing tugboats in wartime, which makes for healthy realism; he was convinced there was a woman in the house. I took him back inside and showed him the little landing at the end of the passage. It had been bricked in on both sides about a hundred years earlier; now it just hung there over the stairwell to the basement, inaccessible except by ladder. He still refused to accept that he had seen a ghost for the first time in his life, but I knew he had. Her name was Anne; three hundred years before she had been locked up by her husband, a man much older than herself, after a passionate adventure with a gardener. He had kept her locked up until her death. At least that was the story.

The ghost as part of daily life was not the only paranormal activity around the Priestley family. Mrs. Priestley's sister, a charming woman called Edith Holland, known as Aunt Ena, was very active in that respect. She lived with a tweedy spinster friend near Oxford; her cottage was a jolly Noah's ark with dogs in armchairs, ducks on the kitchen counter and cats yowling blue murder when mistaken for cushions in the only armchair not occupied by dogs. The kitchen was normally full of people having their fortunes told, drinking tea, or making marital arrangements for their pets.

Aunt Ena was a genuine clairvoyant. She had had many unusual experiences, one of which was used by J. B. in a play called *The Long Mirror*. One evening she described her latest experience. She was visiting a neighbor, a mother with two young children who lived in a sixteenth-century manor house. She casually looked out of a window into the garden and saw, under a tree, a blond young man in Elizabethan dress, holding a flower in his hand. He was in the process of having his portrait painted. He spotted her, waved the flower at her, she waved back and asked her friend, "Who is that charming young man in the garden?" Her friend took a look; there was nobody there. During the days that followed Aunt Ena saw the same young man several times, coming out of doorways in his antique costume, walking toward her down the street. She began to realize he was someone special, and ultimately became convinced that he was young William Shakespeare.

I was fascinated, but the family seemed only mildly interested. In those days, most English families included an elderly aunt who saw Shakespeare. Or Nelson. Or the beast of the moor. Or its footprints.

Some months later the curator of a museum in London, one of J. B.'s Cambridge friends, came down for the weekend. During dinner J. B. happened to tell the story of Aunt Ena and Shakespeare; when he mentioned the flower, the curator cried, "Wait a minute! I think we have that painting in our cellars!"

A few days later the painting was retrieved from the cellars and Aunt Ena traveled to London to see it. The moment she set eyes on it she said, "Yes, that's the man."

Alas, that was where the matter ended. The picture bore no signature, it was of the period but badly painted; the curator could hardly hang it with a notice saying, AUNT ENA SAYS THIS IS SHAKESPEARE. But it was a fascinating story; the family urged her to write it down. She had written a couple of books before which had attracted little interest, but this time her experience and the finding of the portrait would surely have a different reception.

She was persuaded and wrote the book under the pseudonym Ruth Holland. It was called *One Crown with a Sun,* from a list of stage properties found among the Henslow papers. It was published in 1952 by Jonathan Cape; the blurb described it as "A remarkable book—a biography of Shakespeare in the form of a novel."

It was a beautifully written, thoughtful story about young Shakespeare, but the author's personal experiences that had brought it about were not mentioned. Even J. B.'s recommendation on the dustcover said only that it was "A strange, haunting book." And Ena's dedication "To Maud, Elizabeth, and Jasper, in whose house I looked from a window" meant nothing to anyone outside the family.

Her secrecy baffled me; it reduced the book to just another romance about Shakespeare. Why had she not written about her psychic experiences? Maybe in those days one didn't. Interest in the paranormal was far from general in the fifties; it was considered a laughable superstition and the risk of ridicule by reviewers was great. Yet, to me, the most interesting part was her own experience. What effect did seeing the ghost with the flower have on her life? How had she felt when she was shown the actual painting? Did she have any idea what the purpose was of her experience? Was there a purpose?

Those questions remained unanswered. She did not speak of it again and died some years later, taking her story with her to the grave. Thirty-eight years passed. I had forgotten all about her and Shakespeare when suddenly, out of the blue, I found myself facing the same predicament that had bedevilled her.

I am a dowser; I have the gift of locating water underground with the aid of a forked stick or a pendulum—any small weight suspended from a string which starts to swing in a circle when over water. I never attributed any psychic dimensions to the gift; I considered the ability to locate underground streams or buried objects as something that most people could develop if they had a mind to. There are many theories as to how it works; I came up with several myself, but they are irrelevant. The fact is that there is nothing exclusive about the ability to dowse. African bushmen have it, Australian aborigines have it, we all had it fifty thousand years ago when to find water was a matter of life and death. It is one of several human faculties no longer crucial to our survival that have become dormant. But they are not lost; the faculty called dowsing is locked into our genes and can be reactivated in many of us.

In 1981 my wife and I were looking for locations in the west of England for a television documentary on the history of the Quakers which I had written and was to narrate. One weekend, weary of motoring around the countryside writing up locations and making hotel arrangements for the camera crew, we decided to take a few days off and do some dowsing. We were staying in Shrewsbury in Shropshire. I bought a local map and looked for a juicy archaeological site which might have some hidden passages or buried foundations for me to spot by pendulum. The place I picked was the ruin of an old castle in the grounds of a college.

We drove over there, received permission to explore the ruin, and I set out to have a shot at tracing it for buried foundations. There was little left of the castle itself: three walls with holes where the windows had been. Inside the walls the pendulum circled strongly in one specific spot. I wondered why; judging by the strength of the reaction, I thought it might be a substantial piece of masonry, more than just the foundation of an interior wall or even an underground passage. After a number of passes over the site, I concluded that buried under the ruins of the castle there must be the remains of a Roman fort.

The crucial experience, however, was not my locating a Roman fort. Suddenly, in the midst of my dowsing, I found myself asking questions about its history, something I had never done before. I had always limited myself to questions like "Is it deep?" and "Is it made of stone?" The pendulum said yes or no in answer to these questions by changing the direction of its swing. Now, suddenly, I was receiving answers to questions about what had happened sixteen hundred years ago; I picked up, by question and answer, a bizarre incident in which the garrison of the fortress and a centurion had been involved in the year 338 A.D.

My first reaction was: imagination. Obviously, as a writer, I had become bored with questions about foundations and earthworks and started to entertain myself by fabricating this incident. But when I tried a few other locations indicated by pendulum, I was given more information about the same centurion and his company. It was all highly entertaining; then the television series reclaimed me and I had to abandon the fantasy. But it stayed with me and began to germinate into the idea for a novel.

There is a time in the life of almost every writer when he is attracted by ancient Rome. Offhand, I can think of a dozen colleagues past and present who have written novels about Claudius, Julian, Hadrian, Lucan, and Virgil. I don't know why ancient Rome as a subject tempts writers when they get older, but I fell for it too. Out of the episodes I had fantasized grew a story about the Roman reconquest of Britain after the Barbarian Conspiracy in the fourth century A.D. I researched the period, enlisted the help of a Cambridge undergraduate, Andrew Neather, who dug up a treasure trove of information from the archives, and started on the preliminary construction of the novel.

I am a methodical writer. I spent months planning the book down to the smallest detail; after that came the time to check on the atmosphere and nature of the countryside where the action took place. I planned an itinerary of seven locations and took off by car with wife, camera, and tape recorder. On the first location, some Roman remains near Birmingham, I casually asked, after recording the physical aspects of the place, "Can you give me any idea of what actually happened here?" It was a playful question; to my surprise the pendulum responded positively. It was a moment of choice: would I allow my subconscious, or whatever it was, free rein at this point? There seemed to be no harm in doing that.

I soon came to regret the decision. Instead of fleshing out my planned story line, the pendulum demolished the book. All the characters were tossed out, all the locations were changed, and their number increased from seven to thirty. Instead of a Roman general of genius, the story now concerned an anonymous career officer who had played everything by the book, made no waves, and whose name had vanished in obscurity. I received this information by question and answer; occasionally, it was almost as if I saw what had happened. This may sound neurotic or like self-hypnosis; it may have been both. However, I was not alone in this.

In the tenth volume of his *Study of History* Arnold Toynbee describes how he came to write that work: while visiting the ruined citadel of Mistra he had a sudden experience of the reality of the day it was destroyed by barbarians. It was more than creative imagination or an act of identification; he actually lived through that April morning when out of the blue an avalanche of wild highlanders from the Mani overwhelmed the city, forcing its people to flee for their lives and massacring them as they fled. Gibbon's *Decline and Fall of the Roman Empire* owed its origin to a similar experience in the Capitol.

Blake, Kipling, and Yeats describe it. And while waiting for a hansom cab outside a theater one foggy evening, Baroness Orczy saw in the cone of light of the gaslamp nearest to her an eighteenth-century fop take snuff, flick shut the little box, and tuck it up his sleeve, while a voice in her mind said, *The Scarlet Pimpernel.*

So, Aunt Ena saw Shakespeare, I dowsed a Roman centurion and found myself faced with the same dilemma she had faced: do I tell the story of the man or the story of my quest? Aunt Ena had chosen to mention only Shakespeare and leave herself out of the picture; the result had been disappointing. Now, thirty-eight years later, I discovered what had been her real problem: how to make her experience convincing. William Rees-Mogg, ex-editor of the London *Times,* comments in his autobiography on a similar flash of retrocognition:

> If someone who has complete confidence in his senses, and knows himself to be in his right mind, finds that he has a sudden glimpse into the past which is as real in physical detail as an experience of the present, he has no right to call on anyone else to be convinced. But he is very likely to be convinced himself that the materialist explanation, which depends on the absolute character of time, cannot be true.

This may not sit easily with everyone; for those reluctant to accept his conclusion, the late Thomas Lethbridge, keeper of archaeological treasures at Cambridge, offers a formula in *The Legend of the Sons of God* which may enable them to go on reading while retaining their scientific virginity: "I may not believe it, you may not believe it, it is an idea worthy of our consideration."

Arnold Toynbee and Gibbon called their experiences indescribable. To me, as a novelist, that was a challenge, so I started to write my story. I soon discovered that the autobiographical mode was less effective than having another narrator tell it; the subject proved too volatile for an excitable author, bright-eyed with creative imagination. I decided that the narrator of *The Captain* and *The Commodore* was better suited to do my story justice. We were the same age, certain elements in our lives were the same, including our fascination with General Theodosius and Roman Britain in 368 A.D. So I let Commodore Martinus Harinxma, a down-to-earth, sober-minded, canny old realist, stumble upon dowsing and take it from there.

But how about the nature of my experience? What was it? What did it *mean?* The experience itself was real enough, no one can bully me out of that, not even I myself. There are two possible explanations for it. One is that in the ruins of the castle, by some unknown psychic process, I actually picked up the trail of a historic centurion and proceeded to trace his steps with the aid of my pendulum. The other is that, via the pendulum, my superconscious—or whatever it is my brain communicates with while dowsing—made short shrift of the earlier concoctions of my creative imagination and provided me with a better book. I would not know which of the two is the more exciting.

My friend Colin Wilson thinks I came upon a real person and his experiences in 368 A.D. I prefer the other explanation. Either way, in my seventy-fifth year I received a gift from the gods.

To paraphrase Tom Lethbridge: I may not believe it, you may not believe it, it sure beats bingo.

THE CENTURION

CHAPTER ONE

*

In the autumn of 1986 our youngest son Martinus, a KLM pilot with a lethal taste for girls that were too young for him and sports cars that were too expensive, finally married his latest airline stewardess, a Canadian blonde. By that time we had moved to a retirement village in the south of France, so my wife Sylvia and I flew from Nice to Vancouver for the wedding.

I had looked forward to visiting Vancouver again; I had been there several times while still at sea and found it one of the most beguiling cities in the world, but this time the wedding hysteria spoiled it for me. Our new in-laws were in a state of near dementia, especially the women, and the wedding was, like all weddings, dominated by women. The forced gaiety, the despair at hems that were too short, at caterers who were too busy and florists who ought to be hung from a lamppost drove the father of the bride and me, who otherwise had little in common, together in the instant palliness of useless drones. He took me under his wing and we started the protracted binge the occasion seemed to call for. It depressed me to see young Martinus swagger into a situation he did not have the brains to visualize; once the mating frenzy was over, it seemed to me, they would not have an intelligent word to say to each other.

After the banquet, my boozing companion sprang a surprise. Now that they had found a safe haven for their daughter he and his wife were planning to go on a world cruise, starting in Vancouver and ending in Boston eighty days later. How would we like to drive their car to Boston for them instead of flying back to Europe direct? It was the right time of year for a drive down the trans-Canada highway, fall had started with its gorgeous colors; if we did not hang about we might even get to the Adams River in time to witness the salmon run, a spectacle we would never forget. I thought it was a long way to go for two people in their seventies, but Sylvia loved the idea.

1

So, a few days later we set out in a spanking new Mercury
Marquis full of electronic gadgets, armed with picnic basket,
thermos bottles, and keep-awake pills called Nixnap. We
reached the town of Kamloops the weekend the salmon were
running. I had vague memories of movies in which a lot of
wriggling fish tried to climb waterfalls; I was not prepared for
the spectacle that awaited us. The salmon ran in these huge
numbers only once every four years: two million of them battled their way upriver, back to the spawning grounds where
they were born. When they entered the estuary from the ocean
a mysterious change took place in their appearance: from sleek
silver fish they turned into red monsters and the males grew
fangs. They hurled themselves at the first rapids, a near impossible passage which they attacked again and again, a number
of them dying of exhaustion in the process. On they came,
wave after wave; the river boiled with their frenzy. The survivors faced a whole series of further obstacles: thundering
waterfalls, logging operations, a hydroelectric dam. Leaping,
crashing, crazed in the throes of the biological imperative, they
fought their way upriver, back to the still waters of the upper
reaches where those who made it would spawn, fertilize, and
die in the same spot where they were born.

It took us two days to follow the stages of this incredible
journey; we ended up in a forest near the spawning grounds on
the Adams River. It looked as if a village fair was in progress
in the clearing: hot dog stands, tents with souvenirs, native arts
and crafts, and, cruelly, bunches of smoked salmon. The crowd
was in a holiday mood; whole families were picnicking at long
tables in the sun, the children dressed up as Indians with T-
shirts saying I WAS THERE and SALAR THE SALMON.

We made our way through the crowd to the river, now a
clear shallow stream running over a bed of pebbles. It was a
place of amazing quiet. In almost religious silence a long row
of people stood lined up on the river's bank, watching the
drama in the water: thousands of salmon milling around, males
ferociously fighting over females who were trying to find a spot
to lay their eggs that had not been taken up by someone else.
They made nests in the pebbles by circling, digging a hollow
with their tails, laid their eggs which were then fertilized by the

victorious male, shreds of flesh hanging down his body after the fighting. The female stayed around to defend the eggs against intruders; the male, depending on his condition, went on to find another female. Eventually, exhausted by the spawning, the fertilizing, the fighting, they would grow paler and paler to finally turn over, faintly twitching, and be carried off by the current, past thousands of wriggling bodies in the frenzy of procreation. Dead fish literally carpeted the banks of the river downstream.

It was a disturbing spectacle for a man my age. I left Sylvia photographing and wandered upstream, away from the crowd. At a given moment I found myself alone at a stretch of the river as still as a pond, which none of the fish had been able to reach. I sat down on a rock, haunted by what I had seen; suddenly I spotted from the corner of my eye a movement in the clear water. One salmon had managed to get this far.

It was a huge male, already white with encroaching death, covered with scars and bloodless gashes, survivor of the incredible battle. I watched him circle slowly; he behaved as if, freed of the biological imperative at last, he was becoming aware of himself as an individual. Unique, alone, he moved quietly through the water; then he noticed me sitting on the rock on the river's bank. He turned on his side; one golden eye peered at me under the rippling water. He swam away, returned, looked again. I lowered myself to the water's edge, getting my feet wet; he approached me to the point where I thought I could smell him, a faint smell of death. In his new awareness, he appeared obsessed by curiosity for me; then other vistas seemed to lure him on. After one more circling, a last look, he swam slowly upstream, into the forest, the unexplored world. Perhaps he turned to look back, but by then he was out of sight.

I could identify with him totally. I imagined myself striking out for—where? What was there left for me to explore? My life was over. I had said farewell to the sea; the sunlit shimmering days, the starlit nights had ended.

The forest closed over the distant silver of the river. I could not walk any further upstream, virgin brush barred my way. How far would he get, I wondered, before he too keeled over and drifted downstream to the mass grave on the banks of the river?

My God, I thought. My God.

*

That night we stayed in a room in a self-conscious hostelry with chintz curtains, four-poster, brass bed warmer, a bookshelf full of paperbacks and mediocre food. The wine was poor too, and I was out of Alka-Seltzer, but Sylvia loved it. We spent a pleasant evening reminiscing about our newlywed son and his cuddly bride, relishing the thought of no more sports cars, no more long-legged teenagers flashing smiles under thundery skies threatening paternity suits. With our after-dinner coffee we had a local Drambuie so highly perfumed that it would have been better applied behind the ears; when finally we climbed into the swaying four-poster we were both happily sozzled.

In Sylvia's case that meant she fell asleep at once; in my case the wine and the liqueur started to ferment in the warm darkness of my stomach. The result was pure acid; I switched on the bedside light, went to get a drink of water at the washstand, belched at the mirror and expected to see a star etched in the glass. It was going to take forever to get back to sleep; I went down the bookshelf striking matches in search of something to read. *The Altar of Honor* by Ethel M. Dell. *The Kinsey Report. Peyton Place. We Are the Earthquake Generation.* The last of my matches took me to *The Faber Book of Modern Verse;* the match went out and I took it back to bed.

Sylvia had started to snore delicately, almost thoughtfully. I climbed in beside her, opened the book at random at a poem called "East Coker" by T. S. Eliot, an evocation of a rural wedding in the seventeenth century. I skimmed through it, irritated by the lack of rhyme; suddenly a line caught my eye: "Old men ought to be explorers."

I started a few lines back.

Home is where one starts from. As we grow older
The world becomes stranger, the pattern more complicated
Of dead and living.

True. My world had become stranger, the pattern of dead
and living more complicated. My old wireless operator who
had gone down with the ship during World War II was more
real to me than my eldest son Tim, a live bank manager. By
now, I had more dead friends than living ones.

"Old men ought to be explorers." I lowered the book and
stared at the canopy of the four-poster. It was made of pink silk
and pleated in the form of a sunburst. A busy little spider was
abseiling toward Sylvia. "Don't be stupid," I thought. "If you
land on that woman's nose there'll be hell to pay." The spider
seemed to receive my message; it hesitated, then hauled itself
back toward the pink sunburst.

Should I explore the life of spiders? Thought transference to
other species? Antique furniture? It sounded like an old man
doodling. I had been there before, the first time I retired from
the sea at the age of sixty. After a few halfhearted efforts at
carpentry and bird-watching, I had found a hobby that suited
my temperament: research into the life and times of a Roman
general, Count Theodosius, supreme commander of the third
invasion of the British Isles in 368 A.D. What started me off on
him was the casual discovery that he had transported his
troops and matériel across the English Channel in barges built
especially for the occasion and towed by triremes, the first
deep-sea towing job in history. I began to research him and his
period with gusto, even joined Latin evening classes in the
lycée in Cannes where I sat mouthing *Gallia omnis divisa est
in partes tres* among the teenagers and the housewives. I also
joined a barbershop quartet called The Cheerleaders and took
up golf.

I was doing fine when the company hauled me back. Their
newest and largest tugboat had been sold to Taiwan for some
mysterious reason and was about to sail from Antwerp to Kao
Hsiung, towing a thirty-thousand-ton dry dock. They wanted
me to sail on her, not as master, of course, I was too old and
no longer had my license, but as adviser to the Chinese captain;
the ship was manned, they said, by expert Chinese sailors from

a small island north of Taiwan. I fell for it; only when we were at sea did I discover that the giant tugboat was a lemon bent on drowning us all, that the Chinese crew were fishermen who had never seen a tugboat in their lives, and that their captain was so incompetent that he locked himself in his cabin. There I was, master after God *de facto* on a suicidal monster with a crew of Stone Age fishermen who were under the real command not of me but of the cook, an ancient Chinese woman called Ma Chang. The voyage took six months; the tug nearly turned turtle twice, but I managed to keep her upright and to fall in love with her in the process. At the end of the voyage she was sold for scrap. It broke my heart; I had lost the last love of my life. I came home with a tame rat on my shoulder, a canary in a cage, and saw myself through the eyes of our neighbors: a caricature of the Ancient Mariner. I tried to take up life as a retiree again and discovered that everything I had done and liked during my first retirement had turned to ashes. My Roman research was fatuous; by now I knew all there was to know about Count Theodosius and the Barbarian Conspiracy. The Cheerleaders were an excuse for communal boozing. My wife's poodle, which I had taken for daily walks for years, was a pampered creep of minimal intelligence and whining disposition. The walks were not walks but an old man panting up shallow slopes, clutching the skin over his heart at the top. Photographs of my demolished tugboat arrived: a dozen stacks of scrap iron with her name, forlorn, on the bow of a splintered lifeboat. Then my rat, a bright, funny little creature called Louis, was mauled by the dog and died. He had stowed away in Antwerp and accompanied me everywhere since, sitting on my shoulder, rolling over to have his stomach scratched, sleeping at the foot of my bed, sticking his cold little snout in my ear at dawn. I buried him on the top of the hill where I went every day during my walk, and mourned.

Mourning became a full-time occupation. I mourned not just for him but for myself, washed up, useless, an old age pensioner homesick for the sea. I slid into a depression, became morbidly fascinated with death, read books called *The Afterlife, Living On, Is There Life after Death?, Beyond the Veil.* Now I was told old men ought to be explorers.

Explore what? There was nothing left to explore. No mysterious glinting river opened up for me as it had for the salmon. My life was over, all there was left to do was wait.

The busy little spider was still hauling itself back to the sunburst. Its tiny efficiency and humorless determination wearied me; I turned off the light.

*

The trans-Canada highway was spectacular, but there came a moment when we both longed to get off it. Before Montreal we turned south, crossed the U.S. border and motored down a minor road through the riot of colors of the New England fall in the direction of Boston.

It was late in the afternoon when we reached the first sizable village. It was called Danville; we started to look for a motel. To our surprise it turned out to be impossible to find a vacancy; the little town was in the throes of a fair, the streets were thronged with people, there were booths on the village green. I wanted to drive on, but Sylvia felt we had done enough driving for one day and we went on looking. Finally we found a motel on the other side of town that had a cottage available, primitive by Canadian standards, but with television, space heater, and kitchenette. At least we would not have to go into the crowded town for a meal. We had fruit and yogurt Sylvia had bought that morning and made ourselves a cup of tea.

I had been given a complimentary local paper when I registered; while Sylvia made the tea I leafed through it and discovered it was not a fair, the crush in town, but the annual convention of the American Society of Dowsers.

I asked, "Do you know what dowsers are?"

"No. Yes—wait: It has to do with water witching. With a forked stick or something. Why?"

"This whole town seems to have surrendered, body and soul, to the water witches. There are lectures and workshops in all the churches, the Masonic Hall, the firehouse, the high school gymnasium . . ."

"No wonder we had a problem finding a room." She put a cup in front of me. "What's on television tonight?"

"I'll look." I turned to the TV page. "There's only one station. What's the time?"

"Gone five."

"Local news and weather on now. Then the CBS news, then a rerun of M*A*S*H, then a party political broadcast, then Dallas, then—well—some documentary or other." I did not tell her what it was.

But she picked it up, as was her wont. "What's it about?"

"Air raids on Europe during the Second World War."

"Have we seen it?"

"We may have. I don't remember."

The trouble with marriages of long standing is that it becomes increasingly difficult to hide something from one another. She said, "Let me see," and took the paper from me.

I watched her as she read. The documentary was about the Australian Air Force during World War II, with interviews of the survivors; it was the last thing I wanted her to watch. Her first husband Johnny had been shot down over Düsseldorf in 1943, two weeks after their wedding.

But she said, "Sounds interesting. I'd like to see that."

"Are you sure?"

She gave me a level look. "It's considerate of you, but I want to see it. I think I owe it to him. To all of them." She folded the paper and that was that.

We had tea and yogurt while watching the local and the national news, M*A*S*H, and Dallas, then it came. The Wings of the Storm. The Australian Air Force during the Second World War. The past was filmed in black and white, the present in color. First came a long section of the daring young men in their flying machines and the laughing girls who had loved them; then, in merciless technicolor, a series of close-ups of the survivors forty-five years later: turtlenecks, pelican chins, watery eyes, toupees, and jovial reminiscences. What struck me was that I had not noticed the change in myself either. I might carry on about growing old, but in the heart of me lived my true self: a young man in black and white. I had had nothing to do with the Aussies, but I felt closer to them and their laughing girls than to the dentured grumbler I glowered at every morning in the mirror. The young dogs who joshed self-consciously in front of the camera and hugged their self-conscious girls almost moved me to tears, for they were me, not the honking old geezers in technicolor killing themselves remembering.

There was a harrowing color sequence of a still young-looking woman in her seventies remembering her husband who had crashed over Berlin. I did not look at Sylvia, but cringed inwardly for her; when I finally did look she sat watching the screen with what seemed like utter serenity. I didn't understand it. What was there to be serene about? I went on watching the verbose oldsters with dreadful relish, trying to tell myself that I was not like that; the black and white days flickering by on the little screen showed my true self. There I was, arm in arm with my buddies, saying cheese for a snapshot before taking off on what always might be our last trip and for some of us would be.

Too soon the film was over. I looked at Sylvia, ready to slip back into my role of understanding old husband respecting his ghostly predecessor. To my surprise I saw her gaze at me with the same defiance I felt. "How about that?" she said and got up to switch off the set.

"How about what?"

She turned on me angrily. "All those old bags, carrying on as if they're their own grandmothers! Talking about themselves as if they had nothing in common anymore with the young women who loved those men, worked with them, lost them, mourned for them, then picked up their lives again. I *am* that! I still am! This whole age bit is a hoax! I'm older, wiser, funnier, brighter, I haven't died, I'm alive! What you saw was me, not a phantom from the past. Me, Sylvia, Johnny's wife, Johnny's widow, who carried on with her life—"

"And married me."

"And married you, thank God. The same goes for you. You aren't the old dodderer you pretend to be. Much more so of late, I must say."

"What do you mean?"

"You exaggerate your physical age, you pant, you—"

"I pant because I am out of breath! I can't help being seventy-four!"

"Seventy-three. But are you? Are you really? Be honest! How did you see yourself in that movie? In color or in black and white?"

"In black and white."

"Thank God," she said. "I thought I was the only one. More tea?"

"Let's have a snort."

She went to get the brandy-for-colds she carried with her on our journeys and poured a generous helping for each of us into plastic tumblers from the bathroom.

"Cheers!" She took a slug, smacked her lips and heaved a sigh. Then she asked, "Are you going to stop it or aren't you?"

"Boozing? Not likely."

"Acting the old man. Please, Marty, let's go back to who we are, not who we are being told we are. I haven't changed, not really."

"But what about Johnny?"

"He is there, somewhere. Within us, outside us, I don't know where. But he's alive."

"He is dead, love. They're all dead. So will we be, before long."

"I'm sure they aren't. I *know* they aren't. I know they are no different now from the ones we knew."

I looked at her as she stood there, glass in hand, eyes ablaze with determination. What a woman! God, I was lucky. "All right," I said, "you win," and took another sip.

"Why don't we?" she pressed on. "Why not chuck the whole bit of Darby and Joan driving a queen-size bed on wheels across Canada with cruise control? Why not go out and see if there's some place we can dance? Let's go and have a ball."

"You want to go to a disco? Leap around with teenagers in psychedelic lighting?"

"I want to go dancing the way we used to."

"Nobody dances the way we used to anymore. That's now called dirty dancing."

She laughed. "It was, wasn't it?" She took another slug.

"Well, what else can we do? I'm damned if I'll crawl back into
that idiotic car tomorrow and pick up where I left off. I saw
myself tonight for the first time in years. I want to have fun, not
trundle back to boring old Cannes and take the dog to the
beauty parlor and myself to the hairdresser for a blue rinse.
God, I'm glad I saw that!"

She polished off the rest of her drink. She wasn't used to it;
I gave her another ten minutes of coherence. We had to make
the most of them; before she knew it she would be fast asleep
with her head on my shoulder.

"Tell you what," she said, "let's stay here another day and
go to the fair."

"But it isn't a fair, it's a convention of water witches."

"Let's join the water witches and see what happens! It'll be
different, that's for sure."

From the falling night came the most melancholy sound in
the world: the long, drawn-out wail of an American train, far
away.

"All right," I said.

*

The next morning we headed back into town. Despite the
early hour, the place was alive with people, talking in
groups, sitting in clusters on the steps of the churches, troop-
ing in and out of the town hall, apparently their headquarters. They were ordinary American citizens of all ages, most
of them in the jeans and lumber jackets of the New England
fall, including a sprinkling of young men with beards and
young women in robes.

A middle-aged man wearing a lumber jacket and a baseball
cap bearing the name CATERPILLAR accosted us in front of the
town hall. "Are you part of this thing?" he asked, "or just
moseying around kicking tires?"

I said we were moseying around kicking tires.

"Then why don't you go in there and register?" He pointed

at the doorway. "It won't oblige you to anything, gives you access to all the workshops and the lectures, and you can eat real cheap offen the counter up in there."

"How long has this been going on?"

"Just started, you can still slurp the cream offen the top. Know anything about dowsing?"

"No," I said.

"Join the dowsing school on the green. We're a friendly bunch. By the time you leave you'll be able to locate water, noxious streams, radiation—you may have to move your bed."

"Will I really?" I said, lost.

"Go to the workshops," Caterpillar persisted. "Listen to the lectures. If there are things you don't understand, ask any of us and you're in business. Farmer?"

"Sea captain."

"Hot dog! My granddaddy came from the old country. You from the old country?"

"My wife is."

"Hi, ma'am." He held out his hand. "This is a real pleasure."

Sylvia shook hands.

"Well, you go get yourselves some breakfast in there, then hit the circuit. You'll have a ball. See you around."

He walked on, shoulder slapping his way through the crowd.

I said, "I think I've seen enough."

"Why?" Sylvia asked. "You haven't even looked! I have no idea what dowsing is, but I'd like to find out. Remember what we were saying last night? Let's do something different! Let's register and see what it's all about."

"Look, love," I argued with the strained patience of reason, "if we register, we may be caught here for days. We have to get plane tickets, book seats—"

"How long will it take us from here to Boston? Two days at the most. We are not in a hurry, are we?"

"We have to get rid of the car, find—"

"Martinus," she said, "stop being a boring old man." She turned and climbed the steps to the crowded porch of the town hall.

After forty-three years, I knew that if I stuck my ground she would leave me to fend for myself. I was weary after all those miles of driving, too tired for a battle of wills. If she wanted to find out what dowsing was, so be it; I would try to keep it short, diplomatically.

Obeying a sign saying REGISTER HERE! with an arrow, we climbed a flight of stairs crammed with people. On the landing a woman with an official air, installed behind a table full of name tags, asked if we had registered. I said we were just moseying around kicking tires.

"Right," she said. Before I knew it we were briskly processed in the friendliest of ways and moved away from the table thirty dollars poorer, carrying handfuls of paper describing the events of the next few days and our name tags. SYLVIA AND MARTINUS HARINX—the machine had limited capacity—FRANCE. We headed for the buffet.

When our turn came in the queue, we received a plastic beaker with coffee and a sticky bun on a paper plate and joined the others on their slow tour of the hall, carried along by the tide. It was a friendly crowd; lots of laughter, jostling, spilling coffee, cries of "Oops!" At a given moment we found ourselves in front of a long table full of books for sale, forked sticks, bent coat hangers and pendulums. I had a pendulum; Ma Chang had given it to me during a drunken farewell party for two at the end of our voyage. We had boozed it up at dead of night in her galley on Chinese high explosives. It had ended with my ripping my commodore's epaulettes off my short-sleeved shirt and giving them to her as a keepsake; she, cross-eyed with her own evil brew, had groped in a pocket of her smock and handed me her pendulum in return. It had been a momentous present; the wooden bead on a bit of string stiff with chicken fat was as much a symbol of her lofty rank as my epaulettes had been; she also served as ship's doctor and used it to swing over her patients to diagnose their problems. She had done it to me when, three days out of the Cape Verde Islands, I had suffered an attack of extreme high blood pressure. I had been taking pills to control my hypertension for years; owing to a mix-up while packing, I ran out of them in mid-Atlantic. As a result I suffered the attack and lay gasping on my bunk, thinking my last hour had struck, when my Chinese steward called in Ma Chang, who came in looking like a white-haired old witch, smelling of alien herbs. She pulled down the sheet, took her wooden bead on a string out of the pocket of her smock, and started to swing it over my chest and abdomen in a sort of trance. Over my heart it started to rotate instead of swinging back and forth. I had no idea what the change in its movement meant and thought of it as primitive Chinese witchcraft, but she cured me. Once her diagnosis was made, she put me on a diet of unspeakable sludge smelling of cats, five times a day three little bowls of it; after a week it made me feel fit as a fiddle. Without her I might have slid off the plank to the tune of a Chinese dirge, halfway across the Atlantic.

I had not realized that the pendulum was a generally accepted tool not peculiar to Ma Chang and her culture. But her unsavory wooden bead was no match for these pendulums, which went from crystal baubles on silver chains to chrome teardrops marked PROFESSIONAL. On impulse, I bought a crystal one for Sylvia; she was surprised, delighted, and kissed me for it. Somebody behind us said, "Attaboy!"

The current carried us further along past a lineup of photographs on the wall, which turned out to be the speakers. There were workshops on Geomancy, Dowsing for Oil, Map Dowsing, Enhancement of Sacred Sites to Expand Human Consciousness, Dowsing for Original Recipes in Kitchen and Garden.

Sylvia said, "Let's each go to different ones and compare notes later."

She looked so young at that moment that I did not have the heart to voice any rational reservations.

"We'll meet again for lunch." She put her arm through mine. "Come on, choose!"

I looked for a workshop that would tell me how to regress in time far enough to join her in the playground and believe in fairies again, but settled on one given by a Wing Commander Martock on "Pitfalls and Dangers of the Pendulum" in the Congregational Church. Sylvia chose "Further Adventures with Plants" by a Miss Whalen, who looked luscious on her photograph.

*

The wing commander turned out to be a British Royal Air Force character with quivering mustaches and a lazy drawl, oddly out of place in the American crowd. His introductory speech was hard to follow because his pipe frequently went out and had to be relit with a miniature flamethrower. Between incendiary attacks he told us that there was more to the pendulum than a water locator. There were other uses, some of them to be avoided. He listed the pitfalls into which the innocuous tool could lead the unwary. Predicting the future. Determining the sex of an unborn child. All spiritualist stuff. Betting on horses. It sounded reasonable enough, as long as you accepted the basic premise. I could not; despite Ma Chang's diagnosis and cure, the pendulum itself seemed to me pure superstition. As far as I could pick up, it answered questions put either aloud or in the mind by signaling yes or no. It seemed that yes was when it circled and no when it oscillated back and forth. It could also apparently say maybe. I thought the whole thing was a hoot, all these people solemnly swinging their baubles trying to get answers to questions like "Am I in danger of going overboard with my dowsing?" The answer seemed obvious, the gullibility of the audience supported that impression. They seemed eager to explain every phenomenon as supernatural without any attempt to seek out a rational solution first. Life, at my age, was sailing blind in a fog anyhow; it seemed crazy to spike the compass of reason as well.

The association with a compass made me raise my hand when, presently, he asked for examples of practical results of using the pendulum. "I'm not a dowser," I said. "I hold no claim to any paranormal gifts. But I'd like to mention an incident that happened to me during the war. I was master of an oceangoing tugboat leaving the harbor of South Shields in England with a tow of thirteen barges, at a crawl. Just after I had taken a compass bearing of the outer buoy, fog closed in. I stayed on course, but at a given moment something told me I was heading too low. It was important, the buoy marked the entrance to the channel through the minefields. I decided to follow my hunch and steered two points higher, with my heart in my mouth. Twenty minutes later I hit the buoy on the nose. If I had stuck to my compass bearing, it would have resulted in one hell of a bang." I sat down, forgetting why I had told that story and wishing I had kept my mouth shut.

The wing commander puffed at his pipe. "What year was that?"

"Forty-two."

"Navy?"

"W-boats."

"Ah," he said, as to a friendly dog. "I know about those. Now, what was your question?"

"I was saved by an impulse. I just wondered how many answers provided by your pendulum could be reached by simple intuition."

"It's the same faculty, Captain," he said, picking up the title the way the British do. "If you had dowsed your course through the fog with a pendulum, you would have been given the correct heading."

"I'm afraid I can't believe that. And I sure as hell wouldn't have wanted to try. Not while heading for a minefield."

"You could have, you know. Some minesweeper skippers put a rating in the bow with a pendulum and found they were better at spotting mines than sonar. The Navy wouldn't allow it to be reported, of course. Like the Church of England, they don't mind what you do as long as you keep your mouth shut about it. Does that answer your question?"

I said dutifully, "Yes, thank you."

"I'd like to talk to you some more about that. Why don't you and I have a bit of a chinwag afterward over a glass of wine?"

I said I would be delighted.

"Well, now," he continued, "let's hear some more questions."

The meeting broke up half an hour later; I made my way up the crowded aisle to the wing commander. He noticed my name tag. "France? You're not a frog, are you?"

"I'm Dutch, but I live in the south of France. Which part of England do you come from?"

"Where do you think with a name like Martock? Somerset. Where were you stationed during the war with those W-boats?"

I told him while we walked to a restaurant. It served wine only by the bottle, so he suggested we share one and asked for the wine list. When it was brought to him, he took out his pendulum and went down the column, the pendulum oscillating in his right hand. After a moment it started to circle and he ordered. The waiter took it in his stride; he must be used to the weirdos descending on his hometown every year. When he brought the bottle, the wing commander swung his pendulum over it; it started to circle and he said, "That'll do. No need to taste it. Thanks." The glasses were filled, we raised them at each other and drank. The wine was very good indeed, but so potent that it needed a foundation. He called for the menu and we ordered a meal.

"I should have dowsed for the food, really," he grumbled, "but one doesn't want to turn oneself into an eccentric. That's what happens, you know: if you're not careful, you become an eccentric in no time. Cheers." He drank. "A workshop like this morning is useless, really," he continued after sucking his mustaches. "You tell 'em not to do any pregnancy tests, next thing they're swinging a pendulum over their girlfriend's abdomen. You say: no spiritualist stuff, next morning they have a red Indian spirit guide called Holy Smoke. Then they start automatic writing."

"What's that?"

"See?" He raised his glass. "There you go. If I hadn't warned you, you wouldn't be trying to find out what it is." He drank and stifled a belch. "Use your pendulum for selecting ripe melons in the supermarket, testing wines, locating water, oil, or archaeological remains, and leave it at that. The rest is hocus-pocus."

I said, mellowed by the wine, "I might eventually accept that you can test a bottle with your pendulum, but I have a problem with your dowsing the wine list. That strikes me as—well—stretching credulity too far."

"It does, does it?" He poured himself another glass; I was

still having my first. "I can see why. But it works, you're tasting the proof right now. The rest of the wine here is plonk, without my pendulum I'd have been up a tree. This is the only decent bottle in the house."

I picked up the bottle and looked at the label. "But isn't this wine pretty reliable anyhow? I had it in Vancouver. What do you ask when you swing your pendulum over the wine list?"

"I ask, 'Give me a wine that's good for me.' That's the crux of it: ask for what is good for *you,* not the best wine on the list. What's good for you is likely to be good, period. But I warn you: your pendulum may show an expensive taste. Have one?"

"Excuse me?"

"Do you have a pendulum?"

"Er—yes, I have one somewhere."

"But you don't use it. How come?"

"It was given to me as a keepsake at the end of my last voyage two years ago."

"By whom?"

Maybe it was the wine; before I knew it I was blabbing about Ma Chang, how I missed the sea, even about General Theodosius and the Barbarian Conspiracy.

The man listened well, but he knocked back over half of our bottle in the process. When I was through, he poured himself another glass and said, "You are going to need dowsing in your Roman research."

"Oh, I've given that up. By now I know all there is to know about that particular period."

He was no longer listening. "You'll need it to trace your general's movements. Get a map of the Roman roads in Britain, the Ordinance Survey publishes one. Take your pendulum in your right hand, an ice pick in your left. Start at the harbor where they landed, trace the roads slowly with the ice pick, tell your pendulum to signal all locations that are of interest to you. Each time the pendulum starts to spin, prick a hole in the map; you'll end up with a complete itinerary. Don't ask what happened in those locations, go there and find out. Once you're on the spot, ask, for instance, 'Did he pitch camp here?' Your pendulum will say yes or no. Go on asking any questions that come to mind. In the end the pendulum will give you the whole story, even though it can only say yes or no. You'll find yourself asking questions you never thought of before, out of thin air. It's the questions that matter." He smiled. "That's the true mystery: where do those questions come from?"

Wine or no wine, the business with the map turned me off. I could not suspend my reason to the point where I accepted that, sitting in the south of France with a map of the Roman roads of Britain in front of me, I could ask, "Where did General Theodosius go?" and be told where by Ma Chang's bead on a string. But I had to be polite. "Is there a book I could read on all this?" I asked.

"Book?" He frowned.

"There must be a book on dowsing, for skeptical sailors."

"Nonsense," he said, "some of the best dowsers I know were sailors. Military are good too. If you insist, get *Dowsing: One Man's Way,* by General H. Scott Elliot. It's for sale in the town hall. Perhaps we'll have a chance to talk again later."

"Any relation to the poet?" It seemed a silly question to throw at him.

"No," he said surprisingly. "Elliot with two *L*'s. Let me take care of the wine, by the way. I drank bugger all."

"What? Ah yes, thank you. Remarkably civil of you. Next one's on me."

He seemed beyond caring.

*

I located Sylvia in a corner of the town hall deep in conversation with an elegant young woman whom I recognized from the photograph; she was swinging her pendulum.

"Sorry," I said, interrupting, "time got away from me."

"Oh, love! This is Virginia Whalen. Ginny, meet my husband Martinus."

We shook hands; the luscious Miss Whalen gave me a demure but knowing smile.

"Sorry I'm late," I said. "I just had a long talk with a wing commander from Somerset."

"Ah yes," the young woman said. "A very knowledgeable man. A bit unusual. But then, aren't we all?" She smiled. I found myself thinking that maybe I should take some dowsing lessons with her.

"Virginia talks to plants with her pendulum," Sylvia said with eyes that would melt a heart of stone, "and do you know: the plants respond! Ginny says that the first thing to do is to ask them for their names."

Miss Whalen smiled seraphically. If such an obviously sane young woman, without emotional problems other than those she created in passing males, asked plants for their names with her pendulum and received an answer, I might have a problem.

"How do you find out their names?"

"I'll show you," Sylvia answered, taking out her new pendulum. "If you have a plant that isn't doing well, say a jade, you take your pendulum, go up to it and ask, 'Can we have a chat?' If the pendulum starts to circle, like so, it means that the plant says yes."

"They always do," Miss Whalen added, smiling.

Sylvia went on, "Then you ask, first, 'Would you like to have a name?' The plant says yes again."

"They always do," Miss Whalen repeated.

"Your next question is 'Are you a boy or a girl?' "

I wondered how I could get out of this without creating the impression I was fleeing.

"Then you ask, 'Would you spell your name for me?' Yes, says the plant. 'Is the first letter in the first or in the second half of the alphabet?' If it is in the first, you start: 'A, B, C—' The pendulum will circle at a letter. You ask the same for the second letter. Before you know it, you have a name. Say it's Dolly. You ask, 'Tell me, Dolly, what's the trouble? Do you have enough water?' Dolly says, 'Oh yes,' the pendulum circles strongly. Then you ask, 'Have you enough light?' Dolly says 'Yes.' You persevere until you find out the reason why Dolly is doing so poorly: it's because she can't stand her neighbor Anthea, a big aspidistra. So you separate them and, Ginny says, in a day or two Dolly will be doing fine. Am I right?"

Miss Whalen smiled at me as if she guessed, with extrasensory perception, that I was contemplating the future.

"And that's not all," Sylvia continued. I had not seen her so excited for years. "Let me ask Ginny one more question, then we'll have lunch. All right?"

"I'm sorry," I said, "I had mine. The wing commander and I got carried away and we forgot the time."

"Of course," Sylvia said, smiling. "Ginny and I will have a sandwich. Did you have coffee?"

"No, but I'd like to go to the book counter first if you don't mind, I have to pick up something there. I'll be right back."

They both smiled; neither seemed likely to be aware of my absence for long.

I found General Scott Elliot's book among the stacks on the table. His picture on the dustcover showed a rational face. The inside flap told me that he was a soldier turned archaeologist, this book was the result of twenty years of experience in practical dowsing. I glanced at his introduction. "I think it is because I am naturally somewhat phlegmatic that my approach to dowsing is careful and quiet."

I bought it.

*

Sylvia and I read the book together that evening in our motel cottage.

It was she who set the tone. While I was making the tea, she took out her pendulum and started talking to a ratty-looking chrysanthemum in a plastic pot on the table as if it were a baby in a perambulator. Alas, there was no response. Her pendulum would not move.

"Let's read the book," I said. "Maybe you're doing something wrong."

I said so for her sake; I myself did not believe in any of it. Frankly, after a day among the weirdos I was ready to decamp. Sylvia, however, was aglow with the spirit of adventure. In the presence of the ravishing Miss Whalen she had dowsed up a storm, but now that she found herself alone with her pendulum and a skeptical husband the glittering prize seemed to escape her. The least I could do was to give her moral support, but throughout my professional career I had relied on realistic observation and rational deduction; I wouldn't have lasted long without. Was this the moment to heed the poet's exhortation "Old men ought to be explorers"? I had bought *The Faber Book of Modern Verse* in the next Canadian town we passed through and read T. S. Eliot's poem several times since. Now, was I going to explore? Her disappointment when her pendulum refused to move over the chrysanthemum made up my mind for me. Either I lived in black and white or in technicolor. Come on, Harinxma, blow on the dice and let them roll.

I dug up Ma Chang's wooden bead with its unsavory string from my toilet case, where it had been sleeping among razor blades, iodine, bottles of nail fungus medicine and old battle ribbons. It looked revolting; I should have bought one of those silver teardrops in the town hall. "Let's look at the book," I said.

We settled down with *Dowsing: One Man's Way* side by side on the couch, our pendulums at the ready. The tests for beginners opened with:

> Set your pendulum oscillating back and forth, hold it over an electric light cable, such as that of a standard lamp, and ask "Is this cable live?" If it is, and the pendulum changes direction, that will establish your yes. For no, pull the plug and ask the same question.

Sylvia held her pendulum over the cable. Nothing happened, yet it was plugged in.

"Set it in motion first. It may not be able to start from dead center."

"It worked during the lecture . . ."

"You may have been helped by looking at the others. Before you start asking questions, make the thing swing back and forth."

She set the crystal oscillating over the cable and asked the question again. Slowly, hesitantly, it started to circle.

Ma Chang's battle-scarred wooden bead with its sticky string looked so unappetizing that I considered asking Sylvia to let me use hers, but I decided to roll the dice and set the bead swinging. It seemed livelier than Sylvia's crystal and started to circle at once, vigorously. Maybe because it was lighter.

"Let's pull the plug and see." I disconnected the cable; she tried her pendulum over it. It hung still once more.

It was my turn to try. I asked, "Is this cable live?" I wanted to set my pendulum swinging first, but wasn't given the chance. It oscillated briskly at once.

"That seems to be your no," she said.

I put the plug back in. "Is this cable—" The pendulum did not wait for me to finish the question. It circled with a vengeance. It wasn't I who had set it in motion, of that I was certain. It circled and oscillated of its own accord, unless I was fooling myself.

"You may be the more gifted dowser!" I detected a hint of envy in her voice.

"Beginner's luck," I said.

"Well, let's try the next experiment. What is it?"

I consulted the book. "Put four similar coins and one different one under a cloth, move them around and then let the pendulum find the different one."

Sylvia fetched a towel from the bathroom, I hunted for a French five-franc piece to put among four Canadian quarters on the table. I moved the coins around under the towel; Sylvia asked her pendulum, "Would you, please, find the five-franc piece? Please?" She moved her pendulum over the towel; suddenly it circled. She looked under the towel and found she had hit a quarter.

I shuffled the coins under the towel again, set Ma Chang's bead swinging, and said, "Indicate the five-franc piece for me." I moved the pendulum over the towel; at a given moment it started to circle. I looked, it was the five-franc piece.

"You have better luck than I have," Sylvia said.

In the past, during shore leave when the children were little, we would play Monopoly, and there had always come a moment when I felt it would be judicious to let them win. I wished I could do so now; it didn't matter to me if the damn thing picked the right coin or not. "Maybe it's a matter of finding something to which you can relate," I said. "The wing commander mentioned in his lecture that for this to work there had to be a need. Maybe you're just marking time until you can start chatting up your plant again."

She gave me an appraising look. "Are you being patronizing by any chance?"

"Why?"

"I have the impression that you think the wing commander and the general are all right, but that Ginny and I are scatterbrained housewives."

"Don't be ridiculous," I said. "Go on, try the chrysanthemum again."

She looked doubtful.

"Tell you what. I'll take the book into the bedroom with me and study it for a bit; that'll give you a chance to work on the plant in private. Might be easier for you."

"All right," she said. "Are you going to be warm enough in there?"

"Don't worry. Call me when you want me back."

I picked up the book, took Ma Chang's pendulum with me like a dead mouse by its tail, and closed the door behind me.

I wanted to have a look at the book on my own to find out what was going on. My pendulum circling and swinging had not been beginner's luck; it had done so of its own accord. What had made it move? It must have been an unconscious muscular reaction on my part, unless I wanted to attribute it to spirits. Nonsense. I lay down on one of the beds and opened the book at a chapter entitled How Does Dowsing Work?

The answer, on the very first line, was, "To be honest: we don't know." So that was that. But the writer allowed himself some general musings on the subject. Did all objects have an emanation, a sort of energy field comparable to a magnetic field, and did the pendulum react to that? No, he thought it had to do with the mind as opposed to the brain. He gave his definition of the difference.

> The brain deals in tangibles, it is a kind of computer which we train and feed all through life to remember, to reason, to judge situations, to store experiences and much else beside, but it cannot do what the mind can do. The mind covers things known as the superconscious, the subconscious, the unconscious, it includes instinct and intuition.

I believe that the dowser "knows" the answers in his mind. He can get at them simply by using the mind alone, but this is difficult and mistakes are easily made. So, to simplify the process of getting what is in the mind out into a visible, tangible signal he uses a tool, coupled with a code-language of his own.

That was interesting: the circling and oscillating reactions of the pendulum to my questions were a code language my brain had agreed on with my mind: a swing back and forth for no, a rotating movement for yes. It did not make dowsing more acceptable, but this explanation at least partly satisfied my reason. Mind—brain, communicating in a code language agreed upon beforehand, with the pendulum as a messenger boy.

"How this is done and how it works I do not know," the writer continued.

One has to face up to the fact that most of the dowser's work is near miraculous in relation to present day knowledge. For myself I am prepared to accept this and get on with the work of using this ability for good and useful purposes. I do not believe we shall know how dowsing works until more is known about the workings of the mind in general.

Was I prepared to mess with this until more was known about the workings of the mind, not likely to happen in my lifetime? I had an ingrained resistance to all things paranormal; dowsing now seemed to be one of them. Odd, that military men were attracted by it, not a particularly superstitious breed. A wing commander, a general. A commodore would not look out of place in the lineup. The writer was right: if it worked, why not use it even if you don't know how it works? After all, I didn't have the foggiest idea how a telephone worked, but it did not stop me telephoning.

I was about to experiment with Ma Chang's bead some more when Sylvia called from the next room, "Marty!" I got off the bed and opened the door. There she sat, beaming, pendulum in hand.

"She's called Josie!" she said. "And she was *parched.* I gave her some water, she drank half a tumbler from the washstand, then I asked her if she was happy here and she said no! So I asked if she'd like to be close to the window, have a bit more light? She said yes! I put her there and asked her if she was happy now and the pendulum nearly flew out of my hand. Isn't that wonderful?"

"Terrific," I said.

"Shall we stay on and learn some more?" she asked.

"I'd love to," I said.

Out of this granite our heroes are hewn.

CHAPTER TWO

*

We stayed in Danville two more days. They changed the tenor of our lives.

For Sylvia, dowsing became a daily routine. She dowsed in shops without any hesitation to find out if an avocado was ripe or the yogurt fresh; but her main concern was for the houseplants we came across later on the road to Boston, a succession of parched, stunted, or moping philodendrons, schefflera and asparagus ferns, all of whom unburdened themselves to her in intimate dialogues. As a result, motel owners and restaurant managers copped it for neglecting their helpless wards; the looks they gave me were commiserative.

I, just for the hell of it, dowsed down a row of wine bottles in a liquor store near Boston with Ma Chang's pendulum when I thought no one was looking. But a sharp-eyed assistant asked what I was doing; I told him the pendulum was an instrument used by French winemakers to test their product. He asked where he could obtain one; I gave him the address of the American Society of Dowsers in Danville. That was the end of my public dowsing.

In private, I did not fare much better. At first, I fiddled around with Ma Chang's pendulum in the evenings after supper while Sylvia read *The Secret Life of Plants.* I stopped after a while because the results made me feel uncomfortable. On one occasion I mislaid the car keys, looked up Finding Lost Objects in the general's book, made a list of places where the damn keys could be, most of them logical, some way out, such as in my toilet case which I included only to have a fuller menu for the pendulum to choose from. It started to circle at the toilet case; I took it to mean don't be silly until I found the keys inside it. That was the moment my dowsing died on the vine; something deep inside me, something elemental decided I should leave this alone.

In Boston, we had the car washed and left it for our new

in-laws to pick up on arrival; then we boarded a plane for Glasgow, where Sylvia wanted to visit her sister. It was already bitterly cold in Scotland, the visit to the sister was short. We decided to go home via our daughter Helen and her children in Topsham, near Exeter; spoiled by Canada, we rented a car and tooled south in easy stages.

England is a wonderful country to motor through on condition you are not in a hurry. The car was as slow as a turtle and at the urging of Sylvia we took secondary roads rather than motorways. We also spent a long time over lunches in pubs with names like The Silent Woman and The Rose Revived, drank sweet cider, ate shepherd's pie and sherry trifle. We spent the nights in creaking beds, her head on my shoulder, mice discreetly rustling behind the wainscoting, to be wakened at dawn by the buzz, clank and hiss of an infernal machine called Goblin Teasmade.

In the meantime, Sylvia kept up her campaign on behalf of the neglected flora in various hostelries and restaurants en route, which embarrassed me less here than it had in America. The English have a soft spot for eccentrics; a remark like "Your bridal veil is very angry with you!" was received with a smile and the promise to see to it at once. I suppose that at times I may have behaved as if I were indulging the little woman; yet I was unprepared when in a hotel in Shrewsbury, while unpacking my overnight case on the bed, I heard her say behind me, "I *know* you think I'm mad."

"Why?" I couldn't find my comb. Had I left it behind at The Silent Woman?

"Because of the way you behave when I'm dowsing."

She was sitting at the dressing table in her slip, doing her face in front of the mirror. "You're wrong," I said to the mirror. "I think it's fascinating."

"But you don't really believe in it. You don't believe in any of it. Why is that? Huh?"

"Whatever gave you that idea?"

"You've stopped doing it yourself," she said, applying her lipstick. "Why?"

I knew why: because it scared me. I didn't want to be forced to the conclusion that I had a psychic streak in me. Dowsing for coins under a towel was one thing; to be told your car keys are in your toilet case and then find them there was another. I didn't want to go into all that, so I said, "I like watching tennis too, and don't play it myself."

"There you go!" she cried, arching her eyebrows for the pencil. "You treat it like a game, which is ridiculous. Take Terry Ross."

"Terry who?"

"Terry Ross, the famous dowser. He dowses oil and ore in South America for big companies. They wouldn't touch him if it was a game."

"Where did you pick that up?"

"I heard it in Danville. He was president of the society of dowsers three times."

"I see. Ah! There's my comb."

"Dammit," she cried, "there you go again!" She glowered at me in the mirror. "Why won't you, for heaven's sake?"

"Do what?"

"Try dowsing again. Come on, do it just for me, just the once. I'm sure you'll enjoy it when you see the results."

"Quite honestly, I wouldn't know what to dowse for." I didn't want to deliver myself to Ma Chang and her sticky bead, even if the general did call her my Mind.

"Think of something you really like."

"H'm." I rummaged in my suitcase for a tie.

"What's 'h'm?' " the mirror asked.

"I tried in a liquor store on the outskirts of Boston. I started to dowse for a good bottle of wine along the racks."

"Well?"

I told her about my experience in the liquor store and how I had fled after my encounter with the assistant.

"Then what about the car keys?" she asked. "The pendulum helped you find those."

"I suppose I remembered where I had put them, but it had slipped my mind. I wouldn't count that." Why was I lying? What difference did it make?

"Surely you can dowse for other things than a bottle of wine?" She looked at herself in the mirror as if she had never seen that woman before.

"Name one," I said.

"How about General Theodosius?" She looked sideways at her profile.

"What about him?"

"We're in Theodosius country now, as I remember it. Why not dowse for places where he has been, the way Terry Ross dowses for oil? On a map?" She pursed her lips at the mirror.

"H'm."

"Meaning no. You don't believe in dowsing. Go on, say it."

I had joined her in front of the mirror, knotting my tie; I grinned at her reflection. "I'm prepared to dowse for another bottle of wine," I said.

"All right, if that's what you want. Try dowsing the wine list tonight."

"I don't believe in dowsing a wine list. I may believe in dowsing the bottle, the physical thing, in front of me. Not in dowsing from a distance."

"Terry Ross does."

"I'm not Terry Ross."

"Oh, for heaven's sake! Are you so insecure inside your little fortress of reason that you won't venture out and give it a whirl? What are you defending? Where's the threat?"

"Maybe I lack motivation," I replied, moving away.

"All right, I gave you a motivation: do it for *me*."

"H'm."

"See? 'H'm' again. I could be drowning in a bog of superstition and scream for help, all you'd do is peer over the rampart of your little fortress of reason and say 'H'm.'"

"What exactly do you want me to do?"

"Take a map, your pendulum, and dowse for a spot where General Theodosius has been. Or just dowse for Romans."

"How?"

"The book tells you exactly how."

"And if I refuse it means I don't love you after forty-three years?"

"I hate to see you become insecure to the point where you won't even try. What are you afraid of? That you may turn out to have the gift? Is that what you're shying away from? You're not religious, it can't be a sin to you. You have no dogmas—"

"Like hell I haven't! I had it drummed into me, from naval college on: 'Don't speculate, don't waffle: observe, combine, deduct.' To me a chart is not a thing to play games with. I'm stiff with dogmas up to here. What you're asking me is to turn something I took seriously all my life into a game. It's like asking a surgeon to use his lancet for knife throwing." I thought I had put that rather well.

"Pompous ass," she said, getting up from the little bench.

"I'm serious. If I started messing around with my pendulum the way you want me to, I'd feel—"

"What?"

"Like handing in my union card. No more serious business, old man. Go and play."

She sighed. "All right. Start with wine."

I did the next morning. There was a shop across from the hotel with a fancy poster in the window about the new Beaujolais. A real expert; the new Beaujolais would have turned into vinegar by now. But it was a good place to test the pendulum; if it came up with a winner in this grocery I would have to start taking it seriously.

I entered the shop, nodded at a man in a gray dustcoat behind the counter, turned my back on him and faced six shelves full of wine bottles. I brought out Ma Chang's little appetizer and asked, in my mind, "Okay, let's have the best of the lot." Remembering the wing commander, I added, "The best for *me.*" I felt ridiculous even before I started.

The pendulum oscillated with the same independence that had struck me before. The names on the bottles were all unknown to me: obscure châteaux, unknown villages, mendacious French négociants. Plonk was the word; the pendulum agreed. It went on oscillating back and forth over the lot, more forceful over one bottle than the next. I had been right: this was a grocer, not a wine merchant. I reached the end of the first row, the pendulum had spat them all out. I heard the man behind the counter say, "There are more wines in the alcove in the corner."

"Thank you," I said.

The alcove was a sort of doorless cupboard with a few dusty bottles laid out, a *chapelle ardente* for wines. "Okay,"

I muttered to the pendulum, "here we go. Would you select something here, old thing? Something that will leave my innards intact and appease my wife?" The pendulum pulled at its leash like a little terrier. I took it down the row. Nix. Nix. Ugh. No. Brr. Garbage—hallo! Suddenly the thing started to spin in a circle. I tested it by passing the bottle, then coming back to it; there could be no doubt. That particular bottle was the winner. I picked it up, blew the dust off the label, and read CHÂTEAU L'EVANGILE, 1983. Never heard of it, but in for a penny, in for a pound. I took it to the counter.

"Aha," the man said, reading the label. "You certainly know your wines."

"Er—yes."

"In the restaurant business?"

"Why?"

He looked at me, somewhat bewildered I thought. "This is the best wine in the house. Only an expert—"

"Yes—well, how much is it?"

The price was the price of love. Jeepers, creepers, where did you get those peepers. I paid the ransom and took the bottle back to the hotel like a bouquet.

Sylvia was delighted and suggested we open it at once. I knew she was doing a mother-on-the-beach on me: Oh, what a lovely sandcastle! I had a corkscrew in my suitcase, opened the bottle, poured some into one of the tumblers off the washstand. At least it didn't taste of the cork. I poured us half a tumbler each, raised mine, and said, "Here's to the Fifth Dimension."

We drank. Stared at each other. Then she said, *"Woof!"*

Woof was the word. The wine was terrific, the best red I had tasted in many a year. "Good old pendulum," I said recklessly.

Next I knew she had me over a map, asking, "Is there a spot on this map I should visit? Some Roman stuff, of my period?"

The thing went into a spin.

Now I faced the problem of how to pinpoint the spot. The book did indeed give full instructions: "On your map, determine the coordinates with the aid of your pendulum." To a sailor, that was an easy one.

With a pencil in my left hand, I moved the pendulum slowly

down the edge of the map. At a given moment it started to rotate; I marked the spot with the pencil. I repeated the same procedure along the top edge; when the pendulum circled I made another mark. This gave me latitude and longitude; where the two lines crossed should be the location. I looked at it closely. There were no Roman remains in the area; just a blank spot off a minor road. But when I examined the road itself I discovered, alongside it in small print, the words *Roman Road*. Well, hurray for coincidence.

"All right," I said. "Let's go and see what's there, if anything."

"Oh, there will be something! I just know it!" She was a true convert, more Catholic than the Pope. If I had had something Roman in my toilet case, like a coin, I would have secretly dropped it there for, alas, this was going to be a test of her faith.

The next morning we drove down the Roman road, or rather its great-great-great-grandchild, and took the turnoff to a place called Cruckton; my dowsed location was just beyond that. It turned out that the road, Roman or otherwise, changed into a footpath.

Sylvia said, "Ask your pendulum!"

I took out Ma Chang's bead and dangled it from its chicken-fat string. "Is this the right spot?"

No.

"Entirely wrong?"

No.

"Further along? Down this footpath?"

Yes.

We set out on foot down the narrow track until we reached the spot I had marked on the map, or pretty close to it.

"Is it here?"

No, said the pendulum.

"Look, Syl—"

"Don't give up! Ginny Whalen said that Tom Lethbridge, a famous writer on dowsing, called the pendulum "an instrument of absurd accuracy." Be accurate! Ask, 'Is it to the right? To the left? If so, how many paces?' "

"Okay: is it to the right?"

No, said the pendulum.

"To the left?"

No.

"Back a bit?"

No.

"Ahead?"

No.

"Look, this is not going to work—"

"Ask if it will indicate the direction."

"For God's sake, Sylvia!"

"Ask. I saw Ginny do it."

I gritted my dentures. "All right," I said to the damn thing, "indicate."

The pendulum started to swing in a diagonal direction. "What does this mean?" I asked. "Did I hurt its little feelings?"

"It's telling you where to go. Follow the direction in which it's swinging."

"Both ways?"

"Ask."

I asked, "Do you want me to go left?"

No.

"Right?"

Yes.

"See!" she cried, victorious.

I wished I had that coin; this was going to be a terrible disappointment for her. There was nothing here that could conceivably be called Roman, only fields and a few shrubs with quarreling blackbirds. I took a bearing. The pendulum was swinging in the direction of one of the bushes. I headed for it; as I did so I realized I was following an old track. It was barely visible, overgrown with weeds.

"Ask how many paces," Sylvia suggested.

"How?"

"Ask: One? Two? Three? Until it circles."

I obeyed, without faith. At twenty-one the pendulum circled. Of its own accord, I thought, but I could not be sure. It might have been my estimate of the distance.

As I approached the bush, the blackbirds broke up their quarrel and made off with a clatter of wings. I stopped and asked, "Is this the spot?"

Yes, said the pendulum.

There was nothing here. Ah, for the coin!

"Look inside the bush," Sylvia said.

I knelt by the bush and separated its lower branches. "Nothing. A piece of stone."

"What kind?"

"Just a stone. A piece of rock."

"Let me have a look."

She took my place and stayed half inside the bush for a long time. I was about to ask if she was all right when she emerged, eyes shining. "It's an old milestone!"

"You're kidding."

"Have a look yourself!"

I went down on my knees again and stuck my head inside the bush. Well, maybe. It looked like a piece of stone to me, period. There were no markings on it, no numerals. On closer scrutiny, it might have been shaped with a tool. Well, it had better be. I wrestled back out of the bush. "By Jove," I said, "I think you're right."

She stood there like a child that had won at croquet. "I told you so! *Now* do you believe me?"

"I believe." I kissed her.

But she was not to be bought by a Judas kiss. "You don't! I see in your eyes that you don't!"

I said, "Like St. Augustine: I believe, help Thou my unbelief."

"But it's such a wonderful gift! Look how quickly you've picked it up: first the wine, now this!"

"Now this," I agreed. "Let's go."

"Tell you what," she said, putting her arm through mine. "You're going to dowse for another spot on the map while I do some shopping, then we'll have a picnic."

"Too cold," I said. We walked back to the car.

But during the drive to the hotel I wondered what I was defending. Old men ought to be explorers; it made no sense to enthusiastically agree with that notion and then turn tail the moment I faced an uncharted sea. What was more, what was the alternative? The Cheerleaders.

That decided me. All aboard for the Fifth Dimension. "All right, I'll have another go at the map. When we get to the hotel."

"Good," she said, "that's my boy."

*

Before getting another bottle of that wine, I visited an antique shop in Shrewsbury looking for a little artifact, not too expensive, that could be accepted as being a Roman relic by someone eager to believe. I did not find any coins but settled for a shapeless little figurine made of soft stone, two inches high, that looked old enough to preach to the convinced. It set me back more than I had earmarked for this act of flimflam; after I had put it in my pocket and left the shop I suddenly knew she would not accept the little monstrosity but recognize it at once as a cuckoo's egg. Well, no harm in keeping it by to fall back on; she might forget about more dowsing in her eagerness to get to Helen and the children.

But when I returned she had the map waiting for me, spread out on the bed. I opened the bottle; glass in hand, she said, "Go ahead, next spot. The map's ready for you."

"Shouldn't we be getting on to Helen and the children?"

"Since when were you filled with grandfatherly devotion? You usually felt like strangling the little buggers."

"Rarely. Very rarely. Only when there were too many of them and the house was too small."

"Go on, dowse."

Obediently, I took my pendulum out of my pocket, approached the map and started by saying idiotically, "Hallo there."

The pendulum responded with a spin. Hallo yourself.

"Is there another spot on this map I should visit?"

Yes, said the pendulum, in a swinging mood.

"I'm thinking of Theodosius's campaign. Anything in connection with that?"

Yes.

I went through the same routine as before; the pendulum, keen as mustard, gave me the coordinates of a hamlet south of

Shrewsbury called Acton Burnell. Beside it was printed, in gothic letters, CASTLE (RUINS OF).

"What am I supposed to find there? A Roman fort?"

Yes.

"Near those ruins?"

Yes.

"You want me to dowse inside those ruins?"

Yes.

"What would I be dowsing for? An artifact?"

No.

"A coin?"

No.

"Something in connection with the campaign?" ·

The pendulum said yes, but hesitantly.

"Wait till I get there, right?"

Right.

After lunch we drove to the hamlet of Acton Burnell and discovered that the remains of the castle were situated in the grounds of a boarding school. I turned the car into a driveway which led to a building with Grecian pillars. I parked near the entrance, went inside and asked the lady at the desk if I could be permitted to do some measuring inside the ruins of the castle. She was charming; it would be perfectly all right as long as I closed all the gates behind me. She urged me to have a look at the Norman church beyond the ruin too, I would find it worth my while.

Through the coolness of the crisp sunny afternoon Sylvia and I walked toward a tennis court behind the main buildings. The castle loomed behind it: surprisingly fragile; the sky showed through toothless windows; the ruins were no more than three walls kept upright by two square turrets. Beyond were fields and tree-covered hills.

Inside the walls we found a manicured lawn with a paved area in the center. A huge cedar tree overshadowed it.

I took out my pendulum, set it swinging and asked, "Well, now—is this the right spot?"

The pendulum circled.

"We're not talking about these ruins but about the remains of a Roman fort underneath. Right?"

Right.

"Which century? The fourth?"

Correct.

Not quite knowing what to ask next, I said to Sylvia, "I wonder what happened in that fort." To my alarm, the pendulum started to spin in my hand, entirely of its own accord. "Now what the hell does that mean?"

"The pendulum can't answer that," Sylvia said. "It can only answer yes or no."

"It sure as hell answered something right now. I wonder what."

"Ask."

"Ask what?"

"Ask if it was reacting to your wish to know what happened in the fort."

"Did you hear that?" I asked the pendulum.

Yes, it said.

"Can you tell me what happened?"

Yes.

"How?"

"Ask!" Sylvia repeated. "Start from the top."

"Why don't you take over?" I suggested.

"No, no—it's you it's responding to. Ask if it's talking about one particular event."

More for her sake than my own I asked, "Are you talking about one particular event?"

Yes, said the pendulum.

"When did it occur? Theodosius's campaign was during the years 368 and '69 A.D. Was it in '68?"

No.

" '69?"

No.

"It must have been in either one!"

No.

"It *was* during Theodosius's campaign, wasn't it?"

No.

This seemed to be the moment to pack it in; I saw ahead of me a bewildering maze of contradictory answers. But Sylvia was listening with such fascination that to stop now would be like closing a door in her face. "All right," I said. "Was it later?"

No.

"Earlier."

Yes.

"How much earlier?"

No response. I shrugged my shoulders.

"Start counting down from 369," Sylvia suggested, "until it circles."

"All right. I'm counting down from 369, 368, 367—"

"Try one, two, three, that's quicker."

"One. Two. Three . . ." I counted until I was black in the face. At twenty I said, "Look, this isn't going to work."

"Go on," she urged.

I plowed on with a keen sense of the absurd; the pendulum started to circle at thirty-one.

"Thirty-one years before '69? So you're talking about 338 A.D.?"

Right, said the pendulum.

"Now what?"

"Just carry on," Sylvia said, "now you have the momentum."

"This fort—was it built on top of existing Iron Age earthworks, as most of them were?"

Yes.

"Belonging to a local tribe?"

Right.

"Did they defend it when the Romans turned up?"

No.

"It was no longer in use in 338 A.D.?"

No.

"Had it become a settlement?"

No.

"A sanctuary? Like a cemetery?"

Right.

"Now what?" I asked.

"A sanctuary . . . cemetery . . ." Sylvia mused, "was it desecrated by the Romans?"

"Did the Romans desecrate it by building a fort here?"

A strong yes.

"Things started to happen after they built their fort? I mean a curse, an evil spell, something like that?"

Correct.

"Resulting in accidents?"

No.

"Illness?"

No.

"Madness?"

Yes.

"What form? Possession?"

The pendulum went into a forceful spin. I looked up. "Where on earth do these questions come from? What made me ask about evil spells, madness, possession?"

"A form of free association?" she suggested.

"No idea. Well, let's recap. According to the pendulum we're standing over a Roman fort built in a spot that was sacred to the local barbarian tribe. As a result, the Roman occupants—troops, I suppose—"

The pendulum started to circle unasked. This was becoming spooky. "I'm not sure I'm comfortable doing this," I said uneasily.

"Come on, Marty—it's fascinating! The troops in the fort began to show symptoms of possession. Ask what the symptoms were."

"What were the symptoms? Outbreaks of violence? Fights?"

No, said the pendulum.

"Desertion?"

Yes.

"The men just disappeared?"

Yes.

"Did they have somewhere to go?"

Yes.

"A nearby village?"

Yes.

"Ah—were there women there?"

Correct.

"They abandoned the fort to shack up with local women?"

Right.

"And called it possession?"

Yes.

"Fascinating. As a ship's captain I'm familiar with that kind of possession. Did the Roman Army do something about it?"

The pendulum circled vigorously.

"Send a punitive party?"

Yes.

"Commanded by—what? A centurion?"

Right.

"A centurion arrived with a hundred men in the deserted fortress—was it a hundred?"

No.

"Less?"

Yes.

"All right, a centurion arrived with a small contingent. What did he do? Round up the deserters?"

Yes.

"And execute them?"

No.

"They were punished, surely?"

No.

"They were pardoned?"

The pendulum started to swing crosswise.

"Now what the devil does that mean?"

"Either that you're on the wrong track, or that you're almost right," Sylvia said helpfully.

"Almost right?" I asked. "Is that what you're telling me?"

Yes, said the pendulum.

"Not pardoned. Cured? Were they cured of possession?"

Yes.

"How? By exorcism?"

Yes.

"Who performed the ceremony? A priest? A haruspex?"

No.

"Don't tell me the centurion did it himself?"

Yes.

"Did he have any experience of possession?"

A small yes.

"You mean: he had experience of troops going native and blaming it on possession by evil spirits?"

Right.

"He didn't punish anyone?"

No.

"Why not? Was he short of men?"

Yes.

"So they were in effect pardoned after a ceremony of exorcism. Was it to make the army look tough, instead of pussyfooting?"

Right.

"Did he cure them as a group?"

No.

"One by one. What did he do? Make passes, mumble a magic formula, like Captain Bosman and his pharmacy?"

"What do you mean?" Sylvia asked.

I looked up, confused for a moment; I had been concentrating on the questions that seemed to pop into my head. "Captain Bosman, remember? I was an apprentice. He had a pharmacy box with numbered bottles and lost the list. So when a man turned up with a stomachache he would say, 'God bless the grab,' pick one out at random, pour some into a smaller bottle and say, 'One teaspoon three times a day after meals.' " I asked the pendulum, "Is this more or less the way the centurion went about it?"

The pendulum went into a spin.

"He must have been an experienced old bird. What age? In his forties?"

No.

"Older?"

Yes.

"Is he mentioned in the army records?"

Suddenly, the pendulum seemed to go limp, as if it was tired.

"Is this all?"

A tired yes.

"Unbelievable," Sylvia said. "I wish you could have heard yourself!"

"Why?"

"You sounded as if you were there, as if you saw how he handled it."

"What type of man did you pick up from that dialogue?"

"An older professional soldier. Centurion of the Roman army in Britain, in the year 338."

"I can't remember the year."

"You should keep track of these details while you're dowsing. Why don't we buy a little tape recorder?"

"Go on. What kind of man?"

"Experienced, great sense of humor. That, I think, is the main thing."

"Where did you get that from?"

"He comes to an abandoned fortress, rounds up a bunch of sheepish recruits shacked up around the neighborhood with local women, lines them up in front of him—they must have expected to be executed."

"Go on."

"Looks them over and says, 'Possession. I'll cure you.' He must have forced some evil-tasting brew on them three times a day for a month. If that's not a sense of humor! Just the thing you would have done, I think."

She sounded lighthearted enough, but I could see she was shaken by what she had witnessed. Frankly, so was I.

"It's time we went for something real," I said. "Let's go to the Norman church as the woman suggested."

We did. It was small, ancient, its door carried a notice saying KEEP THIS DOOR CLOSED AT ALL TIMES. Inside, high up in the echoing nave, we heard loud twittering and a desperate flutter of wings; a swallow had been locked in and was by now quite frantic. It must have got in through a hole in the stained glass window nearby and now was unable to find its way out again. Sylvia took out her pendulum and asked for instructions; the answer she got was "Open the door."

"But they don't want it opened!" I protested.

"You want to leave the poor thing locked up in here? Go ahead, I'll try and coax it out."

I obeyed reluctantly. Sylvia cooed and made kissing noises in an effort to coax the swallow down from the rafters. I opened the door, there was a whoosh of wings: in flew another swallow. The reunion in the rafters was ecstatic.

Sylvia tried to make them leave, without success. Well, there still was the hole in the window. As we walked back to the car the thought occurred to me that reuniting the swallows might have been the true purpose of our expedition.

*

What with one thing and another, it was fairly late in the day when we returned to Shrewsbury. At Sylvia's urging we did not drive on to Glastonbury as planned but spent another night in the hotel. After dinner she prevailed upon me to do some more map dowsing for a Roman location nearby.

I did so without enthusiasm, but the pendulum reacted in high spirits. Glastonbury Tor was its choice, the sacred hill near the small town of Glastonbury reputed to have some connection with King Arthur and the knights of the Round Table. But it wasn't King Arthur the pendulum was interested in; on top of the hill was the ruin of a tower, another location where our friend the centurion had been active. How, I would be told tomorrow.

I still felt uneasy about the whole thing, especially about those moments when the pendulum started to circle without being asked. I had played around with a Ouija board at sea, I didn't want to get into that again.

The next morning we did some shopping and left too late to do any dowsing in Glastonbury. I booked us into a hotel which the automobile club guide singled out for its excellent cellar. The wine was poor, the dinner stodgy, the service snotty, and we were given a room with a connecting door. As I was drifting off to sleep a couple in the next room started to cavort with chortlings, moans, yelps and a massive twanging of springs. Sylvia slept through it all like a rose. Whoever emerged victorious from the love battle shrieked, "There! There!" in a triumphant bellow, the vanquished gave vent to a death rattle; I banged on the wall. There was a silence, then a bass voice said calmly, "Fuck you." I switched on the light on my alarm clock and saw it was seven minutes to two.

I lay wide-eyed in the darkness for a while, composing

repartees like "What? Me as well?"; then, without transition, I found myself floating above a wild area of woods and lakes mirroring the sun, with a bird's-eye view of a large fortified wall being built by what looked like Roman soldiers. Foundations were laid, ramparts began to rise, day after day wagonloads of stones were brought in, officers moved around directing operations. The days became weeks, the weeks months. There were attacks by bands of natives daubed with woad, firing arrows and scurrying away before the avenging soldiers. Finally the wall was completed. Fires, floods, thunderstorms. The seasons came and went. Years passed. I watched as the Romans finally left; they were followed by a series of nomadic tribes; later still a medieval village grew along the wall. I was watching busloads of present-day sight-seers visiting the ruins when I woke up because Sylvia turned over. I looked at the time again: five minutes to two. The dream that had covered two thousand years had lasted only two minutes.

A church carillon played "Abide with Me" with one tooth of the mechanism missing. Two solemn bangs of bronze reverberated over the rooftops. I fell asleep again and was awakened, with a start, by the racket of Goblin Teasmade.

Later that morning we went to Glastonbury Tor. Gazing up at the ruin of the church tower on its top, I spoke into the little tape recorder Sylvia had bought. "Well, after a miserable night in the hotel I'm ready to climb the sacred hill. The tower on top is where the pendulum wants us to go. It's one hell of a climb, but all right." (Later, climbing.) "This dog turd covered footpath is murder. Whatever the pendulum is planning to tell me had better be good." (Later, breathless.) "Well, we've reached the top. The view is lovely, a blue sky full of sailing white clouds, their shadows sweeping the plain. A lot of wind. Am looking for shelter." (Later.) "Here we are, inside the ruin of the tower, out of the wind. Well, pendulum, let's have it. Am I standing in the right spot?"

Yes.

"What do I do—just stand here and ask questions?"

Yes.

"To do with the same Roman centurion?"

Yes.

"What year? The same, 338?"

Yes.

"Was this a fort at the time?"

No.

"A settlement?"

No.

"A sanctuary?"

Yes.

"Did he come up here to see if it was a suitable spot to build a fort?"

Yes.

"Did he come alone?"

No.

"With another person?"

Yes.

"A woman, perhaps?"

No.

"Another officer? An aide-de-camp?"

Yes.

"Why did I ask about a woman? Was there a woman here?"

Yes.

"A soothsayer? Some kind of oracle?"

Yes.

"Fancy that. Did he consult her?"

Yes.

"Was she an old woman, like Ma Chang?"

Yes.

"Now, let me get this straight: he came up here looking for a suitable place to build a fort, not to consult her."

No.

"He consulted her for diplomatic reasons, so to speak? To soften the news that she had to move, to make room for the fort?"

Right.

"Did she tell him things?"

Yes.

"But she realized he didn't believe a word she said."

Oh, yes.

"Did that amuse her?"

Yes.

It was as if I were seeing him—no, that wasn't right. I didn't see him, just felt I knew him. Did I make all this up? What was going on here? Suddenly I'd had enough. I switched off the tape recorder and said to Sylvia, "Well, that's it."

"Why?" she asked, amazed. "You're doing fine! The whole thing is riveting. Go on!"

"I don't like it. I don't want to mess with Ouija boards and ghosts again."

"But sweetheart, this is not a ghost! You're simply asking what happened here—"

"It doesn't feel right."

"Why not?"

"It isn't my mind that's formulating these questions. It's—well—as if I was there. I don't like it. Let's stop."

She was disappointed. "At least ask who you are dealing with," she urged. "Find out who the centurion is or was. Ask for his name."

"How is the pendulum going to tell me that?"

"The way it tells me what a plant's name is: ask to have it spelled out for you. Remember? 'Is the first letter in the first half of the alphabet or the second?' If it's the first, you start with A, if it's the second with M."

I sighed and switched on the recorder again. "Okay, could you give me the centurion's name, please?"

Yes, said the pendulum.

"The first letter—is it in the first half of the alphabet?"

No.

"Second half? M. N. O. P . . ."

The pendulum started to circle at Y.

"Second letter. In the first half?"

No.

"Okay, the second again. M. N. O—"

Yes.

"The second letter is O?"

Yes.

"Third letter. First half?"

No.

"All right. M. N. O. . ."

This time the pendulum circled at U.

"Is his name Youssuf or something? Was he a Romanized Arab?"

No.

"Okay. Fourth letter. Second half again?"

No.

"A. B. C. D . . ." I went through the first half of the alphabet, but the pendulum refused to swing. I said, "This is ridiculous! Is that all there is?"

Yes.

"YOU—" Suddenly it dawned on me. "You mean it was *me?*"

Yes, said the pendulum.

"That's enough." I switched off the tape recorder and pocketed the pendulum. "Sylvia, this is where I draw the line. Now it's reincarnation, is it? Off we go."

"Now, Marty! We set out on this voyage of exploration with an open mind—"

"Enough open mind for one day. I'm cold, angry and thirsty. Let's go."

"You don't believe any of it?"

I looked at her. Her eyes were full of wonder. "Apart from reincarnation: every word," I said.

*

At Sylvia's urging, I played the tape back over lunch in a roadside restaurant with checkered tablecloths, plastic tulips and a prison menu.

"You know," she said thoughtfully, sipping her coffee, "what fascinates me is the centurion being up there in the company of his aide-de-camp."

"Why?"

"Could it be General Theodosius?"

"Huh?" I stared at her, nonplussed.

"Theodosius had a son who later became emperor, didn't

he? The aide-de-camp may have been his son. I remember your
telling me the boy served under his father during the English
campaign. I don't think a mere centurion could have had a son
serving under him he would take along on such a mission."

"Sorry, love; the dates are wrong. According to the pendulum both episodes took place in 338 A.D. when the centurion
was in his fifties. Theodosius was in his fifties in 368."

"But couldn't the dates be wrong? You have to allow for a
certain amount of error, I should think, when it comes to details
like that. I asked, because you started to research this particular Roman general. Why? Why this fascination with Theodosius?"

"Because he towed those barges."

But I thought it over while the local cider did its evil work
inside me. If I had to consider reincarnation, it would be more
attractive to have been a famous Roman general than some
run-of-the-mill centurion. But then, all loonies imagine themselves to be Napoleon, never a sergeant.

"Let's give it a rest for a while," I said. "What is it you said
about Helen coming to meet us in Bath?"

"She'll be at the hotel in time for dinner."

"But I haven't booked for her!"

"She did the booking herself. It's all arranged, we can drive
there at our ease."

"We'll be early!"

"Splendid, then you can go and shop before she arrives."

"Shop for what?"

"Something for Harry."

"Harry?"

"Yes, Harry. We'll be staying with them, so it's time you put
your shotgun away and treated him like a normal human being
instead of a rapist. They'll marry eventually, don't worry."

That afternoon, dutifully, I went shopping for something for
bloody Harry. After-shave lotion? Toilet water? On second
thoughts it had better be something I could pour into him; that
was our only common interest so far. We had first met in
France, a year ago, on my return from walking the dog. An
unfamiliar car with a British license plate had been parked in
front of our bungalow; I stood peering at its contents through
the windows wondering who the visitors could be when the

front door flew open and out came Helen crying, "Dad!" My heart leaped at the sight of her, we embraced. There was a special tie between us, an intimacy I shared with no one else, not even Sylvia.

"Where do *you* come from?" I asked. "What are you doing here?"

She hugged me. "I'll tell you if you promise to let me talk first, listen patiently, and allow me to finish before you say a word."

I wondered what this was about. "Let's step inside, out of the sun."

"No, let's walk down the street for a moment." She put her arm through mine and led me away from the house. When we were out of earshot she said, "I'm not alone, Dad."

"You have the children with you?"

"The children are with Ella in Holland. The person who brought me here is an English academician, assistant lecturer in medieval history at the University of Exeter in Devon, England."

I stood still with a sinking feeling. "Don't tell me you are starting all over again!"

"What do you mean?" As if she didn't know.

"Goddammit, Helen, you've barely ditched one bully who beat you up!"

She looked at me as if I was a child or, God knows, a lover. "Dad, I'm a grown woman. I know what I'm doing. I can't stand living alone any longer with the responsibility for three young children. I need a man in my life."

"For Pete's sake, Helen! Give yourself a chance! You—"

She kissed me; my anger and anguish collapsed in what felt uncomfortably like shame. Was I jealous? What a mess old age was.

"Come, meet him, Dad. You'll see. He's different from my ex. He's kind and gentle. The only thing is . . ."

I was prepared for the worst. "What?"

"His name is Harry too. Sorry . . ." She giggled.

I said, "Jesus."

The young man who rose respectfully as she ushered me into the living room had one thing going for him: he seemed incapable of lifting a finger against anyone other than in tutorial admonishment. He had to be years younger than she; despite the semitropical temperature he was clad in houndstooth tweeds and perspiration glinted on his balding forehead. He wore glasses which he pushed up his perspiring nose as we shook hands. His was soft and moist. "So pleased to meet you, sir. Helen has told me so much about you."

Sylvia's face was noncommittal.

"Sit down—er—Harry," I said, realizing I sounded like a ship's captain dealing with a shirker. "How about a snort?"

"Pardon?"

"What'll you have? Whisky, gin—"

His face brightened. "Oh," he squealed in a high voice, "do you know what I would love? A Fuzzy Navel!"

I looked at Sylvia. Her face was a study.

"It's the latest in drink, Dad!" Helen gushed. "Harry just came back from a congress in the States and that's what everybody is having over there: half peach brandy, half orange juice . . ."

I said, watching Sylvia, "Sounds lethal."

"In case you didn't have any, sir, we brought you some," the tweedy eunuch caroled. "Helen!"

"I know where it is." She hurried out. Her future was forecast in the eagerness with which she ran to get the creep his cocktail. *Amor fati;* love thy fate.

After the meal she told me, in a cozy aside, that Harry was nervous about getting married. He would eventually, that was a foregone conclusion; she would not be moving in with him with three children if she thought it was a temporary arrangement.

That had been a year ago, they still weren't married, and here I was, buying brandy for his fuzzy navel.

But when I saw Helen on my return to the hotel, all was forgiven. She was a ravishing girl—well, woman. She said, "Mom tells me you've set out on another voyage of discovery. Dad, how exciting! I want to hear all about it."

She did, over dinner. Yes, we had found not only a milestone and a Roman fortress hidden under a medieval ruin, but a live centurion complete with pharmacy—sorry, that was Captain Bosman.

"I don't understand," she said, frowning.

"You swing your pendulum—like so—over a map, it picks out a site, you tootle over there, swing the pendulum again on location, fine-dowse the spot where to stand, and Bob's your uncle."

"How?"

"I'll tell you." It took me until the cheesecake and the decaffeinated coffee. She loved it, this was just up her street. How splendid to do something so different and daring at my age!

"Well, h'm, not much of a dare, you know. It's fun. And healthy, a lot of walking."

"He records every word," Sylvia added. "You must hear the tapes, fascinating."

So it went, merrily, merrily; I didn't see the trap they were setting for me until they sprang it. "Show me, Dad! Let's go somewhere tomorrow where you can demonstrate to me how it works. Please? Please? If you do, I'll type out the tapes for you, I'd love to do that."

I should have kept my mouth shut.

Back in our room, Sylvia spread out the map on the bed and, obediently, I dowsed. The pendulum selected a place called Lullington a few miles southwest of Bath. In a park, off a little road.

*

We had a problem finding the place, hidden as it was in a maze of country lanes like a spider's web; finally we found ourselves at a T junction facing the turreted lodge of the park. The gate was closed and carried a sign PRIVATE, ACCESS ONLY FOR DELIVERIES.

I brought out my pendulum to find out whether we should turn left or right; to my irritation it said "Straight on." Just then a man with a cloth cap came out of a side door, opened the gate and beckoned us through. Sylvia hesitated, then drove across the road and through the gate into a vast park, following a driveway lined with beech trees. After a while she stopped the car to enable me to consult the pendulum. I was told "Further up the road." In the middle of nowhere it circled: here.

"What do I do?" I asked. "Dowse from the car?"

No, said the pendulum.

"Get out?"

Yes.

I got out; Sylvia and Helen drove on to find a place to turn the car. There I stood, in a charged silence. I brought out the tape recorder, switched it on, and set the pendulum oscillating.

"Was there a fort here?"

No.

"Just a meadow, as it is now?"

No.

"A clearing in the forest?"

Yes.

"The centurion made camp here?"

No.

"Another Roman officer did?"

Yes.

"What year are we talking about?"

It turned out to be 368 A.D.

"That *was* during the Theodosius campaign?"

Yes.

"Then it cannot have been the centurion I picked up in the ruins of the castle and on Glastonbury Tor."

The swing of the pendulum went crosswise.

"What do you mean? Yes? No? Maybe?"

I was trying to work that out when Sylvia and Helen joined me.

"How is it going?" Sylvia asked.

"A bit of a balls up, I'm afraid. We are now in 368, too late for the centurion we know."

"The one we think was dad's previous incarnation," Sylvia explained.

"That's what your mother thinks. But let's stay with this for a moment." I asked the pendulum, "If it was 368, my centurion would have been in his eighties. Surely, he no longer can be on active service?" The pendulum went crosswise again. "Look!" I showed it to them.

Both Sylvia and Helen watched the mysterious signal in silence. Then Sylvia said, "I think it means yes and no."

"Thanks," I said. "Let's forget him for the time being and find out what happened here. Something did happen here, did it not, involving a Roman officer?"

Yes, said the pendulum.

"Another officer, whoever he was, made camp here?"

Yes.

"Was he a centurion too?"

No.

"A higher rank?"

Yes.

"General?"

No.

"Tribune?"

No, no—a strong negative signal.

"Praepositus?"

"What's that, Dad?" Helen asked.

"A regimental commander in the fourth century. Nowadays he would be called a colonel. Was he?"

Yes, said the pendulum.

"All right. A Roman colonel and his regiment made camp here. Then what happened? Did he meet someone? Did someone come to see him?" Another of those wingding questions.

Yes.

"Was there a disagreement between them?"

Yes.

"To do with a woman?" Again, a woman. What would a woman be doing here?

The pendulum, of its own accord, went into a positive spin.

"Well, what do you know! Is the woman important?"

The pendulum continued to spin.

"A romantic involvement?"

No.

"What else? Was she a warrior? A sort of Amazon?"

Yes, said the pendulum.

"An ally of the Romans?"

No.

"A prisoner?"

Yes.

"A queen? A princess of some sort?"

Yes.

"Brought here in chains?"

The pendulum went into a halfhearted yes.

"More than just chains? In a cell?"

Yes.

"A portable cell? That would be a cage."

The pendulum spun.

A woman in a cage? Ludicrous. "Was she brought here by the colonel's soldiers, who had captured her?"

Yes.

"Did he set her free?"

No.

"Execute her?"

No.

"Was his disagreement with the other officer about what to do with her?"

Yes.

"Well, if she wasn't set free and she wasn't executed, then what was done with her?"

"They must have kept her a prisoner," Sylvia said.

"Hush, Mom!" Helen was spellbound.

"All right," I continued, "let's find out. Did he keep her a prisoner?"

Yes, said the pendulum.

"How could he, if he was just camping here for the night? Don't tell me he carried her along on his campaign locked up in a cage."

Yes.

"That's ridiculous," I said.

"Why, Dad?" Helen asked.

"A Roman regiment on the march burdening itself with a prisoner in a cage? The whole story is a hoax."

"Don't get discouraged," Sylvia urged. "Persevere!"

"I wouldn't know what to persevere about."

"Ask for a key word!"

"What's that, Mom?"

"Dad will ask the pendulum for a word to help him continue

questioning in the right direction. Ask if it will spell it out for you, Marty. That's what Ginny does when she's foxed by a problem with one of her plants."

The ravishing Miss Whalen had much to answer for. "All right," I said to the pendulum. "Spell out a key word for me. Is the first letter in the first half of the alphabet?"

It wasn't, so I started with M. The pendulum circled at S. "Second letter: first half?"

Yes.

I carried on until I came up with the word *SING*.

"Sing," Sylvia said. "Ask if it has to do with a chant? Like for a wedding?"

"Wedding songs?" I asked, fatigued.

The pendulum was too; it gave me a tired no.

"Ask if she sang alone or with a choir," Helen proposed.

"Girls," I said, "I've had it. Let's call it a day." I switched off the tape recorder and pocketed the pendulum.

They were disappointed but resigned. I took over the driving; on the way to Topsham Helen said, "I think you were too impatient, Dad. It sounded like the beginning of a fascinating story."

I said, "I'm not after stories. I'm after the truth."

Sylvia sighed demonstratively.

I asked, "What was that about?"

"What, dear?"

"You sighed like a sea cow."

"Gee, thanks."

"Was it because I want the truth? Not *Quo Vadis* as a comic strip?"

"If you must know," she said, "I sighed at the thought of such an incredible gift being bestowed on the wrong person."

"Meaning me?"

"For me, dowsing has been like a window being opened, discovering a whole new world, and I couldn't begin to do what you're doing. It's wonderful, watching you work the pendulum. And all you come up with is doubt."

"Love," I said with the superiority of reason, "I enjoy it too, but I'm not about to accept a fat woman singing in a cage while being carried along by a Roman patrol on campaign. Oracles,

Captain Bosman in Roman times—I'm prepared to accept it all, but not a fat woman in a cage."

"Who said she was fat?" she asked, ready for a fight.

"All opera singers are and she sounded just like one."

"Come on, Mom, Dad," Helen said, experienced. She kissed my ear, which nearly sent the car into the ditch. Experienced, she kissed her mother's ear as well.

"All right, Helen," Sylvia said, experienced too, "tell me about the children."

That took care of the rest of the trip; meanwhile, I thought about the woman in the cage and the gullibility of old age. Not me; I wasn't going to believe a damn thing until I received proof. But what proof could there be that sixteen hundred and twenty years ago two Roman army officers quarreled over a woman in a cage who sang, ending with her being taken along on campaign? Wine selection, that's what I should stick with. There at least I had received proof; one Château L'Evangile in hand was worth a dozen caged sopranos in the bush.

I found myself thinking of the old centurion almost with nostalgia. *He* wouldn't have gone in for such a foolish exercise! I didn't like this new, younger officer. I didn't like him one bit. I wanted my old centurion back.

That's how insidious it was: instead of making me dismiss the whole silly business as a hoax, the woman singing in the cage persuaded me to accept the centurion who had cured the deserters of possession as if he was a real person I had known, a fellow captain of the fleet. Good old so-and-so, remember him? Remember the shirkers who hid with the whores and yelled they were under a spell when dragged out of bed and back on board ship? No? Never heard the story? Well, let me tell you. Miss! Two more of the same for the captain and me, please.

"Old men ought to be explorers." I knew another saying, not by a poet but a police inspector: "Some old men don't have the sense to come in out of the rain." Something to do with one foot in the grave and the other on a banana peel.

"Penny for your thoughts, Dad."

"I was thinking about booze," I said.

"He would," said Sylvia.

*

During our short stay in the rambling house on the river Exe, full of dogs, cats, gerbils, kids sliding down banisters and the smell of cabbage, the business about the Roman centurion and his son the colonel really began to bother me. I had messed with the Ouija board during my last voyage, my predecessor Captain Haversma had left it in the bottom drawer of the chest in my bedroom and I had fooled around with it, with some creepy results. But before I was totally hooked, Ma Chang, who had no inhibitions, snatched it from me and flung it over the edge, saying that I should not cross the bridge between the dead and the living before my time. She had even gone so far as to exorcise the ghost of poor old Haversma, who had been dead some time but who, according to her, was still haunting the ship. After that experience I wanted no more part of the supernatural, and the centurion began to feel uncomfortably like it. What I needed, I decided, was a serious conversation about the whole phenomenon with an expert who could tell me exactly what was going on. There was only one I could think of: the wing commander. He had invited Sylvia and me to visit him whenever we were in England; it was time to take him at his word.

According to the map his village was only a few miles off the road to Heathrow, where we were to hand in the car and take a plane to Amsterdam. I telephoned him; he promptly invited us for "sherry and a spot of lunch."

We found the village without difficulty. It was busy with cars speeding through and farmers' tractors dragging clattering trailers; but off the main street it was quiet with the hush of history. Old trees, ancient houses, even the new bungalows seemed to have been there forever. A door in one of them opened and Wing Commander Martock came out: mustache, country tweeds, boots that crunched on the gravel. "Come in, come in! *So* glad you found it!"

He took us to a terrace at the back of the house overlooking a small garden. A decanter and three glasses were waiting on an iron table with three chairs; there seemed to be no Mrs. Martock. He poured out generous helpings while over the neighboring roofs the carillon of the village church clanged out a halting song of praise.

We raised our glasses, which turned out to contain not sherry but straight Scotch. "Welcome! Tell me. You had some interesting dowsing results, you said."

I told him about the so-called milestone, the ruins of the medieval castle, and how I had found myself composing, if that was the word, an episode in the year 338 A.D. When I described the centurion dealing with the deserters, he stopped me. "Can you give me a description of the man?"

My heart sank. I had come to see him because I needed a sober-minded, professional analysis; instead, I had run into another fanatic. "I did not see him, he was a fantasy. The outcome of my research of the period which went on for years. My own impression is—"

"I know, I know!" He waved it away. "If I were a police inspector asking you to describe a suspect, what would you tell me? Not his physical appearance; the feel of the man."

This had gone far enough. "I'm here because I need to be reassured that the whole thing was an improvisation, a fantasy on my part."

"What makes you so certain it was?" he asked.

O, ye gods. "It was a mishmash of memories of my years as a young mate, researched material, and Robert Graves's *I, Claudius,* if not *A Funny Thing Happened on the Way to the Forum.*"

"Describe him to me, please. Let's keep your interpretation till later."

"A run-of-the-mill career officer. Totally undistinguished."

"Do you have experience of career officers?"

I realized it had been close to the knuckle. "I have commanded ships, so I have a certain empathy with professional soldiers."

"I wouldn't be too sure of that," he said dryly. "Tell me about your fantasy. As detailed as you can."

I obliged. I told him about the fortress built on existing

earthworks, the deserters who had shacked up with local women, the centurion who might have punished them but needed them and decided to cure them of possession instead. I told him about Captain Bosman's pharmacy, the origin of the fantasy.

"Fascinating," he said. "What happened next?"

"Two days later, on Glastonbury Tor, I was told by my pendulum—or by my lying subconscious—that the centurion was myself in a previous incarnation. I should have called it a day then, but my wife and daughter strong-armed me into dowsing one more location: a spot in a private park south of Bath. There I dreamed up a crazy story about a woman prisoner in a cage over whom two officers had a row. One wanted to execute her, the other to keep her, they ended by taking her along on their campaign cage and all. Singing, if you please."

"How remarkable."

"This episode took place, according to my pendulum, in 368 A.D., not 338. Neither officer seemed to be the centurion I had picked up before; he would have been in his eighties by then, so it's unlikely he had anything to do with it."

"There may be a link, even so." He wanted to top up Sylvia's glass, she gestured she'd had enough; so he refilled mine and his own. I became aware of the silence; the only sounds were of birds bathing in a pond in front of the terrace.

"Well, now, let's see what we have here. To start with, I take your findings more seriously than you do. The career officer pardoning deserters gone native by pretending they are possessed is not something you would invent."

"I frequently invent things in my dreams that are just as farfetched. A few nights ago I was given a bird's-eye view of the construction of a fortified wall by the Roman Army. I witnessed fights, defeats, victories, people in different costumes in different periods, finally I saw present-day tour buses unloading sightseers. The whole dream took precisely two minutes. I wouldn't put it beyond my creative imagination to produce a dream world while I'm awake. I hope that's all it was. If you were to tell me it was a psychic experience, I'll back off. I won't mess with the supernatural. I have been there and back."

He grunted and lit his pipe. Sylvia said nothing; she obviously was not happy. The birds splashed in the pond. The sound of a truck passing came from the village street. Then he said, "To begin with, your experience is not unique. Arnold Toynbee, the historian, tells of one in the later volumes of his *Study of History*. If he is too illustrious for you, how about the two Oxford dons in Versailles?"

"Who were they?"

"Charlotte Moberly and Eleanor Jourdain. Around 1900 they visited the palace gardens at Versailles as tourists. Suddenly they found themselves caught in a time warp without at first realizing it. They saw people in eighteenth-century costume running back and forth nervously; they thought it was the rehearsal for a historical play. Gradually it dawned on them that they were witnessing the last day of Marie Antoinette. They even became involved in it: a man in a pavilion in the grounds, clearly of the period of Marie Antoinette, noticed them. There are records of other people who experienced the past, either by visiting a place where something dramatic had occurred in years gone by or by holding an object of the period in their hands. The only difference between you and those people is in your mode of perception. You feel the overriding need to remain in control and therefore the only way you can handle psychometry—that's what the phenomenon is called—is by using your pendulum. You can stop it when you like, question your results step by step, even quarrel with your pendulum when you feel it pushes you too hard—forgetting that it is not the heart of the experience. Your questions are."

"I have a problem accepting that," I said. "I studied the Theodosian campaign extensively for years. I have a large number of factual and even visual details stored in my memory computer. I cannot gain access to them by simply pressing my brain for memories, I have to do what we do at sea when you want to spot a ship on the horizon: unfocus your eyes and let them roam idly."

"I know the trick," he said. "Fighter pilots do the same during combat."

"Well, the pendulum does this for me. It makes me look away by forcing me to concentrate on its responses. The memories appear on my computer screen in the form of questions, which are in fact suggestions."

He smiled. "Ingenious, but that won't explain the lady singing in a cage."

"Oh, that was just a bit of nonsense the pendulum goes in for occasionally."

"You see?" He pointed at me with the stem of his pipe. "You are investing your pendulum with wit, high spirits, a sense of mischief. It's *you,* not the bob on the string, who conjured up the lady, the cage, the singing, the deserters in Acton Burnell, the oracle on Glastonbury Tor. Were they in your memory bank? Did you ever come across those incidents in your research?"

He made me uncomfortable. "What are you trying to do? Convince me that I am a medium?"

"We all are, to a certain extent," he replied calmly. "We all have access to other time zones—"

"Speak for yourself," I retorted, more aggressively than I intended.

He grinned. "For a man who dreamed the history of Hadrian's wall from its origins to the present day in two minutes, that's a surprising statement."

"I told you: that was a dream!"

"Dream or no dream, you followed a detailed imaginary sequence of events covering two thousand years in two minutes. You can't get around that. During those two minutes you lived in another time zone."

"I can't accept that."

"Why not? Because a scientist in a lab can't repeat the experience and would therefore tell you it couldn't have happened? Let me give you some advice, Commodore. If you want to get anywhere in this field, you must start by deciding not to allow anyone to bully you out of an experience, not even you yourself. A basic law is that there can be no progress, spiritual or otherwise, without some acceptance of your own experiences as real. Not 'real' in terms of Victorian materialism, real in another dimension of time, like your dream."

"But the dream wasn't real!"

"Not its contents, maybe, but the fact is that you compressed two thousand years into two minutes. You are at liberty to reject the contents as a fantasy, but don't bully yourself out of the central experience, that's all. You're on a voyage of exploration; if you want to feel secure, stay at home. The decision is yours."

Despite the hussar mustaches and the foul pipe, he was an eagle-eyed old buzzard. "You want me to accept the centurion and the deserters as real?" I asked.

"Accept the reality of the experience. Reserve your judgment as to the contents until you have more to go on."

"But where did I get this sudden ability to dowse? I never had the slightest interest in it, let alone gift."

"Look, Harinxma. You're a man of great professional experience. You have commanded ships, you have acted independently all your mature years. Why not now? Collect experiences, arrive at your conclusions at a later date. So far, you have merely flirted with the other dimension. Have the courage to go the whole hog. That's what I'd say." He proceeded to fill our glasses once more after Sylvia had waved the decanter away.

"What about this business on Glastonbury Tor?" she asked. "That the centurion was Martinus in a previous incarnation?"

"Surely you don't want me to accept that!" I cried.

"Don't accept anything at this stage except the experience itself," the wing commander replied calmly.

Well, that seemed to be all there was to be said. We stayed for lunch, which he had obviously prepared all by himself; it was very touching. The booze helped, there was no more talk about me and my centurion, thank God. I had come in order to be reassured; all that had happened, I suspected, was that Sylvia had received a flea in her ear.

As it turned out, I was damn right. From the wing commander we went to our eldest son Tim and his wife in Amsterdam, where I slept in a bunk bed opposite a life-size poster of a pop star in a diving suit zipped open down to his pubic hair. The bed had been vacated for Opa by a teenager with a punk hairdo and a necklace spelling SHIT, who was named after me. Of course, Sylvia had to blab the whole story to the assembled family in the kitchen; before I knew it I was demonstrating how to dowse for Romans on a map of Europe. To my surprise, in answer to my tired question, "Any sign of my centurion anywhere here?" the pendulum gave me the coordinates of a small town on the Rhine, just over the Dutch border, called Neuss.

"Look!" Sylvia said. "It's right across from Düsseldorf."

"So it is," I said. It was where her first husband Johnny had crashed.

That settled it for me. Centurion or no, we had to go to Neuss.

*

It was a rambling, noisy little town just off the autobahn. At her first glimpse of it from the freeway, Sylvia said, "It's odd to be here."

"Must be," I said, watching a German Mercedes angrily flashing its headlights in my mirror.

"He was shot·down just across from here, his friend Mel Stephens saw him go. Three weeks later he went down himself, Mel did. Over Berlin."

I did not respond as I had to turn abruptly down a loop; then we found ourselves in Neuss. It must once have been a pretty medieval city, now it bore the marks of Johnny's terrible swift sword. The houses were mostly postwar reconstruction, faceless and utilitarian. The town seemed to be doing well; the streets were full of traffic, we had a problem parking. I finally managed to squeeze in somewhere a good distance from the museum. Strange, to think that less than a mile away the young boy in his Lancaster bomber had been shot down in flames. This town must have been an inferno worse than London during the blitz, of which I had had a taste. As we walked to the museum Johnny's flaming death seemed to have more reality than we ourselves, strolling arm in arm in technicolor.

"Shall we have a cup of coffee first?" I asked.

"Why? We had breakfast just an hour ago."

"Maybe we should talk about him."

She gave my arm a squeeze. "I only mentioned him because we happen to be here."

"If it was me, I'd like you to take a moment off with your

second husband to remember me. If he's still around, after forty-three years."

"Oh, that he is," she said with certainty. "Look, here's the museum."

The museum, it turned out, was mainly concerned with the city's medieval past; the small Roman section was unimpressive. In response to my query about Roman remains in the town, a young woman in the information booth directed me to a *Römische Kultstätte* on the old road to Cologne. We would have to ask for the key from a lady in the house next door. We were given a city map, as well as a brochure on Roman Neuss. I checked with my pendulum, I had assumed it had indicated the museum. But no, it was the other place.

The *Kultstätte* proved to be a low concrete building, like a wartime pillbox, with a padlocked heavy door. The lady in the neighboring house, who was vacuuming the hall, handed us the key without turning off the machine. There was a strong smell of German cooking.

We opened the heavy door and found ourselves in a humid cavity smelling of toadstools. After some groping I found a light switch; harsh fluorescent light revealed a hole in the ground with a dirt floor, like the cellar of an old farmhouse. A set of stone steps led down to it, another led back up, that was all there was to it. No artifacts, no remains to evoke the Roman past. All the empty cellar evoked was the earnest labor of professors who had overseen the excavation of this bizarre pit and removed everything of interest from it.

Outside, in the bright sunlight, we read the brochure and learned that the hole in the ground had been a baptism-of-blood cellar belonging to the cult of the great godmother Kybele. The poet Prudentius had described the ceremony: a priest with a gold crown would descend into the pit dressed in a toga; once he was inside it was covered up with planks full of holes. A bullock decorated with flowers was pulled and pushed onto the plank floor, its throat was slit, its blood splashed down through the holes onto the priest, who offered his head, throat and tongue to the rain. He had to make sure that his ears, nose and eyes were full of blood before he gave the signal, then the lifeless body of the bullock was dragged

away, the planks removed, and the bloody priest would present himself to the crowd, who would cheer him for now he had
that of God within. *"Renatus in aeternam."* It did not charm
me, yet the barbaric rite was of an appealing innocence com-
pared to the baptism of blood Johnny and his comrades had
rained down upon the city.

We returned the key and thanked the lady; as we were
about to leave we found our way barred by a massive German
woman as intimidating and immovable as a snow plough. *"Ah,
Frau Doktor!"* the lady of the key cried. *"Wie nett dass Sie
gekommen sind!"* She turned to us and explained, *"Frau Doktor* Blankert is a leading authority on Roman Neuss. She lives
across the street, she saw you go in and called to find out if you
were authorized. She says she'll be happy to answer all your
questions. Do you speak German?"

"I do," I said.

Frau Doktor Blankert eyed us sternly. I introduced ourselves, we shook hands, she said in a startlingly masculine
voice, in German, "Tell me what you want to know and I will
try to oblige."

"We—I am particularly interested in the fourth century. In
the garrison that must have been stationed here in the year 367
A.D."

"Why?" she asked sternly.

"I'm—er—researching the third invasion of the British Isles
by the Romans in 368. I have reason to believe that a particular
officer, who was part of the invasion force, may have been
stationed here at the time. With—er—with an older man, a
centurion." I realized it must sound very odd to an outsider.

She looked from one to the other and asked, "What was the
officer's name?"

"I—er—I don't know that as yet."

"What was his rank?"

"Er—well—praepositus. He was a colonel."

"Which legion?"

"I don't know. We are just beginning."

"Must have been a numerus, at that time. Do you have an
idea which one he belonged to? Frisionem Aballavensium?
Batavi? Nervii? Tungri?"

"I'd say Batavi," I ventured, unnerved by a vague sense of guilt generated by this interrogation.

"That would have been a numerus barcarorum. What do you wish to see?"

"Well, I was trying to locate the remains of the fortress on the bank of the river . . ."

"In 367 A.D. there would have been little left." Her voice took on a hectoring quality; she was no longer interrogating but lecturing. I discovered that the canvas bag she carried contained a cat, who started to struggle, meowing plaintively. "During the campaigns of the fifties there was fierce fighting on both sides of the river. Nothing would have been left of the *Koenenlager* except maybe some foundations of the barracks of the auxiliaries. Your Roman officer would have been holding a muddy field strewn with rubble within shattered walls." She made it sound as if it served him right. "Are you planning a book on the period?"

Well, what the hell. "The fact is, I'm a dowser. I'd like to do some dowsing where the fort was."

"A what?"

The cat shrieked; it sounded like laughter.

"A dowser. A water diviner."

"You mean you want to establish the old bed of the river? That is already known."

"Old bed?"

"If you look in your brochure, you'll see that the course of the Rhine is no longer what it was in Roman times. You wish to retrieve the old bank of the river?" Without waiting for a response, she continued, "I will take you there. Come!" She turned on her heel; the cat cried, *"Nein!"* and wriggled in its bag.

"It's very kind of you," I said lamely, looking at Sylvia who stared back, uncomprehending. I explained.

The lady who had given us the key cried, *"Gute Fahrt!"* and closed the door. We followed in the wake of the massive *Frau Doktor* and her cat. We walked for about ten minutes without exchanging a word; then, on the corner of a busy street, she said, "Here. This is where the river's west bank was in 367 A.D."

"Well . . ." I looked at Sylvia, who shrugged her shoulders.

"In that case . . ." I took the pendulum out of my back pocket and, feeling like a flasher, set it swinging. "Is this the right spot?" I asked in English, my voice low, avoiding the frowning regard of our guide. The cat had given up and hung limply in its bag, eyes closed. The pendulum said yes.

"I see . . ." Embarrassed, I didn't know what else to ask. Well, it was fairly basic. "Was the praepositus from Lullington here at that time?"

Yes.

"Did he command the garrison here?"

Yes.

"Did he have the centurion from Acton Burnell with him?"

Yes.

"Er—what weapons did the Romans use? Bow and arrow?

No.

"Catapults?"

No.

What else, for Pete's sake? The *Frau Doktor* was watching me, frowning; Sylvia looked uncomfortable. Some passersby had stopped to watch the eccentric old man swinging a bead in the middle of the street. I pocketed my pendulum and said in German, "Well, that's about all for the moment, I think. Thank you so much for helping me out."

"Ah, but there is more! Much more!"

Sylvia set me free. "It was very kind of you, Dr. Blankert," she said warmly in English. "Would you do us the pleasure of joining us for lunch?"

"Zank you," *Frau Doktor* said. My heart sank, forgetting that in Germany "thank you" means "no." She turned to me. "If you want more information, contact me," she said sternly. "You can reach me via the museum."

We mumbled good-bye and found ourselves alone in the street, still a source of some interest.

"Look," Sylvia said, "there's a sign saying *Zimmer*. The place looks nice, let's ask if they have a vacancy."

"Why? I won't get any answers here."

"Not under these ridiculous circumstances. If we get a room on the street side you can dowse later tonight in private, over-looking the river. Or what used to be the river."

She marched toward the *Zimmer* with determination.

*

The guest house was run by a jolly mop-haired woman with a comforting lack of organization. Toys blocked the stairs, a puppy wagged its tail on the landing above us so vigorously that it lost its balance and came tumbling down, to be caught by Sylvia. I signed a guest slip finally found in a drawer full of papers, pencils and pots of glue. The room we were shown was indeed on the street, noisy as hell, but it had a view, presumably of the nonexisting river of the fourth century.

The twentieth-century one was two blocks down across the road; we visited it that afternoon. Lots of barges, the deafening racket of winches, the shuddering rumble of passing tugboats pushing strings of barges upstream. Not a place for meditation, let alone dowsing. We had a meal in a little restaurant down the street frequented by locals. The wine was young but full bodied; that was how I felt myself after half a chicken, three helpings of *Bratkartoffeln* and a bottle of *Spätlese*. Foolish old sod; two hours later I was fit to be carted off, cringing with heartburn, belching like a ram in rut. It was foolhardy to expect any results from my pendulum in that condition, so we went to bed.

I woke in the middle of the night; Sylvia was asleep. I got up quietly, put on my slippers and robe, took my pendulum out of my trouser pocket and pulled up a chair in front of the window. The street had quieted down, it was very still outside. The sky across the river was lit up by an orange glow as from a distant fire; that must be the lights of the city of Düsseldorf. I set my pendulum swinging.

"First of all, let's settle who we're dealing with here. You said earlier that the centurion was here, but that he was just an observer. Were you serious, or was that a bit of tomfoolery? Was he here in 367 A.D.?"

Yes, said the pendulum.

"You realize it sounds like nonsense? The man must have been eighty. Are you absolutely sure he was there?"

Yes.

"Not as a participant, but merely as a witness? Is that what you said?"

Yes.

"Sounds like hogwash, but never mind: an eighty-year-old witness. Who did command the garrison? The praepositus from Lullington?"

Yes.

"His garrison was a numerus, right? Between five and seven hundred men?"

Right.

"Okay, I repeat the question: what weapons did the Romans use against the barbarians across the river? If it wasn't bows and arrows, catapults, or stone-throwing *ballistae*, then what did they fight with? Could you spell it out for me?"

Yes.

"All right. First letter, in the first half of the alphabet?"

No.

"Okay. M. N. O. P . . ."

The pendulum circled at W.

"Second letter. Again in the second half?"

Yes.

"M. N. O—"

The pendulum circled.

"W. O. All right. Third letter . . ."

I ended up with WORDS.

"That should be *swords,* surely?"

No.

"You mean, the Romans battled the Germans with *words?*"

Yes.

I used a four-letter word. Sylvia said from the bed, "Now act the good cop. You've bullied the suspect enough, now try patience." I had not realized she was awake.

"Sweetheart," I said, "I'm sorry, but this is ridiculous. I'm being made a fool of."

"Believe," she said, turning over. "Say: I believe, help Thou my unbelief."

I went to the bathroom. The puppy was wide awake on the landing and followed me, wagging its destabilizing tail. It insisted on going in with me, so I let it. Words!

I went back to bed, did some halfhearted reading, then turned off the light. Words. The Romans could hardly have engaged in a shouting match across the river with the barbarians, it was too wide. No one could make himself heard across that expanse of water, not even with a megaphone. The whole thing was nonsense.

CHAPTER THREE

*

Novaesium, November 367 A.D.

The Franci had a maddening agility with boats. The river, swollen with winter rains from the mountains, ran furiously under the low black sky heavy with snow, but it did not daunt those savages. A string of five flatboats set out from the opposite bank, attached by a rope to a rock they had dropped in the middle of the stream. Like a chain-ferry propelled by the current the boats slowly swung across in a wide arc until they were within earshot; then they lay still, bobbing and weaving, just out of range of the catapults. They were low in the water with the massive weight of their occupants, fat bearded men decked out in skins and little pot helmets like acorn cups, with horns. In the first boat the old chieftain, plainly recognizable at that distance, heaved himself to his feet, slapped down his helmet and started to shriek catcalls at the recruits marching in rigid drill on the parade ground by the river. He was promptly joined by the rest, heaving themselves to their feet, flatboats scuppering, yelling insults.

The ranks of recruits faltered. "March!" the drill instructor bellowed. "Keep in step, you donkeys! One, two! One, two!"

Out on the river, the Franci parroted, *"Einz! Zwei! Einz! Zwei!"*

The old chieftain unhooked his cloak and despite the icy wind brought out his penis. He made slicing gestures and shrieked, *"Abschneiden! Alle Abschneiden! Kastraten! Ungeziefer! Euneuche!"*

The recruits, shaky to start with, stumbled in confusion. Out on the river all the barbarians had now produced sluglike members and were yelling in unison, *"Abschneiden! Euneuche! Kastraten! Alle abschneiden!"*

The drill instructor, purple in the face with powerless rage, bellowed the command to form turtles. "Testudes! Up shields!

Up!" The recruits regrouped six abreast and lifted their shields in a pitiful display of disunity.

"*Abschneiden!*" the savages screeched delightedly. "*Alle abschneiden! Kastraten! Ungeziefer! Schweinehunde! Hunde!*"

"Lock shields!" the instructor shouted.

The recruits made a mess of forming the marching pill-boxes, symbols of the invincibility of the Roman army. They were a sorry lot, dregs of the tribes on this side of the river, press-ganged by recruiting patrols, branded with irons to deter them from deserting. They were a challenge to any drill instructor; now, spooked by the jeers and boos of the barbarians, they were hopeless.

Colonel Mellarius, Praepositus of Numerus II Batavorum, watched the sorry rabble in dismay. They were degrading the once illustrious name of the regiment. Some dropped their shields, others hit their neighbors over the head as they clumsily lowered the turtle's armor. Out on the river the Franci, drunk with triumph, cheered, whistled, flipped their penises. Under all its previous commanders II Batavorum had been the most decorated regiment on the frontier. Instead of recruits having to be press-ganged, volunteers had lined up to apply. In those days there had been no need to brand them or to bribe them with promises of early citizenship; none would have dreamed of running away.

Colonel Mellarius was not to blame for the decline. The regiment had been decimated twice over the past few years. Fierce battles had destroyed the fortress which, having changed hands several times, was now no more than a bog dotted with ruins. The troops were now housed in leather tents; the *ballistae* and *onagri* teetered on sagging platforms. The neighboring settlement, where once there had been baths and shops and cozy little whorehouses run by motherly matrons, had been destroyed. Skinny cattle roamed among the ruins; under cover of darkness the peasants rustled them to feed their families.

One of the ranks of the second turtle stumbled and fell in a jumble of shields, arms, and legs; there was a chorus of cries and wails as the yokels cut themselves and one another with their swords. The Franci danced in their flatboats; the drill instructor seemed to be on the brink of an apoplexy. Colonel Mellarius gave the order to cease the drill and disperse for meals. It was too early, but there was no point in continuing. The garrison was steeped in a mood of dull disgust.

"Disperse!" the drill instructor bellowed. "Disperse, you rabble! May the gods forgive you for disgracing the army!"

No wonder. What could tie these alien youths, now slinking away to their tents, to Rome, the emperor, the Imperial Army? Maybe he should deliver another exhortation, the colonel thought. Those who had managed to remain upright instead of falling flat on their faces might be rewarded with some baubles. The drill instructor, dispirited, came squelching toward him through the mud. Doctor Fortunatas, the Greek medicus, turned up with his bag of bandages to attend to the remaining heroes who had impaled themselves or been gored by their neighbors. It began to snow.

"Gods!" The instructor spat powerlessly at the river. "Next time, how about giving the bastards a volley of arrows, sir?"

It was a symptom of the demoralization of the regiment that a minor officer presumed to know better than his superior. Colonel Mellarius let it ride, for here was a soul sorely tried.

"Let them have their meal," he said. "Get them back out this afternoon."

"In the snow?"

"Snow or no snow. The inspector can arrive any day. If he sees what I saw this morning we'll be sent to Belgium to grow barley."

It was an exaggeration, but then it was weather for exaggerations. Anything to restore warmth to chilled bones, clammy chests under metal breastplates, weary legs, calves frozen with muscle-knotting cold. The Franci, having lost their audience, sent the string of boats coursing back to the other shore, ululating as they romped home victorious.

The meal was served by the colonel's orderly in the command tent which doubled as conference room for councils of war and interrogation room for high-ranking prisoners, of which there had been none for a long time. The meal was the usual slop of rye, barley and figs sprinkled with poppy seeds. Assuming that he would have a headache after this morning's display, Doctor Fortunatas, anticipating his needs, had provided a cup of celery seeds. There was no wine, not even local beer; he was given mint tea laced with some potion from the doctor's pharmacy to help his digestion.

The orderly came in with the sweet, his shoulders white with snow; the cold wind swirled through the tent looking for chilled old bodies. The colonel was getting too old for this; if the snow persisted he would get a bout of rheumatism again and add a limping commander favoring his left hip to the spectacle of Numerus II Batavorum ready to spring into action. He was staring in mute disgust at the nameless dessert, when he heard a commotion outside the tent.

Shouts, wails, curses; without ceremony two mud-splashed soldiers dusted with snow dragged in a clamoring creature of male gender, haggard, his tousled hair streaked with gray, his clothes torn, the toes of his bare feet black with cold in their sandals. "Lord!" the creature cried in a high keening voice. "Protect me from these ruffians! I am not a common thief! I am an artist!"

The word was a ray of sunshine in the gloom. Colonel Mellarius could not remember ever having heard it uttered during his forty years in the army. "Let him go," he said to the soldiers. "Who are you?"

"Lord!" The scarecrow went down on one knee in a grotesquely theatrical gesture of surrender. "I am a thespian, I have served the army for twenty years with my company of actors, traveling from garrison to garrison, trying to instill some concept of beauty, rhetoric, and virtues into the—" he became conscious of the waiting silence of his captors—"the heroic defenders of the frontiers of the empire."

"Is that so?" Colonel Mellarius contemplated him. He looked like a scruffy brigand caught rustling cattle. "Then where is your company of actors?"

"They fled, lord!" the man exclaimed, his voice swollen with bathos. "We were attacked by bandits who took all we possessed: costumes, cothurni, requisites! They beat us up, they even took our boots! The others fled, the gods only know where. I dragged myself for days through swamp and bog, forest and field, until at last I saw the fort, the army, Rome! Sobbing with relief, I stumbled in, to be pounced upon by these—gentlemen and dragged—conducted into your august presence. For the sake of art, lord, for the sake of the virtues, Rome, receive me for what I am: a victim of circumstance, a thespian felled by perfidy!" The sheer cadence of his phrases seemed to warm him; he struck a pose of humble expectancy and eyed the food on the table.

"Get up," the colonel said. He gestured at the soldiers to leave; they did so without alacrity. "Have some dessert." He pushed the bowl toward the artist.

"Lord!" The man's voice broke with a sob. "You cannot know what it means to a bird lost in the gale, bedraggled, homeless, to be received with such grace. Thank you, lord, thank you." He grabbed the bowl; lamplight glistened in his hair which was no longer gray-streaked, it had been snow. He wolfed down the ghoulish sweet with the greediness of the famished. He must be in his late thirties, old before his time after years of trudging from garrison to garrison to spout Virgil, maybe the *Iliad,* to dumb-faced cretins who did not even understand Latin, like the rabble outside. What struck the colonel was the pointlessness of the man's quest. If the touchstone of art was that it could not be used for anything, then here was a true artist.

"What is your repertoire?" the colonel asked, watching the creature lick the bowl.

"Anything, anything you wish, lord! Any poet, any dramatist, any speech of historical importance: Cicero, Petronius, the *Aeneid,* Sextus Propertius . . ."

"What part of the *Aeneid?*"

The scarecrow put down the bowl and rose. " 'The Passion of the Queen' . . ." He raised his right fist and declaimed:

> Liar and cheat! Some rough Caucasian cliff
> Begot you on flint! Hyrcanian tigresses
> Tendered their teats to you! Why should I palter?
> Why still hold back for more indignity?

His voice was sonorous and powerful, his passion impressive. As Colonel Mellarius sat staring at him an idea formed in his mind.

"Recite that again," he said. "Louder, this time."

"Forgive me, lord?"

"Again, but louder."

The man gamely sallied forth once more. " 'Liar and cheat! Some rough Caucasian cliff begot you on flint!' "

"Louder."

"Excuse me, lord?"

"Louder!"

Baffled, the thespian bellowed obediently, " 'Hyrcanian tigresses tendered their teats to you!' "

"Louder."

The man took a deep breath and roared with a voice that rattled the dishes on the table,

> Why should I palter?
> Why still hold back for more indignity?
> Did he sigh, while I wept? Or look at me?
> Or shed a tear? Pity her who loved him?

"All right," the colonel said, "that'll do. Finish your food."

"Yes, lord . . ." The man stared at him, bewildered; he had already licked the bowl.

"What's your name?"

"Cassius Colonia, lord. Your servant."

Colonel Mellarius clapped his hands; his orderly appeared, snow capped, in the entrance to the tent. "Bring back the dishes. Give Cassius Colonia the same meal you served me."

"Yes, Colonel," the orderly said, with controlled contempt.

*

When it came to putting the idea into practice, Colonel Mellarius almost lost faith in the enterprise. The thespian was quirky, probably even mad. He insisted on someone finding cothurni for him to replace the ones that had been stolen; when he was told that no army outpost stocked them, certainly not the mudhole among the ruins which was now Fort Novaesium, he sulked and said he could not perform without them. Frisius, the regimental carpenter, loved impossible tasks; he fashioned a pair of stilts which were higher than the lamented stage boots and certainly better in mud. Next, the thespian said he could not perform without a mask with built-in trumpet; to this the colonel replied that he had heard the artist's voice and considered it an insult to suggest amplification of such a mighty instrument. The thespian, though still pouting, was prepared to forego the mask and trumpet, but the hairpiece, also stolen, was absolutely essential. Frisius the carpenter, fired now by the spirit of improvisation, fashioned a wig out of lengths of frayed rope from the catapults and dipped them in boiling axle grease, which rendered them green and made them look like a knot of vipers. Finally there was the toga. Essential, the thespian said; without it no artist could possibly perform. The *Aeneid* required a toga, and not just any toga: one of sufficient length to cover the stilts. For a moment it looked as if this would scuttle the plan, but the spirit of improvisation had now spread through the camp and Fortunatas the medicus came up with a shroud for officers, a class of garment higher than the winding sheet used for corpses of lower rank. It turned out to be long enough but on the tight side; as long as the artist did not match his step to his height but minced into position he would be all right. Or he could lift his skirts until he had reached his mark.

The final problem was the thespian's sudden refusal to recite the passage from the *Aeneid* as rehearsed. He had looked at the location, been told about the Franci in their flatboats who would be his audience, and decided that the queen's curse would not do. Now that he had a clear picture of the challenge facing him there was only one oration that would exploit the situation to its full effect: Sextus Propertius's "Warning to a Rival" from the Cynthia cyclus.

This was where Colonel Mellarius lost his temper. "But that's a quarrel between two lovers over a woman!"

The thespian took umbrage. "If your lordship has no confidence in my genius, then I must divest myself of these trappings and—"

"Shut up, man!"

Fortunatas the medicus, always alert to emotional crises which he considered bad for the colonel's health, put a soothing hand on his arm and said, "I know that beautiful ode. A most stirring piece. Admirably suited for the open air, I would say."

Colonel Mellarius knew that Fortunatas knew no Latin poetry, certainly no love lyrics four centuries old, but he relented.
The thespian said, "Thank you, magister," and swept out in his
shroud to go and paint his face.

Once the artist was finally ready to appear, the recruits
were marched out onto the muddy parade ground. It was no
longer snowing, but the clouds were pregnant with sleet and
the wind was icy. The river was dull as lead; the dark primeval
forest on the opposite shore seemed to embody the ultimate
gloom of Ultima Thule. The icy wet cold slid a skeletal hand
between breastplate and sweat-soaked smock; the hungry
grave seemed to reach up the legs of old army officers planted
martially in the mud, arms akimbo, watching stoically as the
miserable rabble formed ranks. Where was the regiment of
yore? Where were the invincible, glittering cohorts that his
predecessors had drilled to triumphant perfection? Rot was
eating at the fringes of the empire, even the river carried the
stench of decay. How could these press-ganged serfs be inspired with the joy, the pride, the sense of mission that had
fired their predecessors as far back as the god Julius Caesar?
The *ballistae* leaned lopsided on their platforms; black birds
of Teutonia came screeching over the leaden river as if bewail-
ing the dying of the light. Then, from the opposite shore, the
barbarian flatboats detached themselves, seven this time, filled
to the brim with beer-bellied brutes, their little horned helmets
glinting in the gloom. No wonder they were fat; in this climate
a man needed layers of blubber to protect him from the groping
hand of death reaching up from the infernal bog. The drill
instructor came marching toward him, his martial stride
marred by a squirt of mud as he stubbed his feet on some
buried rubble. He lifted his arm in salute and said, "Regiment
ready for inspection, colonel."

"Thank you. Proceed as arranged. The moment they start,
have the troops face them. Make it look confident, for the sake
of the gods."

"Yes, Colonel." Another salute, another squirt of mud as he
stamped his feet; he made an about turn and started to bellow
even as he marched, his breath wisps of steam in the chill air.

The troops formed ranks. The seven boats bulging with
human blubber stopped as usual just out of range of the cata-

pults and streamed into line, held in place by the rock in the center of the river. The taunting started: whistles, catcalls, *"Einz! Zwei!"* Despite the cold, there came the pale penises again, flagging their archaic message of contempt.

"Half *turn!*" the drill instructor yelled. "Make *front!*"

The untidy rows of recruits formed jagged lines parallel to the river, facing their tormentors, who stood in their boats shrieking, *"Kastraten! Abschneiden! Euneuche!"* The wind became too cold for penis display; they tucked them away and took out rough wooden crosses which they started to wave, showing they were Christians, freshly converted by some hot-eyed itinerant monk crazed by fanaticism. Suddenly, shocking in its surprise even to the colonel himself who had planned it, there loomed a huge, breath-chilling creature on the river's bank. It stood eight feet high, in a long sinister shroud that fluttered in the wind.

The thespian had painted his face with berry juice and charcoal; combined with the fluttering shroud and the wig like a nest of vipers it made him look terrifying. The jeers and catcalls from the river faltered, but as the apparition took up position on top of a little knoll at the water's edge the Franci resumed caterwauling and waving their crosses. The apparition, outlined in red by the sunset flaring through a tear in the clouds behind him, pointed straight at them and intoned,

> *Invide! Tu tandem uoces compesce molestas!*
> *Et sine nos cursu, quo sumus, ire pares!*

The colonel had not really expected his ploy to have any effect on the brutes screeching in midriver, but to his astonishment they fell silent. They lowered their crosses, their mouths sagged, their little horned helmets suddenly looked like the pricked-up ears of a startled herd of cows.

> *Quid tibi uis, insane? Meos sentire furores!*
> *Infelix, properas ultima nosse mala!*

The effect was magical. The barbarians spoke no Latin, but the sheer majesty of the massive stanzas rolling toward them from the wild spectral figure on the skyline must have aroused the phantoms of their superstition, all the terrors of the primeval forest. They fell silent, confused, fearing bad magic.

Miser ignotos vestigia ferre per ignis,
Et bibere a tota toxica Thessalia!

The command to drink all the poisons of Thessalia, even though not understood, made the Franci turn tail. They jerked at rudders, the string of flatboats started to arc back slowly to the opposite shore, while the thespian, victorious, changed his tone from aggressive power to sonorous melody. What struck everyone, in this sleet-sodden degradation of mud, defeat and hopelessness, was the music of it, the voice singing to the gods. Colonel Mellarius felt a buoyant sense of triumph. There they went, the beer-bellied brutes, back to the darkness of their forest, beaten, not by a feat of arms or a show of military might, but by the voice of Rome which had spoken through a scarecrow in a shroud, perched on stilts on the brink of their eternal darkness.

The thespian turned around, stepped down, lifted the hem of his shroud, and waded through the mud toward the colonel.

"Excellent, Cassius Colonia. That was beautiful."

When the man gazed up at him, the colonel saw to his amazement that the red and black face was smudged with tears. "A failure!" the thespian wailed. "I'm a failure! The gods have deserted me! I am a failure, dwindling to nothing!"

It took the colonel a moment before he realized that the man was actually weeping. It made him angry, for there had been a miracle, a true manifestation of the mystical power of art; yet here stood the miserable mime, parroter of other men's poetry, and wept. "What's wrong, man?" the colonel shouted, hearing the sucking steps of Doctor Fortunatas with his calming potion squelch toward him through the mud.

"No one spoke the stanzas along with me!" the thespian sobbed. "Not a sound from my audience! I am a failure!"

"May the gods strike me dead!" Doctor Fortunatas's soothing hand on his arm cut short the colonel's outburst. "All right! Come to my tent after the evening meal and you may read Virgil to me. I will repeat the stanzas after you if you are good."

"Lord . . ." The terrifying apparition grabbed the colonel's hand and, in an effort to kiss it, daubed it with snot. "Dismiss the troops," the colonel said to the drill instructor who was standing to attention, acting out the Imperial Army all on his own. "Explain to them what they have heard and seen."

It was unfair. He knew full well that the instructor had heard and seen nothing other than the adenoid snoring of his troops' moronic breaths as they watched, open-mouthed, the ghost of a great poet silencing the braying of savages four centuries after his death.

*

The thespian's mellifluous voice, rising and falling in the smoky intimacy of the tent, evoked in the colonel a memory of the little boy he had once been, terrified and lonely, reading to his savior the Roman centurion in a voice hoarse with tears,

> Draw home from the city, my songs, draw Daphnis home.
> Songs can draw the Moon from heaven,
> By songs Circe transformed Odysseus's men;
> By singing the cold snake in the meadow bursts.
> Draw home from the City, my songs, draw Daphnis home . . .

As a boy he had had no idea of the meaning of the words he so painstakingly pronounced the way his grandmother had taught him. She had taught him everything, except how to survive alone, with everybody dead, in an alien world, half prisoner, half mascot, plaything of the stern centurion who had adopted him and now ordered him to read and speak the lines along with him.

> Draw home from the city, my songs, draw Daphnis home.
> Tie the three colors with three knots, Amaryllis;
> Tie them and say: I tie the bonds of Venus.

The lamp smoked. Outside the tent were the usual nighttime sounds: the squelching steps of the guard through the mud, bursts of laughter from the soldiers' tents, the plaintive warbling of a flute shattered by cheers.

Draw home from the city, my songs, draw Daphnis home.
As this clay gets hard and this wax gets soft in the same fire,
So may Daphnis strain and melt from love of me.

Would T. Gaius Virilis really meet him when he in turn was
struck down on some battlefield or in some ambush in the
forest? Would the old centurion embrace him and guide him to
Hades, as he prayed for every night? How the years flew by!
How quickly after the young boy had read those lines, slowly
and fearfully, had the voice of the thespian taken over! A wave
of sadness rolled in from the night at the shortness of life, the
loneliness of the soul, the love that was never spoken and had
left him wondering if it had ever been shared.

"Lord? Is it not pleasing?"

He became aware of the thespian's anguished face looking
at him with the eternal doubt of the artist. "It was beautiful,
Cassius Colonia. But I'm tired now, I need to sleep. Good night,
and thank you. You did well today. And tonight's reading was
a comfort to me."

"You are kind, lord." The scarecrow bowed. "This numerus
is favored by the gods, having for its commander a man of
cultural graces. I bid you good night, lord."

He backed out of the tent, bowing deeply in a mad display
of ludicrous servitude. Almost immediately he was replaced by
Doctor Fortunatas, prim in his clean white gown and little
Greek headband. "Your potion, lord." He took the ritual first
sip himself, before handing the cup to the colonel. "That was
a brilliant tactic today, lord. Most effective."

How seductive! Unlike the thespian's, the doctor's humility
was constant and sincere; it took an act of will to resist the
temptation of confiding in him. But no man other than his own
father should ever be trusted by a commanding officer in the
field.

As if the doctor had heard, he said, "You represented Rome
today, lord."

"Thank you, Fortunatas," the colonel said. "Good night."

"Good night, lord. Should you need me . . ."

"I know. Good night."

Before drinking his potion and extinguishing the lamp, Colo-

84

nel Mellarius kneeled in front of the little pedestal with his
housegod and prayed.

"T. Gaius Virilis, I thank thee for the blessing thou brought
me today, the idea of using the thespian to silence the barbarians. I miss thee, beloved father. I miss thee every day, every
night. Without the awareness of thy presence, thy example, the
memory of thee, I would falter. Wait for me, father, wait—"

A discreet cough behind him made him frown and rise. In
the entrance stood Flavius Maximus, centurion of the watch.
He brought the coldness of the night into the warm tent, as if
he was hewn out of ice.

"Sorry to disturb you, Colonel, but I have just learned that
General Dulcitius and Inspector Marcellus Sabinus may be
here tomorrow. I thought you'd want to know at once."

"Who brought the news?"

"The wine merchant. They're still in town, but are preparing
to leave."

"Thank you, Maximus. Keep me posted."

"Yes, Colonel."

The centurion saluted and took the ice of his presence back
into the night.

What reason could there be for the general's visit? Marcellus Sabinus, the army inspector, had been expected, but General Dulcitius, head of military intelligence? He was too lofty
in rank to be interested in mortals like himself; there must be
a special reason for him to visit this mudhole with its pathetic
dregs of humanity pretending to be a regiment. But then, the
general must be aware of the quality of today's recruits. None
of the commanders of the other frontier regiments could show
anything better. What did this rare and precious French pea-
cock from the emperor's palace want of him?

Well, his record was clean. He had no illusions about himself, but he was a reliable, unambitious officer who did as he
was told and refused to dabble in politics. He was not a Christian, but that was not a requirement for commanding officers,
not yet. He had no private life, no woman, no boy slaves, no
vices other than gluttony, which in this godforsaken place was
like being a prisoner in a cell cursed with the vice of philander-
ing. He was a lonely man, but no lonelier than any other commanding officer on the frontier, which after decades of warfare

and the gradual devastation of fortifications had turned into a no-man's-land of mud, mire, ruins and the stench of corpses, a portal of hell.

Colonel Mellarius drank his potion and resigned himself to sleep.

CHAPTER FOUR

*

Neuss, October 1986

If we had not gone to the trouble of traveling miles off our course to get here, I would have suggested we leave Neuss the next morning. But we decided to stay a second night so I might have another go at dowsing that evening, on the bank of the real Rhine this time, not its ghost in the street below.

We had another Teutonic dinner down the road. After the coffee we bundled up and walked arm in arm down a dark street to the river. It was a clear night; wisps of white cirrus drifted overhead, red across the river with the lights of the city of Düsseldorf. The river itself was a shimmering black sheet crossed by the wriggling reflection of the new moon. There was no boat traffic; some barges were tied up alongside each other in the small basin protected from the current.

We walked around the basin to the end of a jetty with a flashing red beacon and gazed at the string of lights on the opposite bank. Sylvia sat down on a bollard some distance away to give me privacy, without my having mentioned my need for it; after an unsuccessful effort at meditation, I pulled out my pendulum and set it swinging. The bead was invisible in the dark, but I could feel its response.

"Is there anything for me to pick up in this spot?"

Yes, said the pendulum.

"Any particular event, as in the other places?"

The pendulum circled rather hesitantly.

"Do I make suggestions, or do you want to spell out a key word again?"

At that moment a little dog on one of the barges discovered our motionless dark figures and started to bark with a shrill yapping sound. I tried to block it out. "I still have a problem with the old man being here, the centurion from Acton Burnell and Glastonbury. He must have been far too old by now to live in the sort of swamp the *Frau Doktor* described. Tell me honestly: was he here in 367?"

Yes, said the pendulum.

"But why? What was he doing here? Had he any particular function?"

The pendulum went into a strong positive spin.

"What was his rank? Had he been promoted?"

No.

"He still was a simple centurion?"

Yes.

"At the age of eighty?"

Yes.

The yapping of the little dog was very distracting. I became aware of how I was sitting here: cross-eyed with German *Spätlese,* swinging a bead that had belonged to a Chinese ship's cook. The dog went on snipping away at the silence with the sharp little scissors of its yapping.

"Look," I said to the pendulum in a tone of reason, "just spell out the key word to give me some idea in which direction to continue my questioning."

Yes, the pendulum said without enthusiasm.

"First letter. First half of the alphabet?"

Yes.

I started with A, the pendulum circled at D.

"Second letter?"

It turned out to be O.

"D. O. Third letter?"

It was G. Dog. "Goddammit!" I cried, "I *know* it's a dog!"

"What's the matter, darling?"

Sylvia's voice stopped me from flinging the pendulum into the river. "It doesn't work," I said. "Let's go."

"What happened?"

I told her on our way back to the guest house. The little dog went into hysterics as we passed its barge.

In bed, after we had talked it over, I lay staring at the ceiling faintly lit by a streetlamp below. As I listened to Sylvia's breath becoming slow and regular with the onset of sleep, melancholy settled over me.

I was an old man, my life was over. There was nothing left

for me to do except wait for the axe, or the rack, of death. This so-called dowsing was a last pretense that there was something left for me to do; there wasn't. One of our neighbors had a motto on his wall: GROWING OLD IS NOT FOR SISSIES. How true. It meant living constantly on the brink of tears, remembering the dead. It meant living in fear of coming pain, coming darkness, oblivion.

Sylvia was lying with her back to me; I switched on the bedside light. I had nothing to read; *The Faber Book of Modern Verse* was in the suitcase in the car. I took the Gideon Bible in three languages out of the drawer of the bedside table, leafed through the Old Testament, and settled for Ecclesiastes. "Remember now thy creator in the days of thy youth, while the evil days come not, nor the years draw nigh when thou shalt say, I have no pleasure in them! While the sun, or the light, or the moon, or the stars, be not darkened, nor the clouds return after the rain . . ." So it went on, and on, ever deeper into gloom, until "tears shall be in the way, and the almond tree shall flourish, and the grasshopper shall be a burden, and desire shall fail, because man goeth to his long home."

Surely the Bible had something more cheerful to offer old men? I vaguely remembered something cheerful at the far end, in Revelation. I looked it up.

"And I saw a new heaven and a new earth, for the first heaven and the first earth were passed away and there was no more sea." God, that was the last thing I wanted to hear.

I crawled out of bed, put on slippers and robe, found the pendulum in my trouser pocket, sat down in front of the window and looked out into the night. "Come on, pendulum, give me one more word to go on. Will you?"

Yes, said the pendulum.

"The first letter. First half of the alphabet?"

It was. The word, painstakingly pieced together, was *dreams*. I had no idea what that could mean, and no possibility of finding out either. I wouldn't know where to start, what to ask.

I groped my way back to bed, wondering how I could get out from under any further dowsing without deserting Sylvia in her newly found excitement and joy, sending her back to the technicolor world of blue rinse, bridge and bingo.

I believe; help Thou my unbelief!

*

Novaesium, November 367 A.D.

The gods were not favoring Colonel Mellarius on the morning of the general's visit. Behind the first line of well-drilled soldiers of the second century, the miserable recruits were lined up in ragged rows of tilted helmets, flat feet and droopy drawers, ready for inspection. The weather was atrocious: wind, sleet, rags of fog; the river gurgled, burbled and stank, something it did only when the fluvial god was in a foul mood and considered man a vermin infesting his domain. The small group of officers and sycophants accompanying the high-plumed little French general stood huddled together on the tribuna, a platform on the edge of the quagmire of the parade ground. At the sight of their arrival the barbarians had stirred on the opposite bank; this time it was not a string of flatboats that set out but a single coracle. It detached itself from the shore and started the slow arc across the fast-running river. There didn't seem to be anyone inside it; it traveled across steered by a lashed rudder.

This had to signify trouble of some sort. The colonel ordered the catapults manned but he was soon sorry he had done so. The handful of well-trained gunners was instantly in place, but the recruits whose job it was to furnish the stones and arrows were a bunch of clowns. The colonel closed his eyes in shame when he saw them stumble in the mire on their way to the firing platform, dropping rocks, arrows, losing helmets, some of them falling flat on their faces and struggling in the mud like hooked fish. The climax of the farce came when one of them reached up a bundle of arrows, another reached down from the platform to grab it, the top one lost his balance and both of them, together with their load, crashed into the mire with a double scream, to roars of laughter from some morons press-ganged only three days before and kept hidden at the back of the ranks. In an act of desperation, the colonel himself marched to the river's bank to await the coracle with its invisible load, sword drawn. He had no idea what could be hidden in the apparently empty vessel slowly sweeping toward him, but that the Franci were up to no good was certain. Under the curious gaze of the general, the army inspector and their retinue, his centurions moved into place and lined up, swords drawn, shields joined, between their commander and the river.

The coracle seemed to take forever. As it slowly swept toward him, all kinds of possibilities went through the colonel's mind: snakes, poisonous rats, maddened ferrets, a plague-ridden corpse. He was not prepared for the truth. When the little vessel finally bumped across the mudbanks and hit the shore at the feet of the centurions, it was found to contain an old, frightened dog, ears back, with a crude imitation of a Roman helmet made out of cloth and covered with obscene drawings tied onto its head. The old dog rose timorously to its feet; it turned out to have a board around its neck as well, with the drawing of a heap of turd and, misspelt, the word *ROM*.

Instantly both Maximus and Antigonus, centurions of the second and the first, leaped forward to kill the insulting beast. But something in the dog's eyes, its helplessness and degradation, prompted the colonel to call, "Halt!" The centurions froze, swords lifted, the colonel turned to his regiment and shouted with the authority of his rank, "This animal is a Roman hostage returning home! I propose that this Roman dog shall be promoted to regimental mascot!"

For a few seconds his fate and that of the dog seemed to hang in the balance. The troops were baffled by this development; his heart sank as he realized that he had stumbled into a trap the river god had set for him. Then there came, from the tribuna, the small, civilized sound of one man clapping his hands: General Dulcitius, instantly joined by his fawning retinue who all applauded with gusto; one of them, a civilian, even ventured a cheer.

There was not sufficient time for the colonel to register his personal triumph; he called Flavius Maximus, centurion of the first, his second in command, ordered the offending board to be removed from the dog's neck and the mascot to be paraded in front of the troops. Ranks quickly reformed at the barked commands of the drill instructor.

"Bucinator!" the colonel ordered.

At his signal the trumpeter blew *Attentio,* a high, keening sound echoed by the wall of the forest across the river. Flavius Maximus dutifully paraded the mascot past the ranks. The terrified dog, obscene cloth helmet on one ear, tongue lolling, hindquarters dragging in an effort to relieve itself while trotting, was cheered by the ranks with relish. The humiliated and degraded, the branded who had been press-ganged or handed over by their chieftains as tribute to the army, recognized something of themselves in the poor animal. *"Salve! Salve!"* they cheered; when the drill instructor, that most insensitive, hard-hearted of men, entered into the spirit of the moment and roared, *"Salute!"* they all sprang to renewed attention, lifted their arms in one sweeping movement—astounding, from that bunch of untrained rabble—and as if by magic their lines straightened, the chests came out, the chins up. The old dog, now pissing with terror, was dragged past their ranks once more, cloth helmet flopping, while they roared *"Salve! Salve canem!"* It became a roar of pride, totally unexpected, certainly by the Franci who saw their elaborate effort at humiliation mysteriously turned against them.

Colonel Mellarius faced the tribuna, stood to attention, lifted his arm in salute, and cried, "Numerus ready for your inspection, General!"

The slight, aristocratic general looked down on him with a smile, returned the salute and said, "Seen and approved, Praepositus," words traditionally spoken only if a regiment had been drilled to perfection.

Not believing his ears, Colonel Mellarius made an about turn and ordered the drill instructor to dismiss the regiment.

"Regiment! Dismiss!"

The colonel was rewarded with a resounding cheer from the men he despised, and who most certainly despised him with the hatred of the downtrodden.

The dog, tongue lolling, helmet under its chin, looked up at him with uncomprehending eyes, all the helpless of the earth personified.

*

"Brilliant," General Dulcitius said when he was finally alone
with the army inspector in the guest tent. The orderlies and
servants had been sent away; at last he and Marcellus Sabinus
could converse freely over a beaker of wine—their own, thanks
to the foresight of his quartermaster; the stuff here must be
urina.

The inspector grunted.

"You do not agree? Gods, man! That ragtag herd of human
cattle was suddenly transformed into a regiment! This Mellarius is our man. The field marshal needs exactly the qualities
he demonstrated today: inventiveness, quick thinking, authority, sufficient self-assurance to improvise at a moment's notice.
I wish we had more regimental commanders like him."

Marcellus Sabinus sipped his wine, looking gloomy. Why
was he so dour? Envy? Who knows. Native Romans were a
touchy lot; he had been inspector of this section of the frontier
for a decade and was at the age when most veterans settled for
a piece of land and Roman citizenship. But then he didn't need
that, he was a Roman by birth. "Give me the background on
this Mellarius," the general said.

The inspector finished his wine, put the empty beaker down
on the floor and replied in his aristocratic Latin, too perfect to
be anybody's native tongue, "He is a Batavian by birth. The
sole survivor at the age of ten of the massacre of a village on
the Rhine by barbarians from across the river. The story goes
that he hid in a tree in an orchard near his parents' house when
the raid started, heard his family being slaughtered; when the
raiders came to look for fugitives in the orchard he chased them
by calling in the bees."

"Calling the bees? What do you mean?"

"His people were beekeepers. The boy's task must have
been to whistle them home at sunset before the night frost hit

them. When later that day he saw the army patrol arrive, he called the bees again. They were in such a frenzy by the time T. Gaius Virilis got to the orchard that he was stung many times before he could lift the child out of the tree. It seems the boy remained deaf and dumb with terror for weeks after T. Gaius Virilis took him under his wing."

"T. Gaius Virilis? Who's that?"

"The centurion in command. He was with II Batavorum at the time, stationed in Noviomagus. His century regularly patrolled that section of the river's bank. I remember him well. Harsh old man, as tough as they come, but the little boy must have got to him. He had him accepted as the regiment's mascot, gave him the name Mellarius, 'honey boy,' and eventually adopted him. The boy rose through the ranks and has been praepositus of this numerus for six years. Not a distinguished officer. Plays everything by the book. His name will be recorded only on his tombstone, if he's lucky enough to get one."

"I would have thought he'd have done better," the general mused, asking himself why the inspector was so pessimistic about this man.

"I wouldn't know," Sabinus said without interest. "T. Gaius Virilis was a hard man, he may well have intimidated the boy. But Mellarius idolized him, still does. Even made him his housegod."

"The quick thinking he demonstrated this morning would seem out of character then?"

Sabinus said nothing.

"Do you not agree that he saved the situation? Surely it was an example of both initiative and ingenuity?"

The inspector gave him a bleak look. "He may have been sorry for the dog."

Dulcitius reacted angrily. "Nonsense! This fortress is dedicated to Kybele, which means blood sacrifices, priests drinking blood, soaking themselves in blood—"

The inspector froze. Like all native Romans' his toes were so long they virtually crossed the empire. "If T. Gaius Virilis witnessed this morning's scene," he said coldly, "he will not have been pleased."

"I doubt he did," the general snapped.

"He may have," the old soldier persisted. "Remember, he's Mellarius's housegod. To turn an ancestor into your personal god means holding his spirit captive during your lifetime, preventing it from entering Hades."

"I thought you were a Christian, Sabinus?"

The inspector shrugged. "That may be its fashionable name today, but I see no cause to abandon Mithras. He and the Jew god are one and the same."

The general laughed. "Don't let the bishops hear you!"

"They were both born from an unmarried virgin, witnessed by shepherds, on the same day during the festival of the unconquered sun. They both gave a last supper to their disciples before ascending to heaven and promised to return for the day of judgment to gather their faithful. You tell me the difference."

"Well, you may be right. Let's call the man in."

The general clapped his hands; his aide-de-camp appeared after a diplomatic interval to demonstrate that he had not been eavesdropping. "My compliments to Colonel Mellarius and ask him to join us when convenient."

The officer saluted and marched out.

The general refilled the beakers. "By the way, I gather from the state of readiness in which we found the garrison that someone must have alerted Mellarius well in advance. Any idea who?"

"The wine merchant. I told him to."

"You did?"

"It's my practice to let commanders know that I'm on my way by putting the flea into the ear of one of their spies. It makes them feel one stroke ahead of me. Which is good."

The general sipped his wine.

Colonel Mellarius must have been expecting the call, for he entered the tent in parade armor, helmet under his arm. He stood to attention with dignity. The inspector's attitude toward the man had some effect on the general after all, for it seemed to him that there was a faint air of bemusement about the colonel. "Sit down, Mellarius. Have some wine."

"Thank you, General." With a creaking of leather and a small screech of metal when his breastplates shifted, Mellarius sat down on the couch next to Sabinus. The inspector filled his beaker.

"Mellarius," the general said, "I'm here on a special mission, which you are requested to treat with discretion."

"Of course, General." The hint of bemusement was gone; Dulcitius wondered what the man expected. "The rumor may have reached you that a few months ago the British provinces were overrun by a barbarian conspiracy."

"No, sir, it hasn't." Little news of the rest of the empire must penetrate the bogs of the northern frontier.

"For the first time," the general continued, "the Picts, Scots, Attacotti, and Saxons from across the sea banded together and attacked our forts. After a century of peace they were unprepared, most of them were manned by local militia. In some instances the lower ranks deserted and joined the rebels. Field Marshal Fullofaudes, Dux Britannicum, was killed, as was General Nectaridus. The only organized forces remaining are Legio IV in Eboracum and Legio XX Valeria Victrix in Deva, both under siege. Londinium has held out so far by a slapdash reinforcement of the ring wall, but as we sit here it may have fallen into the hands of the barbarians. The emperor sent General Sevirus of the Imperial Guard across; he withdrew after landing to avoid defeat. Then Jovinus, Marshal of the Western Shore, sailed, but he never reached the island because halfway across he received such panic-stricken reports that he returned. In neither case was the force large enough to deal with the trouble; this is a major insurrection. Now Field Marshal Theodosius has been assigned to form an army to crush the rebellion, and I have been appointed his personnel advisor. The army will be made up of four numeri and is due to sail next spring. I'm going to recommend you and your regiment be included, so you will be transferred to Augusta Treverorum shortly to start your training for the invasion."

Mellarius frowned. "As you will have seen, my regiment is made up of raw recruits, General. I have only one century that can be called trained."

"You'll have four months in which to lick them into shape. They need not be prepared for set battles; the field marshal expects his campaign will be fought mainly in skirmishes. He is planning to split up his army into vexillations which will seek and destroy, reclaim loot, free prisoners, reconstruct the defenses of garrisons and leave the local militia to fend for themselves. As the individual officers will have a large degree of independence, inventiveness and speed of reaction are essential qualities. This morning you gave an example of those qualities."

"Thank you, General."

"To be made part of the expeditionary force, Mellarius, is an honor. I expect you to live up to it."

"I'll do my best, sir."

"Modesty and self-criticism are virtues," the general said, "but I see no cause for undue humility in your case. I believe you will be able to inspire your troops to bring the Roman peace back to a province which has relapsed into chaos and barbarism."

"Yes, General."

"Thank you, Colonel. Now we'll bid you good night."

Mellarius rose, stood to attention, turned without salute, and marched back into the night. The guard closed the flap of the tent behind him.

"So, that was that," the general said.

"Well," the inspector admitted after a while, "I cannot share your enthusiasm for this man, but we don't have much choice. He'll do as well as any."

"Indeed. My belief is that he will do better. But enough of Mellarius. Tell me, how did you find Rome on your last visit? I have not been back recently."

"Rome?" Sabinus made a gesture of disgust. "Think yourself fortunate."

It proved to the general that he had been right. Marcellus Sabinus was such an inveterate cynic because the raw ugliness of his native city today disgusted him. He knew Rome, whereas Mellarius had probably never been there and therefore idealized it. As a Frenchman, General Dulcitius could identify with either while retaining his objectivity. Like a poet, he could write a passionate lament on the tarnished glory of the eternal city, while relishing its gamy, decadent beauty. It was all a matter of taste.

*

Colonel Mellarius watched the dog as it lay licking its private parts in a corner of the tent. He drank his sleeping potion thoughtfully. What had made him declare this smelly mutt the regiment's mascot? An impulse from outside himself, alien to his methodical army-trained brain, rather like the impulse that had made him order the thespian to recite Roman poetry at the barbarians in their flatboats. What was it? An inner voice, like Socrates' daimon? No, it had not been a voice. And Socrates' daimon had only told him what not to do.

He rose and kneeled in front of his housegod, but before he started his prayer he heard the dog get up in the corner and a moment later felt its cold, wet nose on his cheek. Eyes still closed, he put his arm round the animal; for a moment it seemed they were both about to pray. Then, suddenly, it was as if a door opened onto a vast high hall full of shades in shrouds, within their midst a presence. The dog stirred, the door closed, the vision passed. But he knew who the presence had been. He bowed and thanked his god, his beloved, revered, stern god, who had loved him even though he had never shown it during his lifetime.

"Lord?"

He looked up; the thespian stood beside him.

"Are you ready for another reading, lord? Or am I too early?"

The man should not have been allowed to enter without being announced. Mellarius had found out from the wine merchant earlier in the day that the man had not been attacked by bandits but kicked out of town by enraged soldiers. He was a liar and a cheat and might turn into a burden. But he had achieved a victory over the Franci without a stone being hurled or a sword unsheathed.

"Not tonight, Cassius Colonia," Mellarius said. "Tomorrow. I'll send word."

"Are we going to war, lord?" The man looked terrified.

Suddenly Mellarius was overcome by a preposterous compassion. "Yes. There will be fighting. Many dead. So we will be in need of your mighty voice and your genius to speak the funeral orations."

"Oh . . ." The thespian seemed to vacillate.

"And I will need your nightly readings. I will be in dire need of beauty, my friend."

"Yes, lord." The man's eyes had now taken on the look common to all who are addressed as what they could be rather than as what they are.

"Come, I need a reading tonight after all," the colonel said, heading for his couch. "Let's hear 'The spell thrown over Daphnis' again."

"Yes, lord."

The colonel lay down. With a sigh, the dog rested its head beside him. Its breath smelled very bad.

"'Draw home from the city, my songs, draw Daphnis home . . .'"

Outside sounded laughter and the voices of soldiers as the rumor took hold that Numerus II Batavorum was destined for glory, loot, and wide-legged women unable to resist the ardor of the victorious. The night's password was "dreams."

C H A P T E R   F I V E

*

Brussels, October 1986

After Neuss, we decided to hand in our rented car in Brussels and go by train to Nice from there. Sylvia wanted to stay in Brussels for a couple of days to visit her dressmaker before the winter; during three solid days I was left to my own devices.

Like all elderly males I need a daily walk; I keep it up wherever we go. In Brussels I walked the same dreary milk round two days running: from our hotel twice around the little park in front of the royal palace, twice across it diagonally, twice at right angles. On the third morning Sylvia said, "Why don't you walk to the museum and maybe include a visit? A brochure at the reception says that they have a Roman collection."

I have reached the age when men listen to their wives, so I set out for the museum situated in the east wing of the imitation Roman triumphal arch at the Cinquantenaire. It turned out to have one of those echoing entrance halls that are the same all over the world; a porter in uniform stopped me as I passed him on my way to the stairs, requesting my umbrella and raincoat. I asked for directions to the Roman collection; he pointed at the ceiling, which might have meant that it was a thing of the past. I climbed the concrete stairs, planning to make a quick round of the top floor and then to head for the open again to continue my walk.

The stairs were in two flights; as I climbed the second and looked up I glimpsed, inside a set of double glass doors on the landing, a white Roman torso. Just a torso, remnant of one of their athletic statues; it had only half of one leg left, no arms, no head, just a hunk of vandalized marble. But its effect on me was that I froze in my tracks.

I cannot find words for the impact my first glimpse of the mutilated statue had on me. A sudden sense of recognition, of

99

total familiarity, a reunion with something I held dear. I had felt a similar emotion at my first glimpse of Holland after the war; I stood halfway up the stairs, gazing at the torso with tears in my eyes as at a long-lost friend. The feeling of reunion was as real and emotionally charged as if I had emigrated as a boy and cherished for all those years the memory of home.

I don't know how long I stood there. At a given moment I got a hold of myself, climbed the rest of the stairs and walked through the doors into the Roman section. It was a large hall filled with sarcophagi and statuary, but I only had eyes for the torso. I stood in front of it, looked up, and suddenly seemed to become aware of having a different body. I felt a weight on my head. My cheeks were encased in metal. A breastplate covered my chest. It was not a hallucination, I had not changed identity, I was still Martinus Harinxma, but no longer a commodore: a centurion of the Imperial Army gazing at a symbol of home with love. It may sound mawkish, but there is no other word for my emotion as I gazed at that remnant of a lost world. The feeling of the helmet on my head was as familiar as the feeling of the peaked cap I had worn for fifty years. The armor and the cloak were as much part of me as the roll-neck sweater and the duffel had been. Had I indeed been a centurion in a previous incarnation, as the pendulum had suggested on Glastonbury Tor? My Roman self now seemed to have been part of me always, unremembered, like infancy; the torso had brought the memory to the surface with stunning immediacy. During the moments I stood there, gazing at it, I felt an entire lifetime stirring within me in all its fullness. I felt as if at any moment I would see my past reel off in front of me the way I had seen the history of the fortified wall in the dream that lasted two minutes. Oh, for a magical two minutes of remembrance like that. I wanted to know, I knew it was there, within reach, just below the surface. But the knowledge was all. I stood frozen in time, waiting, then I realized that this was all there would be: the awareness of having been a man with helmet, breastplate, cloak, and sword, who had loved a statue.

I turned away and walked past the other relics of antiquity on display. As I walked, I felt a scabbard slap against my thigh at each step. I held my head up in a peculiar position—slightly back—to allow for the weight of the helmet; I moved my upper body in an unfamiliar manner because of the breastplate. I paid no attention to the rest of the exhibit; I was too aware of my body, my movements. A group of young men passed me, students probably; I felt anger at their failure to stand to attention and salute.

Turning a corner, I found myself in a room filled with Roman portrait busts. They evoked no emotional response. As I strode past them, scabbard slapping, I seemed to walk out of that previous body, that homeland infinitely dear. My Roman self faded; as I went down the stairs I changed back into the retired old salt, that crashing bore.

Had it been a hallucination? A dream? Whatever it was, it had been an expansion of my sense of self, not a dissociation.

I arrived in front of the porter's desk. I must have looked shifty; he had me walk through a metal-detecting gate, patted my pockets, handed me back my raincoat and umbrella and said, *"Au revoir, Grand-père."* My other half, the centurion, was ready to call on someone nearby to teach him a lesson; it was obviously wishful thinking. I walked out of the door and went down the steps to the park, where panting men with bulging eyes pounded the gravel in sweatsuits.

I walked back to the hotel.

*

The moment Sylvia entered, her arms full of packages, I started to tell her about my experience in the museum. I found it surprisingly difficult; I could not express the reality of it in words. I became emotional, that made me uncomfortable. I had always had problems with men carried away by their emotions; anyone telling me that he had experienced a Roman incarnation while looking at a torso in a museum would have been dismissed as either a liar or a nut. Suddenly, while I was telling her about it, a chilling explanation occurred to me. What if it had been a first hint of the separation of my spirit from my body at death? Before long my body would die. My short thumbs, the creased face peering at me from the mirror, the whole dear complex of flesh, bone, sinew, skin and hair was doomed to decay. Whatever might be left of me eventually, for the moment my body was my self.

Later that day, at Sylvia's suggestion, I telephoned Wing Commander Martock to ask for his interpretation of the episode, but after two rings I put down the phone. Suddenly I didn't feel like talking to him. I wrote him a letter instead, a detailed unemotional report which I mailed at the front desk before leaving for the station.

At the beginning of the long train ride through France, before going to bed in the sleeper, Sylvia and I had an earnest talk and a giggly dinner in the restaurant car as I tried to dowse the wine list while cannonballing along at ninety miles an hour. When we finally arrived home I opened the front door and pushed aside a stack of accumulated mail. Among the bills and the circulars were letters from young Martinus, or rather his bride who had taken over the chore of corresponding with the old folk, from Helen, Ella and Tim, and one from the wing commander. When Sylvia went to collect the dog and the canary from the kennel, I read his letter.

> Dear Harinxma!
>
> What a fascinating experience! Past lives are not my field, so I took the liberty to submit your case to a psychiatrist of my acquaintance who treats patients by regression under hypnosis. According to him, your reaction was typical for someone who stumbles upon an object that takes him back to a previous existence. It would seem that the statue is a link with the old Roman centurion, the one you dowsed in Acton Burnell and on Glastonbury Tor (the younger colonel is clearly not you and of a later date). The slapping scabbard would appear to be a reinforcement of this concept, as does your reaction to the youths who failed to salute you.
>
> Now, where do you go from here? Your experience in the Brussels museum and the episodes from your Roman past you dowsed in the West of England seem to point clearly in the direction of further exploration. Your dowsing could be the key to much more, of both personal and historic interest. Why don't you get yourself a map of the roads of Roman Britain, as I suggested earlier when we met in Danville, and ask your pendulum to give you all locations of impor-

tance, like Acton Burnell and Glastonbury Tor? Start in Richborough, Roman Britain's main channel port, and move an ice pick slowly along the road to London from there. Your pendulum, I would expect, will end by giving you a complete itinerary of either an army campaign or a personal quest.

Let me know if you decide to make this trip and if you do, come and see me. I am fascinated. Yours cordially, Wm. Martock.

My first reaction was a negative one; but when Sylvia came home and read the letter she thought it was a great idea. "Marty, what a wonderful thing to do next spring! Better than the car rally or the tour with the Dickens Society. Imagine: a slow psychic pub crawl through Roman Britain!"

"I object to the word *psychic*," I said.

"But you have no problem with pub crawl, I take it."

The poodle passed, leaving a whiff of cheap perfume like a passing whore. "I'll go and air the dog," I said.

Up on the hill, where I rested while the dog set about undoing the salon's work by rolling on visiting cards left by colleagues, I thought about the wing commander's letter. A voyage of exploration with my pendulum? I wondered if this was what T. S. Eliot had had in mind. The centurion had been with me ever since Brussels. At the most unexpected moments—on my way to the bathroom during the night, walking down the garden path to collect the paper—the ghostly scabbard slapped my thigh.

I could no longer shrug it off as an *idée fixe*. I had better go and find out what else it was.

*

After a while, the impact of the experience in Brussels seemed to wear off. Sober-minded realism made me conclude that the brief sensation of being a Roman centurion had been brought about by my years of researching the period. I put Wing Commander Martock's letter aside for future reference and picked up my life as a retiree again: bridge, golf, walking the dog, boozing at five, snoozing during the news, no snoozing during *Apostrophes* on French TV.

That winter I made a few trips to Roman ruins in the neighborhood and did some dowsing with indifferent results, nothing comparable to what I had been given in England, but my wine dowsing remained successful. Sylvia went on missions to help neighbors' houseplants, losing some friends in the process. A partner at golf warned me amicably, "She's upsetting people with that occult stuff, Harinxma, keep it to yourselves." Then, one day, I overheard in the locker room an otherwise harmless American refer to us as "the Dutch tug driver and his Ouija broad." That made me mad enough to write a letter to a bookstore in London ordering a set of road maps of England, including one of its Roman roads.

The morning the maps arrived, Sylvia had the women of her bridge club in for coffee; I withdrew to my study and spread the one of the Roman roads, southern section, on my desk. It showed not just roads but locations where remnants of temples, villas, forts and towns had been found. I brought out Martock's letter and read it again; then I consulted General Elliot's book, the chapter on map dowsing. Finally I had hyped myself up sufficiently to overcome the inevitable barrier and brought out my pendulum.

Where to start? Roman vessels used to sail with the tide from Boulogne to Richborough, a port now inland. I set my pendulum oscillating, switched on the little tape recorder and asked, "Do I start in Boulogne?"

No, said the pendulum.

"Richborough?"

No.

"Canterbury?"

No.

"Then where, for Pete's sake? London?"

No.

"Now look, everybody passed through London on their way to anywhere!"

Yes.

"But I'm not to go there?"

No.

"Who am I supposed to be following? My previous self, as picked up in Acton Burnell?"

Yes.

"Then what year are we talking about? 338 A.D.?"

No.

"Give me the year, please."

I counted; the pendulum circled at 368.

"Again: that means I was an eighty-year-old man, or pretty close to it!"

No response.

"Still accompanying the praepositus from Lullington, the one with the singing lady in a cage?"

Yes.

I had never, in all my research, come across an eighty-year-old centurion accompanying the army. But how much did we actually know of what went on in the frontier regiments of the fourth century? Many of them had been half barbarian; maybe it was an ancient tribal custom the Romans had accepted to take a doddering ancestor along on campaign. Ancestor . . . ?

"Was there a relationship between the two?"

Yes.

"Father and son?"

Yes.

That explained it: the colonel had taken his old father, the ex-centurion, along on his campaign.

"We're talking about the expeditionary force under Theodosius?"

Right.

"The colonel and his regiment were part of it?"

Correct.

"From Richborough, Theodosius's army went to London. Yet you don't want me to go there?"

No.

"From London the army marched via St. Albans—"

No.

"What do you mean, no? It's a historical fact! Towchester?"

No.

"High Cross?"

No.

"But all these are garrison towns that Theodosius's army

recaptured!" I was baffled. Then it occurred to me. "I'm not supposed to *dowse* in those places, is that it?"

The pendulum circled at speed.

"All right. I now follow the Roman road to Chester, where Theodosius went, you tell me where to stop." I took a pencil in my left hand and began to trace the road leading from London to Chester. The pendulum started to circle halfway between two fortresses, Mandvessedum and Letocetum, now called Mancetter and Wall, northeast of Birmingham.

"You want me to start dowsing there? By the side of the road?"

Yes.

"But what *is* there? And how do I find the location? Do I fine-dowse it on the spot?"

Yes.

I slowly followed the rest of the road to Chester; the pendulum circled at Pennocrucium, a small fortress near Viroconium, now Wroxeter, then at Wroxeter itself. That was odd—Theodosius had headed for Chester.

"You mean, part of the army split off here?"

Right.

"Under the command of my colonel?"

Yes.

"Who took his old father along?"

Yes.

"Well, if you say so."

Once I had got the hang of it, the instructions were precise. I was told to stop by the roadside many times; the itinerary meandered from Wroxeter south through Shropshire, east Wales and Avon and ended, after twenty-eight stops, in the middle of nowhere, a flyspeck on the map called Iford, southeast of Aquae Sulis, the Roman city of Bath. There seemed to have been a villa in Iford, that was all.

"Why stop there? Is that where the old man died?"

No.

"Where peace broke out?"

Yes.

"So from there the detachment returned to base, wherever that was?"

Yes.

I turned off the tape recorder and sat staring for a while at the line linking all those ancient forts, villages, watering holes . . . What was going on?

There could be no doubt, the pendulum had taken the initiative. Each time it circled had been a surprise. It began to feel uncomfortably like messing with the Ouija board; I had felt just as reluctant then, yet unable to deny the facts. The Ouija board had spelled out a warning in mid-Pacific, days before an explosion on board my ship; the word *Beware!* had stared me in the face in exactly the same way, with exactly the same emotional effect, as did the itinerary the pendulum had imposed. Was I crazy to toy with this? Should I ditch the whole thing here and now?

I came close to doing that; then I thought, "Well, I always have freedom of choice. Let me see where this would take us in present-day England, should I decide to go through with it."

I started to transfer the Roman way stations to a present-day road map; then Sylvia came in, flushed with triumph at bridge. "Well," she said, "this time we trounced them! And, thank God, they loved my carrot cake. Sometimes you wonder if people—what are you up to?"

I told her. I played back the tape. She was more than fascinated, she was delighted. "Marty! How lovely! That is *such* a pretty part of England, and so little known! That's real picnic country! When are we going?"

Farewell, freedom of choice.

*

We arrived in Dover with our little Citröen one sunny morning in May. Obeying the pendulum, we bypassed London and motored north to the spot by the roadside near Birmingham, our starting point.

It was a parking area off the A5, known as Watling Street.

We drew up next to a trailer selling tea and bangers, a national sausage that can be smelled upwind. It was an uninspiring location. All I could get out of the pendulum was that a decisive incident had taken place here sixteen hundred and twenty years ago, something to do with horses. Defeated by the smell of bangers and the shaking of the car each time a truck passed at high speed, I asked the pendulum to spell out a key word. I got *QUARRY*. If there had been a quarry here at the time, there was no trace of it now.

"Did the regiment take part in a battle in a quarry?"

No.

"Find something or somebody in a quarry?"

No.

"Am I on the right track?"

No.

"The whole thing is nonsense, is it?"

Yes.

I said, "Screw you," and pocketed the pendulum.

"Shouldn't you spend a little more time on it?" Sylvia asked blandly.

"Let's go on to Wall. There at least are some foundations for me to dowse instead of this concrete strip reeking of sausages."

We headed for Lichfield, a village close to the hamlet of Wall, the Roman Letocetum. It was too late to do any serious dowsing but I wanted to get an idea of the layout of the ruins, maybe buy a plan for some fine-dowsing that evening. We drove to Wall in a translucent dusk scented with flowering hawthorn.

The Roman remains were an anticlimax. A few foundations, gray with age, forlorn, quite dead, as unevocative as the foundations of a present-day post office would be in 3987. We tried the guard's hut, which showed a small display of souvenirs; it was closed. Well, I'd have a shot at it the next morning. We drove back to Lichfield and booked into a hotel.

In the trunk of our car I had two earthenware crocks of Dutch gin hidden in my rubber boots. Rather than sour my stomach with English draught cider, I took one of the crocks with me to the bar, asked for a tonic with ice, gave the tonic to a plant, despite Sylvia's protest, and filled the glass with my gin. Ah! That was better. It probably was all in the mind. At the age of six I had crashed through the ice and would have died of shock if kind bargees had not poured neat Dutch gin down my throat. After forty-three years, Sylvia still maintained it came straight from the lamp; to me it was the elixir of life. What with one thing and another we had a jolly evening; I felt so good after dinner that Sylvia said, at a given moment, "As you now are taking care of my end of the conversation as well as your own, let's go to bed."

I kissed her hand, made sheep's eyes and followed her, humming, up the winding stairs to the usual creaking bed, paperbacks and Goblin Teasmade. While she was brushing her teeth at the wash basin I inspected the paperbacks: this collection ranged from *The Housewife's Handybook* via *Erewhon* to *Poets of the Wrekin*.

"Anything interesting?" Sylvia asked, brushing.

"I'll read to you." I opened *Poets of the Wrekin* at a marker, which turned out to be somebody's parking ticket of three years' standing.

> On Wenlock Edge the wood's in trouble;
> His forest fleece the Wrekin heaves;
> The gale, it plies the saplings double,
> And thick on Severn snow the leaves.

"I know that one," Sylvia said. We learned it at school. 'The Roman on Wenlock Edge,' part of *A Shropshire Lad* by A. E. Housman."

"It's an English lesson for Dutch drunks with dentures," I said. "Listen."

> 'Twould blow like this through holt and hanger
> When Uricon the city stood:
> 'Tis the old wind in the old anger,
> But then it threshed—

At *threshed* my lowers came loose.

Sylvia said, "Read the rest to me in bed."

When we lay side by side, staring at the canopy, I asked, "Now do you want the rest of the poem?"

"I don't think so," she said drowsily. "Good night, love."

I fell asleep in a radiant mood. The whole adventure was charming, never mind the crazy pendulum. Nothing had prepared me for the horrendous nightmare in which I found myself, thrashing and struggling in ice-cold water, sucked down repeatedly before I finally surfaced, gasping, in the present: the darkened room, the still form of Sylvia beside me. It had been a gruesomely vivid dream about the sinking of the old *Isabel Kwel* during the Second World War on the Murmansk run.

Heart pounding, staring in the darkness, I went through it all again: the high whine of a shell passing overhead, then another, and another, then something huge and deadly slamming the starboard flank. Sparks's voice crying out, "Gunfire, skipper! Gunfire astern!" On the starboard beam a sleek, whalelike German U-boat had surfaced, decks awash with the waves of our exploding depth charges. On her foredeck men clustered around a gun; two fierce flashes, an explosion, I was blown clean across the bridge. I scrambled to my feet, screams and yells all around me; the helmsman lay in the windowless wheelhouse, hands on his face, blood spurting through his fingers; on the portside the two British gunners lay dead beside their Oerlikon pointing crazily at the sky. A shrill voice cried, "Skipper! Skipper! They got Sparks!" I saw, on the boatdeck, Cook standing over a mangled mess of flesh and bone and cloth with one foot sticking out of it, back to front. Suddenly I decided: if this is what the human race has come to, I no longer want to be part of it. Every fiber of me, the very essence of me rejected the murderous lunacy of it all . . .

The horror slowly ebbed away; I was back in the dark room, Sylvia asleep beside me. I turned on the bedside light. The book of poems still lay open in the lamplight.

> 'Twould blow like this through holt and hanger
> When Uricon the city stood:
> 'Tis the old wind in the old anger,
> But then it threshed another wood.

> Before my time, the Roman
> At yonder heaving hill would stare:
> The blood that warms an English yeoman,
> The thoughts that hurt him, they were there.

Like the wind through woods in riot,
Through him the gale of life blew high;
the tree of man was never quiet;
Then 'twas the Roman, now 'tis I.

It was as if a cold, groping hand touched me, seeking comfort, the comfort of my living body, my life. Then a sleepy voice said beside me, "There's another meaning to quarry."

"What? What did you say?"

"It also means victim. Prey. Like a robin, chased by a cat. Something small, fleeing for its life. Quarry. Good night."

"Good night, love."

Who had been the quarry, who the hunter? We had managed to kill the U-boat and everybody on board before going down ourselves. I had lost seventeen men, the German captain his entire crew except one: a terrified, half-drowned messroom boy, his face black with oil, whom we had dragged into our lifeboat more dead than alive. I had covered him with my body when a Stuka dived at us and he started to yell, *"Kamerad! Kamerad! Heil Hitler!"* For twenty years after the war he had sent me a box of cookies every Christmas. Then I stopped hearing from him.

Thinking about Heini Rabenschnabel's cookies, I fell asleep again.

*

On the road from Mandvessedum to Letocetum, spring 368 A.D.

Two weeks after Londinium, Colonel Mellarius became disgusted with Field Marshal Theodosius. The order "No prisoners" had brought about indiscriminate slaughter.

The barbarians who had overrun the province of Britain were no more than a disorganized crowd of roving plunderers who scurried like rabbits at the first sight of the army. Those who were caught were not just killed, but mutilated and left to crawl, whimpering, in the fields. After a week of this the troops

began to kill, apart from cattle and chickens for food, anything
that moved: dogs, cats, even birds. Captured deserters from
Roman garrisons with the rank of officers saw their families
massacred before being ordered to fall onto their swords;
lower ranks were crucified. A week later, after the army had
sustained unexpected losses, all deserters were pardoned and
incorporated in its ranks, but the campaign itself remained a
repulsive orgy of cruelty. Colonel Mellarius, who had seen and
committed cruelties himself in the past, was overcome by a
revulsion the like of which he had never felt before; the army
rampaged through the countryside killing for the sick gratification of the killing itself, totally abandoning the Virtues.

The local tribes through whose territories the army ran riot
were Romanized and had been part of the empire since the god
Claudius conquered them three centuries ago, but Field Marshal Theodosius ordered their villages burned to ashes, their
fields scorched, their cattle massacred, all stragglers executed.
Only those who managed to disappear into the forest escaped.

As the spearhead of the army marched down the road to
Letocetum, a flock of small children came running from a spin-
ney in a field. Screaming with terror, they ran straight for Colonel Mellarius's regiment, hotly pursued by a platoon of
horsemen from the Equitis Catafractarii, the Pannonian cavalry, yelling their battle cry. From the head of the column came
the command "Testudes!" ordering the marching ranks to form
into turtles and thereby block the children's way with a wall
of shields. Flavius Maximus, Mellarius's second in command,
gave the order "Shields *up*!" The flanks of the regiment swung
out their shields with rigid precision. Before Maximus could
give the second command, "Lock *shields*!" which would have
welded the regiment into a solid iron wall, the colonel shouted,
"Stay!" The drill instructor had shouted it many times during
their training the past winter; it meant they went on marching
with their shields stretched out horizontally. The rest of the
army, at a ripple of commands shouted down its ranks, completed the turtles; only Numerus II Batavorum kept its flank
open. The children, with the instant reaction of fleeing game,
ran toward the gap and disappeared among the marching legs
as the traditional herd of goats had done during the training.

"Shields *down*!" The children were locked inside the turtle;

the Pannonian horsemen ran up against a steel wall behind which their prey had escaped.

Curses, threats, shrieks of fury; Colonel Mellarius was impervious to verbal abuse from blood-crazed men. No one would dare to attack his marching ranks, even if it looked for a moment as though they might. Sunlight flashed on armor, lances, bridles of rearing horses. The cavalry commander, a fierce Hungarian called Q. Peltrasias Flavinus, came thundering toward the colonel accompanied by his signifer, medaled standard scintillating in the sun. He reached Mellarius at the same time as General Dulcitius, who came galloping down the ranks from the head of the column and arrived in time to interpose himself between the two officers. "What the shit do you think you're doing, you shithead?!" the Pannonian yelled at the colonel, his horse whinnying and rearing. "You can't block my men, you heap of shit!"

"Rome does not massacre small children," the colonel said calmly.

The Pannonian screamed, "You mean only barbarians do?"

"That's right," Mellarius said.

General Dulcitius saw the raised sword and intervened. "Gentlemen!"

The Pannonian backed off among the milling horses. "An insult!" he screamed. "This Batavian shitheap called me a barbarian! I demand revenge! This heap of shit has insulted my numerus! This—"

"Gentlemen!" General Dulcitius raised a hand like a priest in blessing; his rank managed to restrain the outraged Hungarian in the vortex of his trampling, whinnying, snorting horses. "Tonight in Letocetum, the field marshal will receive both of you. Now, please, resume your positions."

Cursing, his rearing horse flinging spittle, the Pannonian shouted a command. The churning horses formed into a unit; with a thunder of hooves they stormed off, clods flying.

General Dulcitius was left with Mellarius, who stood facing him impassively with the vague smile that had struck him at their first meeting. "Most unwise, Mellarius," he said. "What possessed you to do this insane thing?"

"Saving the lives of small children?"

"Insulting Peltrasias Flavius by calling him a barbarian."

The colonel looked at the general with that mysterious bemusement. "It was not I who called him that. He suggested it was my intention."

"But why?"

"Rome does not massacre small children."

There he stood, well into his forties, colonel of a numerus, and still maintained that Rome did not massacre small children. The trouble with this dreamer in armor was that he staunchly believed the eternal city still embodied the virtues.

"Let me give you some advice, Mellarius. Do not mention this when you appear before the field marshal tonight. Find another explanation for your act, say you did not want your ranks to be disturbed because for cavalry to crash through a marching army creates havoc. Whatever you say, do not base your case on ethical considerations."

"Very well, General."

Whatever the man might be, he was disciplined. "I'll be present tonight. Rejoin your regiment."

"Yes, General." His salute was dignified.

Dulcitius sighed and mounted his horse. He cantered back to the head of the column to rejoin the field marshal.

Colonel Mellarius made his way back to his position at the head of the regiment. The men were still marching with their shields joined.

"Well done!" he shouted in an uncharacteristic burst of appreciation. "Shields up, Maximus."

The command was repeated by the centurions; the shields flew up. From the right flank of the second century burst the children, fluttering like birds, to flee hopping and leaping across the fields into the forest. A small flock of little creatures without value, hardly worth the ruin of a colonel's career.

*

Field Marshal Theodosius listened impassively to the angry report of Q. Peltrasias Flavinus. The Pannonians formed the dominant political faction in Rome in bitter rivalry with the Spanish; General Dulcitius realized that, as a Spaniard, the field marshal found himself in a delicate position. The angry man would have to be handled with circumspection, some gesture would have to be made to pacify him or the incident might be blown up out of proportion in the Senate.

The torches sputtered and smoked, throwing a restless multiple light on the Pannonian, whose shadows gesticulated wildly on the walls of the command tent. Servants stood by with wine and sweetmeats, waiting for orders from the supreme commander stretched out on his couch in a civilian toga.

"And when I called for an explanation, the man answered, 'Rome does not massacre small children, only barbarians do!' "

"Excuse me, Field Marshal," Colonel Mellarius said calmly, "that is not what I said. Peltrasias Flavinus suggested that my remark about Rome might imply that only barbarians massacre small children."

"To which you replied 'Yes!' " the angry man shouted.

The fat was in the fire; General Dulcitius could feel the sudden tension as the field marshal shifted the gaze of his brooding black eyes onto the colonel standing to attention, helmet under his arm. "Thank you, gentlemen. Now let us have a little wine."

Was Mellarius to be spared censure, even a reprimand? The wine was poured; the Pannonian studiously ignored Mellarius's invitation to raise beakers, emptied his, and took his leave with the excuse that he had to look to his horses. For an officer to absent himself without being invited to do so by the field marshal was as close to a rebuff as any man in his senses would dare go. It would not help the Pannonian's case; the field marshal was notoriously thin-skinned when it came to breaches of protocol.

After a nod from the field marshal in his direction, Mellarius excused himself too; General Dulcitius was left alone with the supreme commander. After ten minutes' discussion of practical details of the day, the field marshal finally returned to the matter of the officers and the children. Out of the blue, he said in his casual way, "I'm surprised you did not notice it before, Dulcitius. The man is clearly suffering from fastidium. Was that not apparent to you last winter when you visited him on the Rhine?"

This was going a great deal too far; fastidium was a mood of revulsion and nausea which could befall older officers in the field, lethal as far as their careers were concerned. Dulcitius realized he should watch his step now; the army inspector had hinted at this and might be asked for a report. "Marcellus Sabinus seemed to consider the possibility, after the business with the dog."

"Ah yes, the dog," the field marshal said. "You were impressed by that incident, I remember. What was Marcellus Sabinus's interpretation of it?"

"He thought Mellarius might have felt sorry for the dog. The fact is that his innovative idea not to kill the animal but to make it the regiment's mascot baffled the Franci."

"He obviously felt sorry for the children," the field marshal said.

"I'm not so sure, sir. I think he was standing up for the virtues in a somewhat dogmatic way." The field marshal's face stiffened; Dulcitius added hastily, "Be that as it may, what do you wish me to do with the man?"

"He cannot be maintained as part of my army. I cannot afford two staff officers involved in a blood feud."

"Would it be that serious?"

"Peltrasias Flavinus is a Pannonian. He will not rest until he has avenged what he considers a personal insult. I cannot spare any cavalry, so it will have to be Mellarius. I want you to find an assignment to remove him from the scene."

So that was going to be the punishment: send the man into the wilderness. He was a deep fish, this Spaniard; it was like dealing with a conger eel permanently poised to attack. "We have an isolated Welsh tribe on the rampage in the west, sir. He might go and deal with them," the general said.

"Which tribe?"

"We don't know, exactly. Probably the one that sacked Lavobrinta."

"I'm not going to waste any manpower on Wales, Dulcitius. Think again." The field marshal shifted the gaze of his black eyes to the general's chin, a habit which unnerved his officers.

"It would not be Wales, sir. The latest report puts the raiders just south of Viroconium. They are probably on their way to the villas in the southwest, which are rich pickings indeed.

They must be stopped somehow; the local militia can only defend their own cities, out in the field they are useless."

"H'm. How many men would you suggest he take with him?"

"Three centuries, Field Marshal."

"Let's give him two."

That was tantamount to ordering the man never to return. "Is he to have any cavalry?"

The field marshal smiled, shifting the black gaze from Dulcitius's chin to his forehead. "You must be jesting. Have your scribe write out the order."

"Yes, sir. What shall I state as the objective of the operation?"

"To seek and destroy the raiders. Tell him to report back to me when his mission is completed."

"Very well, sir."

"On the other hand, we don't want the Pannonian to get above himself," the field marshal mused.

"Maybe Mellarius's assignment could be upgraded somewhat?"

"I'm not going to give him more than two centuries, if that's what you mean."

"I mean: present it as an honor, rather than a punishment."

"Punishment?" The black eyes opened wide. "Who talks about punishment? Those raiders have to be exterminated, you said so yourself. Somebody has to do it."

"Then would it be in order for him to recruit an additional century from the local militia as he goes along?"

"He may help himself to whatever is left, and good luck to him."

"What would you say, Field Marshal, to granting his detachment the regiment's eagle?"

The black eyes narrowed. "You mean promote him?"

"No. Prevent his successor from assuming he is permanently taking Mellarius's place."

"Who would that be?"

"Flavius Maximus has seniority."

"Any good?"

"Reliable. No initiative."

There was a silence. Then the field marshal said, "Have

some more wine, Dulcitius." He filled the beakers and raised his own. "The emperor."

"The emperor."

They drank. Outside the tent, the bucinator shattered the silence with his signal for the changing of the guard.

*

On arrival in Pennocrucium, the army's next way station on its march north, Field Marshal Theodosius ordered Colonel Mellarius into his presence.

The colonel hastily changed into parade armor while his orderly laid out a fresh set of leggings. When he appeared in the august presence, he found the field marshal lying on a couch in civilian toga as if he had not stirred since the night before, even though that morning he had participated in a chase of fugitives through a wood and killed seven. It had been another day of blood and the screams of women, a day of sunlight and small white clouds, a dark day for Rome.

"Sit down, Mellarius," the field marshal said, gesturing toward the visitors' couch, "I want to talk to you."

"Thank you, Field Marshal." The colonel handed his helmet to a servant, unclasped his sword and sank down, trying to find a comfortable position. Lolling on a couch in parade armor was like making conversation while clamped in a vice.

"Wine for the colonel."

A servant filled a beaker and put it in front of Mellarius. It would have been less awkward had he handed it to him.

"The emperor."

Mellarius managed to grab the beaker without rolling off the couch and raised it in response. "The emperor." They drank. The colonel held out the beaker for the servant to put down; the ass refilled it instead.

The field marshal seemed not to have noticed. "I'm going to send you on special assignment, Mellarius." He waved the servants out of the tent. "A tribe of Welsh bandits is on a rampage in the west. They are sacking villages and slaughtering every living thing in sight." It sounded pretty much like what the army was doing. "They have to be sought and destroyed, which calls for an experienced staff officer who can act on his own cognizance. I have chosen you."

"Thank you, sir." So that was it: banishment in the wilderness.

"I'm sorry I cannot give you the number of men you need, I'm under strength as it is. I'll let you have a detachment of two centuries, but it shall be considered as the regiment. The eagle, the mascot and your medicus will go with you."

"Thank you, Field Marshal."

"General Dulcitius will give you the details. May the good Lord and His Holy Son be with you."

That would be the day, when T. Gaius Virilis's son marched under the aegis of a crucified criminal. Colonel Mellarius put down his full beaker, a hazardous feat, rose and saluted. The field marshal clapped his hands, the servants came hurrying back with the colonel's sword and helmet. He did not turn at the exit for a second salute but marched straight out, ignoring the sergeant of the watch's howled "Present *arms!*"

When he approached his tent, Fortunatas the medicus materialized out of thin air and whispered, "The general is inside, lord."

Mellarius entered, his face set, ready to hear the details of his punishment. Two centuries! A slap in the face.

The general, in civilian toga, was waiting for him in the uncertain light of the torches which his orderly must have hastily lit, as they were still sputtering and hissing. "My sympathies, Mellarius," the general said pleasantly. In toga he looked even more delicate; without the insignia of his rank he could be taken for an accountant or a medicus.

"Thank you, General."

"Make yourself comfortable." General Dulcitius gestured at the orderly, who helped the colonel out of his armor, took his sword and helmet, and unlaced his leggings for him after he had sat down. The general watched the process with an air of melancholy, as if seeing a man being freed from his armor revealed his mortality. "You have been told that you will retain the eagle?"

"Yes, I have."

"Who are you going to appoint as your stand-in while you're gone? Flavius Maximus has seniority, but you may wish to take him along."

"I haven't thought about it, General."

"Well, there is some urgency. You march tomorrow morning at first light."

"Where am I supposed to march to?"

"Uxacona. The next day Viroconium."

"And from there?"

"In Viroconium you'll be joined by a scout who will give you the latest information on the whereabouts of the raiders. He'll accost you in the marketplace, where you should mingle with the crowd as a civilian; Viroconium is certain to be full of spies. He'll either make himself known or send a messenger. You take it from there."

"What strength are the raiders?"

"Nobody knows. All we know is that it's a Welsh tribe who leave nothing but ashes and bones wherever they go. You've been told Lavobrinta was ransacked?"

"No, sir."

"A unit of Cohors IV Brucorum was decimated there, the rest of them captured. All survivors were forced to swallow their genitals before being crucified." The general gave him a look; its meaning was obscure. "I'm telling you this because there is a possibility we have not discussed. They may be women."

"Women?"

"You may be dealing with a tribe of Amazons."

"What gives you that idea? Ah—you mean . . . ?"

"Indeed, the nature of the mutilation. The army has had to deal with tribes of women before, as you may remember. Anyhow, they have cavalry, you won't."

"So I gather." A hundred and twenty men in the wilderness without cavalry, without mobile catapults, nothing but their swords and shields. It was suicide; chances were the survivors of his two centuries would suffer a similar fate, himself included. All that because he had stood up for the Virtues.

"I trust the field marshal made it clear to you that you have been selected because of your experience."

"He did indeed, sir." He said it wryly; the general was head of military intelligence, not a function in which sympathetic identification played much of a part. Or perhaps it did.

"I would suggest, Mellarius," the general continued, "that you profit from your authorization to enlist local militia. You may even find some cavalry among them and heavier weaponry than you'll be given tomorrow."

"Very well, General."

The general gave him a rueful smile. "You'll have to use the same ingenuity you showed in the case of the Franci's dog. This tribe, Amazons or not, is not likely to have much subtlety. Outwit them, Mellarius, do not confront them. The advantage of a small unit like yours is its mobility and its capacity for camouflage. When they do attack, make sure they find nobody there. Your father, now with the gods, was very good at that. Be worthy of him."

It was startlingly crude for a man whose profession was supposed to be subtlety. The Frenchman could not possibly have known T. Gaius Virilis, he was too young, and a centurion was too lowly for him to have noticed anyhow. But he obviously was at pains to sweeten the pill.

"Yes, sir. I'll do my best."

"Well," the general said, rising, "I'll leave you to it. You'll have your marching orders before dawn. May the gods be with you, Mellarius, and may your father have his hand on your shoulder in the days to come."

Mellarius stood to attention.

When the general left he was almost instantly replaced by Flavius Maximus, saluting.

"At ease, Maximus. There has been a change of plan."

"I know," the centurion said, his face grim. "Everyone knows."

The effectiveness of the grapevine was one of the mysteries of regimental life. "What is the men's reaction?"

"They're not sure how to take it, Colonel. I think if this could be presented as an honor—"

Flavius Maximus was an intelligent man; pity he would have to be left behind. "Well, why not? That's what has been conveyed to me. It's too late to call the men together, so spread the word that the assignment is an honor to those who are selected. The eagle will go with us, so will the mascot and so will Fortunatas. Tell the men that the two centuries will be hand-picked by you. Let me have the list tonight."

"Yes, Colonel." The centurion did not say it, but the question must be uppermost in his mind.

"You will be in command of the remaining centuries. I'll take Secundus along, but not his optio. The second will be commanded by Antigonus. Ask them to come and see me."

"Very well, Colonel."

"Thank you."

The moment he had left, the medicus appeared.

"Lord . . . "

"Not now, Fortunatas, I have work to do. I'll see you later."

The Greek disappeared without a word; Mellarius sat down at the crude table and was about to drop his head in his hands when his eye caught a movement right in front of him, close to the ground. The skirt of the tent was lifted surreptitiously, no more than a crack. He said, "All right, Cassidile, come in." It was the soldiers who had given the mutt a name: Little Helmet.

The dog's wet snout appeared, then the eyes, dark, liquid, pleading, the way they had looked up at him from the coracle.

"It's all right."

Reassured, the dog crept into the tent, tail wagging, and put his head on the colonel's knee.

"Sorry, old friend," Mellarius said. "I have to take you along. Amor fati."

CHAPTER SIX

*

Water Eaton, spring 1987

The night before Water Eaton, the Roman Pennocrucium, Sylvia and I spent in a hotel in Shrewsbury that was so historic there was nowhere to park the car. I was getting into the spirit of the adventure, a mixture of holiday mood and the excitement of a paper chase. I had had no personal experiences comparable to the one in Brussels, it was just a round of the way stations and the daily effort to squeeze out of my pendulum forgotten bits of information from my years of research—I was convinced that was all it was.

Water Eaton was a good example of our daily procedure. Sylvia drove so as to leave me free to dowse on the way. We set out with only a vague idea of where the place could be; it was not on our modern map, we had to deduce its location from the map of Roman roads, hoping we would happen upon some locals who might be able to direct us. We left the motorway for a road indicated by the pendulum; just short of another main artery I was told to stop. Sylvia pulled in to the side of the road; at that moment a jeep passed us and turned into a farmyard. I got out, made my way to the two men in the jeep and wished them good morning. They looked unforthcoming but told me how to find Water Eaton: "Down yar road, follow him to the crossroads, turn yar right."

By the time we had followed their directions the morning fog had lifted and revealed a warm, sunny day. Water Eaton was no more than a couple of houses and a mailbox; I got out to try and find a fellow human in the bird-haunted silence. There was a large old house in a garden; an elderly lady with a straw hat was doing some ritual gardening in what appeared to be a patch of weeds. She smiled at me, then unsmiled and something dropped from her eye socket. It was a monocle. I said, "Good morning. I'm sorry to trouble you."

She said, "Oh, that's perfectly all right. What can I do for you?"

I started to talk Romans; she screwed her monocle back in place, tipped her hat on the back of her head and said, "Well, how very interesting. There's nothing left, don't you know. Absolutely nothing. Above ground, that is. Here, right where we are standing, is where the barracks were. At least, that's what my grandparents told me their grandparents told them. There are Roman remains all around in the fields; quite recently a man with a metal detector came and walked through the garden and indicated a number of places where metal is buried underground. Coins, don't you know. We decided not to dig because of the roses. Are you an archaeologist?"

"No, I'm just an interested amateur. So is my wife, in the car there."

She peered at the car. "Ah, you are from the Continent. What country?"

"France."

"I have a cousin living in France," she said, as if that created a bond between us. "At first, she was quite the odd one, you know. At least, that's how she seemed to us other young girls. Always knitting. Now she has a flourishing business of knitted garments in a place called—let me think—Lille, and is quite well off. Are you from Lille?"

"No," I said, with the feeling I was taking part in some alien ritual. "But one of our neighbors was prima ballerina of the opera in Lille. The comic opera, that is."

"Of course," she said. "Do you have a metal detector?"

"No, I don't." I decided I had better come clean; she might see me working the pendulum and ask herself what in the world I was doing. "I'm a dowser," I said.

She looked at me amazed, making her monocle drop from her eye once more. "How absolutely riveting."

"Well, I think I'll try and see if I can pick up something here or there. Thank you very much. A very good morning to you."

"How awfully kind. And to you. Happy—well, whatever it is. Good-bye."

I walked back to the car. Sylvia, camera in hand, asked, "Where do we go first?"

Suddenly I felt exhilarated by the radiant morning, the

birds, the monocle, the straw hat, the treasure in ancient coins remaining undisturbed because of the roses. "It seems there are Roman remains all around us," I said. "I'll try to find out where." I took out the pendulum, set it oscillating and asked, "Can you tell me where to get some feedback about my colonel and his old dad?"

Yes, the pendulum said.

"Where? Would you point in that direction?"

The pendulum slowly changed direction until it indicated a lane to the left of where we were standing.

"Do I go down that lane?"

Yes.

I walked down what was in fact no more than a track running parallel to the wall of the old house; after a hundred yards or so I reached the gate to a field.

"Here?"

Yes.

I leaned on the gate and let the pendulum swing on the other side of it. "I understood from what you told me when you gave me the itinerary that a detachment commanded by my colonel separated here from the main body of the army, which went on to Chester. Is that correct?"

Yes.

"Can you give me an idea how many men he had? A century? Two centuries?"

Two centuries.

"Any cavalry?"

No.

"The whole thing was done on foot?"

Yes.

"He must have had a wagon train with supplies."

Yes.

"Drawn by mules?"

No.

"Horses? Oxen?"

Oxen.

What else could I ask? So far it had been tame stuff, clearly based on my own research of the period. "Near here, it seems, were the barracks."

No.

"I mean, further back, where the house is."

No.

"No barracks?"

No.

"That's odd. Pennocrucium was an important army post on the way to Chester, it must have had barracks . . . "

So I ground on, one humdrum question after the other. Sylvia was through with her part of the work; there was a distinct lack of photo opportunities in this dusty lane. I felt I had to come up with something worthy of her expectations. I asked for a key word.

After the usual spelling procedure, the pendulum came up with *priest*.

"Well," I said to Sylvia, "that's it. All I've got is another word for our collection: *priest.* "

"I wonder what all these words add up to?"

"No idea. *Sing, words, dog, dreams, quarry, priest.* Where does the pendulum get them from?"

We started back toward the car. A blackbird on a telegraph line carried on a conversation with a distant neighbor, talking rubbish. "All I can think of is that those words are somehow in the air," she said.

"Why should they be?"

"I don't know. I'm not sure they sum up anything, rather like 'Kilroy was here.' "

That dated us all right. "Let's go and find a pub," I said, taking her arm.

After all, the Romans were only part of the crawl.

*

Pennocrucium, spring 368 A.D.

The fort of Pennocrucium had been almost totally destroyed, only its baths were still standing, probably because they had looked empty to the barbarians. At this hour of the night Mellarius did not expect anyone to be there except the attendants, but when he entered the caldarium he discovered to his dismay that all the slabs except one were taken. Only after he lay down did he realize the naked man next to him was the field marshal.

Army tradition dictated that in the baths no rank prevailed; yet it was an awkward situation. The masseur appeared; Mellarius shook his head. The naked man beside him lay eyes closed, but his arrival had not gone unobserved.

"Well, Mellarius? Is all ready for your departure?"

"Yes, sir."

"And who will succeed you?"

"Flavius Maximus."

"Ah, yes."

There was a silence, during which Mellarius felt the sweat run down his breastbone. He asked himself how soon he could leave without insulting the field marshal.

Suddenly, a voice on Theodosius's other side asked, "Where is he going, Father?" That must be young Theodosius, adjutant of the field marshal, a presumptuous youth who during the past weeks had distinguished himself in ferocity, which was saying something in this company.

"He is leading an expeditionary force into the far west," his father replied with a hint of coolness.

"How far west are you expecting to go, Colonel?" the voice asked.

"Wherever the enemy takes me," Mellarius replied. He had come here to calm his soul, not to be badgered by young Spanish aristocrats.

"Do you have a priest to accompany you?"

"Yes, I have my haruspex."

"I don't mean a pagan sorcerer, I mean a Christian priest."

Young Theodosius was a notoriously zealous Christian; only the rabid ones called priests pagan sorcerers. Mellarius did not answer.

"I have just the man for you, Colonel. His name is Father Ioannis. He is courageous and devout. I recommend to my father that he be added to your expedition."

The field marshal, silent as if asleep, must be exasperated by his interfering son; yet he might like the idea of having a personal spy in the expeditionary force. May the gods make him refuse, Mellarius prayed. The sweat on his chest was chilly.

The field marshal asked, "Any objection, Mellarius?"

"I do not feel the need for a Christian priest, sir."

"I know the man," the field marshal said presently. "Great experience in dealing with soldiers. It's your decision, of course, but you would be passing up an opportunity of providing your troops with spiritual sustenance in what are likely to be trying circumstances."

Mellarius allowed the silence to remain between them for as long as he could without it becoming offensive. Then he said, "If that is your wish, sir, I would appreciate it if you would make it an order. To avoid complications with my haruspex."

"If I had a haruspex in the habit of making complications, I'd get rid of him," the youth sneered.

It was insufferable. Mellarius was reaching for a response that would put the snotnose in his place when the field marshal said calmly, "That's enough."

Mellarius slid off the slab; the masseur put a gown around his shoulders. "Good night, sir," the colonel said, ignoring the youth.

"Good night, Mellarius. May the blessing of the Good Lord and His Holy Son be with you."

"Thank you, sir." The prospect of being separated from the main army began to look attractive.

The medicus, the orderly and the thespian were waiting for him in his tent; the doctor with his potion, the orderly with his nightgown and the thespian, haughtily, with his Art. The potion tempered his anger at young Theodosius; the gown had been warmed and scented with night-flowering jasmine; after he had laid down his head on the pillow, the voice of the thespian started soothingly:

> They walked obscured by darkness, in the lonely night, through the shadows,
> Through the vacant homes of Pluto and the empty kingdoms;
> Under the dim light of the wavering moon,
> A journey in the woods, after Jupiter had hidden the sky in shadows
> And the black night had taken away the color from all things.

"Are you aware of the fact that we are going on expedition, Cassius Colonia?"

"Of course." The man's outrage at being interrupted was obvious.

"Are you aware of the dangers?"

"Of course. May I continue?"

"You may stay behind if you wish."

There was a shocked silence. "Are you not pleased with my readings?"

"It's a beautiful section. You read it very well."

"How kind of you," the thespian said waspishly. He continued,

> Before the very entrance and in the very jaws of Orcus
> Grief and avenging Cares have placed their couches,
> And pale diseases dwell, and sad old age,
> And fear, and hunger, persuading evil, and base want,
> Forms terrible to see, both death and toil . . .

"Son?"

The unfamiliar voice made the thespian stop. Mellarius opened his eyes and saw in the uncertain light of the last torch a priest, in cassock and sandals, his head shaven, gaze at him with the unseeing eyes of zealotry. The shock of the interruption, the insult of this man penetrating into his tent without permission, broke the camel's back. Suddenly the colonel's fury at the accumulative insults of the day flared and the storm broke over the head of the cleric.

"I am not your son!" he roared, raising himself on an elbow. "You shall never call me that again! Next time have yourself announced! Get out of my tent!"

"I am Father Ioannis," the priest said, puffing himself up like a blowfish. "I have been sent by—"

"I don't give a damn who sent you! You are not my father! You are not anybody's father in this regiment! Get out!"

The priest fumbled in the folds of his gown and produced a cross, which he held out as if to exorcise an evil spirit.

"Get out!" In his fury, Mellarius hurled a slipper at the man.

In the entrance, the priest collided with the medicus, who came running at the sound of altercation.

"I'm all right, Doctor, leave me alone."

The doctor knew enough to retreat.

"Continue, Cassius Colonia." He lay down again.

The thespian took a deep breath.

> Then sleep, the kinsman of death,
> And evil pleasures of the mind and death-bearing
> War on the threshold opposite,
> And the iron chambers of the furies, and mad discord
> Entwining her snaky hair with bloody fillets—

"Enough! I need something soothing."

There was a silence, another intake of breath, then the voice, mellifluous, caressing, continued.

> Scarcely had he spoken, when beautiful Venus, visible
> To no one, stood in the middle of the Senate House.
> She snatched the newly arisen soul of her Caesar from
> His body, and, not suffering it to be dissolved into the
> Air, bore it to the stars of heaven.
> As she bore it, she perceived that it acquired a
> Radiance, began to burn,
> And she let it go from her bosom.
> It flew higher than the moon, dragging a fiery tail
> On its long path . . .

"Thank you. That will be all for tonight."

When Mellarius opened his eyes he saw that the thespian was of two minds whether to accompany him on the expedition or withdraw in disgust. For some reason the man's emotions, intense and evanescent, were more soothing than his recital. How wonderful to be thrown into the depths of outrage so readily and then to rise from the rubble a moment later, like the Phoenix. "It was beautiful," Mellarius said, "but I have to perform my venerations, and we march at dawn. I am sorry, it is my loss."

The Phoenix rose from the ashes. "It will be an honor to feed your soul with beauty after the ravages of battle," the thespian said, still caught in the meter of Ovid's *Metamorphoses*. "To serve the fearless is the essence of my calling."

"Ask my orderly to serve you a libation," the colonel said, to restrain the Phoenix's ecstatic swooping. The thespian bowed with a sweeping gesture, as if thanking a crowded amphitheater for a standing ovation. "Soft dreams, my lord," he whispered and swept out.

Wearily, Mellarius rose to kneel in front of the little statue on its pedestal in the corner. "Father, I know thou art aware of me at all times. I know thy presence is unshaken. But there is a sense of urgency within me that reaches out for thy hand, the experience of thy love." He should not have said that. T. Gaius Virilis would be embarrassed. Yet Mellarius knew that no one had ever touched the old man's heart the way he had. "I mean, Father, make the reality of thy presence known to me, make me feel the shelter of thy wing, give me thy power to be Rome." For a moment, like a hallucination, there strode toward him the ramrod white-haired old centurion, scabbard slapping, between the rows of supplicants of a liberated town. Never had Rome been personified with such dignity, such awesome authority.

A discreet cough asked for his attention. It was the officer of the guard. "Excuse me, Colonel. Could I have the watchword, please?"

"Yes," the colonel said. "It is 'Priest.'"

*

Wroxeter, spring 1987

I began to enjoy dowsing for my colonel and his old father. It was an inoffensive pastime to be indulged in between picnics and nights in Ye Olde Holiday Inn, and the weather held. My sunny mood suddenly darkened in Wroxeter where, out of the blue, I changed from a harmless tourist into a maniac torn away from his moorings.

We had spent another night in the hotel in Shrewsbury. I had enjoyed a relaxed breakfast with the local paper, savoring a story headed RAPIST FOILED BY MOUSETRAP. After an easy drive down quiet roads to Wroxeter we arrived at the open-air museum, all that was left of the Roman Viroconium. A huge old wall in its center had been part of the baths; by the look of it, this was going to be another collection of foundations as in Wall.

We parked in the otherwise empty car park and strolled to the ticket booth. I bought from the unforthcoming lady attendant two admission tickets and a plan of the exhibit. The pendulum, extremely keen this morning, indicated where to start my dowsing: in the *marcellum,* once a marketplace surrounded by a gallery of little shops. We made our way over there and found it was now no more than a rectangle of weeds surrounded by a fence. The gate was padlocked; restrained by Sylvia from climbing over it, I dutifully went back to the lady in the booth.

"Could I have the key to the *marcellum,* please?"

She looked at me as if I had belched. "I *beg* your pardon?"

"I would like to do some research in the center of the marketplace."

She stared at me. "Are you an archaeologist?"

"I'm a dowser. I'd like to go in there and dowse. You know, swing my pendulum."

Her eyes became wider.

After long professional experience with customs officials and the like I decided to change my approach. "My name is Commodore Harinxma. I am a member of both the American and the British Societies of Dowsers. I am researching the Barbarian Conspiracy in the fourth century and need to go into the *marcellum* area to try and find out what happened there."

She had had time to regroup. "Absolutely out of the question," she said briskly.

"Why, may I ask, should a person like myself not be admitted to that patch of weeds? Are you growing something there?"

She bristled. "That patch of weeds, if you must know, is the archaeological dig of Professor Wasprick."

"Then where is Professor Wasprick? I'll go and ask him myself."

"Professor Wasprick is in Edinburgh," she said with some satisfaction. "Now, if you'll excuse me . . . " She swiveled on her stool and started to finger the keyboard of an adding machine.

Bar reaching through the ticket window and spending the rest of my life in an English jail, the only thing I could do was stamp back, glowering, to the patch of weeds, where I stood among the Roman remains telling the world, in Dutch, what I thought of the lady in the booth and Professor Wasp and his prick.

"Can't you dowse from a distance?" Sylvia asked soothingly. "Look, there's some scaffolding over there, a footbridge. It overlooks the *marcellum,* ask the pendulum if you can dowse from there."

"I don't want to dowse from there! I want to get in!"

She smiled; I climbed the footbridge with enough noise to make neighboring farmers' wives peer out of their kitchen windows. Standing up there was meaningless, like surveying the foundations of Giggleswick two thousand years from now. But I brought out my pendulum and asked meekly, "Can I dowse the goddam marketplace from here?"

It circled as if it was of great importance for me to find out what happened in that marketplace sixteen hundred and twenty years ago.

"Why?" I asked. "Did my praepositus get into a fight? Or his father get drunk?"

No.

"Did he meet someone there?"

Yes.

"A woman?" Again: a woman.

No.

"Good. A man?"

No.

"A child?"

Yes.

"A little girl?"

Yes.

"Did she have a message for him?"

No.

"Took him somewhere? Where?"

The swing of the pendulum changed direction and pointed toward a shed on the edge of the exhibit.

"You want me to go there?"

Yes.

I rumbled down the steps of the viewing bridge and said to Sylvia, who was taking pictures, "I'm supposed to go to that shed over there for more information."

"Want me to come with you?"

"No, leave me to it for the moment."

I hurried to the shed, expecting the dragon lady to come out of her booth and shout that I should not go there because it belonged to Professor Wasprick, but I reached the building unchallenged. Its door was padlocked, its windows shuttered. "Is this where you wanted me to go?" I asked the pendulum.

No.

"Further along?"

Yes.

"In the same direction?"

Yes.

"How many paces?"

I was given six. I walked past the shed into a stubbled field and stopped after six paces.

"Here?"

Yes.

"Is this where the centurion was taken by the little girl?"

Yes.

"Was there a house here?"

Yes.

"Who was he supposed to meet here? The mayor of the town, or whatever he was called in those days?"

No.

Of course not. If so, he would have been given an official reception.

"Was it a secret meeting?"

Yes.

"With a scout?"

Yes.

"Let me see . . . A scout . . . A house . . . What kind of house? A brothel?"

No.

"A private house?"

Yes.

"Belonging to an important citizen?"

So-so.

"A soldier? A retired soldier?"

Yes.

"A Roman veteran who had married a local woman?"

Yes.

The wing commander was right. It was the questions that were odd. Where did they come from? The little girl, the scout, the veteran married to a local woman?

"Was the child theirs?"

Yes.

"Was she present when the centurion met the scout?"

Yes.

"What could a little girl—ah! She served refreshments!"

Yes.

Suddenly I saw, clearly, a little girl from the back, slowly walking into a high-ceilinged room with couches and a mosaic floor. She carried a tray with refreshments which she put down on a low table in front of a couch; on it a heavyset man in a toga was reclining. The toga looked like a disguise; I knew he was an army officer in civvies. On another couch, facing him, lay a mousey little man with a big nose, eyes very close together, peering at the little girl with pedophiliac interest. The child bowed and solemnly walked out through the doors by which she had entered; then Sylvia said, "Are you all right, dear?"

I came to with a start. "Never do that again! Don't interrupt me when I'm dowsing! —Oh, I'm sorry . . . I didn't mean to snap. But it was—I don't know—I was lost there for a few moments."

"What's going on? Can you talk about it?"

"It was a bit like Brussels. I saw the inside of a house, a room with couches. A little girl. I also know now what our colonel looked like. But I didn't see his old father. Unless—no, it couldn't be."

"Was it a vision? A dream?" She sounded concerned.

"No, just a flash of something. Two men, one as trustworthy as a pickpocket, the other an untidy middle-aged military man in a creased toga, if that was what he was wearing. And this little girl, serving refreshments."

"What if we went and had a cup of coffee? Then you can tell me exactly what happened, from the beginning."

"Oh? Yes, all right," I said. "You know, I was right there for a moment or two."

"So I gather," she said and gently steered me back to the car. The lady in the booth was on the telephone, probably calling an ambulance.

*

Viroconium, spring 368 A.D.

Viroconium, as Colonel Mellarius found it after a day's march, was a dismal village of wooden houses and a half-finished bathhouse. Full of sullen people, the town was defended by a local militia under the command of a runt wearing too large a helmet which obscured his view; he looked as if he was perpetually peering from under a bed. The town had not been attacked; the pipsqueak with the bed helmet greeted the liberating army as if they were a detachment of slaves. The barracks were occupied by his own militia; the two centuries were told to make camp in the courtyard of a farm within the walls, the owner having left to be on the safe side, leaving his bailiff in control. He was a bluff man who, while not running over with deference, proved civil enough.

Once the tents had been put up and a foraging party organized, the colonel changed into his civilian tunic and short fringed cloak. He made his way to the marketplace, as he had been instructed to do. It was full of shoppers and noisy with vendors touting their wares; despite their apparent prosperity, the people's mood seemed to be sullen. After wandering around aimlessly in the crowd for quite a while he was about to return to camp when someone tugged at his cloak. A solemn little girl gazed up at him and disappeared again in the crowd without a word. Presumably she was the one to lead him to the scout. He started after her; it was like following a mouse in a cornfield. He caught sight of her again on the edge of the square and saw her turn a corner into a street leading from the marcellum.

It was further than he expected. He caught only occasional glimpses of the little figure; finally he found her waiting for him in the doorway to a patrician house behind the baths. When he entered the marble-tiled hall he was met by total silence. The house must belong to a wealthy citizen, the furnishings were luxurious, with statuary, portrait busts and mosaic floors. It felt as if its inhabitants had fled.

The door clicked shut behind him. He swung around; the little girl must have been hiding behind it for there she stood solemnly gazing at him, her hand on the bolt. They stared at each other for a moment, then she shot the bolt and tiptoed past. He followed her into a large room with couches and wall paintings. The child invited him with a gesture to sit down.

After a few moments an elderly man came in, stoop-shouldered and tired, his sallow face lined with sadness. "I am Cunorix Maqqo Colini, lord, a foederatus. At your service." An alien settled in the provinces? This must be the scout.

"I am T. Gaius Mellarius, praepositus of Numerus II Batavorum. I gather that you have some information for me?"

"Yes, lord."

"Sit down."

The man sank gratefully onto the couch.

"What sort of tribe are we dealing with?"

The man sighed. "Murderers, lord. Savages, torturers, arsonists. All the vileness of the beast, in one bloodthirsty pack."

"Welsh?"

"Yes, lord. Otherwise, little is known about them. They make no prisoners, all they leave is corpses. Judged by their trail they have horses, but not many. Very elusive, impossible to approach. No other details, apart from deathbed rumors."

"Such as?"

"It is said that every night, at dusk, someone sings in their camp. Maybe a boy. Also, they leave something outside every villa they destroy. A token of their passing."

"You mean excrement?"

"No, lord, toys. A stack of children's toys outside each doorway."

"What kind of toys?"

"Just toys: dolls, miniature animals, little carts, doll's houses, toy soldiers."

"Any idea why?"

"No, lord. They are an enigma even to me. I may find out more once we're under way. That's to say, if you wish me to act as your scout."

"Where are they now?"

"My latest information is that they are headed south, in the direction of Bravonium. They go for isolated villas, open villages. If a town is defended by militia they circumvent it. If they expect no organized resistance they sack it and leave no life within its walls. Cats, dogs, cattle, women, children, old people—they leave nothing but the raven. And the flies."

"Any hope of my raising any volunteers here? I have one hundred and twenty men, all told."

The man gave him a melancholy look and said, "Not among the militia, lord, under their present commander. You might talk to the owner of this house, Honorius Simplex. He is a veteran, Primipilaris of Legio II Augusta. A Christian."

A retired senior centurion would be a good man to enlist. "Where is he now?"

"Staying with his wife's family, lord. His brother-in-law was killed by the raiders, so he can no longer live here."

"Why not?"

"The local custom—" He was interrupted by the little girl carrying in a tray with refreshments. They watched her in silence as she put it down on the low table, curtsied, and tiptoed out.

The old man helped himself to a sweetbread. Then he continued, "He married a local woman supposed to be a Christian, but like all of them she still adheres to the tribal customs. If a male member of the family is murdered, the eldest brother or brother-in-law must vacate his house and set out to avenge the crime; the spirit of the murdered man must have a place to live while waiting for his murderer, whom he'll take with him into Hades as his slave. As Honorius Simplex wants to go on living among his wife's tribe, he had to leave his house to his brother-in-law's spirit and set out to kill his assassin. He has not done so yet. He cannot tackle the raiders alone."

"And you, Colini? What is your interest in this?"

The old man gave him a mournful look. "I'm searching for my daughter, lord. She disappeared after a raid."

"When?"

"Six months ago."

"I see." It seemed a pointless quest; but then, it might be a pack of lies. The rule of thumb was never to trust any scout, not to the point where he could lead you into an ambush. But this was going to be a cat-and-mouse assignment, different from the straightforward advance and retreat on the frontier; he would need the man's local knowledge. "What's the next step, Colini? Are you prepared to go down to Bravonium or wherever? I'd like to enlist you as a scout."

"Thank you, lord."

"You travel alone?"

"Yes."

"On horseback?"

"Yes."

"Where do you suggest we meet next?"

The man shrugged his shoulders. He really was a sad sack; Mellarius wondered how much use he would be. "All right, I leave it to you to be in touch. Now, if Honorius Simplex is here, ask him to come and see me."

"Yes, lord." He rose arthritically, then added, his voice low, "He's a proud, lonely man, lord. Not your usual Christian: a Gnostic. The church considers him a heretic." He shuffled out.

The little girl came back with more refreshments. Unlike the terrified little creatures whose lives he had saved, she was very self-possessed. He watched her as she moved about, determined and elegant, a hostess in miniature. How nice to have a little daughter like that, after your retirement. Maybe, one day—

He heard a sound behind him and looked round. A tall, bearded civilian had come in. His bearing betrayed the soldier; despite the toga, the sandals and the trim grizzled beard it was as though he wore armor.

"Honorius Simplex?"

"Yes."

"T. Gaius Mellarius, praepositus of Numerus II Batavorum. I would like to thank you for allowing me to use your house."

"My pleasure, Colonel. You wanted to see me?"

Mellarius was about to gesture him to one of the couches, then he remembered it was the man's own house. The veteran dismissed the little girl and settled on the couch opposite.

"Maqqo Colini has told you about my situation?" he asked, helping himself to a sweetbread.

"That you are obliged to avenge the murder of your brother-in-law?"

"Yes."

"Who killed him? When?"

"The raiders, while he was inspecting a field outside town, a week ago. They must have surprised him; he was decapitated, the head was missing, and atrocities were performed on other parts of his body." He sounded matter-of-fact and unemotional, a military report.

"What do you know about the tribe?"

"No more than Maqqo Colini." The cool blue eyes sized him up. "I have known many scouts in my time. Like all of them he needs not only trust but respect."

The colonel smiled.

"Where are you stationed normally, Colonel?"

"In Novaesium, on the Rhine."

"Ah, yes, I know it. Passed through there as a young officer a lifetime ago."

There was a silence; then Mellarius asked, "Would you care to join me with a century of volunteers from the militia?"

The blue eyes lit up. "Don't expect to find any volunteers among the militia, Colonel. I might round up a few untrained or semitrained freedmen and slaves, serving my wife's family. It depends on the bounty."

"I leave that to you. They would be placed under your command. I have a hundred and twenty men on foot; from what I've heard, not a match for this tribe."

"Except that you represent Rome," the man said, observing him.

The colonel smiled.

The man rose. "I'll come to see you tomorrow, Colonel. I may have results by then."

"You know where to find me. Present yourself to the officer of the watch."

The man turned on his heels; at the door he stood to attention and saluted.

The girl came to collect the tray. How fragile she was, how vulnerable! On impulse, the colonel rose to his feet. With perfect aplomb, she curtsied and disappeared with her tray.

Thoughtfully, Mellarius made his way back through the empty streets to the farmyard where his regiment was encamped. He looked forward to a beaker of wine and a meal

with his centurions to talk over the situation. To his irritation
he found young Theodosius's priest waiting for him, all humility and pious smiles, making a sign of the cross as he entered.
"I want a word with you, my son."

This had to stop. "Priest," the colonel said with restraint, "I
told you: I am not your son, so you will not address me as such.
And next time, have yourself properly announced."

The priest's unctuous smile survived. "I was told by the
young Theodosius that . . . "

"The young Theodosius is a minor officer in another regiment. You are now serving under my command; if you want to
see me, speak to the officer of the watch, he'll make the proper
enquiry as to whether I am prepared to receive you. Dismiss."

The infernal priest stood his ground. "All I wish to say,
my—Colonel, is that the civilian you spoke with is a heretic. He
may not be made part of this expedition." He turned to go, but
the colonel, in an uncharacteristic gesture of outrage, grabbed
him by the scruff of his habit, brought his face close to the pious
eyes and said, "If you interfere in my decisions, I'll have you
trussed up and shipped back to where you came from. I'm of
a mind to do so now. Get out!"

He thrust the priest away; the man stumbled over his habit,
looked as if he would end up flat on his face, but managed to
remain upright. He fumbled for his cross.

"If you wave that thing at me once more," the colonel said,
"I will ram it up your rectum."

"Blasphemy—!" the creature started; then the centurion of
the watch came in, attracted by the altercation. "Take this man
out of here and do not readmit him unless it's on my personal
order."

The officer saluted and held open the flap of the tent for the
priest, who hurried out, hands in the sleeves of his habit.

In came Doctor Fortunatas with his calming potion.

"I don't need your concoction, medicus. I need to be left
alone."

The doctor smiled in perfect understanding. "I know you
would like to strangle him, lord," he said soothingly, "but you
must realize he is not what he seems. He is a spy from headquarters who should be treated like a beautiful rich young
widow."

"Fortunatas," the colonel said, mollified, "you are a manipulator. All right, I'll have it." He took the beaker. "Tell me one thing from your wisdom: how does that priest know of my discussion in a private house twenty minutes ago?"

The doctor thought it over while his patient drank the draught; then he said, "Either someone eavesdropped, lord, or he knew beforehand what was going to be discussed."

The colonel stared at him. "The scout," he said, and handed him the empty beaker.

*

A café in Shropshire, spring 1987

"But how, exactly?" Sylvia asked. "How did you slip into that dream?"

"It wasn't a dream." I beckoned the waitress of the little café where we had ended up after our visit to the museum. "Two more coffees, please."

"It's very good," Sylvia said to her, with the radiant smile English women exchange on such occasions.

"So glad you like it." The woman took our cups away; a few moments later the gurgle, hiss and hawk of a coffee machine sounded from a doorway, in which a ginger cat had appeared at ankle height, blinking.

"I was questioning the pendulum," I continued.

She put a hand on my arm. "Love, listen to me. Are you listening?"

"I'm listening."

"You were *not* questioning the pendulum. You were seeing something."

"Well—"

"The pendulum, love, is a little ball of wood on a string which can only indicate yes, no, or maybe. It's nothing, just a bead; you are the one who puts the questions, and this time they led to a sort of trance."

"All I did was visualize the scene. I've done it all my life.

During the war, for instance, after I was given the old *Isabel,* the navy put on our aft deck a catapult and four rows of depth charges painted blue and orange. I didn't need to go into a trance to see what a German fighter pilot would see, I had to think of a way of camouflaging those things and I did."

"Marty, that's hardly the same thing. You were visualizing something familiar, something that was right outside."

"Well, I'm familiar with the Roman army in Britain. I researched it for years."

"Are you telling me that a room with a mosaic floor and wall paintings and couches and a little girl serving refreshments and two men you saw in detail—"

The woman brought two coffees. "Thanks awfully," Sylvia said.

The woman said, "That's all right."

"Can't you accept that what you experienced was a form of clairvoyance?" she continued.

I looked at her eyes, their concern and love and worry, and said, "Sure."

She stirred her coffee. "Tell me again: what did the little girl look like?"

"Little. Nine or ten. Long dress, feet in something like ballet slippers. Plaits pinned on top of her head, a fragile little neck. The way she carried the tray was adorable: very self-important, all alone in the house, serving two gentlemen. The older man I wouldn't trust any further than I could throw this building. The praepositus in mufti looked like any ship's officer ashore. He seemed to spot at first glance that he was dealing with a sea lawyer."

"What's that?"

"A double-tongued bastard."

"Pity your tape recorder isn't running. I'd like you to play all this back and listen to it. You were describing a child in great detail, two men as if they were sitting right in front of you, and the praepositus as if you could read his thoughts."

"So?"

"My question is: did you actually see that child, those men? Did you read the praepositus's thoughts?"

"Let's call him colonel, that's what he was. I'm sure that if I ask the pendulum, it'll confirm everything."

"But where does it *come* from, Marty? Don't you understand? I'm a listener, an onlooker. I heard your questions and I swear to you: no one could have come up with those details unless—"

"What?"

"Unless he was clairvoyant."

"But I didn't see anything! I simply imagined it as it could have been."

"All right, describe a Napoleonic hussar for me."

"I'm not interested in Napoleonic hussars. I don't know the first thing about them. But I do know Romans, especially Theodosius's expeditionary force in 368. I'm not a clairvoyant. I'm just an expert by now who knows a lot about his subject and has no problem visualizing it."

"Like little girls with fragile necks and ballet slippers and plaits pinned on top of their heads?"

"I must have seen her a dozen times on illustrations in books. Maybe even on television. What about *I, Claudius?*"

"If it worries you, I won't insist."

"It doesn't worry me, dear heart. I just don't want to put a ten-guilder price ticket on a pencil sharpener worth fifty cents."

"Well . . . " She looked around her as if for support; the woman had kept her eye on us and came with the bill.

I paid. The cat was necking with the doorpost. Sylvia said to the woman, "It's a lovely day, isn't it?" and the woman said, "Last night, when I heard the weather on the telly, I thought we were going to have rain. Aren't we lucky?"

The cat turned around and showed its behind.

*

On the road to Bravonium, spring 368 A.D.

The morning had been soft with mist rising from the valleys. The abandoned fields had had no color yet when the detachment marched out of Viroconium. The aquilifer had taken up position at the head of the column; the centurions joined the colonel behind him; the mules started pulling the wagons stacked high with tents, cooking gear and mouseproof barrels of grain.

It was now a long column, with the addition of the sixty volunteers under Honorius Simplex. The veteran himself marched with the centurions and the colonel at the head of the detachment. At the other end, behind the wagons, the thespian and the dog tagged along, the thespian gesturing and declaiming at the sky, the dog, tongue lolling, looking up at him with the permanent guilt ingrained in its humble soul.

The sun rose high, the road was straight. The officers at the head of the column carried on the traditional debate, so as to combat the monotony which could lead to inattention. After all subjects were exhausted and no new issues of importance came to mind, one of the centurions would read from the classics. It was the secret of the erudition of the officers of the Imperial Army.

This morning, a new mind had joined the regiment: the veteran. He was given free rein and turned out to be worthy of the honor; Colonel Mellarius thanked his god for sending the man his way. After four hours of marching he knew more about the western province and its tribes than he cared to know.

At noon, the detachment halted for a meal. Cassidile the dog made the rounds for scraps and had his head scratched. When the sun was at its zenith the haruspex, after a shrill altercation with the priest, sacrificed a chicken. When the troops rose at the colonel's command and continued their march the haruspex came to the head of the column; to the colonel's irritation, the infernal priest turned up as well. "I did not ask you to join us," he said. "This is a private consultation."

The priest replied with a smile of long-suffering patience. "I have been ordered by my bishop and Field Marshal Theodosius to join this expedition as a representative of Our Savior and his Holy Church. I may not be excluded from any discussion that bears on my religious duties."

"Priest—" the colonel restrained himself as he saw, from the corner of his eye, that his officers were trying to suppress amusement "—as long as we are in the field, there is only one authority for you to obey: me. Your Jew god is not here, your bishop is not here, the field marshal is not here—"

"But Jesus is here!" the priest intoned, lifting a hand at the sky. "As He said unto us on the shores of the Dead Sea—"

The colonel was overcome by the insane impulse to run the bugger through with his sword; the watchful Felicius Antigonus led the man away.

"What does today look like, haruspex?" the colonel asked, breathing heavily.

"Propitious, lord." The haruspex sounded pleased with himself. "No danger, maybe some slight adversity."

"Such as?"

"That the omen did not say. The liver was slightly discolored, so perhaps an interference by a minor god. Nothing serious. We are still under protection."

"By whom?"

"A strong but so far anonymous god, lord. There is hope he will become attached to us and decide to act as our protector. It's too early to press for his identity, it could irritate him. This is a critical stage."

"Well, the sooner you know, the sooner we can start sacrificing to him. Or her."

"It is a male god, lord. Perhaps even a military one. I will inform you as soon as—"

"Very well, haruspex. Thank you."

The man bowed and stepped aside to let the column pass, in order to resume his place in front of the wagons with Fortunatas the medicus, the accountant, Frisius the carpenter and the infernal priest.

"Forgive me, Colonel," a voice said at his shoulder, "but be careful. That so-called Christian priest is dangerous. They all are."

"I thought you were a Christian yourself, Honorius Simplex?"

"Not of his ilk. I'm a Gnostic, a heretic in his eyes."

"I thought all Christians believed the same?"

"No," Honorius Simplex said. "I follow the teachings of Christ but I won't allow bishops or priests to put themselves between Him and myself. The man is a zealot."

"I see." To the colonel, Christianity was a private affair like any other religion and none of the army's business, but the subject was interesting and good to march by. All the while his ever-alert eyes scanned the fields and the hills to his left, the woods to his right; after long practice he could take in his surroundings during any discussion. "What's a zealot?" he asked.

"A mad sect we had to deal with in Judea. They killed themselves when their last stronghold was surrounded. Did you serve in the east?"

"No, only on the Rhine. Except for one foray into this province thirty years ago."

"What were you doing here?"

"One of those uprisings. More localized than the one we are dealing with now. We were brought over in support of Legio II Augusta."

"That's interesting," the veteran said. "I was here too at that time. I don't remember you."

"I served as adjutant to my father, T. Gaius Virilis. He was centurion of the Second."

"Ah, yes."

"What were you doing?"

"Equerry to C. Mannius Natalis of the Secundani Britones."

They marched in silence for a while.

"As I said," the veteran resumed, "you must be careful in your dealings with that priest."

"I know he is a spy, if that's what you mean."

"More than that, he is dangerous. Do not give him a free hand. Do not let him preach to the troops. His gospel is not the true gospel. His message is not what Jesus preached."

"I see," the colonel said neutrally, hoping to stem the religious outpouring.

"His preachings have nothing to do with mercy or compassion, only with hatred and revenge. His god is a jealous monster whose angry eyes are forever fixed on his so-called chosen people, telling them to destroy all places of worship in which others serve their gods, overthrow their altars, break their images . . ."

"Quite," the colonel said.

But Honorius Simplex continued with the passion Christians showed only when maligning each other, "Jesus was a

148

man of mercy and tenderness unlike the official church, founded on his death rather than his life. Its 'poor in spirit' are anarchists without country, without tradition, contemptuous of all government, all public services, all civic virtues, all education, the army, the arts, philosophy. Unless they are stopped, the illiterate and the ignorant will undermine the empire. That is no idle threat—"

A shout, passed up the marching ranks from the rear, reached the head of the column. "Accident!"

The colonel lifted a hand; the centurions shouted their orders, the detachment drew to a halt. A messenger came running. "An accident, Colonel! One of the wagons broke an axle!"

"When?"

"Just now, as it crossed the ford!"

The colonel had not noticed splashing through any ford; so much for the hypnotic power of oratory. "At ease!"

The command was echoed by the centurions. He marched down the resting column. The men were laughing and chatting; the new volunteers looked somber and suspicious. Finally there was the wagon: on its side, two wheels still turning. Its contents were strewn about the road, some in the brook. The haruspex would be pleased; he always was when his predictions came true.

The head wagoner took the incident as a personal insult inflicted by a mischievous little god, now shaking with laughter somewhere among the hills on the horizon.

"It's not your fault, plaustrarius," the colonel said to the man shaking his fists at the hills. "The wagons have seen a lot of service since Rutupiae. Even then they were not new."

"It's the mules, Colonel! They're too rough on the wagons, they tear through the fords at high speed. The oxen we left in Viroconium would have tested the water, then lumbered across."

"Well, go ahead and repair it. Be as quick as you can."

"Ah, but this is going to need time!" the man wailed. "If it had been a wheel, I could have changed it quickly, but it's an axle!"

"How long is it going to take?"

"Hours, Colonel. First I have to retrieve the load from the

water, then the cart has to be righted and pulled onto dry land—"

"All right. Do your work."

"Yes, Colonel."

Mellarius rejoined the centurions at the head of the column. "Repairing the wagon is going to take a while," he said. "We'll make camp here. Antigonus! Have a look at the high ground over on the right. Take the camp prefect with you. If it's suitable, go ahead. Honorius Simplex, are your men fit to act as guards yet?"

"Oh yes, sir."

"In that case, you'll be officer of the watch."

"What's the watchword, Colonel?"

"That can wait until nightfall, after we've made camp."

"It would be helpful if I could give it to them now."

Mellarius thought of the capsized wagon, the sodden stores. *"Patience,"* he said.

Within the hour, camp was made. The leather tents were put up in a square around the praetorium; in the corners smoke started to rise from the cooking fires. The men squatted in groups, gossiping, drinking wine. The guards were in place. Evening was falling.

The colonel had looked forward to a quiet hour before the meal, but it was not to be. He had barely entered his tent when the thespian barged in, accompanied by the dog.

"Lord! This is the time! At last! I know exactly what I will recite: the death of the warrior girl:

So when the javelin whistled from his hand
The Volscians as one man looked up at their Queen,
Oblivious of the air around her, of the whistling shaft—"

"Calm down, Cassius Colonia," the colonel said. "What's all this about?"

"Lord, I have waited for this opportunity ever since Londinium! It's perfect: the weather, the setting, the little elevation in the far corner for me to stand on. I'll need some torches, maybe the bucinator to support me by blowing the attack when I give him the signal—"

"What the devil are you talking about? What attack?"

"In the recital, lord! By the treacherous Arruns!

The Queen, oblivious of the air
around her, of the weapon
Gliding from high heaven, remained
Until the javelin swooped and thudded home
Beneath her naked breast—Aah!"

There he stood, unkempt, bestubbled, the old mutt panting at his feet. His obsession with reciting Virgil to press-ganged yokels who would not understand a word gave him a mad nobility. "Very well," the colonel said, "talk to Honorius Simplex, he is the officer of the watch. If it's all right with him, you may organize it."

"Lord!" The scarecrow kissed his hand; the dog, which had lain down, pricked up its ears in apprehension. "This is why I followed you through all the horrors of this campaign: to, one night, relieve the ugliness of your existence with the glory, the music, the poetry of the *Aeneid!* Come, Cassidile!"

The old dog farted as it rose and waddled after him.

*

A ford in Herefordshire, spring 1987

The Roman road south of Wroxeter led via Church Stretton to Craven Arms; the spot I had dowsed on the map in France lay somewhere along it. The pendulum had been precise: where the road crosses a brook, near a farm. The car bumped and bounced down the badly paved lane full of potholes toward the expected bridge.

It turned out to be not a bridge but a ford. I got out of the car to see if we could make it across; at my signal Sylvia drove through slowly. While she parked on the shoulder of the road, I walked to the narrow footbridge to one side of the ford, but had to wait for a little boy on a tricycle racing at me like a beetle. Halfway across the bridge I stopped and looked down at the water.

It had recovered from the turbulence of the passing car and

I saw, as under a glass plate, a section of paved road. I could not believe my eyes: the pebbled center, the track of larger stones on each side of it, the curbstones, the shoulders—I gazed at the ghost from the past in its glass case with a feeling of awe. A section of a Roman road no more than sixteen feet square, yet the pendulum had pinpointed it from seven hundred miles away!

Sylvia joined me, marveled at it with me, and started to take photographs. I took out my pendulum. The little boy on the tricycle had turned around and pulled up to watch.

"This is a piece of Roman road?"

Yes, said the pendulum.

"Something happened in this particular spot?"

Yes.

"Was it a ford then, as now?"

Yes.

"My colonel passed this way?"

The pendulum went into a diagonal swing.

"Did he pass here or didn't he?"

A small yes.

The tepid response foxed me; then I understood. "You mean, he passed after having stopped?"

Yes.

Suddenly, like a breakthrough, it came to me. "Had there been an accident?"

Yes.

"Something to do with a wagon?"

Yes.

"Did they repair it quickly?"

No.

"They had to make camp?"

Yes.

"Anything else I should know?"

No.

"Okay." I put the pendulum in my pocket. The little boy stood there kneading his private parts. "For God's sake," I said, "go and have a pee!" He pedaled off.

"I can't get over it," Sylvia said.

"What?"

"This!" She pointed at the ford. "You're sure it's an authentic section of Roman road?"

"The pendulum says it is. I can't see anyone in later years paving the bottom of a brook in just this way, certainly not during the Dark Ages, the Middle Ages even."

"Why not?"

"The Roman Army had a road department with permanent crews; if a tree fell across a road or a pothole developed they took care of it within twenty-four hours. The roads were vital to them; after 410 A.D., when they left, the whole system collapsed, the locals used the paving stones as building material. It took until 1764 before Parliament finally passed the Turnpike Act and the government became responsible for the roads again."

"I think it's magical," she said, gazing at the paving stones in their glass case. "*Now* do you believe?"

"I think it's extraordinary," I said.

She sighed. "All right, let's have our picnic."

"Where? Here?"

"Why not? It's a pretty spot. Go get the basket."

"It's barely eleven o'clock!"

"We needn't eat straightaway. We can sit and look at the birds, you can read your paper. Go on!"

I got the picnic hamper out of the car and lugged it, with blanket, up the road. Sylvia spread the blanket at the bottom of a rise underneath whispering trees. I put the hamper between us; she started to take out the dishes, the jam, the thermos flask, the beakers. Forty years ago I had seen her do this in exactly the same way. How fast the years had gone!

She poured the coffee and we sat for a while listening to the birds. Suddenly she said, "I've been thinking. I may have the answer."

"To what?"

"To your picking up things that happened two thousand years ago. It's like starlight."

"Huh?"

"The light of distant stars travels thousands of years before reaching us. Maybe happenings are like that: they travel in time until someone who has the gift picks them up and says, 'Two thousand years ago a column of tired, dusty Roman soldiers marched down this road, led by a middle-aged colonel. As they crossed the brook one of their wagons broke a wheel, it had to be mended, so they made camp.' "

"Interesting thought."

"All it needs is a man like you who opens himself up to faint impulses that travel through time, like the light of a distant star."

"That's all very well," I said, "but, if you ask me—"

Suddenly she whispered, "Don't move! Don't look around! Don't reach for anything!"

It sounded as if she had spotted a man with a shotgun taking aim. Then she whispered, "There's a very nervous wagtail right behind you . . ."

If this moment too were to travel through time and be picked up sixteen centuries from now by someone with a pendulum, he would wonder what had made the woman warn her husband not to move. After many fruitless guesses he would ask his pendulum for the key word and it would spell *Wagtail.* He would feel exactly what I had felt when my pendulum told me that the Romans and the Franks had slugged it out across the Rhine with *Words.*

"Okay now?" I asked.

"Yes, it's gone."

"Good."

I started to read the editorial in the London *Times,* but the sun and the fresh air made me drowsy. I lay back, hands under my head, and gazed at the white clouds sailing over Shropshire, a fleet of dreams. I must have dozed off, for suddenly I was back in the dream of the Romans building a fort. Only it wasn't a fort, it was a camp with tents and fires. Someone standing on a platform was addressing the troops, rows of squatting figures; even the ones on the periphery of the camp were spellbound. I was outraged by the sloppiness of the commanding officer sitting in the front row. Couldn't he see his guards were distracted by that bellowing ass? What was the matter with him? Bungler! Half-wit! Good-for-nothing! A hand shook me by the shoulder. "Marty! What's the matter?"

"Huh?"

"Are you all right? I was talking to you just seconds ago!"

"So you were," I muttered, sitting up.

"You were dreaming again, weren't you? Something upset you?"

"I'm not upset, I'm furious. Absolutely furious at an incompetent commanding officer who failed to notice that his guards were being distracted."

"Tell me about it."

"Well—a camp, at night, tents, smoking fires. Some bellowing ass making a speech to the troops . . . "

"But what was it that upset you?"

"The guards! The soldiers on the edge of the camp, they were listening too, watching the man with their backs to the outside world. I was mad as hell with the officer sitting in the center of the first row for not noticing that his guards were being distracted."

"But where were you? In the camp?"

I tried to remember; the dream was drawing away. "As in Glastonbury: floating overhead, with a bird's-eye view."

"Incredible . . ."

"It was just a dream."

"I believe it. It's all so consistent."

I looked at her; this was becoming ridiculous. "Don't be silly," I said and picked up the newspaper.

It was her turn to be exasperated. "One of these days, my boy, you may suddenly find out that everything you saw really happened. Then what will you do?"

"That day seems pretty remote."

She sighed. "I never met anyone who was given so much and accepted so little. I mean that."

"Darling, the danger in this business is gullibility."

I drank my cold coffee, while wagtails hopped in the branches and the white clouds sailed on over Shropshire.

*

Bravonium, spring 368 A.D.

Colonel Mellarius and his detachment were approaching

the city of Bravonium when the scout came to meet them in full gallop. The sky was blue and innocent, the city walls and the banks of the river were garlanded with the white lace of hawthorn in bloom, it was a scene of peace.

The scout dismounted and came running toward the head of the column. He looked as if he had escaped from Hades. "Lord!" he panted, "the city . . . "

"Are we too late?"

"Nobody, not a soul! Even the children have been murdered!"

"How long ago?"

"Last night, maybe early this morning!"

"Where is the tribe now?"

"Gone, lord. Not a trace of them anywhere."

"The city was not defended?"

"The people must have believed the raiders left cities alone. That's what they did so far."

Honorius Simplex asked, "What about the sacking of Lavobrinta?" It was against army discipline for an officer to put an oar in like that. Maybe he had relatives in Bravonium.

"Thank you, scout," the colonel said. "We'll go in and have a look. What's the next town down this road?"

"Magnis, lord."

"How far?"

"Two days' march, lord."

"At walking speed," Honorius Simplex commented. Something would have to be done about him.

"Go and alert the people of Magnis."

"But lord—"

"Someone has to warn them. Go, now!"

"Yes, lord." The man mounted wearily and swung his horse around.

They marched for a while in silence. The birds were in full voice; it was a warm day.

"You're planning to march into the town?" the veteran asked.

"I'll go in with one turma while the rest of you march around the walls."

"Take my men! Some of them have relatives here."

"That's why I don't want them. I'll give permission later."

"But I would have thought—"

"Enough, Simplex!"

"Yes, Colonel."

The walled city looked somnolent and bucolic. Within, the city seemed asleep; there was nothing to alert the untrained eye. But there were no birds, only crows winging skyward from behind the walls, then swooping down again. A whiff of wind carried a smell: nauseous, sickly sweet. The raid must have taken place earlier than the night before.

The city gates showed no signs of violence; the attack had come in broad daylight, when they were open. The colonel marched in with his platoon. He had seen many sacked cities and was familiar with the refuse of enemy raids: corpses, flies, stray dogs, blackened ruins. Each time he was struck with revulsion at the sight; this time it turned into rage. Most of the corpses in the streets and in the doorways were women and children; the men must have fled. The walls of the gardens showed tufts of flowering lilac and laburnum; in the doorways were neat piles of children's toys: dolls, wooden swords, little carts, toy crockery, right beside the mutilated corpses of the children themselves. It was not easy for raw recruits to keep up a steady march; too many corpses, too many fear-crazed dogs barking and snarling at them. Crows feasting on the corpses' eyes took off, wings clattering, and circled overhead, cawing.

"Send some men to search the houses for survivors," the colonel said.

"Yes, Colonel." The optio made up four groups of three men who started a systematic search of the houses while the rest of the platoon marched to the center of the city. There, in a small forum innocent in its rural simplicity, lay the men, a veritable pile of them, their throats cut. This meant a mass burial; the troops were not going to like it. And there was not likely to be any loot left for them in the ransacked town except the stacks of toys in the doorways.

The gate on the other side of the town was also open; across a meadow, strewn with the carcasses of sheep, Mellarius saw a glint of water. The rest of the detachment stood at ease on the opposite bank of the river.

He was on his way to the bridge when the optio overtook him. "Colonel!" The man was carrying a child, its head hidden in the shoulder of his cloak. "This is the only one, Colonel. I found him in a tree behind one of the houses. Come on, boy, say something! Say something to the colonel!" He put the little boy on his feet and turned him around to face his commander. At the sight of the child's terror, Mellarius was deeply moved. There stood he, himself, forty years ago. "Good boy," he said kindly.

The child came toward him, slowly at first, suddenly at a run. It threw its arms around his hips and pressed itself against him.

Mellarius touched the soft, silky hair. O, T. Gaius! Bless thy memory! When it had happened to him, the hand stroking his hair had been the touch of life.

"Come, boy," the colonel said, taking the small hand in his.

Together they walked across the bridge to where the army was.

*

The mass burial was executed in the usual silence. When it was over, the colonel ordered the men to bathe in the river and cleanse themselves. On the opposite bank, the sacked town was slowly being reclaimed by a few survivors who had been able to flee into the forest. Presently they sent a delegation to ask for the army's continued protection.

At their approach the little boy scurried and hid. Doctor Fortunatas went after him and brought him back to be handed over, but it soon became evident that his parents and all his relatives had been killed. The child pressed himself against Colonel Mellarius. The haruspex as well as the infernal priest insisted that the boy be left behind, orphan or no orphan. But the colonel picked him up, lifted him high for all to see, and shouted, "This boy is hereby adopted by the regiment! Give him a name!" This was what, forty years ago, T. Gaius Virilis had done.

The men shouted names; the optio who had found the boy

said, "Why not call him after the tree he was hiding in? A hazel tree."

The colonel said, "All right, his name will be T. Gaius Corylus, after the tree in which he was found."

The men, some of them still in the water, applauded. The delegation from the town withdrew gloomily after being assured that the raiders would not return. They were told to form their own militia.

The detachment made camp in the ruins of a military depot outside the city walls. It had been pillaged by the raiders. The thespian was ordered to recite standing on an empty barrel, not a tragedy this time but something amusing. His gifts were not those of a stand-up comedian, but there was enough mead left in some barrels undiscovered by the raiders for the soldiers to become more appreciative as the recital wore on. In the end, they roared with laughter at mere winks.

Meanwhile, the little boy hid under Mellarius's cloak, pressed tightly against him; finally he fell asleep with exhaustion, the dog at his feet.

After the thespian's performance the colonel made the rounds of the tents to talk to the men and thank them for performing the revolting labor of burying the victims. Halfway, after all that mead, he had to absent himself in the bushes. As he stood there, humming with relief, the little boy rustled through the shrubs, took up position beside him, and followed his example.

Suddenly, he had the strange feeling that there were three of them standing side by side under the stars. He was about to pray to his divine father when there was another rustling in the bushes; the dog had finally found them, now they were four.

*

Leintwardine, spring 1987

The discovery of the perfectly preserved section of Roman road softened my skepticism. No creative imagination, however compelling, could have pinpointed on a map a minute spot like that at seven hundred miles' distance. Calling this coincidence would mean that skepticism had turned into a closed mind. The dream had been merely a dream; the section of Roman road was real, and the pendulum had led me to it.

I tackled the next location I had map-dowsed in the south of France in a new spirit of openness. It was a village called Leintwardine in north Herefordshire, built on the remains of the Roman Bravonium. As Sylvia drove into the village I spotted an old wall down a side street. "Hold it," I cried, "that looked like a Roman wall!"

It proved impossible to stop the car because of the traffic; she had to drive across a bridge before we could park. We walked back into the village and discovered that if Leintwardine had anything, it had Roman walls. I dowsed five different sections, the pendulum rejected them all until we reached the one I had glimpsed from the car.

Unlike the other locations so far, this one was very public. In a row of terraced houses nearby curtains moved in the windows; children playing in the street were fascinated by the old man standing facing the wall. I was muttering my first question into the tape recorder, held close to my chest, when a woman's voice behind me said, "I must say! Some people! There are toilets right around the corner!"

Sylvia joined me and I asked, "How the hell can I convince people that I'm not standing here pissing against the wall?"

"Maybe a small sign around your neck?"

"Do something!" I urged, as I saw the children close in.

"I'll take their pictures, you go ahead."

She walked over to them and managed to capture their attention. I returned to my pendulum and the tape recorder.

"Again: is this a Roman wall?"

Yes, said the pendulum.

"Important in connection with my colonel?"

Yes.

"Had this town been sacked when he got here?"

The pendulum went into a spin. Behind me I heard Sylvia talking to the children in the same way as she did to plants.

"A sacked city. Corpses in the street?"

Yes.

"Any survivors?"

Yes.

"Many?"

No.

"A few? One?"

One.

"An old woman?"

No.

"A child?"

Yes.

"A little girl?"

No.

"A boy. Was he taken in by the army?"

The pendulum spun so strongly that it slipped from my grip and flew into the street.

When she saw me pick it up, Sylvia asked "Any luck?"

"It's rather spirited today, to coin a phrase. Anyhow, the town was sacked, only one survivor, a little boy who was taken in by the army." The children began to crowd us, clamoring for more photographs. From one of the houses opposite a woman's voice called, "Jo—seee!"

"Let's go," I said.

We returned to the car through quiet streets, past somnolent houses with tufts of flowering lilac protruding from behind garden walls. Sylvia and I walked across the bridge; as we did so I heard the splashing of a weir. It had the same effect on me as a running tap on little boys; I had to disappear into the bushes on the other side.

As I stood there relieving my bladder, I suddenly had a similar experience to the one in Brussels. I felt the weight of a helmet on my head, my chest was encased in a breastplate, a cloak hung from my shoulders. For a few seconds the Roman centurion and I were reunited in a rush of ecstatic joy at having come home again; but this time there was another element, a disturbing one. Beside me stood another man, the officer I had seen in the house in Viroconium. Beyond him I sensed the presence of others, but to him I felt tied by a bewilderingly emotional bond. Then the hallucination, or whatever it was, let go of me. Again I stood alone, old man peeing in the bushes. I zipped up and stepped into the open.

Sylvia had been waiting for me. "Hallo there," she said.

"You're not going to believe this."

"What happened?"

"I had another Brussels experience, but this time—Well, let's have lunch and I'll tell you about it."

"We'll picnic here. Get the hamper."

"Here?"

"Down there, by the river. Why not? It's pleasant and beautiful."

"All right."

While she made her way down to find a spot to spread the blanket, I went to the car. I was confused, bewildered. So far, this had been fun; now I suddenly felt I was no longer in control. The hallucination of being a Roman centurion had been just as real, just as emotional as in Brussels, but this time my alter ego had suddenly sprung an alien emotion on me concerning the other man beside me. I no longer wanted any part of this. This was sick.

"Lovely," Sylvia said, taking the blanket from me. "Here— put the hamper beside me."

I twisted my knee as I tried to squat and cursed old age.

"Tell me!" She started to unpack the basket.

"You're not going to like it."

"Why not?"

"I had a return to my Roman self in those bushes, just as in Brussels, only this time there was a new element. An emotional involvement. I don't know how to put it. I suddenly seemed to touch a well of deep emotion and didn't like it one bit."

"Within yourself?"

"Between myself and the man standing next to me, the one we have been following so far. In my previous incarnation, if that's what it was, I was in love with a man."

"I see. But I thought he was your son?"

"Out of the question. That was not paternal love. They were homosexuals." There was a silence. "Well?" I asked. "Do we react in black and white or in technicolor?"

"This happened in classical times," she said. "Maybe we should allow for the mores of antiquity."

"The hell with antiquity." I picked up a beaker and held it out to her. "A queer is a queer at any time in history, and I want no part of them. I feel the need for a breather."

She poured the coffee. "What makes you so sure they were?"

"You want details?"

"Yes." She unwrapped the bread. I watched her, amazed. There she sat, calmly preparing sandwiches, eager to hear the details of love between men. Maybe women were more sanguine when it came to male loving male. "Perhaps nothing fazes you," I said. "I happen to find this repulsive."

"I can't see why." She reached for the mayonnaise. "You mentioned a well of deep emotion. That doesn't sound as if there had been actual—well—was there?"

"Buggery, you mean? No. Not on the spot, at least."

"Then what makes you think—"

"I never felt for another man what I felt for the one standing by my side."

She handed me a sandwich.

"I seem to have a clear choice," I continued. "Either I pack it in, or I start dismantling lifelong convictions. I'm too old for that."

"Which convictions?"

"Well, hell! I never could accept love between men. I always felt like kicking the bastards off my ship."

"I would call that a prejudice, not a conviction."

"Well, whatever."

Sparrows were gathering, noisily debating the risks of hopping onto the blanket.

"All right," I said, "so it's prejudice. My prejudices are part of my identity. I can't just toss them aside at random. And why should I, at my age, begin to accept something that has repulsed me all my life?"

"If the centurion is indeed you, in a previous existence—"

"I tell you: it's just too damn late. I'll be damned if I'll start identifying with queers and their wing-flapping emotions at my age."

"But the centurion is important to you! I remember how

moved you were in Brussels, what the experience meant to you. Are you going to dump all that just because you are not a homosexual yourself and won't even—"

"I am an old man preparing for death," I said with finality, adding in my mind, "stupid old ham."

"Preparing for death?" she said sweetly. "To me, it sounded like bad temper."

"Bad temper? What *are* you talking about?"

"The usual negative stuff: grumbling at restaurant food, lousy service, punks being noisy in the street when decent people are trying to get some sleep, that sort of thing."

"You call that bad temper?"

"I should say so. Before you were made aware of your Roman past your standard mood was rage."

"Against whom, for God's sake?"

"Football hooligans. Muslim extremists. Corrupt politicians. Spineless bishops, with or without gaiters—"

"What is this? Chicken?"

"Yes."

I took a bite. "What else?"

"What what?"

"You were ticking off my prejudices."

"Want more? Snarling mopeds. Ghetto blasters. Graffiti. Tuneless music. Rhymeless poetry. Sculptures made of a thousand slices of toast called 'bed.' "

"You want me to accept all that?"

"It happens to be the times we live in, dear love."

"I must accept the present in order to understand the past? Is that what you are saying?"

She smiled. "I never took 'old men must be explorers' to be the motto for a kneeler."

"How cunning! How like a woman, to slip that one in!" I took an angry bite of the sandwich.

She said peaceably, "I never expected this to be just a guessing game with picnics. From the very beginning I've taken it more seriously than you. I knew it would take guts."

"More than that," I said, chewing. "It takes swallowing discrepancies the size of coconuts and pretending I don't notice them."

She frowned. "What do you mean?"

"Old men of eighty taking part in campaigns. Singing women in cages being carted along by the army."

"Careful," she warned, "your sandwich is coming apart."

I stuffed the rest of it in my mouth; that silenced me for a while. The sparrows plumped for boldness and hopped onto the blanket. She started to feed them crumbs.

"Well?" I asked finally. "Now what do we do?"

She thought that over while feeding the sparrows. Then she said, "Let's carry on. Forget about all this; I'm sure it is a red herring. It will all become clear in the end, believe me."

"I don't."

She looked up and took my hand. "You're doing a wonderful thing, Marty. Exciting, fascinating; neither of us ever dreamed that we had something like this ahead of us. Just carry on and let it happen. You don't have to analyze any of it right now, all we need for the moment is your intuition and your pendulum. Keep the faith, it will all fall into place in the end."

We sat for a while in silence, hand in hand. The sparrows pecked and bickered. It was a scene of tenderness, England in the spring. There was a dreamlike quality about it all which suddenly deepened. Suddenly, I had the sensation that we were the dream and that the Roman with his helmet, breastplate and sword was the reality in which I was about to awaken: harsh, violent, brutish, darkly lit by love between men.

CHAPTER SEVEN

*

Weston-under-Penyard, spring 1987

Our next location after Leintwardine was off a narrow lane further south, near a village called Weston-under-Penyard. The pendulum had been specific when I map-dowsed it in the south of France: I had to go to a hillock in a meadow.

The meadow proved to be a wheatfield, the "hillock" a deep hollow from which the tops of trees protruded. I made no attempt to reach it, the young green sprouts were still too delicate for me to trample across. I asked the pendulum, "Can I dowse the hollow from here?"

Yes.

I looked about me. A lovely spot, very remote. Green, hilly, hazy shifting sunlight, a chorus of bird-song from the trees in the hollow. I switched on the tape recorder; Sylvia, who had been taking photographs, sat down on the grass nearby and turned her face to the sun.

"Are we talking about that hollow in the field?"

Yes.

"Good place for an ambush. Did an ambush take place here?"

Yes.

And so on, and so on; before long, the pendulum had given me a rough idea of what had happened here. For some reason the Romans had stopped in the road; while they were dawdling, unprotected by guards, a volley of arrows had been fired at them from the hollow, killing one of them. I tried to find out who; I got no further than "a noncombatant." It might have been a cook or a carpenter.

I was surprised at my own reaction to this information. Instead of registering dispassionately what the pendulum told me, I found myself getting angry at the carelessness of the officer in command who had allowed his troops to present such an easy target. His attention must have wandered; he had done this before, in my dream after the picnic at the ford. Then, as now, I had felt like kicking his ass, the stupid bungler.

I told Sylvia about it; she was amused by my passionate involvement. I did not need that either, so I turned off the tape recorder and said, "The next spot seems to be another half mile down this road, around the next bend. Shall we take the car or leave it here?"

"We need the exercise," she said. So we left the car where it was and set off down the road.

Ten minutes or so later, after checking with the pendulum, I found myself at a spot in wide open country with a lovely view of rolling hills. Straight ahead was an unusual-looking hill, shaped like a crocodile, facing north. It would have been there in Roman times, as striking a landmark as it was now. There were hills all around us, higher than I had seen so far; in front of us, in the valley, were the roofs of the village of Weston-under-Penyard.

I started my questioning and found out that the army had made camp nearby. The dead man had been buried here and my centurion received a visit from the scout.

"Anything else I should know?"

Yes.

"To do with the little boy picked up in Bravonium?"

No.

"But he is there, isn't he?"

Yes.

"Was anybody else hurt?"

No.

"Then why do I see an army doctor around? Sorry, you can't answer that question. Well—anything else I should know about this particular spot?"

No.

"This is the end of this location?"

Yes.

"Okay." I switched off the tape recorder and said to Sylvia, "At least we know now that someone was buried here, for all the good it does. Let's go back to the car."

We set out down the hill. Sylvia asked, "Did you actually see someone?"

I looked at her, startled. "Who? What are you talking about?"

"I heard you ask, 'Then why do I see a doctor?' Did you?"

"Oh, that. Hell, I don't know; I can't remember if I saw him or just thought about him. Saw him, I think."

"Was it like Wroxeter? The little girl, the officers on couches, in that house with the wall paintings?"

"I suppose it was. Sometimes I pick up images."

"That doctor, can you describe him?"

"A man in white. Wearing a tunic, I suppose. A narrow headband. A short black beard. But, as in the case of the house in Wroxeter, I may be visualizing accumulated knowledge. All Roman army units over a certain size had a surgeon with them on campaign and I know what they looked like. Must have seen an illustration somewhere."

"It's very intriguing," she said. "I wouldn't dismiss it out of hand."

I said nothing.

A little way further down the lane we passed the driveway to a house; nailed to a tree was a sign we hadn't noticed on the way up.

"Look at that!" Sylvia cried.

The sign read BURY HILL COTTAGE.

*

Ariconium, spring 368 A.D.

When the detachment reached the small town of Ariconium, center of the local iron industry, they found it empty of all life, like Bravonium. But this time there were no corpses, no signs of violence or pillage, no stacks of toys in the doorways. It looked as if the populace had fled into the forest to escape the fate of the Bravonians. The raiders were obviously still in the area: cooking fires were smoking, in the smithy embers were still aglow, the iron was still warm. To Colonel Mellarius, marching down the main street at the head of his troops, it was alarming. There had been no untoward omen this morning when the haruspex performed his sacrifice, yet there was danger in the air, treachery. There were no dogs either. And where was the scout?

Outside the town, as the detachment headed down the highway leading to the distant hill sanctuary of Nemetobala, there suddenly came a furious sound of barking and a number of dogs strayed into the road, snarling. Honorius Simplex, who marched beside the colonel, said, "Their owners must be around somewhere. What about that compound on the left?"

The compound was hidden by trees and shrubs, a storage place, it seemed, for wagons or farm equipment. As they passed, the colonel glanced inside and saw a mass of people, squatting, heads bent, their hands tied behind their backs, as if waiting to be sentenced. He raised his arm, the detachment halted. He paused; then something, a feeling, made him order, "Testudes!"

The order was passed down the ranks; in a flash the troops were encased in shields. The colonel looked around, wondering what had alerted him.

There was nothing to be seen. To the right a field of waving tall grass undulating in the wind; to the left the compound with its crowd of motionless people, silent as the grave. The dogs barked and pranced. Together with Honorius Simplex, he cautiously approached the camp, certain now this was some kind of a trap. So far, the tribe had slaughtered every living creature in sight during their raids; why suddenly make a whole village prisoner if it was not to some nefarious purpose? No one moved among the crowd, not even the children; they must be paralyzed with terror. Yet there was no one to be seen. No guard, not a soul. Just this mass of people squatting, heads bent, in total silence.

"I think—" Honorius Simplex started; there was a shriek of warning from the road, the whoosh and clatter of a volley of arrows hitting the turtles. Horsemen burst from the field like ghosts and galloped away, out of range of the detachment's archers who instantly responded. The colonel hurried back to the road, sword drawn, and gazed at the field; there must be a hollow, hidden by the tall grass, deep enough for the dozen horses now disappearing into the distance. "Any casualties?" he cried.

"One, sir," Felicius Antigonus of the Second replied, "the thespian. He refused to take shelter inside the turtle."

"Where is he now?"

"The medicus is looking after him, sir."

"At ease!"

As the command rang out down the line and the testudes were dissolved, Colonel Mellarius hurried to the rear of the column. Doctor Fortunatas was kneeling beside a still form, watched over by the dog.

He was too late. The thespian gazed up at the sky with glazed eyes, his face blank with amazement. The arrow had struck where Arruns's javelin had hit the Virgin Queen; he had, like her, tugged at the shaft, but the steel point between the ribs had held fast in the deep wound. He looked less convincing now, stunned with disbelief, than when he acted out the queen's death that night at the ford. The dog licked his face.

"Any hope?" Mellarius asked.

"No," Doctor Fortunatas replied. "He's gone."

Aelius Rufinus of the First caught up with him, out of breath. "Colonel!"

"Yes?"

"What do you want me to do with the prisoners, sir?"

It took a second before the colonel realized he meant the crowd in the compound. They should be set free, but there was no time for that. "Cut one of them free, let him take care of the rest."

He watched the centurion go back down the road and was overcome by a sense of defeat. This was not an episode to be proud of. Where was the damn scout?

He rose to return to the head of the column and realized that the little boy Corylus was clinging to him. "God," he said, as he touched the silky hair. "Dear god."

"Do we bury him here?" Honorius Simplex asked when the colonel joined him.

"We'll make camp on that hill ahead and hold a funeral service for him tonight."

"Silly brute," the veteran said.

"I wonder what happened to the scout," said the colonel.
"He should have warned us."

The veteran spat in the road.

*

The thespian was buried at sunset, after they had made camp
on windy high ground with a view of distant hills.

No sacrifice was offered for the dead, no service held by
either the haruspex or the priest, who bickered over the matter
of precedence. The colonel recited Virgil at the graveside.

The detachment, lined up behind him in formation, stood in
silence; the little boy, pressed against him under his cloak, was
silently crying. The dog lay panting beside the grave.

Lo! Hylax is barking in the doorway! May we believe it?
Or do lovers make up dreams for themselves?

There lay the mad thespian in his shroud, far away from
home. Maybe he had had no other home than the army. He had
been a friend, despite his need to stay aloof which had become
his downfall. If he had not lagged behind with the dog, he
would have been safe inside a testudo from the arrow that
killed him. Farewell, my friend, may thy guardian god guide
thee safely into Hades.

The command "Present *arms!*" rang out, followed by the
orchestrated sound of two hundred men saluting the departed.
The colonel saluted too and remained motionless while the
bucinator blew the *Ultimum Vale,* a quavering sound in the
wind. Then he lowered his arm, commands rang out, the detachment marched off toward the field where the tents stood,
orange with black shadows in the sunset. The gravedigger
filled the grave. Overnight, Frisius the carpenter chiseled the
lettering on the tombstone, for which the colonel had given him
the text.

CASSIVS   COL
ONIA TRAGOE
DVS   NVMERI
II BATAVORVM
MORTVS   EST
PRO ARTE

*

Late that night, after the meal, the scout finally turned up, his cavernous face set in a lugubrious scowl of guilt. In the old days he would have been executed for failing to alert the army to the ambush, but the colonel was not in a mood to add blood to blood. It would not bring the thespian back from the banks of the Styx where, if the gods showed grace rather than exasperation, he would be reciting poetry to those waiting until the ferryman called his name.

The scout groveled before him. "I could not have known, lord! I was just a few ells away from the main body of the army, I had to hide many times like a badger, I did not see the posse leave that killed your thespian. But I have important information . . . "

Colonel Mellarius silently contemplated the miserable man, wondering whether he was indeed a traitor or just looked that way. The medicus came in with the nightly potion, trying to look discreet but if ears could express fascination, his would have grown to twice their size.

"You may stay, Fortunatas," the colonel said. "Massage my foot."

"Yes, lord."

The Greek knelt by the side of the couch and started to manipulate the colonel's left foot which occasionally had the ague, but not that night. "Speak up, scout," the colonel said.

"I know now who they are, lord."

"So do we. They are a band of bloodthirsty assassins from Wales."

"They are a small tribe from the mountains, led by a woman whose name is Agrona, meaning 'divine slaughterer.' "

"Very apt," the colonel said. "Not so vigorous, Fortunatas. Go on, scout."

"They are a sick tribe, lord. Two of Agrona's relatives are mentally retarded, her son and her sister. She has both of them with her to prevent their being killed in her absence. The boy is twelve, but mentally no older than five. The stacks of toys they collect are for him to choose from. The singing heard at dusk is her sister Eos, meaning 'nightingale.' She travels with them in the cart with the victuals because she can barely walk, she is too fat. The Divine Slaughterer wears a cloak, a bearskin, with the skull on her head."

"Like a standard bearer's?" the colonel asked, surprised.

"Yes, lord. It belonged to the signifer of Cohors IV Brucorum. They captured and crucified him in Lavobrinta after feeding him his manhood."

On the couch behind Mellarius the sleeping boy Corylus made soft yapping sounds, like a dog dreaming. "Where did you obtain this information?" the colonel asked.

"It is my profession, lord."

"It's also your profession to alert us to ambushes."

"Sorry, lord. I was like an eagle obsessed by a panther, ignoring the snake."

Doctor Fortunatas suggested, "A pantheress, perhaps?"

The scout grasped the straw. "Indeed! I obtained this information between the thighs of a woman. I am at your mercy, lord."

If the tribe was indeed led by a woman, this wrinkled old prune would be the last to be allowed to mount her or any other woman among them. But the information was probably genuine.

"Where are they now?" the colonel asked.

"Not far, lord. Maybe three miles, headed for the forest. They may already be there."

"How and when am I supposed to corner them?"

"I'll keep a close watch, lord. From now on I'll report to you every night. I'll alert you to the first opportunity. Bear with me, lord, thank you for bearing with me."

Gratitude, contrition; the thespian would have done a better job. But the thespian was gone forever; no reading of Virgil or Sextus Propertius would take place tonight or any other night. "You may go," the colonel said.

"Yes, lord." The scout backed out, bowing. There went one lucky man.

"Enough, Fortunatas."

"Yes, lord. Drink your potion."

"Next time do not interfere."

"Forgive me, lord."

A lot of forgiveness was called for that night. "Very well. Enough."

"Lord, a word of warning—"

"Enough."

"Yes, lord."

The doctor left, unruffled as always.

"Wake up, Corylus." The little boy moaned when his shoulder was shaken. "It's time you started to speak, little friend. I want you to speak poetry for me every night from now on. Do you speak Latin?"

The boy looked at him, blinking sleepily.

"Repeat after me: *Vidi te in somnis fracta, mea vita, carina.*"

The boy's eyes filled with tears.

He himself must have wept like this when T. Gaius Virilis first forced him to speak after it happened. He remembered how the man who was Rome had looked at him.

He gazed at the small tear-streaked face, mirror of the past.

*

On the banks of the Wye, spring 1987

Our next dowsing stop pinpointed in France was a picnic area on the banks of the river Wye.

It was a pleasant spot: a grassy bank in a bend of the river. White water ran fast and noisily through miniature rapids; a red and a blue canoe full of squealing children paddled to and fro; towels and bathing suits covered the only bench in the little park. The view beyond the river was lovely, all of summery England caught in a prism: green meadows garlanded with white flowering hedges; on the crown of a hill a large ocher building outlined against a pale blue sky. An old gray wall looped down through the meadows and the hedges to a stop in the middle of a field. Nothing made sense, yet everything was in harmony; it was one of those moments when the foreigner thinks he has at last caught the England of the poets, the land dreamed of by young subalterns in the trenches of Flanders during the First World War. I was gazing at it when suddenly a piece of pie dripping honey appeared in front of my nose.

"Open!" Sylvia said.

I obeyed; at the first taste of the crumbly crust perfumed with honey, present and past crossed wires again. With a suddenness that seemed to be the hallmark of these experiences, I was worried that the honey would drip on my tunic. I was reclining on the slope of a hill. There were goats in the olive grove; one was standing up against a tree on its hind legs, trying to get at the leaves. A woman smiled at me and asked something tender and loving. I could not hear her, but knew it had to do with the piece of pie she had popped into my mouth. I said, "Delicious!" She smiled and said, "Glad you like it. When I bought it in that little shop I wasn't sure. It must be homemade after all, not from some factory called Auntie Lee or Mother Love." I was back in the present: Sylvia, the children squealing in their canoes, the rapids, the dotty blind wall meandering down the hillside and then just sitting down. How precious all this was, how vulnerable, how brief. "I don't want to lose you," I said, stretching out my hand.

"What brought that on?" she asked, startled, putting her hand in mine.

"Another flash of the past. Very strong this time."

"Tell me."

"When you said, 'Open,' and surprised me with that piece of pie—"

"I had to, it was dripping honey!"

"I know you had to, dear. Only it wasn't you."

She took her hand away and stared at me, frowning. "I don't understand."

"I was afraid the honey would drip onto my tunic, so I hastily opened my mouth and tasted it and—there I was."

"Was where?"

"In an olive grove, on a hillside. A woman was smiling at me, a ravishing woman—at least I thought so, I must have been in love with her. That's a relief."

"I have no idea what you mean."

"If it was I, the centurion, which I'm sure it was, I must have been normal after all. I was in love with a *woman.*"

"Oh, that," she said.

"It was like a very vivid dream, lasting only a second or two. All I can remember is that she said something and smiled, and I said 'Delicious!' "

"That you did."

"And you replied, 'So glad you like it' and something about the shop where you bought it. I only realized it was you when you mentioned a bread factory called Auntie's Love."

"Mother Love. It does exist, really." She opened the thermos flask and poured two beakers of coffee. I watched her with the feeling that I would wake up any moment now and find myself back in the grove with the ravishing woman, the goat standing up against the olive tree reaching for its branches. I forced myself to hold onto the river, the rapids, the red and blue canoe, the cheering children daring the torrent of their fantasy. Was I simply in love with ancient Rome and slipping into a wish dream every so often? The taste of honey? The love of a woman? "I can't understand it," I said.

"What, dear?"

"Why did I, in Leintwardine, love another man?"

"Ah, that," she said. "Do you want another piece?"

"Small, please. I'm serious, things are difficult enough as they are, why do I have to be fed the notion that as a Roman centurion I was bisexual?"

"Maybe you're wrong." She handed me a paper plate with the piece of pie.

"No. What I felt, in those bushes—"

"I've been thinking about that," she said, wiping her hands.

"The colonel we've been following all this time was your son, right?"

"Darling, I told you: the way I felt about him was not the way a father feels about his son."

"How do you know?"

"Excuse me?"

She sat there smiling and said nothing.

"I'm a father, aren't I? I should know."

"I'm not sure you do."

"What *are* you talking about?"

"I've been thinking about that episode. I didn't mention it at the time, I was afraid you might get worked up about it."

"Why should I? Are you suggesting that I'm lacking in paternal feelings?"

She looked at me steadily and said, "I suppose I do."

"Well, of all the— What on earth gave you that idea?"

"I think I have the answer."

"You do?"

"Tell me—do you ever think about Tim?"

"Why?"

"Do you have any particular feeling for him? We all know you're his father and so on, but when he's with us you always give the impression you can't wait for him to leave."

"Well, he's a splendid boy, but— Jesus! There's only a limited amount of interest I can generate in triple interest bookkeeping or whatever it's called. He can be a crashing bore."

"Right. One down, one to go: Martinus."

"Well—"

"A 'phallus on wheels.' Or was it 'with wings'? An immature philanderer with a taste for expensive cars and brainless girls."

"Well, he has been a worry for a long time, not just to me, to you as well, until he married Miss Vancouver 1963, or whenever it was."

"Now, just listen to yourself. No—just listen. In one sentence, there goes your son, there goes his wife, you'd just as lief drown the lot like a batch of kittens. That's what life has done to you."

"What has life done to me, dear heart?"

"You were a sailor, not on a liner or a freighter, on oceangoing tugboats. In the old days you were away for eight or nine months at a time, eighteen when your ship was lying on station in some foreign port. When you finally did come home on leave it was only for four weeks or so, then you were off again, towing a dry dock or whatever. The weeks you were home, you went through the motions. I'm sure you had genuine feelings, but you simply weren't given a chance to be a father. Can't you see? The boys never had a father for the simple reason that you were never there."

I gazed at her, perplexed. "Are you saying that I have so little concept of paternal love that when I get a whiff of it, as I did in those bushes, I take it to be homosexual passion?"

"Something of the sort," she said lightly.

"Well, of all the—!"

"You see? There you go. That's why I didn't mention it earlier. I knew you'd take it the wrong way."

"Well, goddammit, wouldn't you?!"

"No. If someone, someone I trusted laid it on the line and explained it to me, I would have the good sense to recognize that was how it was. You never saw them, they never saw you. By the time you were allowed to come home more often they were teenagers, and when you came home for good they were gone. One was married, the other—"

"Arsing around with floozies! And what about Helen? Must I become a lesbian before I can be accepted as loving her with the required depth of feeling?"

"Martinus," she said, unfazed, "get it off your chest first, then we'll talk about it. I'm certain I am right. The way you described yourself in Brussels, in those bushes, and again now, it simply isn't possible that you had a sexual relationship with a man who was your son. It was not so. I know it."

"Then you know more than I do."

"I do. To love a child takes effort. It takes being there. You have to *be* there for love to grow. You cannot do it by correspondence or by an occasional visit. It was not your fault, you have been a good father within the limitations imposed on you, but you never had the opportunity to reach the depth of feeling that can exist between father and son—"

"Helen and I are very close. I love her, I really do—"

She sighed. "Love, all I'm trying to define, together with you, is the true nature of the feeling for the other man that you experienced in those bushes. You were suddenly struck by the realization that he was dear to you. You didn't say, when you came out of those bushes, that you had lusted after him."

"Well—"

"Your exact words were: 'I touched a well of deep emotion.' You experienced, in those seconds, an abiding love. It bewildered you, you could only interpret it as a homosexual relationship. Is it not possible that you experienced the love of a father in those few seconds? The love you would have felt for your sons if life had given you the chance to nurture it?"

"Jesus," I said, "this is not what I had in mind."

"Then what did you have in mind?" she asked patiently.

"I did not expect this to turn into an exploration of myself, like an onion being peeled."

She said, "Maybe that's what we should all be doing at our age."

"Rubbish," I grunted. Then I took her hand again.

So we sat for a while. I remembered our sitting like this at the very beginning, during the war.

As so often, of late, she must have picked up the thought, for suddenly she said, "Maybe that's our soul."

"What?"

"The ageless ones, in that film on the air force we saw in Danville. The young women and the young men in black and white. Maybe that's the part of us that will survive in the other dimension."

"Would be nice," I said.

After a while, we walked back to the car.

*

Silva Silurum, spring 368 A.D.

After the world the marching detachment left behind, which had been full of light with fleecy clouds and zephyrlike breeze, the forest was dark, dank, and silent. Its humid caverns, haunted by shadows and unseen presences, were another world; the stagnant air was scented with the nutty smell of toadstools. This was goblin country.

The soldiers, especially the volunteers from Viroconium under Honorius Simplex, were nervous; some of them might panic inside the steel boxes of the turtles which the colonel had ordered as they entered the forest. It felt totally alien to the colonel too, malign, full of menace. Its god was an unknown hostile deity, served by a host of sylvan spirits known only to creatures of the forest: half animal, half human, roaming the dank fern-shielded wolf runs. Misshapen fauns with chinless dog's faces, goat's legs and huge red-tipped erections, emitting eerie shrieks hopped, rustling, in the crowns of trees or leaped in the undergrowth with sudden startling sounds which made the volunteers of Viroconium bark like puppies in their gnashing steel boxes.

Colonel Mellarius, marching alone in the open in full armor, complete with shin shields and skirt of mail, wondered how little Corylus was. He must be terrified inside the turtle where Frisius the carpenter, whose turn it was, carried him not on his shoulder this time, but in his arms. The other officers, even the aquilifer, had taken shelter inside the boxes.

Like an evil cloud, the threat from the forest became more oppressive as they marched. Their muffled steps, dulled by the grass between the paving stones, pounded softly in the silence. It was not fear of the tribe's archers that had caused the colonel to order testudes, but an elemental wickedness in the air, the sylvan god and his court of bat-voiced goblins, billy goats and incubi that came bouncing weightless from the shadows, invisible blobs of evil that might bring about craziness and slackening of the bladder muscles in the untested troops. Honorius Simplex would need all his authority to keep the weak-kneed volunteers from bolting into the very forest that filled them with such terror. The stench must be stifling in the testudes.

The trouble with marching in turtles for a length of time was that frequent rests were needed which were worse than the march. The noonday meal was passed over; this meant that camp would have to be made early, somewhere within the forest. The colonel hated the idea; if he had not been burdened with the inexperienced volunteers he would have forced his troops to march on until they reached open country. The scout, who had described the road before disappearing in the dark haze of the forest on his horse, had said it was a two-day march; but about halfway there was a pond with a meadow and a brook, suitable for making camp in some security.

Whether the man had been optimistic in his estimate or the march had slowed down to a crawl as the hours crept by, evening was falling when the detachment, testudes swaying like gutless wagons, reached the scout's pond, meadow and brook. The brook was no more than a trickle, red with rust from iron deposits in the hills; the smell of the pond was not to be believed. Here, in the heart of nature, they should have been cradled in the purity of Diana's breath; the pond stank like a sewer, the brook reeked like rusty armor when wet, and the meadow was a swamp. Colonel Mellarius wondered who the sylvan god was who relished playing with them like a peasant child with beetles. They would need the full protection of T. Gaius Virilis and his century of ghostly legionnaires to keep them safe that night and shield them from the bat squeaks, goat cries, toad barks of the forest god's noisy minions. As the colonel stood contemplating the glassy black surface of the pond there was a gurgle, a blob, a snicker; sleek concentric rings came sliding his way as if to say, "Welcome in my parlor, succulent sweetmeat of my dreams." He called the haruspex.

"Whoever our god is, let's sacrifice to him right here, right now!"

"Yes, lord . . . "

The priest hurried off to consult with the cook as to where to find a suitable warm-blooded creature to satisfy both the appetite and the vanity of the detachment's protector. He came back at a trot, like a woman, toes out.

"Our god has just told me that he will need no sacrifice tonight, lord."

This meant he had been unable to get a pig out of the cook and that the wagoner had said he'd be damned if he gave him one of the mules. In the meantime, the testudes had been dismantled; the volunteers, faint with exhaustion, staggered in clusters into the meadow to relieve themselves; Honorius Simplex, purple in the face and hoarse with un-Christian rage, cursed their apple-buttocked cowardice, calling them pissing frogs and three-legged newts, quite a mouthful for someone who had been out of the army for seven years.

The little boy Corylus, pale and limp with fatigue, was handed to the colonel by the optio of the Second, the last to have carried him. The child collapsed in his arms.

It seemed safe now to carry him on his shoulder as he went to check the troops, the tents, the location of the guards, his army eyes restlessly roaming the edge of the forest, the pond, the tunnel where the brook emerged from the trees, the darkening road. So far, no sign of the tribe's archers. He did not doubt that they were there; he and his troops had been observed and followed from the moment they set foot in the forest. Darkness was the enemy now, fires had to be lit around the periphery of the camp, guards had to be posted, not apple-buttocked volunteers but battle-hardened warriors of experience. It was an optimistic definition of his own recruits, but he needed to shore up his confidence as commanding officer of this horde of knock-kneed, swallowing men with ill-fitting helmets, armed with swords that represented more danger to their own soft flesh than to the hide of their enemies. Ah, if only the thespian had been here! He needed firing up with poetry and heroic oratory from the glorious past of the Roman Army. But the thespian lay, frozen in stunned surprise, in a grave on a hilltop which might as well be a thousand miles away. *Mortus est pro Arte.*

The command tent went up; the colonel put the little boy inside as soon as the prefectus gave the word. But the child was restless and would not be left behind, so he told him to go and find the dog; after that, then they would eat together. As the little boy ran off, there came the wagoner to ask what he should do with his mules; there was nowhere for them to graze. Frisius the carpenter came to complain that someone had made off with the portable fences without asking his permission first; where were they? Doctor Fortunatas appeared with his soothing smile to report that seventeen of the volunteers had suppurating blisters and intestinal complaints; would it be all right if he put them together in one tent so he could keep an eye on them during the night? And there came the infernal priest, bog eyed with indignation, brandishing his cross, to express outrage at being refused access to the sick who might be in need of absolution. The colonel directed him to Doctor Fortunatas, who was as impervious to priests as he was to madness, bad breath, explosive diarrhea and fallen arches, all of which he interpreted as continuous tests of his equanimity to which his Greek gods subjected him.

Finally, the camp settled down; it was only as the meal arrived and the colonel collapsed on his couch with a groan of fatigue that he realized, with heart-stopping alarm, that Corylus had not returned. He sprang to his feet and ran outside.

"Officer of the watch!"

"Yes, Colonel!" the man came running.

"The boy! He went off to find the dog some time ago. Have you seen him?"

"No, Colonel. Shall I—"

"Let's hope he has not left the camp. Make a search immediately. Report back to me at once!"

The officer saluted and left at a run. He returned quickly with the information that one of the guards had seen the boy leave camp to follow the dog as it ran into the forest. The colonel's heart sank; he stood still, eyes closed, and prayed, Oh god, Father! For the sake of my soul, protect the child, protect him, I beg of thee . . . Then he bellowed, "Silence!"

Night was falling, the forest had changed from a brooding menace into an encroaching threat. All voices, even the nibbling of the mules, the grunting of the pigs and the wailing of the sick in the doctor's tent, fell silent. In the silence forest sounds murmured. Rattled. Chirruped. In the pond, frogs croaked like rolling dice. A night bird, drunk with sleep, woke up in a nearby tree with a sound like a yawn. Bats swooped low on the water with high-pitched squeals. From the pond's depths came, once more, the gurgle, the blob; again, sleek rings slithered across the black glass toward him.

The colonel took a deep breath and shouted, "Corylus! Where art thou? Corylus!"

His voice was echoed by the wall of the forest. Everywhere

around, in field, shrub, reeds, hollow, brook and meadow, startled creatures pipped, hopped, fluttered, squealed, rustled. The sleep-drunk nightbird squawked with early-morning indignation. Somewhere in the forest something laughed hysterically. One of the cook's oxen mooed; the wagoner whacked it across the rump with a smack that resounded in the silence.

No answer from the boy. The colonel realized that, still mute, he could not have responded. There was only one solution: a search patrol had to go and look for him before it became too dark to see, despite the danger. The colonel was certain that the tribe's archers were all around them, watching.

Orders were given, a patrol was formed. The guards were removing a section of fencing to let it through when, tongue lolling, Cassidile came lolloping back from the forest and collapsed in front of the colonel, who went down on one knee, stroked the dog's head and said, gazing into his eyes, "Here, beast, is thy chance to repay me for saving thy life! Go, take me to him! Find Corylus. Corylus! Take me to him! Go!"

The dog, obliging, guilty, old, overcame its obvious bone weariness, rose to its legs and turned around to trot back into the forest, tail dragging, back concave with age.

"Follow me!" the colonel cried. "Testudo!"

The patrol's shields came up, interlocked; inside their steel box they proceeded cumbersomely into the forest, following the dog. Branches scraped. Twigs cracked. Indignant birds exploded, shrieking, from under their feet. Rustlings, howls, rattles sounded, high up. The testudo made its clumsy way around shrubs, fallen trees, trying to keep up with the colonel who was following on the heels of the dog. Suddenly, in a clearing, there stood the beast, ears cocked, tongue lolling. The colonel ordered, "Halt!" Slowly he moved forward, step by step, until he almost stumbled on the body of the child, lying behind a low shrub.

He kneeled down, stretched out his hand and touched the flaxen hair, the soft cheek, the open lips; his little finger felt a sigh.

"Corylus!" He lifted the small body off the ground. Instantly, the boy's arms came around his neck, squeezed tight. "Thank thee, god, thank thee! T. Gaius Virilis, thank thee . . . "

On his command the testudo turned around messily to crash and bump its way back to the camp. Branches scraped, twigs cracked, birds cursed, wet blobs thudded onto the shields from the trees. When they finally arrived in the camp and the gap in the fence had been closed behind them, the colonel ordered the guards doubled. No solitary soldiers anywhere on the periphery, only turmae of six men forming half turtles, facing outward. It meant that half the detachment would be on guard duty that night, to be relieved every three hours. The watchword was *Gratitude.*

Colonel Mellarius carried the little boy to his tent. The medicus paid a hurried visit to see if the boy was all right and gave him a potion. If only the child would speak!

"What happened?" Mellarius urged. "What did they do to you?"

It seemed they had done nothing to him. The child had just lain in the heart of the forest paralyzed with fear, so terrified that when found he had appeared lifeless. What had he seen to frighten him so? He must have seen something.

"What did you see, Corylus?" Mellarius asked, stroking the silky hair. "Did someone attack you? Did someone go for you? Who was it that terrified you?"

But the child could only stare at him with those huge eyes full of mystery.

"You're safe now. Let's thank our god together, shall we?"

He took the child's hands, so cold, so small, and held them tightly. He was filled with a surging sense of grace. "Thank thee, Father," he said.

How still the forest was! But somehow the fear had gone. The little boy—helpless, defenseless, tiny quivering bundle of terror in abject surrender—had remained untouched. The spirit of T. Gaius Virilis must have manifested itself to whoever had approached the child and frightened them away. It was the only explanation as to why the human predators who massacred Bravonium had left this helpless prey inviolate in the vastness of the forest.

If ever Colonel Mellarius had been convinced of the presence of his god, it was as he sat there, the child's small cold hands in his own, listening.

*

The Forest of Dean, spring 1987

The Forest of Dean came as a surprise. I had no idea that in present-day England there still were forests that had not changed since the beginning of time. It was an anachronism, not the forest but the road which ran through it. I could identify totally with the colonel of the detachment of Roman infantry which must have followed the same road sixteen hundred years ago.

He must have been continuously alert; the dark caverns of shadows among the trees, the eery, secretive movements of slivers and patches of sunlight seemed made for ambush. Even two hundred men in this primeval forest must have felt vulnerable as they penetrated deeper and deeper into this ancient, timeless world. What had given them self-confidence? Faith in their invincibility because they were Rome? In front of the torso in the museum in Brussels I had felt like that; in those moments I too had been Rome, an indescribable feeling of power, invincibility, mission. The half-naked natives who slunk through the primeval forests of Europe and unleashed volleys of arrows and assegais were, to me, no more than savages; as I gazed up at the torso that for some mysterious reason broke my heart I was an instrument of civilization, a bringer of human dignity, harbinger of the observed life, the life worth living. As I stood in front of that statue the light of Rome had radiated from me into the darkness of a savage world.

The pendulum, back in France, had selected the next station: a meadow and a pond in the heart of the forest, near a brook. I had imagined something gentle, sunny, but that was not how it was. The pond was a black pool of stagnant water, the brook no more than a ditch, the meadow a swamp into which I sank up to my ankles.

But that was only the beginning. I can only do justice to

what followed by quoting literally what I recorded on that occasion, as later typed out by Helen.

Location 16—The Forest of Dean

I am standing in the heart of the forest. A brook flows among the trees with a soft, gurgling sound. The water is rusty, the forest dark. Despite the playful sound of the water this is a ghoulish spot.

"Did the detachment make camp here?"

Yes.

"Was there an attack?"

No.

"Was somebody wounded? I seem to pick up something."

No.

"Did someone fall ill?"

No.

"Get lost in the forest?"

Yes.

"It must have been somebody inexperienced or dotty. Wait a moment—was it me, the old father? Gone gaga, wandered into the forest?"

No.

"Not dotty, not old. Young? The little boy they picked up in Bravonium?"

Yes.

"Did he call for help?"

No.

"Climb a tree?"

No.

"Odd, I seem to pick up a tree. Never mind. Did he see something that frightened him?"

Yes.

"An animal? A wolf or something?"

No.

I put a series of questions and finally come up with the answer "another boy."

"That's odd. Must have been a barbarian child."

Yes.

"And that boy frightened him?"

No.

"Then what? Showed him something? A toy sword? A bow and arrow? Something of that sort?"

Yes.

"The little Roman boy must have been relieved when he saw a boy his own age appear who showed him a toy."

Yes.

"Yet he was frightened, I pick up fear. Did someone else appear?"

Yes.

"Who? A woman? Dammit, another woman! What would a woman do in a forest?"

Yes.

"What do you mean: yes? It *was* a woman who appeared from the forest?"

Yes.

"Who was it? The mother of the barbarian boy, looking for him? Is that right?"

Yes.

"Did she look threatening? The little boy got a tremendous fright."

Yes.

"But why? Was there something alarming about her?"

Yes.

"The way she was dressed? She wasn't naked, I suppose?"

No.

"What was she wearing? A harness? A coat of mail, or something?"

No.

"Furs? A suit of animal skins?"

Yes.

"What was frightening about that? The little boy—"

Suddenly, as in Wroxeter and the bushes of Leintwardine, I see the scene, looking down upon it from above. The little Roman boy in a short tunic, kneeling behind a shrub, facing him a larger boy, older than I thought, with a toy soldier in his hand which he is showing to the Roman boy. Behind him a woman, slight, fairly young, wearing a pelt with claws around her shoulders, on her head the skull of the animal, a bear. Indeed, to a child who never saw anything like it she must be frightening. She is armed, she pulls a sort of sabre, a rapier, and advances on the little Roman boy. But now her attention is distracted. She sees something that makes her freeze: above her, in a tree—she is looking straight at me. Suddenly she grabs her son and pulls him with her, back into the forest. The Roman boy, frightened, cowers behind the shrub, trembling, even though she has left. How odd: she did not just grab her child and make off with him, she saw something that scared her away. She saw *me*. But where? How? When?

Now the vision or the hallucination or whatever the hell it was disappears. I am standing on the bank of the brook, the tape recorder in my hand, with wet feet, the pendulum spinning like a top in my hand.

"Was it true what I saw? Did it really happen that way?"

Yes.

"You mean: that woman really did see me, in a tree? An old man of eighty?"

Yes.

"Hell, come on now! I'll accept most anything, but this—are you sure?"

Yes.

"Well, this is enough for one day, I would say. Or do you want me to ask more questions?"

Yes.

"Look, I'm tired, my feet are wet, I'm cold. Must I?"

Yes.

"What else is there? Somebody else in trouble? Or up a tree?"

Yes.

"The colonel?"

No.

"I, the old father? Did I crash out of that damn tree by any chance?"

No.

"Well, who else? Someone we know?"

Yes.

(Pause)

I have run down the list of characters we picked up so far: scout, doctor, the lot, and—wait! "The dog?"

Yes.

"You can't be serious! It *was* the dog?"

Yes.

"What was the matter with him? Did he fall ill?"

No.

"Was he killed?"

No.

"Hurt?"

No.

"Worn out? Refused to go on the next morning? Is that it?"

Yes.

"So they left him behind."

No.

"Did someone kill him, a mercy killing?"

No.

"They could hardly take him along."

Yes.

"Come on now!"

Yes.

"Then they would have had to carry him."

Yes.

"Those tough, hard-bitten Roman soldiers carried a dog along because he was tired?"

Yes.

"He must have been pretty heavy all the same. Did they take turns? Did they carry him in a sack?"

No.

"On a sort of stretcher?"

Yes.

"Sorry, I don't believe a word of this. The hell with it."

(End of tape)

I stuffed the pendulum in my pocket; when I came sopping through the swamp toward Sylvia she took a damn picture of me. Then she asked, "Well, how did it go?"

"What would *you* say if you were told that a Roman detachment, in wartime, carried a dog along with them on a stretcher because he was too tired to tag along?"

"Why not?" she asked. "That's what I would have done."

I went to change my shoes at the car.

When I was standing up again, in carpet slippers, like an escapee from a nursing home, she said, "I found a little parking area on the map, in the open, with picnic tables. It's a little further down the road. Let's go and sit in the sun."

I was exhausted, she drove. On the way I told her about the boy lost in the forest and his little barbarian friend who had been dragged home by his mother, scared out of her bearskin when she spotted an eighty-year-old man up a tree. God only knew how he had got there.

"How amazing," she said. "A bearskin around her shoulders and the skull on her head? I've seen that picture somewhere."

Pictures remembered. Dreams. Pieces of pie dripping honey. Snowflakes in the blizzard of time.

The picnic area overlooked one of those scatterbrained English landscapes with everything in it: houses, spinneys, hills, churches, farms, dovecotes, and a toy train running in a valley. After finishing lunch I brushed my tie with my hand because it had crumbs on it. Sylvia said, "It's the blue one, love, with the white spots."

"God," I said. "I *am* getting old."

She put her hand on mine. We listened to the distant train in the valley. A gust of wind rustled the leaves. The forest came briefly alive with a vast rushing sound.

> Like the wind through woods in riot
> Through him the gale of life blew high.
> The tree of man was never quiet,
> Then 'twas the Roman, now 'tis I.

*

Nemotabala, spring 368 A.D.

The dog did not make it. When by the end of the day's march the detachment reached the small sanctuary where they were to camp for the night, Cassidile was dead. It was a bitter blow to little Corylus, who had taken the thespian's place in the dog's affection; his heaving sobs as he embraced the dead beast on its litter spoke louder than words.

But for the boy's grief, Colonel Mellarius would have ordered the cadaver to be buried on the spot; now a proper funeral seemed indicated for the old mutt. After all, he was the regiment's mascot. While he looked around for a suitable spot for its grave, Frisius the carpenter was ordered to prepare a headstone.

The sanctuary was on a hilltop overlooking the river Sabrina, a lonely spot of gale-stunted trees, high grass, and brambles. On a neighboring hill the remains of ancient earthworks could be seen, now a village populated with primitive people dressed in cloaks like mats. On the river below, a trireme was working its way seaward; from this distance it looked tiny, with oars like the legs of a centipede.

The raiders had passed but not stopped here. There was nothing to steal or plunder; the slack-jawed, mop-headed women peering from the huts were a remedy against rape. Whoever had built the temple to Nodens on this godforsaken hilltop must have been guided by a dream.

The colonel walked slowly around what was left of the temple's forecourt. Everything was in ruins, the temple itself a jumble of broken white pillars and friezes; to one side lay the giant cup of the upturned roof, overgrown with brambles. The statue of a god had been toppled, only its marble legs were visible now, pointing skyward from the brambles like those of a tumbling clown in a circus. No trace of worship was left in this junkyard; either the likes of young Theodosius had smashed the shrine in honor of their god's crucified son or a cave-in of the hillside had destroyed it.

The scout emerged from the elephant grass like a pollen-dusted garden gnome. Eager to please, he provided the unsolicited information that the sanctuary was now a place of worship for the simpleminded females of the village on the other hilltop. The statue of the god was still revered; if a woman wanted a son she approached its legs at full moon, unclothed, on her knees, grasped the god's testicles while uttering a prayer, then threw a votive offering in the hole that had once been a pond. The water must have disappeared down the same hole into which the god had toppled. Well, maybe the god would like a dog to keep him company. The colonel ordered the grave to be dug among the remains of the little temple.

Frisius, impressed by the religious setting, fashioned a memorial for Cassidile in the shape of an effigy, something to which the thespian had failed to inspire him. He set out to chisel a dog out of sandstone; apart from his limitations as a sculptor, the block was too small, so the dog was lying down, looking over its shoulder. It was a worthy monument to a mutt all the same; the troops were impressed.

There was a simple ceremony later that night. The colonel assured Corylus that dogs waited for their masters on the banks of the Styx, to join them on the ferry to Hades; but the little boy stared at him uncomprehendingly. The detachment was lined up in front of the grave; the colonel spoke a brief funeral oration ending with the passage about Skylax barking, then the troops saluted and the bucinator blew the *Ultimum Vale*.

At bedtime that night, the colonel explained to the boy about the spirit of T. Gaius Virilis awaiting him on the banks of the Styx. Maybe Cassidile would be waiting too, in which case he would tell the dog to wait for Corylus. To the shades in Hades time no longer mattered; even a wait of fifty years would, to the dog, be like a single breath. But the boy was too worn down by sorrow or homesickness to listen. He himself, forty years ago, had been homesick for months. Not for home itself, but for his grandmother Drusilla, the feel of her lap, the soft cushion of her breasts, her sheltering arms. T. Gaius Virilis had been understanding of tears and the lonely shrieks of a nightmare in the dark, but he had not lifted him onto his lap, nor put sheltering arms around him. He had occasionally stroked his hair, and at one time held his hands; only at the very end, in a ditch across the river, as he lay dying in his arms with the broken javelin protruding from the growing red stain, had his true feelings broken free from his dying heart. "With thee . . . " he had whispered, "always . . . "

So he had been. Now more than ever; consoling the little boy after the death of the dog was like praying to T. Gaius Virilis, guardian spirit, protector, daimon, keeper of the chalice of his love. How much there would be to talk about once they were

reunited on Charon's landing! All the words left unspoken during their lifetime, all the laughter that had never gone beyond a
wrinkling of the eyes. "Father," Mellarius whispered as the boy
fell asleep under his stroking hand, "I love thee..."

There came the modest cough of the minor officer, as always at the wrong moment, the embarrassed look from under
a helmet dull with wear. Then, the regulation bellow, "Watchword, please! Colonel, sir!"

Mellarius gave him *Family*.

*

Lydney Park, spring 1987

Our next way station, dowsed in France, was a deer park
near Lydney on the north bank of the river Severn. The road
map indicated RUINS OF ROMAN TEMPLE, IRON AGE FORT AND MU-
SEUM.

At the entrance gate to the park a boy of ten sold us tickets
and a plan. We drove through a somewhat moth-eaten deer
park to a manor house which was the museum, and parked the
car. Guided by the plan, we climbed a steep hill with ancient
trees. Maybe it was the trees that gave this place its atmosphere of mystery and timelessness, giant old beeches, leprous
with age.

At the top, while catching our breaths, we looked at the
view of the river. The hilltop opposite must be the Iron Age
earthworks. Still, a tree dominated the scene: a gigantic sweet
chestnut that looked as if it might have been here sixteen
centuries ago.

A short way to the right were the Roman remains, the usual
collection of bland foundations of temple and bathhouse. I
asked the pendulum where to start and was directed to the
temple, some crumbling foundations with broken stone steps in
the center which, the plan said, had led up to the statue of a
god called Nodens, about whom not much was known other
than that he was connected with hunting.

I asked the pendulum, "Is this where the detachment pitched camp?"

Yes.

"Had they been attacked on the way here?"

No.

"So, no casualties?"

Yes.

"What do you mean: yes? There was a casualty?"

Yes.

That was the trouble: the occasional inconsistency. Then a thought struck me. "Don't tell me it was the dog?"

The pendulum circled.

"They arrived here carrying the poor beast on a stretcher?"

Yes.

"And it was dead on arrival?"

Yes.

"Well, it's not exactly earthshaking."

Yes.

"What, yes? You want me to go on asking about the dog?"

Yes.

"Did they bury him near here?"

Yes.

"Not in the temple, surely?"

Yes.

"Come on, now! It may not look like much today, but this was a religious site! They can't have been so callous as to bury the carcass of a dog inside a temple?"

Yes.

"It *was* a temple?"

A small yes.

"Now what does that mean? Was it a temple or wasn't it?"

A small yes.

"The ruin of a temple? You mean a heap of rubble from which the statuary had been removed?"

Yes.

"Had the barbarians done that?"

No.

"Then was it struck by lightning or something?"

No.

"Well, never mind. The ruin of a temple. They decided to bury the dog inside. Just a hole in the ground and slam?"

No.

"They gave it a funeral?"

Yes.

"And a tombstone?"

Yes.

"Of course: the regimental mascot. An effigy, perhaps?"

The pendulum nearly flew out of my hand, as if bells rang after I hit the jackpot.

"All right! A tombstone with an effigy on it. Of the dog itself?"

Yes.

"Did they have a stonemason with them?"

Small yes.

"All right, somebody had a shot at it. The dog was buried. They put the tombstone with its effigy on top."

Right.

"Can't have been a great work of art."

No.

"Then what? Do I go on asking?"

Yes.

"About the temple?"

No.

"About the other foundations?"

No.

"About the colonel?"

No.

"About myself, his old dad?"

No.

"More about the damn dog?"

Yes.

"Am I in the presence of the dog's ghost or something?"

Yes.

I had been right: it was one of those mornings. The pendulum seemed to take the whole thing as a lark.

"Thanks a lot," I said and turned off the tape recorder.

Sylvia was taking photographs nearby. As she saw me approach she said, pointing, "Look—that looks like part of a frieze."

It was a square stone, half buried in the grass, with what looked like a hind leg and the tail of a dog in low relief. It just went to show what state I could get into by dowsing. I crouched beside it to have a closer look.

"Remember the dog they carried on a litter?" I asked.

"Yes."

"I just dowsed that it was buried here, with its effigy on top."

She kneeled beside me. "Think this is it?"

"According to the pendulum it was some sort of statue. But I may be way off beam this morning."

As if in agreement, a cuckoo sounded off in the trees.

We shuffled back, down the steep footpath—*cuckoo, cuckoo!*—trying to keep each other upright on the rolling stones.

At the bottom, we went to have a look at the museum. It was obviously a private enterprise, an untidy one at that. The head of a Roman statue in the entrance acted as a doorstop; nearby a girl no older than twelve sat at a little table doing her homework, with an exercise book and a dictionary in front of her. We wandered over to the first glass case. When I saw its contents I stopped in my tracks.

The case was filled with statuettes of dogs. Very small, very primitive, dozens of them. I went to ask the girl what they were; she pointed to a book lying open on the windowsill secured by a chain.

Lydney, the book told me, was called Nemetobala, an elegant temple complex in the fourth century. It had probably been destroyed by a mudslide and excavated in 1928. It seemed to have been dedicated to a god connected with hunting, as a number of small votive figures of dogs were discovered during the excavation. These might have been thrown into a pond by worshipers to sustain their prayers. Dogs were also associated with healing in the ancient world, so, on the other hand, the sanctuary might have been a sanatorium or a healing center. It had remained a place of pilgrimage long after the Romans had left; at its center had been the statue of a dog, known as *The Dog of Lydney*. This was reputed to have had magical powers to do with fertility. On the opposite page was a photograph of the statue of a supine dog, head turned, looking over its shoulder.

I was staring at it when I heard Sylvia say beside me, "Here, this is for you."

She held out a small copy of the statue of *The Dog of Lydney* on a little marble slab.

"Where did you get that?"

"They're for sale over there. Here—with my love."

"How sweet of you! Thank you ... " I kissed her and stared at it. A brief vision of Roman soldiers lined up on top of this windy hill. A bugle blowing. The commander saluting the grave before they marched on ...

The word *dog* had been given to me as far back as Neuss. During our journey I had occasionally been aware of a dog accompanying the detachment, lastly this very morning, in the Forest of Dean. And here it was.

Sylvia asked, smiling, "Now do you believe?"

All I could come up with was a lame joke. "Hot dog!"

There are those of you not worthy of salvation.

*

Venta Silurum, spring 368 A.D.

It was thirty years since Colonel Mellarius had last been in Venta Silurum. At the time, he had served under his father, centurion of the second century, Legio II Augusta. It had been during a regular patrol of the southwest, a force of only sixty men without a standard, let alone an eagle. Yet their reception had been as if they were the whole legion marching into town in splendor, with meticulous drill. His father had marched at the head of the column like a victorious general who had been granted a triumphal entry into Rome. Mellarius, as his optio, had marched by his side feeling like the slave who rode along in the victor's chariot with the task of whispering in his ear, "Remember you are mortal."

The present Venta Silurum was a badly frightened town, unlike the one he remembered. The local authorities welcomed him in front of the temple outside the east gate, ashen-faced; he could almost smell their fear. Yet there had never been a real threat; the walls of the city were massive and studded with impregnable bastions, this was not a soft-bellied fortress like Bravonium; the Divine Slaughterer and her tribe had given it a wide berth. But the detachment was received as if they were the city's saviors, ghost of Legio II Augusta, the remnants of which had long since been scattered all over the province.

They marched into town to the wild cheers of the inhabitants, led by Colonel Mellarius painfully aware that he was impersonating T. Gaius Virilis, even though by now he heavily outranked him. The flowers, the laurel wreaths pressed upon him—how magnificent they had been then! But this time the speeches, delivered by local orators on the steps of the basilica, were embarrassing, full of misquotations from Cicero and Catullus. They too were impersonators, trying to revive a reality which was gone forever.

The memory of the army's triumphant entry thirty years ago was like a dream. The shabby wooden houses with their flaking paint could never have been the white marble mansions of his memory. The little forum with its fly-buzzed shops and stench of open sewers could never have been a resplendent arcade surrounding a square full of cheering people. When the colonel's time came to address the populace from the steps of the basilica, the memory of his father doing the same made him feel like a caricature. "When I first marched into this town at the side of my father T. Gaius Virilis thirty years ago, it was an occasion of great joy and festivity . . . " Nobody applauded; there must be few indeed who remembered the glorious occasion. He proceeded to reassure the crowd, whose fear was expressed by a massive silence, that there was no longer any threat from the raiders. A local militia would be organized, the city was invincible if properly defended, the army was in hot pursuit of the bandits and would deal with them forthwith. The officials beside him applauded, the crowd went on staring at him in silence. The local tax collector, a plump, swarthy man slung with the gold chain of his office, announced that those desiring to present personal requests to His Excellency should make themselves known to the officer of the guard at the guest house two hours after noon.

The guest house, one of a row on a street close to the basilica, turned out to be no more than a shell. At one time it must have been the home of the governor of the district; now there no longer was such a person. Even so, no one had dared to move into the house after the man's departure; it did not even appear to have been cleaned for his arrival. There were bird-spotted marble benches in the atrium, its central flower bed was a tangle of shrubs, the mosaic in the reception room was peppered with mouse turds. The place smelled like a mausoleum; when the first supplicants arrived they laced the musty atmosphere with the stench of unwashed bodies. The range of their requests was piteous: tax relief on fifty bushels of corn unjustly requisitioned; a restraining order on a neighbor who allowed his dog to defecate in the litigant's backyard; a permit for the sale of combs and trinkets for which the authorities said there was no room in the arcade, whereas two shops were empty; permission for a son to marry a stepsister; the complaint that a statue of Machus the Usurper was left standing in the courtyard of the House of Justice, despite his damnatio memoriae seven years ago. Then, suddenly, a silver heron among the ducks: a tall, dignified old man with sad eyes.

"May I speak with you in private, lord?"

There were seven supplicants left. "In half an hour. If you wait for me in the atrium, I will be happy to hear you."

"Thank you, lord."

Something about the man hinted at a military past; he looked like a centurion who had retired under a cloud.

Half an hour later, Mellarius joined him on one of the marble seats in the atrium. The birds who ruled the place resented the intrusion; as they talked, they were beset by diving starlings.

"What can I do for you?"

"I won't give you my name, Colonel, it would mean nothing to you. I have not come with a request, but with information that weighs on my conscience. If I were not to tell you—well, all that is of no importance."

The times were treacherous and rumors were rife. It was not the first time that the colonel had been approached by a stranger purporting to have information; most of it could be discarded out of hand. Yet there was something about the man that commanded respect. The information he brought might prove to be useless or outdated; the man himself was not one to be sent packing.

"Tell me."

The stranger looked around uneasily; there was no one about but the starlings. Then he said, his voice low, "Through certain circumstances, I have become aware of the existence of a plot against the life of Field Marshal Theodosius."

"By whom?"

"The Pannonian exiles in Londinium. A man called Valerius is the ringleader. As you may know, he was exiled from Rome six years ago because of corruption."

"How did you come to know this?"

The man's eyes, weary with caution, gazed at him without response.

"Have you any proof?"

"No, lord. All I have is the knowledge. Now that you are here, I felt I could not remain silent."

"You have not informed the local authorities?"

A hint of a smile. "No, lord. Now the burden is yours. Forgive me if I retire."

The man rose with dignity without asking permission. He must have been of considerable rank; what in his past had made him take refuge in this outpost of the empire?

"I must know your name if you want me to pass on the information."

"Lord, I am not personally involved. I have no wish to become so. Good day."

Mellarius watched him as he walked away. For whatever it was worth, his information would have to be passed on as quickly as possible or he himself might become implicated. He would have to find a messenger he could trust. But there were no frumentarii among his troops . . . Ah, wait! A brilliant idea.

He was about to call for the infernal priest when he heard a commotion outside. Shouts, commands, scurrying steps, then silence. Antigonus, the day's commander of the guard, came running. "Colonel! Are you all right?"

"What's going on?"

"A man has been killed! One of those who came to see you, right on the doorstep! It was done so fast that—"

"Who was it?"

"No idea, Colonel. An older man in a dark blue cloak."

"His assailant? Was he caught?"

"He escaped. It was done in a flash, with a dagger. I wasn't aware that anything was wrong, I thought the man was having cramps, the way he held his stomach. The assassin just walked away."

Mellarius suddenly had a sense of great personal danger. It made him rise to his feet, clasping his sword. "Have a search made for him at once. And call the priest."

"The priest?" The centurion looked startled.

"Not the haruspex, the Christian priest. Quick!"

"Yes, Colonel."

The centurion saluted and rushed off.

Minutes later the rosy countenance of the infernal priest beamed at the colonel. "Yes, son? You called for me?"

"You are aware that someone was assassinated in front of this house a few minutes ago?"

"I noticed the commotion, I did not realize—"

"Moments earlier he had given me some information that may have been the reason."

"You mean he was killed because—"

"He warned me of a plot. Against the life of the field marshal."

The sly eyes of the priest sharpened. "A plot? By whom?"

Something in the man's reaction decided the colonel to keep this vague; the less the creature knew about it, the better. "I can't tell you, the man wouldn't say. But he mentioned the Pannonian exiles in Londinium."

"The Pannonian . . . " The priest's face brightened; obviously, this was good news. "Are you sending a messenger? Send a messenger at once! The one to be told as quickly as possible is General Dulcitius. Who will you send?"

"You," said the colonel, watching him.

The priest's face was a study. He might be a bore, but he was as quick-witted as a weasel. "Why me?" he asked.

"Because you're the only one I can entrust with this message," Mellarius said. "You are the only one among us the assassins will not suspect. If I sent someone else, he would never make Londinium. You, as a priest—"

"But that's not so! I would be running a far greater danger! I'm closely associated with the young Theodosius . . . "

All this was music to the colonel's ears. "Because you are so closely associated with the field marshal's son, it is your sacred duty to inform him of the danger to his father's life." So there, he thought, you devious bastard.

The priest gazed at him somberly. "Will you provide me with an escort?"

"That would draw attention to your importance. If we want to be sure the warning reaches the field marshal, you must go alone."

The priest looked as if he were reaching for a theologically acceptable curse, but could not find one. "As you wish," he said, "son."

The colonel resisted the temptation. "Have a good journey, priest," he said earnestly. Then he called the guard.

"But where do I find a horse?" the priest cried.

"I would requisition one for you," Mellarius said, "but that also would draw attention to the importance of your journey. You will have to walk. Pretend you are an itinerant priest. Forget you ever were part of this detachment." He could not resist adding, "I will try to do the same."

The priest left, sulking.

"Thank you, T. Gaius," the colonel said to the scudding clouds above the atrium. "May he arrive safely and may I never set eyes on him again."

Outside, the bucinator blew the signal for the changing of the guard. The scruffy scout came scurrying in, as trustworthy as a seller of carpets. The raiders, he reported, had marched south and reached the river. They had massacred the inhabitants of the fishing village of Pescadora and stolen their boats. They were last seen heading across the Sabrina. The colonel gave orders for the detachment to leave at once.

Just before departure, the identity of the murdered man was revealed. His name was Maenius Peregrinus, ex-prefect of Numerus IV Exploratorum, now stationed on the Saxon shore.

How he had come by the information was not known; his oath
as an officer must have forced him to alert the army to the
danger.

Mellarius thought about the man in his tent that night, after
the medicus had made him drink his potion and sleep began to
rise like mist. Reclining on his couch, little Corylus curled up
by his side, he mused about the mysterious officer and his
secret, and how Fate had caught up with him as a result of his
decision to honor his oath.

His prayer remained one-sided that night, as if it fell on deaf
ears. He did not know what he could possibly have done
wrong, but his god's disapproval was almost tangible. He
would have to sacrifice a ram tomorrow, better still a bullock.
But for reasons he could not fathom, deep within his secret self,
the thought of a blood offering was repulsive to him. Too much
blood had flowed. Too much, too much. Red was the color of
his lonely world.

*

Caerwent, spring 1987

Caerwent, a village in South Wales, was the next item on
our itinerary dowsed in France. After the dog of Lydney I went
there with high expectations; maybe it was the mood of ready
acceptance that tripped me up.

The spot I had dowsed turned out to be inside the fiefdom
of another archaeological professor, who had covered the excavated area with sheets of blue plastic and left it guarded by
a workman doing some desultory digging in the back. His task
was to keep everybody out. "The professor has ordered—" I
had been there before. Dowsing from a distance became a
mess; misunderstandings, circumlocutions, misinformation,
nonsense. In the end we packed up and left.

The next dowsing station on our list was south of Bristol.
As this was Friday, Sylvia decided we should spend the week-

end with Helen, the grandchildren, and the Fuzzy Navel; Topsham was only an hour's drive from where I was supposed to swing my pendulum come Monday. So, off we went to Helen.

She and the children were delighted to see us. She could not wait to hear all about our experiences; Harry, however, found the subject so intellectually embarrassing that he could not bring himself to even acknowledge it. First, he retired behind a smoke screen produced by his pipe, one of a kind that used to be advertised with the slogan THE THINKING MAN SMOKES A PETERSON. Later, he introduced me to his own worries: the little apple tree he had bought for the garden. It had lost all its leaves and was about to die; a severe setback, it had been very expensive.

I looked at the poor little thing: very thin, very small, spreadeagled against a wall without a stitch on, clearly expiring. He cursed, in academic terms, the colleague from Agriculture who had advised him to spray the tree with Fairy Liquid to combat leaf curl. I did not know what Fairy Liquid was; it turned out to be liquid soap. He had applied it undiluted, which even I, the world's worst horticulturist, realized was pretty stupid. This created a bond between us; he confided to me the price he had paid for the naked stick, which was steep even for a certified descendant of the tree which had hit Newton on the head with one of its apples and made him discover the law of gravity. I pondered upon the mystery of how he could be intellectually offended by a dowsed section of Roman road in a ford while paying through the nose for a little apple tree proclaimed by some snake-oil salesman to be a descendant of Newton's.

Sylvia, when she heard there was a sick little tree in the garden, made Harry flee as she started to diagnose the problem by pendulum. After half an hour of delighted squeals and laughter in the garden, Helen and she came back indoors, flushed with excitement; Helen nailed Harry to the wall with the information that the little tree's name was Sally. "At first it just sulked, Mom's pendulum refused to react to her questions—"

"Then it relented," Sylvia added, "said that it felt awful, that it hated the spot it was in—"

"And hated the half-wit who had doused it with undiluted Fairy Liquid," Helen said sweetly.

Harry's face was so screwed up with embarrassment that I simply had to come to his aid. "You mean mother suggested he was a half-wit and the tree agreed."

"I suggested it, not mother," Helen said. "Look at him! Crestfallen with guilt, as well he might be."

The thinking man with the Peterson looked ready to dematerialize, but did not utter a word. Anything to avoid being drawn into a discussion that acknowledged the paranormal.

"In the end," Sylvia said, "Sally summed up the conditions for her survival. She wants Harry to visit her daily for the next few weeks and talk to her."

"She wants him to learn how to dowse," Helen gloated, "so he may take over after Mom leaves, for Sally feels lonely and miserable and was about to pack it in. Harry, boy, over to you."

If ever I saw a man smile under torture, it was he.

Helen saw it too, relented, gave him a kiss and said, "All right, Piggy, I'll do it."

Piggy. For the first time I shared Sylvia's calm assurance that they would marry eventually. She would marry *him,* pipe and all, and he would never be seen again. What happened to old Harry, chaps? Oh, she tied the knot and he choked, don't you know.

"How about a glass in The Locomotive, Harry?" I suggested.

"Oh. Yes. Certainly." He was ready to be towed into port, like any stingy freighter captain who balked at the price of the salvage after yelling Mayday for six hours.

We had two lagers in the pub. After the second glass he blurted out, "I must say! You and Ma are really snarled up in this stuff, aren't you?"

"Spot on, old boy," I said. "Up to our navels. How about a proper snort, instead of this? Let me give you a taste of the real world."

"Taste of what?" he asked uneasily.

"Something from a rubber boot," I said.

CHAPTER EIGHT

*

Abona, summer 368 A.D.

Looking back at the south bank of the river from the ferry, Colonel Mellarius saw his troops lined up in single file, under a blue sky strewn with small white clouds. The grass was full of daisies; the reeds were heavy with bullrushes.

He tried to ignore the sobbing of the girl behind him; it seemed to have no place under this sky, on this peaceable river mirroring the clouds. Ashore, the wagoner had difficulty holding onto the girl's frenzied horse, trying to calm it down by talking to it the way he talked to his mules. The mules themselves were asleep standing on three legs, switching ears, eyes closed, impervious to the frantic horse, the dance of the wagoner, his helmet flashing in the sun. Sun dance. Naked maidens, garlands of flowers, a potbellied Bacchus.

The girl wept; long, heaving sobs; finally the ferry landed and they trooped in to the ferryman's house. The ferryman's wife was fat and motherly, her kitchen fragrant with the homey smell of baking bread. Despite the intimidating presence of the colonel in armor, creaking with leather, his cockscombed helmet on the table, the frantic young woman was calming down. The ferryman's wife proved surprisingly adept at getting information out of her; it had been a good idea to have her interrogated by a woman. The girl's disheveled state and torn gown could not hide her wealth and breeding; the woman managed to coax out of her that her father had been the head of a sanatorium. Had been. So he was dead.

"Sanatorium for whom?" the colonel asked.

"Officers and men stricken with consumption."

"Where?"

"Everyone was killed, everyone! Even the children!"

The questioning went on, frequently interrupted by the girl's sobbing. Mellarius tried to put himself in her place:

206

daughter of a physician caring for dying soldiers in a remote sanatorium, who had suddenly seen her gentle world invaded by a tribe of blood-crazed barbarians in a killing frenzy.

"How were they killed?" the woman asked casually, as if it were a daily occurrence.

"By axe . . . Like cattle . . . Even cattle are killed more humanely!" The girl started to weep again.

Suddenly Mellarius asked, "Do you want revenge?" An odd question; a spoken thought.

She became aware of him for the first time. After a sudden stillness she answered, "No. There is no revenge for—for this. Nothing will bring him back. No sorrow. No prayer. No—no hunger for love . . . "

What an odd thing to say. He found himself thinking: I wish I could give it to her. Hunger for love was a wish for peace, private happiness. He had gradually come to understand the deserters his father had pardoned thirty years ago. Their urge to desert had had nothing to do with fear, but was brought about by the hunger for love. For a woman. For peace.

"We are about to move on," he said. "We will stop there on our way. Would you like to come back with us?"

She shook her head, aghast.

"We may return this way after completing our assignment. I'll come to see if you are still here." But would he? What had made him say that? It was not kind, not honorable, it was nonsense. "Tell me your name," he said.

"Lavinia."

"Farewell, Lavinia."

He was ferried back to his troops. Little Corylus came running and clung to him; he must have feared he would never return. The detachment resumed its march in single file. The tinkling of the mules' bridle chains sounded like wind-bells on the porch of a villa in the evening breeze, a villa deep in the country. Inside would be a woman and a little boy, and a dog like Cassidile, and the thespian who would recite Sextus Propertius's *Dream of Cynthia*. Toys would be strewn all over the porch; Lavinia would say, "Clear those up, Corylus, do you hear? Grandfather is coming." In the wine-red dusk, a chariot would rattle up the driveway. Servants would come running to catch the horses' bridles; T. Gaius Virilis would walk toward the porch, heavy with armor. Corylus would run to meet him, crying, "Grandfather!" and throw his arms around him. T. Gaius would lift the little boy off his feet and press him against his breastplate, not knowing how painful that was to a small body.

"Did you hear the singing last night?" Honorius Simplex asked behind him.

"Singing?"

"She was at it again, whoever it is. Why do they allow it? They're taking quite a chance. It must have a purpose; could it be religious?"

"I did not hear it," Mellarius said.

"Tonight's going to be another dark night. We'll probably hear her again. Shall I send one of my men to trace the sound?"

"No," the colonel said, "I'll talk to the scout about it." Then he added, saddened by his return to war and death, "While he and I are talking, take away his horse."

*

Cadbury Hill, spring 1987

Cadbury Hill, the next location dowsed in France, could only be reached by climbing a muddy track starting at a public house northwest of Congressbury. When we had left Topsham that morning the weather had been clear, now it was turning into another blustery day with squalls sweeping the hills.

The track ran through a wood of cypress trees soughing in the wind. We worked our way to the top and had to put up our umbrellas as rain was starting, sweeping in from the west, while the sun still shone on the hills to the east. The view was like an English watercolor: rain, rainbow, hills, all done in greens.

I stood under my umbrella in the rain, surrounded by brambles, wet high grass, wild flowers. In the distance, on one side of me, black clouds scudded over a black landscape; on the other side patches of sunlight swept the green hills. There was a scent in the air. It took a while before I recognized it: the smell of cypress trees. In antiquity their aroma had been considered beneficial for patients with weak lungs. This had not been a fort, there was a fort nearby which had been ignored by my pendulum in the south of France. This must have been a civilian settlement. I brought out my pendulum and tape recorder. Cypresses. Lungs. Tuberculosis?

"Was this a hospital?" I asked.

Yes.

"For civilians?"

No.

For the military. Here, on this hill, consumptive Roman soldiers and officers must have lain staring at the alien view, dreaming of home. A statue. There must have been a statue somewhere if this had been a hospital. "Was there a statue of Minerva Medica?"

Yes.

"I seem to pick up pain, death. Is it because this was a hospital or because of an attack? Was there an attack?"

Yes.

"A massacre, as in those other places?"

Yes.

"Of all the patients and those who cared for them?"

Yes.

"Any survivors?"

Yes.

"Another child?"

No.

"A woman?"

Yes.

"I seem to pick up that she was *not* the sole survivor. There was a doctor. A Greek doctor, who managed to hide. Is that so?"

No.

"Then where does he come from? Was he with the army?"

Yes.

"The same one I saw in Ariconium?"

Yes.

"I see."

I looked around. The rain rustled on my umbrella. "It's a

strange, empty landscape. Empty of people. Had the entire population of the surrounding villages fled?"

Yes.

"What else took place here on this hill? Something did, apart from the massacre."

Yes.

"To do with the raiders?"

No.

"An encounter?"

No.

"An omen?"

No.

I went on questioning without success; finally I said, "I don't seem to be able to sort this out. Give me a word to set me on the right track. Would you do that?"

Yes.

I went through the usual procedure and came up with *Child*.

"What does that mean? Did he pick up another child here?"

No.

"Just a word, grabbed out of a hat?"

To my dismay the pendulum replied yes.

"Well," I said to Sylvia, "that seems to be all this morning."

"What happened?"

I told her. The rain had traveled on; suddenly we were standing in bright sunlight. I closed my umbrella. She said, "Maybe it's just a word like the others."

"What others?"

"Dog. Song. Priest. Quarry."

"I don't understand what you mean."

"Perhaps the fact that it stands alone is its meaning."

"What would be the purpose of a word by itself?"

"I don't know. A random word. A word that lingers long after. 'Words in the air,' I called them . . . "

Then the answer hit me. It had been staring me in the face ever since Lullington: *Song, Words, Dog, Priest,* now *Child.* They had been passwords. Suddenly I saw, clearly, as if they were real, ruined barracks, cottages gutted by fire, roofs blackened by smoke, corpses in doorways, wide-legged, disemboweled; little bellies white as snow. Children! Slaughtered children, surrounded by toys.

Suddenly I was overcome by anger, the same flaring anger as at the ford. A word came to mind: *Ass.* Not a watchword; I was furious with the bungler. Sooner or later he would find himself in a hopeless mess, and there was nothing I could do to prevent it. I asked the pendulum, "Which I? The one with the sword or the one with the umbrella?"

"Don't get cold," I heard Sylvia say. "Let's go back to the car, but take it easy. It may be slippery after this rain."

We started to walk back down the trail through the wood with the cypresses. "I don't understand it," I said, hanging onto her; she was as surefooted as a mule. "I had a son whom I loved. He must have loved me too for him to take me along on campaign at the age of eighty. But do you know what I got just now?"

"Careful!" she warned.

"It turns out he was such an idiot that I was about to pack it in. Pack it in? At eighty, in enemy country? Where could I have gone? Yet I was mad enough to walk off into the night and the hell with him."

"Fathers often feel that way," she said. "It's par for the course."

I said, "Not that again!"

*

Collis Mortis, summer 368 A.D.

When Honorius Simplex came to ask where the dead were to be buried, the colonel said, "First, take the scout for a tour of the place." The unsavory creature had been clearly upset about the loss of his horse; let's upset him some more. "Show him the children. Then bring him back here."

Honorius Simplex took his time. The colonel became aware of sounds: birds singing, bees buzzing from flower to flower. All of nature humming with joy, and dead children with their guts hanging out.

Finally, the scout was brought before him. He looked at the

creature and wondered what could have motivated a man to bring about the horrors of Bravonium, the ambush in Ariconium, and now the massacre of the children with their toys by their side. He asked. "Now are you satisfied?"

"Lord!" The man looked about to burst into tears. "Why do this to me?"

"I'll tell you," the colonel said. "Because I'm at an age when I don't want to kill a man unless he leaves me no choice. So, leave me a choice. Where are they headed?"

"Oh, lord . . . " The man started to cry. "They'll kill her, they'll kill her . . . "

It had to be the daughter he had mentioned at their first meeting, in Viroconium. What else could make him beholden to that tribe of murderers? It had to be the daughter. "Does the Divine Slaughterer hold your daughter as a hostage?"

The scout wept.

"All right," the colonel said. "Where are they going next?"

"They will kill her," the man repeated hoarsely.

"They have her with them?"

He nodded.

"I will make no promises, but I'll do my best to spare her when we attack."

The man shook his head so vigorously that a tear detached itself and sparkled in the sun as it fell. The birds sang, the bees hummed. From behind the cottages came the sounds of the men digging.

"Where are they now?"

The man went on shaking his head, eyes closed. Not so long ago, the colonel would have had him tortured.

"Are they just hitting places at random or are they going somewhere?"

Silence.

"Scout, I'll try to save your daughter, but if you don't answer me you leave me no choice. Do you understand?"

The man nodded, weeping.

"Take him away," the colonel said.

"I am supposed to lead you there!" the man cried, when Honorius Simplex grabbed him by the arm.

"Where?"

"They are planning to ambush you further down the road! An old fort, abandoned . . . "

The colonel was overcome by pity. He knew, and the scout knew, that it would be impossible to kill the murderers and save the daughter. "Where, scout?"

"Iscalis."

In the silence spades clanked behind the cottages.

"The fort at Iscalis?"

"Yes."

"Why there?"

"It is abandoned, on a hilltop, close to the road. They cannot be seen, but they'll see you. There's a field by the roadside. I'm supposed to lead you there to pitch camp. It's the only level site in the hills, and there is a spring."

"How far is it from here?"

"One day's march, lord . . . "

He stood there, broken, crying among the bees. After a silence the colonel said, "I want all officers for a planning session. Now."

"Yes, Colonel."

"We will not make camp here, just put up the praetorium. See that the men have a meal. We will march after sunset."

"Very well, Colonel."

The moment the command tent was up, the officers and the colonel squatted around a square of sand that had been cleared. "Go ahead, scout," the colonel said, "draw the road and the location of the field and the fort." He handed him his dagger.

The scout hesitated, then took it and drew in the sand.

"Is there cover for us on the slopes to the fort?"

"Yes, lord, shrubs, small trees. The fort has been abandoned for a long time."

"You know the road well enough to lead us there tonight? Without torches? There will be no moon."

"I can, lord."

"I need men with owls' eyes to spot any guards posted along the road. How about some of yours, Simplex?"

"No need, lord," the scout said. "They won't expect you until after daybreak."

"Even so. Simplex, do you have six men who can see in the dark?"

"Yes, Colonel. I'll go with them myself."

"Very good," the colonel said. "This is what we'll do . . . "

*

On the road to Iscalis, spring 368 A.D.

After an hour, Colonel Mellarius was overcome by a feeling of unease. The night was pitch dark. The road could barely be seen; but for the scout, the detachment would have slowed to a halt. The troops were marching barefoot to maintain silence; he was convinced no one, unless he were crouching by the side of the road, could hear their approach. Honorius Simplex and his six men, reaching into the night ahead of the silent mass of the detachment, like sensors, scoured the shrubs and ditches. The scout had been right, the Divine Slaughterer had not thought it necessary to put out guards on the approaches to the fort.

The colonel's unease became suspicion. It was too silent. Was the scout leading them into ambush? If so, he must be insane; neither he nor his daughter would survive; he would be killed by the colonel at the first volley of arrows, the tribe would not spare his daughter because of a promise made. She would be either abused and left for dead or kept as a slave— if indeed she was still alive, which the colonel doubted. But why was there no sign of life, no nightbird squawking in alarm, no howl of a vixen warning her cubs? Something was wrong.

Dawn broke, a high, faint brightening of the dark blue sky. The detachment reached the fork in the road where, according to plan, they were to split up into four prongs to attack the fortress in a double pincer movement. The colonel commanded one contingent, Honorius Simplex another, the two remaining ones were under the command of the centurions of the Second and First. Surely, once they started to move into position in the

growing daylight they would be seen by guards on the earthworks?

The pincer movement was executed in silence. Now there
were birds, alerting the unwary; but no one showed on the
ramparts of the fortress as they emerged from the morning mist.
The occupants must be waiting until the enemy started to climb
the slopes, then hit them with everything available: arrows,
javelins, they even might have ballistae. In any event, it was
going to be a bloody battle. According to the scout there were
no more than a hundred of them, but the colonel did not believe
him. The fear of a trap was thick in his throat.

The contingents were in position. The dawn brightened into
day. The birds were out in force now, screaming insults. Still
no sign of life from the fortress, not even the moving speck of
a guard's head. There must be guards; despite the stealth of the
army's approach it was unthinkable that its presence had still
not been detected. And they were expected that day.

The sun rose. Shadows were born. Field flowers started
to perfume the air. Parent birds began to hunt for food for
their young. Still no sign of life from the fortress. Trachius
Donatus, optio of the First, volunteered to try and take a
look inside.

He climbed the slope stealthily, a beetle crawling. Nothing
happened. He reached the top unmolested. Finally, he rose to
his feet, outlined against the sky. The colonel expected him to
be hit by an arrow and fall over; instead, he turned and beckoned.

At a sign from the colonel, Honorius Simplex set out to join
him. The scout wanted to go too but was held back. Then
Trachius Donatus came running down. "Dead, Colonel! They're
all dead! Everybody is dead in there! Everybody!"

Colonel Mellarius climbed the rampart. It was a long climb
in battle armor. Finally, panting, he looked down into the fort
and saw hundreds of corpses, some in orderly rows, some
scattered about at random.

"It's like Masada," the veteran said beside him.

"What's that?"

"The stronghold in Judea I told you about. We found nine
hundred there."

Incredulous, the colonel scrambled sideways down the

slope to look at the corpses. Those ranged in rows lay apart from the rest. There were no more than seventy, all young, long-haired and bearded, dressed in skins. Their swords were unwieldy; some carried bows and quivers with arrows like the one that had struck the thespian. Then he came upon the corpse of a woman.

The Divine Slaughterer was younger than he had imagined her to be. She looked delicate and beautiful in the signifer's robe. A dead child lay beside her, open-eyed, an older boy, too old to be holding a toy soldier. The toy had a little mouse's skin around its shoulders, with the top of the mouse's skull for a hood. This must be the retarded boy, for whom all those children had died so he might pick over their toys.

The colonel walked slowly past the corpses. How young they were, how finely chiseled their faces, despite the long hair and the wild beards! Some had daisies woven in their hair, like the defenders of Thermopylae. How could these beautiful youths have committed such unspeakable atrocities? At a stone's throw from their ranks lay mounds of corpses of slaughtered villagers, the men castrated, the women disemboweled, the children cleft in two like hogs after slaughter. What insane rage had possessed the youths to indulge in this orgiastic frenzy? No wonder no one had noticed the army encircling them; they must have been besotted by castrating men, raping women, hacking to death fleeing children. "Poison," Honorius Simplex said. "She is still holding the beaker, she must have been the last to drink it."

"Why?" the colonel asked, bemused. "Why not put up a fight? They could have killed half of us before we reached the top."

"That's what we asked ourselves in Judea. The zealots had women and children with them; when we forced our way in everyone was dead, nine hundred of them. Here there are only seventy."

"I cannot understand it," the colonel said.

The veteran shrugged. "No one will ever understand. See the daisies in their hair? 'Adorn yourselves with flowers, drink poison rather than surrender.' Like the Spartans." He surveyed the sickening scene. "All these people, these children, must be their servants now in their hereafter. Even Romanized tribes like my wife's believe that. I'm here to provide her damned brother's spirit with servants, while his spook loiters in my empty house. What you are seeing—"

"Colonel!"

Mellarius looked up; it was Antigonus.

"Yes?"

"She's not among them!"

"Who isn't?"

"The woman who sang. This is the only woman. Unless it was she who sang?"

"The scout mentioned a retarded sister called Eos, the Nightingale."

"There are no horses and no carts either, Colonel. Their support column must have gone ahead, no sign of it here."

"No one saw them?"

"No, Colonel. They have horses. There must be many loose ones now."

"Send the scout to me."

"Yes, Colonel. Shall I organize a search party?"

"Yes. Go with them. Leave immediately, report back to me as soon as you have sighted them. Do not attack."

"Very well, Colonel." He left.

Honorius Simplex asked, "Do we bury the villagers?"

"Let's leave them to the crows. We must be on our way."

"As a Christian, I need to see them buried."

"Then have your men bury them. Bury the others too."

"The enemy?"

"Christians don't bury their enemies?"

Honorius Simplex stared at him for a moment, then said, "As you wish."

Mellarius looked around. The scout was searching among the corpses. Rivers of blood and no sea to flow to. What had been the woman's name? Lavinia. Maybe after this campaign was the time for him to ask for retirement. A plot of land in the west of this province, a house with a porch . . .

Even as he thought it, he knew it was a dream. Like T. Gaius Virilis, his fate was his sword. "Your sword is your friend," the old man had said, teaching him. "Your only friend."

218

*

Charterhouse, spring 1987

The Roman road to the earthworks of Iscalis led through a gorge with high steep banks; if my praepositus and his detachment had come this way he must have been watchful, it seemed the perfect place for an ambush. But according to the pendulum nothing had happened here; our map-dowsed location was beyond the gorge.

As we came out of the dark ravine the landscape changed dramatically. The gloomy morning had turned into a bright day, the air was so clear after the rain that the woods on the horizon seemed etched in the bright blue sky. The gray road ran straight among the green fields; after a few miles there was a fork, the right branch led to the fort I had dowsed in the south of France.

It was now called Charterhouse: a small, lonely set of earthworks amidst low hills, as remote as the ruins of Palmyra in the Syrian desert. The landscape was bucolic, a grazing ground for sheep. In the Iron Age the fort must have been surrounded by a moat, now it was a dry gully swept by the shadows of clouds. We parked the car near a billboard rocking in the wind on squeaking posts; it showed a plan of the fort.

After studying the layout I climbed to the top of a rise overlooking the ramparts; Sylvia stayed below. The wind was cold up there; I moved into the shelter of an outcropping. The clouds' shadows drifted across the landscape. The only sound was the distant bleating of sheep. It was very peaceful, yet something brutal had happened here. Below me, Sylvia was spreading the picnic blanket out on the grass, small image of domesticity in this heart of darkness. What could have happened here to leave this memory of violence and brutality? I switched on the tape recorder.

"This was the final encounter?"

Yes.

"Was there a battle?"

No.

"Did the tribe escape?"

No.

"I don't understand . . . No battle, no escape . . . Did they surrender?"

No.

It took me, in hindsight, a surprisingly long time before I finally came up with the answer.

"They committed suicide?"

Yes.

"All of them?"

Yes.

"Even the barbarian boy I saw in the Forest of Dean?"

No.

"He escaped with his life?"

No.

"He was killed?"

Yes.

"By the Romans?"

No.

"By his mother?"

Yes.

Briefly, I saw him in my mind's eye, as real as the clouds and their fleeting shadows. His haunting image was right in front of me: a blank child's face, vacant eyes, mouth open as if frozen in a scream. Nothing had meant anything to me, emotionally, until then.

We had our picnic beside the car, with sheep mournfully bleating behind the ramparts. I told Sylvia about the communal suicide and the child's face I had seen. I couldn't wait to get out of here; the child's ghost seemed to be wandering around us, calling for someone, a mournful, inarticulate lowing like a small animal that had lost its mother. Whoever the call was meant for did not respond. It seemed this was all there was left of the massacre long ago: the lost spirit of a child holding a toy. It might all be in the mind, but if ever I visited a haunted place it was Fort Charterhouse.

After the meal I hastily packed the hamper and lugged it to the car; Sylvia drove.

An hour later we passed a signpost saying LULLINGTON. "Shouldn't we go back there?" Sylvia asked, braking hard. "That's where—"

"I know: where I picked up the lady singing in a cage. No, thanks. Drive on."

She shook her head and accelerated. "Honestly, Marty, occasionally I wonder," she said after a while.

"About what?"

"After all you've been given, why do you refuse to go back to a place where you got the most fascinating input?"

"Because at this stage of the game I don't want to be sidetracked by something so grotesque and obviously garbled."

"But here you were told that your son had a confrontation with another officer! About a woman prisoner—"

"I don't want to go into it now."

"Have you asked your pendulum?"

"I don't need the pendulum. The experience I had in that park was distinctly unpleasant and I don't want to repeat it. That's all."

"What was unpleasant about it?"

I did not want to say "The pressure you women put me under." "All right, I'll spell it out for you. There was a conflict in that place over what to do with the woman prisoner. The colonel wanted to keep her alive; someone else . . ." A thought struck me. More than a thought; a sudden knowledge.

"What's the matter?" Sylvia asked, glancing at me.

"I—watch the road!—I just realized who the officer was who disagreed so violently: his father. It was I." The knowledge widened. "I was disgusted, furious. That's why I don't want to go back there and drag up that anger again. I must have been a nasty old man. Fancy having me around while trying to fight a campaign! Me and a fat lady in a cage who sings."

"How do you know she was fat?"

"I just said that for effect. The whole episode was a farce."

But as we drove on in silence, I became uneasy. I had no grounds for any of this. It would have made a good story to be told at a messroom table, where the ancient craft of storytelling still survived. That's what it was: a story. Somebody was telling me a story.

But who?

*

On the road to Aquae Sulis, spring 368 A.D.

Antigonus and his search party returned two nights later when the detachment was making camp in a clearing off the road to Aquae Sulis. Their arrival caused the soldiers putting up the tents to pause and gape, for they brought with them a strange contraption: a large cage made of willow branches, like a giant birdcage, mounted on a flat wagon pulled by mules. Inside the cage cowered a huge, half-naked woman, dirty, drooling, with roving eyes and wild stringy hair, more animal than human. Alerted by the guard, the colonel came out of the command tent; the officer marched up to him, saluted and said, "Colonel, I thought you would wish to see the prisoner before we put an end to her. It's the Divine Slaughterer's sister, the retarded one."

"Where are the others?"

"There were only six men, Colonel. They ran, I had to deal with them on the spot or they would have got away."

"You had orders not to attack! You were told to report to me."

"I know, Colonel. But under the circumstances—"

"Where are their horses?"

"They got away. When we attacked they broke loose and made off into the forest."

The colonel suppressed his anger. Disciplining him out here in the wilderness was pointless. The young man knew that he was needed; he stood waiting, with humble arrogance. Soldiers flocked around the cage, poked branches through the bars at the huge idiot woman and laughed.

Antigonus said, "Sorry, Colonel. May I have the order now, sir?"

"For what?"

"To execute her, sir."

"Rejoin your men. You and I will talk later."

"Very well, Colonel. Thank you, sir." The young man saluted, made about turn and marched off to join his patrol, who were telling tall stories to the rest of the detachment, competing for their attention with the fat woman.

The colonel went to have a look at her for himself; the soldiers made room for him. The cage smelled of excrement and rancid sweat. The woman stared at him, drooling, a large beast without comprehension. She did not react to the sticks prodding her, she was not of this world. A creature of mythology, lost among mortals.

"Enough!" the colonel cried. "Back to work! Everybody!"

The men obeyed. When he was alone with the woman in the cage, he asked, "Where are you from?"

No response. The stench was overpowering.

"Fortunatas!"

The medicus had been watching from a distance; he came running. "Yes, lord?"

"See to it this woman is cleaned, the cage too. Make sure she gets something to eat and to drink."

"You are—er—keeping her?" the doctor asked.

"I thought your business was to save lives?"

"But this—surely—tomorrow morning, when we leave—"

"Do as I tell you!"

The doctor, unaffected, sought out the cook and whispered instructions. The eavesdropping soldiers were bewildered.

Later that evening, after the cage had been cleaned out and the woman washed down by the medicus, Honorius Simplex came to see the colonel in the command tent.

"Everyone is asking what you are planning to do with the woman, Colonel."

Mellarius looked at him with surprise. "What would a Christian do, Simplex? Kill her?"

"This is not a matter of doctrine, but of common sense. When we march tomorrow—"

"Common sense? Is that your religion now?"

"It has nothing to do with religion."

"Everything has to do with religion!" the colonel shouted with sudden anger. "If yours does not, it's a fraud!"

"I did not know you were religious—"

"I live by the Virtues!" the colonel shouted.

"But—"

"Because it is my office to represent Rome!"

Honorius Simplex realized he had better leave well enough alone. Common sense would return with the dawn. He left the tent and went to have a look at the woman again, now guarded by four men at Fortunatas's orders. Night was falling, time to extinguish the fires.

When the last fire had been doused and the watchword whispered to the guards, the stillness of the surrounding forest pervaded the camp. A nightingale started its solitary song; suddenly, it was joined by a high-pitched human voice. Rising in volume in the still of the night, the voice had no melody, yet its song was of an eerie beauty, pure and free of all mortal troubles, fears and sorrows, singing in another sphere. Soldiers woke, guards froze in the shadows; the colonel on his couch, little Corylus by his side, did not realize at once it was the barbarian woman singing. He had not heard her at close quarters before, only far away in the forest, a faint, birdlike fluting. As he listened, caught in the spell of the human beast's otherworldly voice, he understood why the Divine Slaughterer had taken her along with her on her rampage. It was like being accompanied by a captive goddess.

From the forest the nightingale responded. The voice fell silent until the nightingale had finished a phrase, then paraphrased it with a sound so serene that all of nature seemed to listen to the duet. The nightingale sang, fell silent; the voice answered. Not a goddess, a giant bird of legend had alighted in their midst.

When finally the woman and the nightingale fell silent, the guards whispered the watchword for the night.

*

Camerton, spring 1987

The next way station was in a field near a hamlet called Camerton. We were unable to locate it, although Camerton was clearly marked on the map; after meandering down endless country lanes like the bottoms of ditches I realized why we were led astray: someone had turned a signpost around; it now pointed in the wrong direction.

So, at last we found the spot: a muddy field with a brook. There was no room for the car until half a mile further down the road; we walked back to the field.

It had been raining overnight; the woods smelled of mushrooms. The birds were active, whirring and fluttering among the trees. A young fox lolloped ahead of us down the lane, unaware of our presence; when it got wise it tripped up in an inexperienced start at speed and crashed into a hedge. Somewhere, a cow blew a Roman tuba, a mournful sound in the happy frolic of birds and little foxes.

The field proved to be messy with liquid manure. The public footpath alongside the brook was impassable without rubber boots, and we had left them in the car. I asked the pendulum if I could dowse leaning on the gate; the answer was yes.

"The detachment must be on its way to Iford now?"
Yes.

"Why did they stop here? Any particular reason other than to make camp?"
No.

"Then what am I doing here? Is there a reason?"
Yes.

I labored for about ten minutes; all my suggestions to the pendulum were rejected. Finally I got a yes to the question "Am I supposed to inquire about someone other than the colonel or his father?"
Yes.

"The scout? The Christian legionnaire? The little boy?"
All of them: no.

"The army doctor?"
Yes.

"Is he relevant?"
The pendulum hung limply in my hand.

"Sorry if I hurt your feelings, but I'm not about to stand here up to my armpits in shit and go in for some blather about a minor character. If it isn't about the colonel or his father I'm going to call it a day."

Yes, said the pendulum.

I switched off the tape recorder. Sylvia asked, "Why did you stop?"

"Because I'm tired. Dowsing drains me."

"But it sounded interesting—"

"Love, I have my hands full with the colonel and his angry old father. I'm too tired to start identifying with army doctors, ladies singing in cages, or cooks slinging hash. I must draw the line somewhere."

"All right," she said, "you're the boss."

We walked back to the car taunted by the birds, but saw no more little foxes.

It occurred to me only that night that I had been too hasty. I had had contact with the army doctor before; interrogating him might have thrown some light on the odd relationship between the colonel and his father. Why was the old man so exasperated with his son at times? It could not just be the short temper of the elderly who feel their authority and ultimately their independence slipping away. Where was it I had shouted, "Stupid ass"? Or had I thought it? Anyhow, "stupid ass" was too gentrified by far. The old man had no need to worry about his authority slipping.

I wondered about practical things, like the detachment being ordered to frequent stops to enable the eighty-year-old centurion to pee by the roadside. Did his left knee ever give him trouble during the march, as did mine?

I drifted off to sleep and a series of disconnected dreams, one about trying to awaken a sleeping dog. Talk about Sigmund Freud.

*

A field by the roadside, spring 368 A.D.

Doctor Fortunatas wished there were a colleague he could consult about the colonel, for he was deeply perturbed.

The suspicion had first entered his mind in Letocetum when

the colonel had protected those children from the Pannonian cavalry and made a mortal enemy out of their commander. Then he had spared the scout, clearly a traitor, saved a boy, ordered a dog to be carried through the forest, and now they were lugging a retarded enemy woman along in a cage. What was he planning to do with her? If he set her free she would be killed by the relatives of murdered villagers wanting to revenge the dead. It made no military sense; he was losing the respect of his officers, the troops were asking what was the matter with their colonel.

Clearly Colonel Mellarius suffered from the psychological deterioration that could befall old commanders in the field: fastidium. They became disgusted with the killing, a growing revulsion which, if discovered, spelled disaster for them. Doctor Fortunatas had been with the colonel for years, they had lived through many campaigns together. He was devoted to his charge; this latest development confirmed his worst fears.

The army pitched camp in a field by the side of a brook with a wooded hill on the other side, from which, as dusk fell, came the hooting of owls. The tents were erected in the falling night, cooking fires lit up the faces of the men; overhead, the first stars quivered in the darkening sky. The password for the night had been given, although after the defeat of the enemy there was no longer any danger of raids. In this newfound security Doctor Fortunatas wandered past the guards. Out of sight and earshot, he sank to his knees in the damp grass. He had never prayed to another man's god before; it was a hazardous thing to do. He had no idea how his plea would be received or whether the colonel's god would even hear him. He started bravely, "Divine Lord Virilis, guardian of my master—"

His prayer was interrupted by an eerie high voice singing a single long-drawn-out note. The barbarian woman started her nightly monody. She distracted him; after a while he rose from his knees and went back to his tent which he shared with Frisius the carpenter and Scilla the cook. In the old days there had also been the thespian and occasionally the scout, but Cassius Colonia was dead and after Iscalis the scout had disappeared.

The carpenter and the cook were quarreling about something in hectoring voices; the doctor stepped back into the night. On impulse, he went to the tent of Simplex the veteran. He was an older man, an experienced officer who might have seen such cases before. He obviously had a high regard for the colonel; they marched side by side at the head of the detachment every day and spent hours in lively discourse.

When the doctor entered the tent, Honorius Simplex was having his evening meal all by himself. The doctor was surprised to see a crucifix on the table. Did Christians pray to their god with their mouths full? His knowledge of Christians was limited; all he knew was that they were a quarrelsome lot who caused more trouble in the empire than any other cult.

"Doctor? What can I do for you?"

"I'd like to have a word with you, Honorius Simplex, if this is a good moment."

"Of course, of course. Sit down. Have you had your meal?"

"Yes, thank you," the doctor lied. "I wanted to talk to you about the colonel."

The veteran's face seemed to close. His eyes became hooded and watchful. What was he expecting? Malicious gossip?

The doctor hastened to put his mind at rest. "I want to talk to you because I am worried about his health. I wondered if you might have any advice for me in this—well—delicate situation."

The expression of disapproval softened. "Did something happen?"

"I am afraid the colonel may be suffering from a serious disease, which presents a danger not only to him but to us all."

"Which disease?"

"Fastidium."

The veteran might have arrived at the same conclusion; he did not seem to be surprised. "What in particular gave you that idea, Doctor?"

"Early in the campaign, before you joined us, there was an incident with a unit of the Pannonian cavalry." He told him about the business with the children; for good measure also about the dog whose life the colonel had saved in Novaesium. He knew, of course, about the orphan from Bravonium.

"In that instance he only did what T. Gaius Virilis had done for him," the veteran remarked.

"You are familiar with his background?"

Honorius Simplex dipped his bread in the sauce. "I knew T. Gaius Virilis. I served under him briefly as a young man."

"Where?" the doctor asked, surprised.

"In this province. I was part of a garrison occupying a fort near Viroconium. We were all very young, the province was at peace, we let ourselves be lured away nights by local women. Technically, it was desertion. T. Gaius Virilis turned up with a punitive patrol, rounded us up, we expected to be executed. But he declared we were all possessed by evil spirits cast upon us by local sorcerers, whom he executed. Us, he subjected to some hocus-pocus and a nasty potion that gave us the trots. We knew that he probably needed us; even so, after that we were ready to give our lives for him in battle. He was a very tough man, a centurion of the old school, but we were jealous of Mellarius, his adoptive son, who seemed much too young to serve as his optio."

"Does the colonel know you served under his father?"

"No," the veteran said, chewing. "He did not recognize me and I never mentioned it. Fastidium. Do you have any other reasons to suspect he may be suffering from it?"

"The way he ordered the dog to be carried. This business with the singing woman. She should have been executed for her own good, he can't release her. What's he going to do with her? Take her back with us to the Rhine at the end of the campaign?"

"I don't know. He has not discussed her with me."

"All these are symptoms of fastidium."

"No," the veteran said.

The doctor could not believe his ears. "No? What else could it be?"

"This may sound alien to you, good doctor, but I think the colonel has been the recipient of a gift from Jesus Christ, our Savior. Unwittingly, of course."

Doctor Fortunatas's heart sank. He had hoped to talk sense with this man, now he found himself facing a fanatic. He wanted to mutter an apology and make a getaway, but that would be an insult. "An interesting thought," he said lamely.

"It has become the central conviction of my life these later years," the veteran continued, "that Jesus Christ seeded a new

element into human nature which may save us all in the end. A
gift, distributed among Christians and pagans alike, at random."

"You don't say . . ."

"At present we are, at best, intelligent, inventive, but at
heart we are wolves. Christ's gift will start a transformation
which may finally turn us into human beings, if we live to see
the day."

The doctor did not want to enter into a theological debate,
but found himself asking, "What gift?"

"The gift of compassion."

It was a bit of a letdown after the rhetorical buildup. The
Supreme Command was made up of Christians, but the doctor
doubted Christ's gift would make a dent in their attitude toward fastidium. He said mildly, "You know the penalty for
fastidium."

"Ah!" the veteran exclaimed. "That is the dark side of the
gift. Like Christ himself, he may be crucified for it in the end."

"But he is not a Christian! What will his god think of all
this?"

The veteran thought that over. "As I knew T. Gaius Virilis,"
he said finally, "he will be disgusted. To him, mercy equaled
weakness."

"Very interesting," the doctor said politely. After a brief,
meaningless exchange of polite pleasantries he bade the veteran good night.

Outside, under the stars, he thought, "The colonel cursed by
a gift from the Christian god? Ridiculous! He is a sick man.
What am I going to do?"

In the darkness, the caged woman sang an ecstatic phrase,
like a glimpse of audible light. In the wood across the brook a
nightingale answered.

*

Iford, spring 1987
Iford, indicated in the south of France as the end of our

English expedition, was a flyspeck on the Roman roadmap, with the symbol for villa beside it. I expected at best the remains of a floor mosaic and the usual foundations; the guidebook gave no hint that in the backwoods of the West Country a treasure lay hidden. All I knew was that the pendulum had picked out this spot on the map as our final way station; Neuss on the Rhine was the next.

I located Iford on a large-scale map of the area I bought that morning: a tiny hamlet that could be reached only by country lanes. I balked at the prospect of again driving down those narrow winding tracks between high hedges peculiar to England, my heart in my mouth because of locals zooming around the bends at fifty miles an hour, forcing Sylvia to stand on the brakes in clouds of dust, to end up with our bumpers touching.

But this time there was no traffic on the winding lanes. After a few miles the road widened and we found ourselves facing a honey-colored Queen Anne house across a narrow bridge, Roman by the looks of it, with the statue of a goddess in its center. I consulted my pendulum; it wanted me to cross the river. We parked the car beside some cottages and set out on foot toward a set of iron gates in the wall surrounding the house. As we crossed the bridge I heard the sound of a weir; it was so evocative of the location that I switched on my tape recorder and said, "I'll record for a few moments the sound of the weir at Iford," and held it over the water. As I did so, I saw that the statue was not Roman; it was Britannia holding a trident and a shield.

"Aye," said a croaking voice behind me. "You're looking at him, I see."

I turned around and saw an old man with a flat cap and a pipe standing behind me. He had materialized out of thin air; I had not seen or heard him coming.

"Aye," he said, as if in answer to a question, "my grandfather stood model for him." He pointed at Britannia with his pipestem. "He was the gardener at the time, old Mr. Peto told him to take a pitchfork and the lid of a dust bin and stand on the bulwark of the bridge facing the river. He had to move back and forth until he stood in the spot old Mr. Peto wanted. That's where they put him."

"Who?"

"Him." He pointed at the statue.

"I see," I said. "And who was Mr. Peto?"

"Ah," he said, gazing at the river. "Mr. Peto. Long gone, him. Never knew him meself. Him's the one who built the gardens. Mad about the gardens, him was. Him went to Rome for statues. You'll see 'em when you visit the gardens. One's of a bitch suckling two toddlers. Roman, they was. You aiming to visit the gardens?"

"If they're open."

"Oh, him's open Wednesdays and Sundays, two to teatime. Summers, that is. You get yourself a ticket inside, in the loggia, from Mr. Peters. Reckon he'll be asleep right now, but just bang on the table, gentlelike. He'll sell you a book too, all about Mr. Peto and the gardens. Used to be sixpence, reckon it's a pound now."

"Thank you," I said, "we'll go and have a look. Thanks for the tip."

"Tip?" He frowned.

"For telling me about it."

"About what?"

"Your grandfather and Mr. Peto."

"Oh, him," he said, turned away with his pipe and dematerialized. As I walked further across the bridge I saw steps leading to the river down which he must have vanished.

The house was exquisite, its walls covered with pink and yellow roses. The gates were open; an arrow pointed the way to the loggia, where we found an elderly man snoozing in a chair behind a table with leaflets, brochures and a book of tickets. I tapped gently on the table as instructed; the man awoke smiling and sold us tickets and a brochure. We entered the gardens.

It was like entering a time warp; the gardens were almost aggressively Roman. A flight of lichen-covered steps led to a wide stone path flanked by a colonnade. Among the pillars stood Roman portrait busts, stark white against a background of black trees noisy with the cawing of jackdaws. To the left, at the end of the colonnade, I spotted a half-moon-shaped seat next to a fountain. On our way there we passed, set in a niche in a privet hedge, the life-size statue of a girl standing, ankles crossed, one hand on her hip, one elbow leaning on a tree trunk. She stared down on me haughtily; if my colonel had walked these gardens and she had been there, he must have stopped in front of her. How would she have affected a man fresh from a war, haunted by what I had seen with the aid of my pendulum? She was a vision of peace.

I found myself thinking of these gardens as Roman, but that was nonsense. The statues might be Roman, the original gardens could not possibly have survived. Sylvia and I sat down on the bench by the fountain; I read to her from the brochure.

There had been a Roman settlement nearby; traces of Roman occupation had been found on both banks of the river. The gardens were mentioned in the Domesday Book as part of the lands of Count Morton, brother of William the Conqueror. There had been several houses, which had changed hands many times over the centuries. In 1899, when this house had become dilapidated and the gardens had run wild, a landscape architect called Harold Peto had visited them out of curiosity. He had walked down the weed-covered paths, and suddenly seen a vision of men in togas and women in white gowns, sitting by the side of an ornamental pond. He became smitten with the idea that these had been Roman gardens, decided to buy the house and restore the gardens as they would have been in Roman times.

We walked down the stone pathway past the colonnade and the statues, toward the pond. Steps sprinkled with violet campanula led down to it. There was a fountain with the statue of a grinning old man cutting the throat of a deer; the water squirted from its throat. Carp moved slowly among water lilies and bullrushes. This must be where Harold Peto had seen men in togas and women in white; I saw in my mind's eye a soldier in rusty armor, weary after weeks of pursuit and battle, gazing at the carp. I took out my pendulum. "Was my praepositus here?"

Yes, said the pendulum.

"The house and the gardens were untouched by war at that time?"

Yes.

"Why was he here? Had his detachment pitched camp nearby, in a field belonging to the villa?"

Yes.

"The owner invited the commanding officer for a visit?"

Yes.

Harold Peto had had his vision of ancient Romans strolling by a pond ninety years ago; now the gardens looked as if they had indeed survived intact since Roman times. I could see a small man in a toga, and my colonel, still in armor—

At this point, Sylvia unexpectedly passed right in front of me, taking pictures. The shock she gave me was disproportionate, but typical for the dowsing state which I had come to recognize as a sort of trance. After the interruption I was too shaken to pick up the thread again and we decided we would come back here later, toward sunset, when I would try to recapture what had happened here in this magical place sixteen hundred years ago.

*

Hortus Tribuncius, summer 368 A.D.

Walking in the garden untouched by war, General Dulcitius observed Mellarius as he reported on the campaign against the Welsh tribe. What could have possessed the murderous woman to lead her band of marauders, probably all the adult men under her rule, on such an orgiastic rampage of slaughter and torture, taking her child with her to boot? Mellarius told the tale of her death factually; the impersonal style of the military report could not hide his emotions.

Again, Dulcitius found himself thinking of the man as a relic from the past. He must be about the last of the keepers of the Pax Romana, whose lives had been ruled by their dedication to the virtues. How their simple devotion had been corrupted! This very villa was a monument to greed and ruthlessness, masked by "culture." The warrior in rusty armor walking beside him, smelling of sweat, bone weary after the hardship of pursuit and battle, formed a piquant contrast with the statue of the owner's daughter posing as Diana when they passed it. Seen through the eyes of the man by his side she must seem civilized, feminine, precious, tender, all that he and his sword defended and kept from harm. Reality was a pampered nymphomaniac who took her wealth as well deserved and who was so bored that all male guests, short of impotent old dodderers, were treated as amusements presented to her by a lecherous god. Life was an entertaining pageant of follies to the objective observer; even so, it was an irony of Fate that poor Mellarius had to be sacrificed for political reasons.

"Tell me," the general asked, "did the informer in Venta Silurum mention any names? All the priest could tell me was that the Pannonian exiles in Londinium were plotting against the field marshal. Did he mention who their leader was?"

"Yes," Mellarius said ingenuously, "a man called Valerius."

"You're sure the name was Valerius?"

Mellarius nodded, unaware that this made him the main witness against one of the most powerful men in Londinium. Secret documents never remained secret; he would incur the wrath of the Pannonian clique in that city as well as in the Senate and at the Imperial Court; there was no way in which his name could be kept out of the records. The informer had been assassinated, he was now the only one on whose testimony Valerius and his conspirators could be executed. One last thing could be done for the man: remove him from the scene, send him back to his fortress on the Rhine. As long as he did nothing to attract their attention, the Pannonians might consider it was too much of an effort to get even with him in that far-flung outpost on the frontier, and too expensive, unless the army could be made to foot the bill.

Dusk had fallen, deepening the peace. In the twilight a billowing white ghost came to meet them, Tribune Octavius Montanus, owner of the plantation. He invited them to sit down with him on a bench by the fountain; he was a wheezing fat man, heavily scented, like a ripe white rose. The evening breeze ruffled the pond; the smell of the tribune's perfume was briefly defeated by the stench of Mellarius's body under his armor.

"Our baths are at your disposal, Colonel," the tribune said pleasantly. "May I invite you and your officers to use them before we dine?"

"Thank you, Tribune."

"How many officers are there in your detachment?"

"Six, including the optios, Tribune."

"Well—"

Suddenly dusk seemed to be given a voice as, beyond the garden wall, a woman began to sing. There were no words to her song, but the sound was so serene that it seemed unearthly, celestial.

"Ye gods," Octavius Montanus exclaimed, "who's *that?*"

"A prisoner, Tribune. Sister of the chief Amazon of the tribe we defeated."

"But she's extraordinary! Does she sing often?"

"Every evening at dusk, Tribune."

"Where is she?"

"In a cage in the camp."

"A cage?" The tribune rose. "That I must see."

He walked down the colonnade in the falling darkness. General Dulcitius followed him, under the spell of the singing woman in spite of himself. The tribune opened a gate in the wall; they found themselves among trees bordering a field where the detachment was encamped. Cooking fires were smoking, soldiers walking about; on the edge of the camp stood a cage made of branches with a huge female, shapeless, moronic, inside. The creature was singing to herself, oblivious of her surroundings, warbling like a bird, long-drawn-out, haunting notes of bliss. Her soul seemed to wander enraptured in a mythical landscape, where Pan played his flute and the nightingale sang, where life was immortal, love eternal and death a dream from which she had just awakened.

"She's incredible!" the tribune whispered. "She would grace any party as a cantrix! What do you intend to do with her, Colonel?"

"Ah," Mellarius said, gloomily, "that's the problem, Tribune."

"Where are you going next?"

"Aquae Sulis. I may have to leave her there."

"Aquae Sulis?" the tribune cried, aghast. "What would they do with her there? Make her sing for the entertainment of people taking the baths? That would be a scandalous waste!"

"I wouldn't know what else to do, Tribune. I have to leave her somewhere. She is retarded, she cannot look after herself."

"You are not going to Aquae Sulis, Mellarius," General Dulcitius said casually. "Your detachment is returning to base from here."

"We are—?"

"We'll talk later. Thank you."

"Yes, General. Tribune . . ." Mellarius left them, obediently, his armor squeaking in the silence.

The tribune asked, "What does she eat, do you think?"

"Eat?"

"What do they feed her? She must have been given temple food to sing like that."

"I'll have to ask their cook."

"Very well, ask their cook, and I'll put her up in my garden. He said she sings every night?"

"You intend to keep her as a musical instrument? For the entertainment of your guests?"

The fat man laughed. "Wouldn't you? I can see us sitting by the pond in the evening, listening to her. I shall not keep her in a cage, of course. She must be given suitable quarters. I'll have something built for her, a little temple, perhaps. Dedicated to Diana." The man had Diana on the brain.

"If she's retarded, the temple should have bars," the general said.

"You mean, she would try to get away?"

"People from the villages her sister massacred will be after her."

"In my gardens," the tribune said proudly, "she is perfectly safe. Nobody sets foot in them unless invited by me."

General Dulcitius wondered at the man's unworldliness. How narrow are the horizons in which we live!

The voice in the darkness rose to ecstasy, a long, tremulous note of pure bliss. From the black trees on the hill a nightingale responded, questioningly.

CHAPTER NINE

*

Neuss, summer 1987

The landlady of the *pension* in Neuss did not recognize us but the puppy did; this gave us sufficient authenticity in her eyes to cash a check for us. We went to have a look at the river; the racket on the quayside was as discouraging as it had been last time. Barges were unloading with a roar of winches; push-boats butted loads of lighters upriver with engines that made the air shudder. Better to wait until later that night when I would have the river to myself, seated in front of the window.

Before supper I lay down on the bed with my shoes off to have a snooze; Sylvia went to do some shopping. She came back on tiptoe, took half a minute closing the door without a sound, then slowly, cautiously, started to unwrap her purchases on the table by the window. In the end I said, "For God's sake, unwrap the damn stuff!"

She came to kiss my forehead; I opened my eyes and refused to believe them. She had bought a monster of Teutonic kitsch: a beer mug the size of a chamber pot covered with pink elephants, dancing.

"I love German china of the worst period," she said, pleased with herself.

"This was the worst you could find in this town?"

"Come," she said. "Let's go for a drink and dinner."

We had dinner in the same restaurant; when we returned to our room I put my robe and slippers at the ready on a chair, together with pendulum and tape recorder; then we went to bed and watched *Dallas* in German on a black-and-white television set. A woman with a ten-gallon hat said, *"Nanu, Schatzerl,"* followed by the sound of galloping hooves. I closed my eyes and lost the thread, then I heard J.R. snarl, *"Verdammt noch mal, das ist ja Dilettantendreck!"* I sank below the surface again until I heard a voice say, "The old buzzard is dying."

Bemused, I opened my eyes. J.R. cried, *"Alles Unsinn! Ich*

habe das Land ja nicht gekauft!" Sylvia's bedside light was out; she had gone to sleep without telling me. I got up, turned off the set, put on my robe and slippers, dropped the tape recorder, waited for Sylvia to mutter, then sat down by the window.

"Now then. What happened here? Are you prepared to tell me?"

No, said the pendulum.

"What do you mean, no?"

No.

"There's nothing left for me to find out here?"

No.

"You made me come all this way for nothing?"

No.

"No yes or no no?"

The pendulum went dead in my hand.

"Come on, wake up!" I said, shaking it.

"Huh?" Sylvia asked. "Whatsamatter?"

"Sorry, I didn't mean you. I'm having problems with my pendulum."

"Come to bed. Tomorrow."

Well, I might as well. As I climbed into bed a word popped into my mind: *butcher.*

"Did we talk about butchers at any time today?"

No answer. She was asleep.

I turned off the light on my side of the bed and lay staring at a patch of light from the street lamp on the ceiling. It had never happened before that my pendulum refused to respond. It had been as if the current that made it move was turned off, a psychic power failure. Only the word *butcher.* But that had come from elsewhere.

I must have fallen asleep, for I found myself involved in a dream about buses. I was running to catch one; a gawking, grinning boy watched me run from the rear window. "Ma . . . Ma! Look at the funny old man!" It wasn't a bus, it was an oriental house with a balcony full of Chinese. "Ma! Look!" With immense relief I stopped running; somewhere in the house a cuckoo clock clanged three. *"Clang-cuckoo! Clang-cuckoo! Clang—"* I lay waiting for the final *cuckoo* when the goddam puppy licked my hand and banged the side of the bed with its tail. The landlady pulled open the curtains and gave us the tea tray I had ordered and the morning paper. When she was gone I said, "I had the most extraordinary experience last night. My pendulum ceased to function."

Suddenly, on the landing outside our door, the cuckoo clock called, *"Cuckoo!"* About time too.

*

Novaesium, early autumn 368 A.D.

When the detachment, together with the rest of the regiment, returned to Novaesium it was autumn. The woods were turning, the river, a colossal sheet of dull pewter with flashes of steel, slid massively past the muddy bank. It was silent; only occasionally a splash could be heard as a clod of mud caved away and fell into the water. Black clouds drifted overhead; there was a distant rumble of thunder.

The opposite bank of the river seemed unusually quiet. The colonel had expected a riotous welcome from the Franci; but no flatboats, no jeers, no penis display. There should at least have been some spectators lined up across the river, watching their return from under their houses on stilts, but there was not a soul to be seen.

Mercatius Massavo, senior centurion of the skeleton garrison, joined the colonel as he stood gazing at the village across the water, little Corylus pressed against him. "It looks deserted," the colonel said. "Where have they all gone?"

"The old man is dying, Colonel. Everybody is staying indoors, waiting for him to go. That's their custom."

To his own surprise, the news struck Mellarius with a sense of loss. He had never before felt any kinship with the bellowing old chieftain who had taunted his recruits for years. Occasionally, they had met in battles, always bloody and always undecided. Now here he stood, overcome by a sense of mourning. Or was it a revolt at the pointless suffering, the brutish slaughter, the meaninglessness of it all? Not a rational reaction, the

aftereffects of the campaign, the mutilated corpses, the slaughtered children, the bearded young warriors with flowers in
their hair beside the mound of carcasses of their final killing
frenzy. He felt a deep revulsion, the unreasoned urge to honor
life rather than destroy it as Q. Peltrasias Flavinus, the cavalry
commander, had done, and Field Marshal Theodosius. He said
to the man by his side, "Massavo, prepare a boat for me."

"Boat?" The centurion stared at him, openmouthed.

"Also a white vexillum, to be raised when we approach the
other shore. How many men does it need to row me across?"

"You are not planning to go to the village, Colonel?" The
centurion sounded alarmed.

"How many men?"

"I wouldn't know, Colonel. I'll have to ask . . ."

"Find out, and have a boat ready in half an hour."

The news that Colonel Mellarius was planning to have
himself rowed across the river, with a white banner of truce,
stunned his troops. It also brought about a protest by the infernal priest, who, like a curse of the gods, had rejoined the
regiment just before sailing. The colonel told him in uncom-
promising terms that it was none of his damn business. The
priest left in a huff, gathering his skirts. Doctor Fortunatas
appeared, smiling, with a potion against the vapors; the colonel grabbed the beaker and flung it out of the tent. After that,
everyone got the message. No more protest was voiced. The
colonel started to change into his parade uniform.

When the boat was ready he reappeared in full dress,
watched in silence by his men as he strode past, scarlet cloak
billowing in the wind. They watched without a word as he
climbed into the boat, ordered the rowers to cast off and head
into the current. The boat slewed across the river slowly, the
scarlet cloak a spot of blood on the pewter.

It took them a long time to reach the other shore; by then,
people had appeared over there, helmeted men, groups of
women and children. They all watched incredulously as the
boat with its white banner and scarlet-robed figure slowly
drew nearer, askew in the current.

Finally the boat ground ashore. Colonel Mellarius jumped
out and walked toward the flabbergasted barbarians standing

motionless among the stilts of their houses. "I have come to pay my respects to your chieftain," he said slowly, spacing the words to make himself understood. "Please lead me to him."

A young man with sword and helmet came up to him and said in excellent Latin, "I am his son. My father is dying."

"That is why I am here," Mellarius said. "I want to say farewell to him before he sets out for the hereafter. We may have been enemies, we are both honorable men."

The bewildered young man stood for a moment in indecision; then he beckoned the colonel to follow him. Together they walked past the stilted houses watched by their stunned inhabitants. He marched, cloak swinging, scabbard slapping, the cockscomb of his parade helmet flaring in the sun, by the young man's side until they arrived at the largest of the dwellings. There, the young man held aside a leather curtain and gestured him to enter. He stooped inside.

As his eyes adjusted to the semidarkness he saw he was standing at the foot of a bier on which the old man lay, lost to the world. He was almost unrecognizable: shrunken, gasping, his forehead and eyelids glistening with sweat. He looked crushed, degraded, not a warrior giving up his soul on the battlefield but a beetle stepped on by Fate. If Mellarius had harbored any doubt as to the validity of his impulse, his presence in full regalia transformed the helpless twitching of the stepped-on beetle into a warrior's death. This might not be on the battlefield; it was, mysteriously, better: a farewell, a last clasping of the hands in honor of their honorable profession, on the banks of the Styx; Charon would hold up the ferry in respect.

The son must be feeling this too as he stood by the colonel's side, looking down on his dying father. Then he took one step back in tribute to the extraordinary occasion. As they stood there, in silence, Mellarius felt, incredulously, that peace on the frontier was within their grasp.

Then the dying man slowly opened his eyes. They roamed, unseeing; then they caught sight of the resplendent figure looming at his feet. He gave a shuddering gasp, whispered, "Rome!" his eyes glazed over, his head fell aside. Mellarius realized, horrified, that he had died of fright.

He looked at the son. The young man stared at his dead

father speechlessly. Peace was slipping from their grasp; in a last effort to save it Mellarius took off his helmet and put it at the dead man's feet.

Bareheaded, he was escorted back to the river's bank by the son. The boat cast off and started its laborious crawl back to the other side. Thunder rumbled over the forest.

Then the Franci recovered from their shock. They started to scream, to catcall, to shout incomprehensible curses at the disappearing boat. The colonel looked back and saw, to his startled disgust, that they were using his helmet to vent their rage. They kicked it around, relieved themselves in it, wiped their behinds with the cockscomb, in utter humiliation of the army.

On his arrival Mellarius saw, with a feeling of fatality, the infernal priest gaze at him smirking with gratification. Little Corylus came running toward him and disappeared under his cloak. Together they walked back to the command tent, where Doctor Fortunatas welcomed him with a funereal air. "Never mind, lord," he whispered, handing him a beaker with some potion, "most of us understood."

On the opposite bank of the river the Franci went on abusing the helmet until darkness fell, then they lit bonfires, howled, shouted obscenities, and ended by making an effigy of a Roman soldier, grotesque, with a limp pale penis of impotent shame. They ended by burning it and dancing around the fire.

*

Castellum Arbeia, autumn 368 A.D.

General Dulcitius was present in the field marshal's headquarters in Arbeia, easternmost stronghold of Hadrian's Wall, when the report came in from Father Ioannis on the Rhine. The field marshal read it, then handed it to him without a word.

Mellarius had crossed the river with a banner of surrender and humiliated the army by leaving behind his helmet for the enemy to desecrate, in a bizarre desire to pay homage to a dying barbarian chieftain.

It was fastidium turned virulent. The man had to go, of course. Dulcitius was shocked when he heard the field marshal dictate to his scribe the order, for the emperor to sign, that Praepositus T. Gaius Mellarius was to fall on his sword but that as an act of grace he might be buried with military honors. Why this savage sentence? Mellarius was a good man, his record was exemplary, he had just defeated a tenacious and elusive enemy; his paying tribute to a chieftain of the Franci on his deathbed had been an effort to establish the beginning of a code of honor between foes, of which the army would clearly be the beneficiary. Only on reflection did the real reason for this overreaction occur to the general. Theodosius was above all else a consummate politician; personal feelings such as gratitude toward a man who had in effect saved his life did not prevail. The Pannonian plot had been dealt with ruthlessly, Valerius had been executed, the participants punished; it had been done discreetly however, so as not to upset the balance between the Pannonian and Spanish cliques in the Senate and at the emperor's court. But Valerius had been executed without a proper trial, on the word of one witness who had not been called; this needed a calming of the waves, not with oil but with blood. Effective, no doubt, but it shamed Roman law to a greater extent than had Valerius's hasty execution.

The choice of a fellow officer of equal rank to take the fateful message, first to Amiens for the emperor's signature, then to Colonel Mellarius, was a delicate one. Theodosius, looking grave, with only the good of the army in mind, appointed Colonel Q. Peltrasias Flavinus, the Pannonian cavalry commander with whom Mellarius had clashed on the road to Letocetum. It was an astute choice; it would give the Pannonians a sense of getting even with the man who had cost their leader his life; Q. Peltrasias Flavinus himself would derive great personal satisfaction from the assignment. Thus the balance was restored with finesse and discretion.

Dulcitius watched as the field marshal gave the instruction for the document to be sent by messenger to the emperor's headquarters. If Valentinian Augustus had ever met Mellarius he might amend it, but there was little chance of that.

As the messenger left with the scroll the general reflected, with the objective observer's detachment, on the life and death of the Roman who had never been to Rome, the loyal servant of the virtues to which no one adhered any longer. The gods must be weeping, or laughing. He wondered how T. Gaius Virilis's spirit would take it; not well, one would think. The old father must be about the last person, alive or dead, to tolerate his son humiliating the army and dying by his own hand, the Imperial Officer's ultimate shame. For a guardian spirit to desert his ward during the man's lifetime was considered an impardonable sin by the haruspices; it carried the punishment of being strapped to the merciless wheel of birth and death *ad infinitum*. But from what the general knew of the old centurion, he might well be mad enough to jump onto the wheel of his own volition rather than hang around to watch the ultimate disgrace of the orphan he had loved.

It was a tragedy worthy of a good singer, with a well-tuned lyre, after an elegant meal.

*

Novaesium, winter 368 A.D.

The news, a few weeks later, that Q. Peltrasias Flavinus had arrived with a message from Imperial Headquarters came as a pleasant surprise to Colonel Mellarius.

Ever since the old chieftain's death and the business with the helmet he had felt depressed. He did not doubt the rightness of the impulse that had sent him across the river to pay homage to his old enemy before the man's soul set out for Valhalla, but the effect on his officers, his troops, even the haruspex, bewildered him. The only one who seemed to approve of his action was Doctor Fortunatas; he at least seemed to accept the impulse as having been inspired by the Virtues.

Most alarming of all had been the reaction of his father's spirit. In the past, T. Gaius Virilis had responded to his prayers with a secret physical signal, a twitch of the scalp invisible to others, as a sign that there was contact. Of late, much as he needed his housegod, there had been no reaction. Ever since the incident, he found himself praying to a mere figure of stone that was blind, dumb, and soulless. His tender thoughts, his yearning for a word of comfort to ease his anguish remained without response. In that darkness, the news that the Pannonian colonel had come to see him was a ray of light.

"Ask him to come in!" he cried, checking the impulse to go outside himself and welcome the man who had, obviously, come to let bygones be bygones. For a colonel to be dispatched to deliver a message to a fellow colonel meant that he must have asked for the assignment himself.

When he came in, Q. Peltrasias Flavinus was accompanied by Marcellus Sabinus, the army inspector. Their entrance was uncommonly formal; they saluted in unison, without the usual comradely greeting, then Peltrasias Flavinus held out a sealed roll of parchment and said, in a tone that made Mellarius realize he had not come to let bygones be bygones, "I hereby hand you a personal message from our emperor, Valentinian Augustus."

Surprised, Mellarius took the parchment, broke the seal, and unrolled it while the two officers remained standing to attention. Could it be that he had been promoted to tribune at last? No wonder the Pannonian looked so dour. But then, why would it be he who brought the news?

> We, Flavius Valentinianus Caesar Augustus Germanicus Imperator, to Trajanus Gaius Mellarius, praepositus of Numerus II Batavorum: salutations.
>
> It has been brought to our attention that by acting against military tradition and practice you have brought about a humiliation of our army and thereby ourselves and Rome. As this cannot be tolerated, it is our decision that you shall, upon receipt of this order, draw your sword and fall upon it in punishment for your actions. In view of past services your corpse shall not be beheaded, nor shall your name be subjected to a damnatio memoriae. You shall be recorded as fallen in action and buried with military honors within the confines of for-

tress Novaesium, before sundown on the day of your death. May our Heavenly Father and His Holy Son our Lord Jesus Christ have mercy on your soul. Valentinianus Augustus, on behalf of the Senate and the People of Rome.

Devastated, numb with shock, Mellarius stared from one to the other. How was it possible? What had happened? Who had reported this to the emperor? The priest! Then, staring at Q. Peltrasias Flavinus, who stood rigidly to attention, he knew why the Pannonian had been selected. This was not the punishment for leaving his helmet at the dead chieftain's feet, but for his having allowed the children to escape. "Rome does not massacre small children." He had been wrong: Rome did. Then he thought of Corylus. His first reaction was, The boy must not know!

As if reading the thought, the Pannonian said, "I am told you have a son. I will allow him to hold the sword. Immediately afterward, he shall alert us so that we may view the body and report to the emperor that his will has been done." Both he and the inspector saluted again in unison, made about turn with military precision and marched out.

The moment they were gone, Doctor Fortunatas appeared in the doorway, white as a sheet, eyes wide with horror. "Lord . . . !"

With death now cold in his stomach, as if the sword had already pierced it and cut the silver cord, Mellarius gazed at him, speechless.

"Shall I bring the boy in, lord?"

"No! I do not want him to know about this until after it's done. He is too little. Tell him later." He could not bear to see the child, it would weaken him to the point where he might not be able to go through with it, which meant that Q. Peltrasias Flavinus would have to execute him by hacking off his head.

"But then who—?"

"I do not need anyone. I will hold the sword myself."

"Oh gods, oh lord! Let me—just one moment—I—let me . . ." He rushed out of the tent.

Cold, without emotion, Mellarius knelt in front of the statue. "Be there," he prayed. "I am coming, be there. I beseech thee, be there." He waited for the twitch of the scalp; it did not come.

Maybe because of his state of shock; maybe his soul was already in the process of separating from his body. When he rose he found Doctor Fortunatas standing behind him, holding out a beaker.

"Lord, drink this."

"What is it?"

"A sedative, lord. Drink it, please."

"But I am calm, Fortunatas. I don't need this. Death has walked beside me all my life, I am not afraid. I am going home to my father."

"I know, lord, but just as a farewell, a last token of my esteem after all the years I have looked after you—I beg you, let me do something!"

Moved by the man's anguish, Mellarius took the beaker from him, raised it, said, "Thank you, dear friend," and drank.

The moment the searing pain hit his stomach he screamed, "No! Not that! Not that!" A furious flight of images swept past him: his woundless corpse, his sword still in its scabbard, Q. Peltrasias Flavinus spitting at him for being a coward. He fell to his knees, groaning, "Not that! Not that!" and saw, in a rippled image, as if under water, Fortunatas unsheathe his sword and raise it above him. He fell on his back. There would be no shame, no—

The sword struck. Terror struck. With his last breath he tried to whistle.

But this time the bees did not come.

C H A P T E R   T E N

*

Cannes, France, summer 1987

It was a despondent homecoming when I finally drove into
our village. To have gone through all this, to have been given
the complete story of a Roman officer's experiences on assignment in Britain, his thoughts and emotions, only to end up with
a pendulum that refused to function at what had to be the
catharsis was infuriating.

But for Sylvia, who disliked Dutch rages, I would have flung
the damn pendulum out of the window. Instead, I made a few
telephone calls and went to join a rehearsal of *The Pirates of
Penzance,* to the accompaniment of tinkling ice cubes in whis-
key glasses.

It was a dreary month. The heat was murderous and I had
nothing to do. In desperation I joined a physical exercise class
made up of hollow-eyed old men clad in sweatsuits running
like dervishes, mousy hair flying, at five o'clock every morning.
I did it once, collapsed halfway, and saw a ghostlike oc-
togenarian come back for me like an apparition in the first flush
of dawn, crying, "You must *live* for your exercises!" The idea
of living only for the sake of prolonging life made me decide to
accept the part of Admiral Farty, or whatever his name was,
in *The Pirates of Penzance.* The melancholy of it all was indescribable. Never before had I felt so dispirited, facing a void of
boredom. Finally I telephoned Helen to ask her to send the rest
of the typescript of my tapes; she told me she had been too
preoccupied of late but would get with it at once.

"Preoccupied?" I said to Sylvia. "What the hell does she
mean? Too fucking busy, or the other way around?"

Sylvia looked at me coolly and said, "This may be the
moment to tell you."

"Tell me what?"

"I've been waiting for an opportunity ever since we left
Topsham, but you didn't seem to be very receptive. Maybe

you're not very receptive now, but it's time you knew. Helen is going to have a baby."

I gaped at her. "Helen?"

"Helen."

"Out of that creep? That jackass who refuses to marry her?"

"In English," she said calmly, "the term 'out of' is used only in connection with horses or dogs."

"How can you stand there, as if—now he *shall* marry her! Even if I have to—"

"You see?" she said. "Now do you understand why I was waiting for the appropriate moment?"

"If that man still won't marry her, I'll go and shoot his balls off!"

The dog started to bark enthusiastically. I shouted, "Shut up, you creep!" and shoved it into the kitchen. It disappeared under the wine rack.

"Home sweet home," Sylvia said, strolling to the pantry.

"Good God, Syl!" I cried. "Why didn't you tell me?"

"Because of this," she replied, pointing at the dog nervously wagging its rump that stuck out from under the wine rack.

"But what are we going to *do?* There must be something we can do!"

"Acting the heavy father and threatening castration by pistol is not a promising line of action," she said, opening the icebox. "Would you care for some orange juice?"

"Orange juice, hell!" I grabbed the jug of Dutch gin.

She took it away from me. "Not at two o'clock in the afternoon," she said firmly and closed the door of the refrigerator. "Leave him to Helen and me. For God's sake, Marty, stay out of it! Haven't you recognized yourself in the old centurion? My God, you haven't changed in two thousand years!"

I wandered over to the window and looked down the empty street. Suddenly I heard her say behind me, "Dear love, how difficult it must have been for you to be an absentee father. What a lonely life you must have had."

I did not know how to respond. I said, "Well, I'd better go and let the dog out. Just to the top of the hill and back."

There was no florist in our village, all I could do to make amends after that heartbreaking remark of hers was to pick some lousy heather on top of the hill spiraling with heat in the burning sun. When I came back and handed her the measly posy, she was touched.

"Dear Marty," she said, kissing me, "how lovely. I'll put them in water at once."

She did; I hoped they wouldn't die of shock.

*

A week later, the typescript of my final dowsing sessions in England arrived, with a letter from Helen.

> Dear Dad. Well, here they are, all complete. I hope I didn't miss out on anything; occasionally your voice faded away when you obviously were talking to Mom. It is a fascinating story that goes on haunting me. Cold, old, long dead Roman soldiers with their iron breastplates in this climate, homesick for the smell of lavender. Why do they want to be known by us twentieth-century people? Why do they come back again and again through the ages, misunderstood in every century, to tell us their story? Maybe the story is just a dream in which we can dwell for a while. Maybe it is more. I keep thinking about this.

I lowered the letter. I had never asked myself that question: why? What had been the purpose of the experience?

Haunted by the question, I went through the dowsing log once more, from the beginning, alert to anything that might hint at a purpose for this pilgrimage, my pendulum going dead in Neuss. Nothing could be considered a clue until I hit the Forest of Dean.

I took the typescript to the kitchen where Sylvia was preparing the dog's noonday meal. "There's something here I don't understand," I said. "I've assumed all this time that I was tracing the footsteps of the colonel, or rather myself as a decrepit old man tagging along with him. Can you explain how in that case I could have dowsed the experience of a little boy, alone in the forest? The way he felt, what he saw, what he thought, what happened to him? He had lost his way, the colonel was nowhere around, neither was his old father. Right?"

"I suppose so. Why?"

"Where did I get the information from? How did I *know*?"

She thought that over, spoon in hand; the dog started to whine with impatience. She put the dish on the floor. "Maybe the boy told them his story later. Maybe that's what you came up with, the telling of the story."

"No. The boy did *not* tell his story. Not that night or any other night: he was mute. So, where did I get his story from? Where *was* the old man, the observer? Up in a tree somewhere, looking down, seeing the whole scene? That's how it felt as I dowsed it: I saw it all, heard it, heard the night birds start their song, smelled the forest. I was there. But *where?*"

"It's odd, I must admit. Well, read on," she said, as to a child that wanted to know how a bedtime story ended. "It will all become clear in the end."

"I sure hope so," I said.

I read the rest of the typescript; it did not provide an answer. Unless—but that was crazy. That was where I drew the line. I was prepared to swallow previous incarnations, eighty-year-old men hobbling along on campaign, singing ladies in cages, but I refused to consider that I might have accompanied the colonel as his father's ghost. No. Hell, no! I slammed the door on the risible idea and went to the rehearsal, where I proceeded to bellow the third bass in "O Come Let Us Adore Him"; it had been decided we would start our Christmas carol rehearsals early this year.

But the thought went on nagging me. How did I know what had happened to the boy in the forest? No one else knew. The more I thought about it, the more certain I became that Helen had put her finger on it: I would only find the answer after I had discovered the purpose of my quest.

But how? I forced myself to concentrate on other things, for I was in the process of turning into a crackpot. Then a death notice arrived in the mail from Germany.

I had no idea who it could be, until I pulled the black-framed card out of the envelope. It was Heini Rabenschnabel, the German cook's mate we had fished out of the sea after our ship and the U-boat that sank her had gone down together in the

Arctic. *"Lieber Mann, Vater, Onkel, und Neffe,"* followed by the names of his widow and seven children, *"und Familie."* The funeral would be in two days' time.

I told Sylvia I had to go; she understood at once. I asked, "Any idea why I feel I have to go?"

She answered, "Don't ask, just go. Want me to come with you?"

"I would love it."

On second thoughts she could not make it because she had a committee meeting. Frankly, I don't think she wanted to. Heini was part of my life; better I deal with it alone.

*

The burial took place in an impersonal cemetery near Wiesbaden. I had planned to see his family, make myself known; but during the drive north the decision took hold to see no one. I still had no idea what had made me go; it was all so long ago, forty-six years. I had not heard from him for twenty.

I arrived in a gale after an exhausting drive. The church service had already started; I slipped inside and sat in the back. When the coffin was carried out I followed the procession of mourners.

There was quite a crowd of them, the majority overweight. It was like a convention of fatties, mourning one of their number who had died young. In fact Heini had been sixty-three. The burial itself meant little to me. Nothing evoked the fateful occasion forty-six years ago. Standing on the edge of the crowd, listening to the surf of the September gale in the trees, I felt an odd disappointment. Nobody seemed to live up to the occasion, least of all the minister in his black robe and white lobster bib, who bellowed a prayer in competition with the foaming trees. I left without having seen anyone.

I had a lonely meal with half a bottle of *Spätlese.* In the middle of the night I suddenly found myself wide awake in an unfamiliar hotel room. Staring in the dark, I was beset by a dreamlike, distorted memory of the ship I loved being lifted bodily out of the water, her stern gone, her foreshortened body capsizing as she rose. An avalanche of boiling milk came combing toward the lifeboat; with my face in my hands I heard the mountain of water breaking over us, a deafening, hissing sound. Then it drew away; in the sudden silence a voice like a child's shrieked, *"Hilfe! Hilfe!"* The lifeboat lay wallowing on a smooth black sea; close by the head of a black boy was screaming, *"Hilfe!"* I realized it was a white boy, drowning in oil; I ordered the boat over. The first mate leaped up, brandishing a boat hook, and started slamming at the water, jabbing the hook at the head, yelling, "Bastards! Bastards! Sadistic bastards!" The others pulled him down, he lost his balance and collapsed screaming shell-shocked abuse, fighting, kicking. I leaned over the edge and grabbed the boy. I thought I would lose him; the oil made him as slick as an eel. The others helped me drag him into the boat; he slumped in the bilgewater on hands and knees, vomiting, reeking of crude petroleum. The deafening roar of a plane came diving down on us; I heard the same twangs I had heard before and I realized, incredulously, that it was trying to sink us with its cannons. It missed, the boat was rocked by the explosions; I heard it banking, then it came back for another pass. The boy screamed *"Halt! Halt! Ich bin Heini Rabenschnabel! Koch's Hilfe, Zweite Klasse, U-237! Kamerad! Heil Hitler! Kamerad!"* He had risen to his knees and was giving the Nazi salute, shouting at the plane as it came roaring down guns blazing. I pulled him down and threw myself on top of him.

I lay on top of the trembling body for an eternity. I smelled the oil, felt his breath on my cheek, heard his voice whisper, close to my ear, *"Mutti, Mutti, Mutti . . ."* The plane's roar became deafening. I put my hand under his head and pressed his face against my shoulder. As I did so, it suddenly was as if I touched upon the meaning of life, the purpose of my existence. I felt an indescribable peace, an utter serenity, total acceptance; it came as a shock when the roar of the plane drew away and the world fell silent. I lay, in an unearthly serenity, on top of him. I saw his eyes stare at me, the eyes of a terrified child. I said in German, "Lucky boy, Heini. They missed again." His lower lip began to tremble, he burst into tears. And now he lay buried in that cemetery.

Why had the moments I lay there, his head pressed against my shoulder, seemed so important? Why had I been given the answer to the enigma of life, only to forget instantly what it was? Whatever the answer, I had proved unworthy of the moment of revelation. It had not changed me; it had just happened and was gone.

I had come to Heini Rabenschnabel's funeral in the hope of finding the answer at last. I had come in vain.

*

After my return home I was at a loose end. I read the damn typescript over and over until I knew it by heart. I walked the dog, yelling Dutch curses under the alien sky when it rolled on other dogs' turds. I sang "O Come All Ye Faithful" and boozed with the choir. I read Thomas Lethbridge's *The Power of the Pendulum*, Stefan Schwartz's *The Secret Vaults of Time*, Colin Wilson's *The Psychic Detectives*, and wondered if I should try holding an object of the period in my hand instead of dowsing.

Sylvia must have worried about me, for one morning at breakfast she asked, "How about a visit to the wing commander?"

"Huh?" I froze in midmotion, dangling a rind of cheese above the dog.

"I think we should pay a visit to Helen. Why don't we go by car, in easy stages, and take in the wing commander on the way? I think it's time you had a word with him."

"But—ouch!" The dog had snapped the rind, nearly taking some of my skin with it.

I telephoned the wing commander; he sounded delighted. "Splendid, old boy! Jemima and I would love to see you!" So there was a Mrs. Martock after all.

When we got there, a week later, Jemima turned out to be

not his wife but a cat. It lay stretched to its full length, which was that of a dog, in front of a fire doing its best in a chilly room in his cottage. He was garbed in sweater, tweed jacket, hunting pants and flying boots lined with sheepskin; his pipe, spewing sparks, was a better source of heat than the fire blinking sheepishly in the hearth. The cat lay virtually under the fire basket; it lifted its head with a scowl of disapproval when he cried, "Sit down, sit down! Mrs. Harinxma, take this seat! Now what can I give you? It's weather for a hot toddy, isn't it?"

"Maybe a tad early," I said, after a stern glance from Sylvia.

"Oh, come on! You don't mind a small libation, do you? Or would you rather have a cup of tea?"

"I don't think so, thank you, Wing Commander," Sylvia said.

"Well, then!" He poured something from a bottle into a glass in the background. "What is this I hear about hitting a roadblock in Germany?"

I told him about the pendulum refusing to respond, and about the feeling that the answer to the enigma was within my reach, if only I knew where.

I remembered from our first meeting that he was a good listener; he let me tell my story without interrupting. "H'm," he mused, when I was through. "Curious, the business about the pendulum going dead on you. There must be a reason. Off the top of my head: did you ever arrive at a conclusion, with the aid of your pendulum, which you decided to reject?"

"I don't quite understand."

"Did you, at any time in the recent past, arrive at a conclusion with the aid of your pendulum and then refuse to accept it?"

Extraordinary question, but I might as well give it a shot. Had I rejected any conclusions? Yes, I had. "There was an episode," I said, "about a little boy in the Forest of Dean who lost his way. He encountered a barbarian child of his own age who showed him a toy, they were interrupted by the appearance of a woman, the boy's mother, dressed in a bearskin with the skull of the bear on her head. If I accept the premise that I have been following the trail of the old centurion, the colonel's father, then how could I know what happened to that child in the forest when he was alone? I seemed to see him from above, but I could hardly have been up a tree, could I? So I did arrive at a conclusion which I rejected."

"That you were the Roman commander's guardian angel? His father's spirit?"

"Well, yes."

"The concept is as old as mankind. You rejected that as a possibility?"

"Out of hand."

"Why, may I ask?"

"Because I have to draw the line somewhere. I refuse to go in for spiritualism. I have been there, I want no part of it."

"I see." He sipped his drink. "In that case, I'm afraid, your pendulum will consider the matter closed."

"My pendulum, friend Martock, has no power of decision. It is a bauble on a chain which serves as a go-between."

"Between what?"

"My mind and my brain. It's not my idea, by the way, but General Scott Elliot's, whose book you recommended."

"Quite right. Well, in this case your mind decided: that's it. If you won't accept that conclusion, finish."

"And if I were to accept it?"

He puffed at his pipe. "That might remove the obstruction blocking your pendulum. Why don't you ask your mind, 'Have I been dowsing the experiences of the Roman colonel's father?' If your pendulum says yes, ask, 'Was it during his lifetime?' If the answer is yes we may have a problem. My guess is that the answer will be negative."

I had to admit it was pretty astute. There was a silence.

Sylvia asked, "So you believe that it was the old man's ghost he has been following?"

"Yes," he said.

I had known this all along, but refused to acknowledge it. I had known it as far back as Leintwardine, when I first became conscious of my love for the man standing by my side in those bushes.

"There's something else," I said. "As I stood beside my son in the bushes by the river in Leintwardine, I was in my thirties." I turned to Sylvia. "I went into those bushes in technicolor, the transformation into my Roman self was a change to black and white."

"I see," she said. "You had better explain this to our friend."

I proceeded to do so. The cat stretched, yawned under the fire basket and sank back into sleep, felled by boredom.

*

The moment our car pulled up outside Harry's door in Topsham, Helen came out in a state of high excitement. "Mom! You're *not* going to believe this! You *must* see it! It's a miracle!"

"What's happened?" Sylvia asked, alarmed. I fussed with the luggage.

"I'm not going to tell you! Come quick! Dad! Leave the suitcases, Harry will help you in a moment. First, come and have a look—come!"

We stumbled through the dark hall and the kitchen as she said breathlessly, "I've been telling Sally, every day after you telephoned, for days, 'Mom is coming, Sally! Mom who saved your life, who taught me how to talk with you! *Mom* is coming!'"

"Jesus Christ," I muttered, as I nearly broke my neck over a skateboard outside the door to the garden.

Helen didn't notice. "Twice a day I told her, 'Sally, Mom's coming a week from now! Three days from now! Two days! Tomorrow! You must *do* something!'"

"Do what?" I groaned.

"Hush, Marty," Sylvia said, "let her finish."

Helen pulled her along the garden path to where Harry's little apple tree stood spread-eagled against the wall. "Look!" she cried. "*Look* what Sally did for you!"

She pointed at the little tree. It was already losing its leaves. In its center was one white blossom.

I could not believe my eyes. Apple trees do not flower in October; she had stuck it on, the slyboots. Sylvia kneeled in front of the little tree and said, "Sally, how marvellous!" She touched the little flower, then looked up at me with eyes full of wonder. "It's real . . ."

I could not believe it. I inspected it myself; to my utter amazement there was no doubt: the crazy little tree had produced one blossom, which had opened that morning. All I could come up with was "Fancy that," then I patted Sylvia on the shoulder and fled for a period of private reflection on the Old Goatwalk.

Alone in the wind, among the old men and the giggly young girls, I faced my moment of truth. Ever since Danville I had indulged Sylvia and her embarrassing "communication with plants." She had calmly continued coaxing names out of drooping African violets, molting ferns and lice-infested jades brought in by neighbors for her to fuss over: dwarfs, cross-eyed hunchbacks, flatfooted morons of the plant world, to whom she talked as if they were individuals aware of love and affection. She had called them—or they had called themselves—Beulah, Josephine, Yvonne and Dolores. Now, on behalf of them all, a crazy little fruit tree which she had coaxed back to life presented her with a blossom in October. I could sneer, reject, close my eyes and my mind; I could not deny that the blossom was real. Sally, egged on by Helen, had presented Sylvia with a posy of thanks from the plant world.

Well, the least I should come up with was the same. I walked back to the village, found a flower shop in the high street and bought her a bouquet of red roses with a card saying, FROM A CRESTFALLEN SKEPTIC TO HIS BELOVED OUIJA BROAD, signed HER CENTURION.

*

That evening, Sally's blossom dropped off. Harry, smiling benignly, was not impressed. "An aberration," he said. "The little tree was sick to start with. It's off its stroke, that's all."

A few months ago, as recently as yesterday, I might have thought the same; now I knew he was wrong. Like myself, he had lived his life boxed in by three dimensions, refusing to acknowledge that we were surrounded by a vast world of miracle and mystery subject to laws that had nothing to do with linear time. It was Sally who had finally taken the blinkers from my eyes.

Helen said to him indignantly, "*Surely* you know about the garden in Scotland called Findhorn, where similar results are routine? Whole books have been written about it! People go to visit it in droves! You should at least have the intellectual honesty to look at the evidence before you come out with your pompous verdict!"

He smiled, unsullied by doubt. "Let's give the parents their present now," he said.

Sylvia and I exchanged a look at the word *parents.* Helen said, "Whenever you're ready."

He ambled off; it seemed a good moment for me to hand Sylvia the roses I had smuggled in. I had her in my arms when Helen tapped my shoulder and said, "Come on, you lovebirds. Harry has something to show you. He brought it all the way from America especially for you, and had it adapted at great expense. So, be suitably impressed. Come."

I had no idea what she was talking about. In the living room benign chaos reigned; at our entrance the television set was blaring *Top of the Pops.* It was turned off under howls of protest from the children; they were chased off the sofa to make room for Opa and Oma. Then Harry produced a videocassette. "I saw this in Princeton last month," he said. "I thought it was just up your street, so I asked the friends I was staying with to tape it for me. American videotape doesn't fit English sets, so I had it copied here. It'll work on your set in the south of France too. Let's have a look at it. Shut up, children! Upstairs!"

There was a sulky show of creeping protest as the children, in slow motion, pawed their way upstairs along the banister.

"Ready?" Harry switched on the television.

The video showed an episode from a talk show in America. An eager young reporter had visited the dowsing convention in Danville; he must have been there at the time we were. He set up a test by digging a row of holes and putting empty bottles inside all of them except one. In that one, in full view of the camera, he put a bottle of water. Four elderly dowsers, whom I recognized by sight, were called upon to demonstrate their magic by determining with their pendulums which hole contained the full bottle. All of them failed dismally; a scientific expert in a white coat, surrounded by microscope, computer, retorts and pipettes to accentuate his objectivity, said, "Dowsing for water is complete nonsense. You will find water anywhere in the world, on condition you dig deep enough." Commercial well drillers might not agree, but to each his own.

In the next segment the sheriff of an upstate New York county told a story against a background of shots of the scenery. Last winter two young men had set out from a diner in a small lakeside town during a blizzard in a pickup truck. They were born in the county, knew it like the backs of their hands and wanted to get home before the snowstorm made the roads impassable. They were never seen again. The sheriff sent out descriptions of the men and the pickup truck all over the county and the neighboring counties; nobody had seen them. It was a mystery so bewildering that the sheriff quietly called on a dowser called Ben Kaufmann, who had located missing persons before. Mr. Kaufmann, a small old man with a beard and a beaming wife, agreed to try but would not promise anything. He asked for a large-scale map of the area, dowsed over it with his pendulum and came up with the information that the pickup truck and the men were at the bottom of the lake. The sheriff said that was impossible, the lake was frozen, the two men knew the neighborhood too well to have blundered onto it. He went back to headquarters, sorry he had succumbed to superstition.

Next spring the lake thawed and the body of one of the young men was washed ashore. Back went the sheriff to Mr. Kaufmann. It now appeared that, indeed, at the height of the blizzard the two had blundered onto the lake with their pickup truck, hit a soft spot in the ice and crashed through it. Did Mr. Kaufmann think he could locate the other body, maybe the truck? Mr. Kaufmann said he would do his best, but could not guarantee any results. He dowsed over a large-scale map of the lake, then they set out by boat for him to fine-dowse the exact spot. It took a bit of maneuvering; Mr. Kaufmann, consulting his pendulum, said, "Back a bit," and "To the left. This is it. Yes!" They dropped anchor; it fell onto the bed of the pickup truck on the bottom of the lake. The truck was brought up by crane; the body of the other young man was found behind the wheel.

The scientific expert in the white coat, asked what he thought of it, shrugged and said, "Coincidence."

"Where the hell did they get that moron?" I cried. "From central casting?"

Helen said, "Dad . . ."

Fuming, I watched the sheriff as he respectfully accepted the scientist's expertise and agreed it must have been coincidence. "Goddammit!" I cried. "Of all the stupid, asinine—"

"Dad!" Helen put a hand on mine. "Harry and I have something to tell you."

"What?" I asked, glaring at the thinking man and his Peterson, who sat smiling smugly in his armchair. Helen turned off the television. "Tell them, Harry."

"Well, to coin a phrase," Harry said, smiling, "you may have lost an argument, but you gained—"

"Lost an argument?" I shouted. "What do you mean? That so-called expert—"

"Dad!" Helen slapped my hand. "Harry, go on."

"As I was saying: you may have lost an argument, but you gained a son." He closed his eyes in humble appreciation of his own pun. "Helen and I have decided to get married."

"Harry! How wonderful!" Sylvia jumped to her feet, embraced them both, crying, "Wonderful! Wonderful!" Helen hugged me and whispered in my ear, "Don't say high time too . . ."

I rose arthritically, pumped his hand, and said, "Wizard prang."

"Oh, for God's sake, Marty!" Sylvia cried. "He's your *son!*"

"So he is . . ." I pumped his hand some more. There was a silence. "This calls for a Fuzzy Navel," I said, and headed for the icebox.

*

"Well?" Sylvia asked when we finally lay in bed. "What did I tell you?"

I was about to say, "High time too," but admitted, "You were right. When's the wedding?"

"They talk about next month."

"They had better, or there'll be an infant squalling in the back of the church."

"There's not going to be a church. The Church of England does not marry divorced partners, they just bless them. Or maybe they do now."

"Whatever," I said.

"You were very rough on him after all the trouble he took to get us that video."

I stretched under the blankets, flexed my muscles, and said, "Sorry about that."

"Well you might be! You may not agree with him in some respects—"

"I don't agree with him in any respects. After the apple blossom in October I've decided I'm not going to genuflect any longer in front of the altar of science. It's time the burden of proof was put on their shoulders, not ours."

"I told you that ages ago."

I ignored it; I wanted to make a speech. "All my life, whenever there was talk about the paranormal, I've clung like a drowning man to the axiom that nothing shall be accepted until it has been scientifically proven. When I heard that donkey in his white coat bray 'Coincidence!' without so much as looking at the evidence, I decided the time had come for those closed minds to prove their point, instead of demanding that we prove ours. They've taken everything away from us: religion, inspiration, intuition—"

"Don't get excited, love, not now. It's too late." She kissed me. "What's more, I told you all this as long ago as—"

"No, goddammit, I want to talk about it *now!* I went through a conversion today. Doesn't that interest you?"

"I'm delighted, but it's going to be a busy day tomorrow—"

"I don't give a damn! This is important, this is what the whole thing has been about, don't you understand?"

"I understand. I understood as far back as Danville."

With all this understanding, the steam was taken out of my conversion. I had seen, in a flash of revelation, how all my life I had been bullied into submission by the mullahs of science;

but I could not deliver a lecture lying down, at ten to midnight, while being kissed by a woman who had, after months of silent patience, been vindicated by an apple blossom in October.

"I think they'll be very happy together," she said dreamily.

"They had better," I muttered. Another opportunity for a great catharsis had passed me by. But something had changed: I believed, and the hell with unbelief.

CHAPTER ELEVEN

*

So I believed. Belief did not provide the answer to the central question: why? but I now was prepared to accept that what I had been following with my pendulum, all over the west of England, was a ghost.

It sounded crazy. Still, at odd moments during walks or while watching television, I was hit by the sensation of being Roman. During those brief flashes I experienced the world of the centurion with breathtaking reality, a world inaccessible to outsiders however knowledgeable, even the wing commander.

After our return to France I went through the typescript of my dowsing sessions again, without becoming any the wiser. No wonder; I knew them by heart. Then something happened.

Sylvia and I watched television every night and often dozed off for minutes at a time. One night we were watching an American movie called *Romeo and Juliet of the Convent,* in which a novice fell in love with a young priest. The novice looked like a baton twirler and the priest like a quarterback; the whole story was ludicrous. Sylvia gazed at the set with the reverent expression she reserved for religious movies and dozed off. I scowled as I watched the baton twirler say good-bye to her mother, a tearful farewell; then the whole thing crashed into darkness, a deeper, colder darkness than I had ever experienced, and I was standing on guard in helmet, breastplate and cloak, gripping the hilt of my sword. I could feel the shape of the round, hard hilt in my hand and heard a voice say, "My sword is my friend." I was back in the world of a fourth-century centurion, a murderous world of violence, brutality, hacking into living flesh, killing, a world devoid of light and love. Yet, to find myself back in that world was like returning home; this was my body, my sword, I felt no need for light in the darkness, all I needed was my sword. Then a whining female voice cried, "Sister! Don't *do* that, honey! We aren't allowed out after prayers." I opened my eyes. There was the baton twirler, the priest with his neck wider than his head.

"For Christ's sake!" I bellowed.

Sylvia woke with a start. "Huh? What's that?"

"Nothing," I said. "A dream."

"Oh . . ." She dozed off again.

I slumped in my chair, feeling as if I had been involved in a pub brawl and flung out by the bouncer. I shook my head, opened and shut my eyes; everything was functioning. I was back in a body that was creaky, feeble and old, instead of strong and young as the other had been. I knew now what the word *butcher* had stood for: "My sword is my friend." I had been a stone-hearted killer, brutal instrument of Rome in the darkness of the prehistoric world.

When the movie was over Sylvia woke and we made the usual bedtime conversation: cat, dog, canary, windows. The next morning at breakfast I tried to recapture the experience but found that all I could tell her was that my sword had been my friend.

"How fascinating," she said.

"You already gave me sugar," I warned.

"Sorry. Shall I pour you a new cup?"

"No, don't bother, I like it sweet."

The canary greeted the day with its little dentist's drill. The poodle stood by my chair wagging its rump, ears cocked, ready for walkies.

"Cold, old, long dead Roman soldiers, with their iron breastplates in this climate . . ."

A dream, in which I had dwelt for a while.

*

But the brutal centurion whose grip I had felt tighten on the hilt of his sword would not withdraw into the background, the way he had done before. This time he stayed with me, sword arm swinging, scabbard slapping, throughout the day.

Was I going insane? Was I possessed, haunted, or simply too imaginative for my own good? He was there as I got out of bed; when I stood shaving he stared at me over my shoulder in the mirror: bright eyes in deep sockets glinting under the visor of a helmet with a red cockscomb. He was there when I set out for my daily walk with the dog. He stood beside me in the wind at the top of the hill, gazed with me at the distant blue sea. He was there in my dreams: a dark shadow, the glint of a helmet, moonlight in the forest. He was not a ghost, not a ghoul accompanying me. He was me, part of my soul, God knew, my soul itself.

After a few days I had to tell Sylvia. I did so at an inopportune moment, while I was holding up with both hands a skein of wool she was rolling into a ball.

"I'm being bothered by my centurion," I said casually.

"Well, punch another hole in it," she said, whisking wool. "I did notice you've put on weight lately."

"What the devil are you talking about? A hole in whom?"

"Your whatchamacallit—belt. Isn't that what you said?"

"*Centurion,* woman! *Ceinture* is French!"

"Oh," she said. "Your hands a little lower, please, then you won't have to wave about so much. Bother you when?"

"Oh, forget it. Finish your damn ball."

Of course she persisted, and I told her. I had thought it would worry her the way it worried me, but she took it in her stride. The centurion in the bathroom was as acceptable to her as an aspidistra called Beulah or an apple blossom in October. I saw myself in a previous incarnation in the mirror while shaving? No ghost, large or small, could cause her heart to miss a beat; she was at peace with life in all its dimensions.

"Maybe I have some unfinished business," I said. "Maybe I should go back to Neuss and find out what this means."

"When you last tried Neuss, your pendulum packed up."

"Maybe I should go and try again."

"My dear man," she said peaceably, whisking wool, "you're too old to go on whizzing about the way you used to do. I don't think you'll find the answer in constant motion. I think you are mentally tired. Why don't you forget about the whole thing for a while? Go and play golf, sing in the choir, take up your morning exercises with the others again and forget about Rome for a while. In three weeks' time we have to go to Topsham for the wedding; if you still feel you want to go to Neuss, take the car and stop there on your way to Amsterdam. Take me to the plane, I'll wait for you at Tim and Ella's and we'll leave for the wedding together, the lot of us in two cars. How does that sound?"

It sounded terrible, but it was one of those tribal trials one has to live through. "Good idea," I said. "Let's do that."

And so it happened that in the darkest days of November I found myself once more—shivering, nose dripping, ears bitten by the wind—facing the dull expanse of the river Rhine sliding past massively. The barges were powdered with snow.

I brought out my pendulum and tried to get a reaction out of it in the vicious wind.

"Will I get to know the truth?"

Yes.

"Here?"

No.

I couldn't think of any further questions, not with the cold wind blowing in my ear and my nose dripping.

I moved into the same *pension,* but this time the room on the street was occupied by a honeymoon couple. The jolly lady who owned the place offered me the adjoining room, but I was not keen to probe previous incarnations with a couple of newlyweds squealing next door. It seemed that all she had left was a single room overlooking the backyard, very comfortable, but I might not be able to open the window because of the wind. The puppy, now a dog, leaned against my leg, slamming its tail against my coat. I invited it in Dutch to bugger off.

Maybe it was the surroundings, maybe the whole thing had turned into a wild goose chase. When I tried to lower myself into my prenatal past behind a window overlooking other people's windows, nothing happened. The pendulum responded with a brisk humorless yes when I came up with the question, "Should I do my dowsing somewhere else?"

"Back on the river's bank?"

No.

"Where the fortress was?"

No.

Then one of those Frisbee questions came winging out of nowhere. "Do I need help?"

Yes.

"Where do I find it?"

To that, no reply. No wonder; the pendulum could not be expected to bark the answer.

"Help from a book?"

No.

"In the museum? By going to the museum?"

The pendulum went into a diagonal swing. At least I was getting warm.

"Help from someone there?"

The pendulum rotated.

"Someone connected with the museum? An expert, a professional historian? What's her name—*Frau Doktor* Blankert?"

Yes, said the pendulum forcefully.

I wasn't charmed by the idea. The woman was a scientist; to try and involve her in dowsing seemed doomed from the start. But she had seen me dowse during our first visit, in the middle of the street; after that she had suggested I contact her if I wanted more information. Well, it was worth a try. I asked the pendulum, "Do you really want me to contact Dr. Blankert?"

The pendulum said yes.

I went downstairs, telephoned the museum, was given her number, and dialed again. A woman's voice answered *"Ja?"* Not encouraging; I resisted the cowardly temptation to say, "Sorry, wrong number."

"Frau Doktor," I said in my best German, "you may not remember me, my name is Harinxma. I was here more than a year ago, together with my wife. You were kind enough then to give us some information on Fortress Novaesium in 367 A.D. I was the elderly Dutchman with the pendulum."

"I remember," she said in a surprisingly pleasant tone. "How did you fare? Did you find your officer?"

"Oh, yes. I was given a substantial amount of information on his experiences during the Theodosian campaign of '68. But I ran up against a wall after his return to Neuss."

"Who gave you the information?"

"I'm sorry to say my pendulum did."

There was a silence. I thought she had put down the receiver in scientific disgust. Then she said, "How interesting. I'd like to hear more about that."

"You would?" I asked, astounded.

"I'm not close-minded, you know."

"Ah, yes. No, of course not! Well—er—that's nice to hear."

"The formula for ignorance is contempt prior to examination."

"Quite," I said in a small voice.

"So, let's meet and discuss the matter, maybe I can be of some assistance. I could be in the *Kultstätte* at three o'clock this afternoon. Would that suit you?"

"How very kind, thank you. I'll be there."

"Very well, I'll see you then." This time she did put down the receiver.

It seemed an odd place for a rendezvous, but at three o'clock sharp I turned up at the door of the concrete pillbox Sylvia and I had visited a year ago. I did not relish the prospect of a meeting in a cellar with fluorescent lighting but, after the icy wind outside, it turned out to be almost welcoming.

Dr. Blankert greeted me in riding boots, short fur coat and red pixie hat, suitably garbed for a reindeer hunt. "There you are," she said.

"How very kind of you, *Frau Doktor.*"

"I thought this was a good place for us to meet. Your pendulum reacts to locations, I presume. This cellar is the least disturbed link with the period you're interested in. Nothing much has happened here since the last bullock had its throat slit."

"I see," I said.

"Tell me about your findings, if you think that would be helpful."

"Yes, of course . . ."

We sat down on a wooden bench and I proceeded to tell her about my quest for the praepositus who had commanded this fort and returned after the British campaign, only to vanish into thin air. I told her about the man's adoptive father, a centurion who despite his age had accompanied the praepositus during the campaign and returned with him to Novaesium, only to disappear like his son. I did not tell her that the old man might not have been physically present; a guardian angel seemed to be one wrinkle too many for her scientific forbearance.

"Well," she said, fumbling in the pocket of her fur jacket, "after you telephoned I searched my files. I did not find anything specific, the *Notitia Dignitatum* does not mention the names of commanding officers of that period. There was a *doctorandus* called Heinkel who came up with some unsubstantiated information in 1924, but I don't know how reliable he is. Are you familiar with his name?"

"Not him, personally," I said. Heinkel bombers had been the bane of the convoys to Murmansk: black swarms of them, dropping bombs in slow, tumbling clusters on the ships below.

"He came up with a list of names of army commanders in the second half of the fourth century, but I don't know where he got them from, he never published his sources. Here is his list, for whatever it's worth." She handed me a piece of paper.

"Very kind of you," I said uncertainly.

"Well?" she asked. "How about checking it out with your pendulum? Isn't that what it's for?"

I gazed at her, perplexed; then I obediently produced it, put down the piece of paper between us on the bench and asked, "Is the name of my praepositus on this list?"

The pendulum circled.

"How interesting," she said.

Her ready acceptance confused me. "I'm surprised you believe in this."

She gave me a stern look. "Professor Emerson, founding vice-president of the Canadian Archaeological Association, gave the keynote lecture during the 1973 conference. In it he announced that after many experiments he accepted dowsing and psychometry as legitimate aids to archaeology. If he had been a less important figure he would have been laughed off the stage, but his opinion carried enough weight to induce some archaeologists to give it a try. I was one of them."

"You mean, you've seen other examples of this?"

"If you think you're alone, *Herr* Harinxma, you are naive indeed. I can give you the titles of a number of books which may restore your self-confidence."

"I would appreciate that."

"Very well," she said, "let's get on with it."

There were fifteen names on the piece of paper. I went down the list, speaking them slowly for the pendulum to react.

"P. Saturus Erasinus
Albanus—(?)
C. Pomponius Secundus
P. Sisenna Rutilianus
T. Mannius Honoratus
P. Aelius Secundus
T. Caius Malarius . . ."

The pendulum started to circle forcefully.
Startled, I repeated, "T. Caius Malarius?"
Again the response was yes.
"So, you have your man," she said briskly. "What happens now?"
I looked up and found her staring at me, blue-eyed, fired by the spirit of the chase.
"I don't know," I confessed. "I didn't expect this. Well, suppose that was my praepositus, where did he go from here?"
"Perhaps he didn't. Have you considered that he may have been killed? They were at war with the Franci, you know."
I asked the pendulum, "Was he killed?"
The answer was yes.
"In battle?"
No.
"Illness?"
No. The pendulum started to lose momentum.
"Old age?"
No reaction.
"I'm afraid my pendulum has packed up again," I said. "It has done that to me before, here in Neuss."
"In this instance you may need a stronger stimulus," she said. "Perhaps you should hold an object in your hand, something of the period, something small, while you work your pendulum."
"Psychometry, you mean? I have never tried that before."
"The museum," she continued masterfully, "has a small collection of votive objects excavated from graves of the period, military graves. Now that your pendulum has selected the name of—who was it again?"

"T. Caius Malarius . . ."

"Dowsing the collection of votive objects in the museum may give you access to more information. Should your pendulum react positively to one of them you might try dowsing over it, or just hold it in your hand, close your eyes, empty your mind, and vocalize whatever comes to you in the way of impressions or information. I have witnessed it before; on several occasions the method produced valuable information which was later confirmed by research. It needs someone with the necessary gift, of course; you seem to have it. Shall we try?"

"I—er—could you arrange that?"

"Of course," she said curtly. "I suggest you and I meet tonight in the museum at closing time. We will view the collection in private, for your pendulum to make its choice undisturbed. If it does, I'll take out the object and leave it for you to dowse over for the length of time needed. How does that sound?"

"Well—"

"Very well, six-thirty in the hall of the museum. I'll be waiting for you. Good day."

With that she strode out of the *Kultstätte,* leaving me standing in the dark as she switched off the light.

I managed to scramble past the pit in the semidarkness, then I heard her say *"Verzeihung!"* and the light came on again.

*

After an early frugal supper, I met her in the lobby of the museum. The staff was in the process of locking up; the way they greeted her on their way out indicated that she was a big fish in this modest pond. She had exchanged her pixie hat for something funereal with a veil rolled up on the brim, ready to be lowered for either an interment or beekeeping. It made her look more intimidating still than in the *Kultstätte.*

The last lady to leave the premises handed her almost surreptitiously something small, which she pocketed. The front doors closed, she went to bolt them, said, *"Komm!"* and led the way down an echoing passage to a door at the end. She opened it, switched on lights; at her command I entered a small exhibition room lined with glass cases. She turned on the lights inside one of them; it contained three shelves of small stone objects, all of the Roman period, lined up in single file. Oil lamps, small vases, votive animals rather like the little dogs of Lydney; the rest were small human figures, crudely shaped, some nude, some squatting, others draped in cloaks or wearing hats not unlike the one the *Frau Doktor* was wearing.

"All these," she said beside me, "were found in graves within the confines of the fortress. As you see they are strictly pagan; the latest of them must date from the period you are researching. Under the Emperor Theodosius, Christianity became the official religion of the army and the burying of house-gods, lamps, or other symbols with the dead was discontinued. After that, all we find is crosses. I suggest you have a good look at these, check them with your pendulum, and make a selection. There may be one among them that has some meaning for you. Give it a try."

"Well . . ."

"Oh—excuse me! I'll open it up." She took from her pocket the object the last lady had slipped her, the key to the glass doors of the display case. She slid them open and said, "There you go."

I took out my pendulum and asked, "Could you tell me if any of these objects provides a connection with T. Caius Malarius, or his father?" I set the chrome teardrop swinging and moved it slowly down the rows.

Oil lamp? No. Another little oil lamp? No. A squatting female? No. A hatted female? No . . .

So it went, down the top row and the next; then suddenly something happened. Just before the pendulum started to circle I felt a presence behind me. I was now familiar with the sensation; it was my old friend the centurion. The pendulum started to spin over one of the small objects in the third row.

It was the figure of a male warrior, crudely made, worn by time. The features of the face had been obliterated, one arm was missing, the comb of the helmet broken. Nothing distinguished it from its neighbors: just a soldier in helmet, cloak and sword. He wore his sword on the left, which meant the little figure was made after the end of the third century when the shift from right to left had taken place. It seemed to excite my pendulum, which had been businesslike in its rejection of the others.

"I think this one," I said.

She joined me and looked at it. "I'll tell you what we'll do: you take it out of the case yourself and put it on the table. I'll pull up a chair for you. Then take it in your hand or try dowsing first, whatever you prefer."

"Thank you very much."

"Don't mention it. It's not often that the collection is of some practical use. Here's a chair. I'll be in the room next door. If you need me, call." Before opening the door she turned around and added, "Do not try to censor your intuition, *Herr* Harinxma. That's for *Dummköpfe.*" The way she stood there, in the shadows, wearing that hat, she looked like Erasmus in Holbein's painting. She swept out and closed the door; I was alone with the squatting, grinning, sleeping, hopping, headless and armless statuettes from sixteen-hundred-year-old graves.

I took the little soldier to the table; it was the first time I actually touched something that went back to late Roman times. I put the figure on the table cautiously and sat down. I took out my tape recorder and switched it on. Picking up my pendulum, I looked at the little soldier with the broken arm and the damaged helmet. What an ungainly little piece! It must have been so from the start, shaped by unskilled hands. What had its function been? A companion for the soul of the man in whose grave it had been found? A little housegod, an idol he had worshipped? All I had to do was ask.

"Was this a housegod?"

Yes, said the pendulum.

"It looks pretty crude. Who did it belong to? A military man?"

Yes.

I hesitated. The next question was an obvious one, but I felt a strange reluctance to make a discovery that might confirm my own experience, tell me it was real. It was as if my whole quest suddenly hung in the balance; but there was the centurion again, standing behind me.

"Tell me, honestly: does this object have any connection with either the colonel or his father?"

Yes.

"The last thing I know was that Caius Malarius, if that was he, returned to base here in Neuss accompanied by his father, either in person or as his guardian spirit. Which of the two? Was the old father still in the body?"

No.

"So, after his death he did indeed accompany his son as his guardian spirit?"

Yes.

"They arrived here together. Then something happened that made the father's spirit turn around and leave."

Yes.

"Was it because his son was safely home now and could do without a guardian spirit?"

No.

"Can you tell me the reason why?"

No. A faint no.

I became aware that my pendulum was hanging limply from my hand again, with that peculiar feeling I recognized. It had packed up on me once more.

I stared at the little soldier. He was standing, feet apart, his left hand resting on the hilt of his sword; the broken arm must have been raised in salute. I felt like stopping the whole thing right now. I wished Sylvia were here. I spoke to the tape recorder as if it were she.

"Love, I have in front of me the little figure of a soldier, found in a military grave of the fourth century. It is five inches high, badly damaged by time. It's made of soft sandstone, the face is totally obliterated. He's wearing breastplate and parade helmet, the crest of which is broken; he must have been at least a centurion. I've been dowsing over him and had some interesting feedback, but now, again, my pendulum has packed it in. For a moment there, I felt like doing the same thing, but now I'm here I might as well push this as far as I can. Dr. Blankert told me, surprisingly, that in Canada psychometry and dowsing are accepted as legitimate aids to archaeology; it was her idea to have me hold an object of the period in my hand and see if that, maybe, will stimulate the pendulum. So now I'm going to see if I can get any response from this little guy. I am now picking him—Jesus!"

The tape recorder purred in the silence.

"I don't know how long that took. It was like the dream I had in Glastonbury, of the building of the wall. As I picked him up I was given the whole story, the man's entire life in one fell swoop, just as if I was handed a ball of wool like the one you had, with the baby's jumpsuit inside it. I have to unravel it for it to be of any use. I don't really know how to go about that, but we'll see."

I picked up my pendulum again, which I had dropped, and set it swinging over the little soldier in my hand.

"I am now dowsing over the figure. I'm not going to bother with questions, I want to try to unwind the ball of wool by extemporizing, starting at the beginning. Hopefully, the pendulum will tell me if I go off the track. Here goes."

I tried to empty my mind of all thoughts, a blank surface for my intuition to write on. I began to speak the words as they came into my head: "You were a sinister man, friend. I cannot believe you were me once. Were you? God, yes, the pendulum starts spinning of its own accord. What I get is that you were a brute. A powerful, ruthless man, not an idealist by any means, a servant of Rome, a killing machine . . ."

No.

"The pendulum says no. All right, let's say killing was the main aspect of your world. Impossible now to identify with that world. Dark, primitive, full of superstition, violence, screams. Man-to-man combat. Plunging swords, spilling guts, blood. Screams, screams. No saving grace, no ideal, no concept of mission . . ."

No.

"The pendulum says no. Why? What's wrong? Ah, there *was* a sense of mission. But what a brutish, dark, horrendous life! No light anywhere. No hope, no tenderness, nothing. You didn't even know what tenderness was . . ."

Yes!

"Ah! The pendulum circles strongly. There *was* tenderness. To do with a boy. A little boy in a tree. A frightened child's voice, calling. Something draws me toward that voice. Bees! They sting, I slap them, curse, but walk on, furious bees buzzing all around me. There he is, in the tree: a terrified little boy in a short shirt, knees drawn up, eyes wide with terror, shivering. Tears, tears. I reach up to lift him out of the tree. The moment I do so he jumps into my arms and throws his around my neck. We stand for a few moments among the angry bees. Long moments. Then I carry him through the swarm to where my men are waiting. I am aware of their curiosity, I say, 'Well, seems we got ourselves a mascot.' They laugh and shuffle their feet, not quite sure how to take this. Neither am I. Here comes the medicus. 'Centurion, you have been stung. Let me put some vinegar on those stings.' I say, 'Look after him first, they must have made a meal of him.' But the little boy won't let go of me when I try to hand him to the medicus; he hangs on tightly, his arms around my neck, his wet face against mine. 'He doesn't want to let go, so let me carry him for the moment. No, I don't need any vinegar. *Form!*' The ranks form with relief; this is the reassurance they have been waiting for. *'March!'* My optio asks, 'Are we leaving the rest of the village be?' I hear myself say, as if I'm drawing away, 'Enough . . . Let them bury their own . . .' "

Overcome by a wave of tiredness, I switched off the tape recorder and leaned back, eyes closed. It felt like half waking from a dream, part of me still dreaming, but I had to come up for air, a glimpse of the room, the fluorescent lights, the display case with the figures, the table, the little centurion in my hand. I closed my hand around it; the dream sucked me back with such force that I barely remembered to switch the tape recorder on again.

"Just now, for a few moments, it seemed like a dream: the whole thing about the centurion saving the little boy. Now it speeds up, like a film running faster. I see the boy trying on a little tunic. Having his hair combed. Being carried on my shoulder as we march, on the shoulder of my optio, of other soldiers, they vie for the privilege of carrying the boy. It is like carrying a candle flame, the small face with the large frightened eyes, the small hands holding onto sleeve or shoulder. At night the torches splutter and smoke in a tent. The watchword is given. The steps of the guard draw away into silence. The teaching of poetry begins. Poems are beauty, hope. The little boy stands before me with earnest eyes, sleepy but alert, eager to please.

'Repeat after me,' I say, 'slowly, clearly. Open your mouth, don't swallow the words. Say: *Ibant obscuri, sola sub nocte, per umbram.* Each word clearly! Slowly!' The high timorous voice repeats: 'They walked obscured by darkness, in the lonely night, through the shadows . . .' 'Good! *Perque domos Ditis vacuas, et inania regna.* Go ahead!' 'Through the vacant homes of Pluto, and the empty kingdoms . . .' 'Very good. *Quale per incertam lunam sub luce maligna*—Let me hear it.' 'Just as under the dim light of a wavering moon—' *'Est iter in silvis, ubis caelum condidit umbra Iuppiter.'* 'Is a journey in the woods, when Jupiter has hidden the sky in shadows . . .' "

I was startled by a buzzing noise, nagging, persistent. It was the recorder; the tape was finished. More in the dream than in the white light of the room, I took the tape out, turned it over, and switched the machine on again.

"I see the boy grown up now, a youth. A soldier in his father's century. More than a soldier, his father's optio. It starts out light, and happy, and proud—now it darkens. Sinister, crude: war. The young man marches by his father's side, fights at his side. I see battles. Battles upon battles. Violence, blood, screams. Smoking villages, mass graves. Dead cattle, horror, pain. Then, suddenly, death."

Yes.

"The pendulum says yes. At a moment nobody has foreseen, a searing pain in my side—'Gods! What happened? Where? What?' The youth's arms are around me, his face is looking down on me. Those eyes, I see them through water. I want to say something . . . something . . . He bends over me and kisses me. I die.

"But I'm still there! Nothing has happened, I'm there! I'm not dead! I'm not myself, not in my body, but I'm standing beside him, he's there, his arms around the body, sobbing, holding it, kissing its face. Soldiers turn away, form a ring around him of swords and shields, a circle of privacy in which he sobs, *'Pater . . . ! Pater . . . '* But I am still there! I am standing right here, *here!*

"He does not hear me. I shake him by the shoulder, he does not feel me. I cannot understand it—how can he not see me? 'I am here! Here, me, alive, exactly as I was, here: helmet, breastplate, cloak, sword, I'm here! All of me!' But he does not hear me, nor see me. He rises, orders the soldiers to lift the body. They carry it away. I see a funeral, at night. Torches, smoke, a bugler. He stands by the grave, his face expression-less with grief. I go to him, put my arm around him, say, 'I'm here, I am with you, please, see me! Hear me, please!' He does not see, he does not hear, he does not feel me. His face is like marble, his eyes are downcast. Then he stands to attention, the bucinator blows the farewell. But it is *not* a farewell! 'I am here, you ass! I'm here, right beside you! What do you mean, *Ultimum Vale?* Here I am, here! Listen! *Look!*' But not a sign, not a flicker. How is it possible? I am dead, yet I am not dead. I am there, and not there. I was buried, and watched them bury me.

"Do I realize I am dead? Does it matter? I am there, I follow him, I stay with him, always, everywhere, day, night, day, night—I am there, by his side, behind him, overhead, watching him, trying to talk to him; then he does something that breaks my heart. He goes to a quarry, alone, and picks a piece of soft stone. That night in his tent, he tries to carve it with his dirk. He can't, the dirk slips, he cuts himself. He asks the carpenter to chisel me for him. I watch, I see the little figure come to life. It does not look like me, it does not look like anybody, it's just the crude little effigy of a centurion with helmet, breastplate, cloak and sword, standing with one hand on its hilt and the other raised in salute. When it is done he puts it on a stool, kneels in front of it and prays . . ."

I pressed the little statue against my chest. It contained it all, all of it: battles, conquests, expeditions, postings, the cam-paign in pursuit of the Amazon and her tribe. In a tumble of images, emotions, sounds, a new feeling is born: impatience. Disapproval. Anger. He is stupid, weak, woolly-headed. I argue with him, shout at him, put myself in front of him to forestall idiot gestures of weakness, like stopping a cohort of cavalry chasing some children, letting some idiot thespian distract his guards at night, walking straight into an ambush, ordering his men to carry an old dog on a stretcher through enemy country; what in the name of the gods is happening to him? What pos-sesses him? He was such a promising boy, I trained him so carefully, shaped him in my own image, loved him, and look at him now! Look! The river. Huts on stilts, barbarians lined up underneath, watching. There he goes, the fool: in parade uniform, crested helmet, leather harness, scarlet cloak, by boat. Talks to a young man who meets him on the river's bank, a barbarian. The enemy. They walk away together. Walking with the enemy, unprotected! In the name of the gods: *you are Rome!* Then, there he goes, back across the river, by boat. Without his helmet? There it is! Barbarians are kicking it around, shrieking, tossing it to one another, fouling it . . . I can stand no more. He is no son of mine! I turn away and flee. Flee into one of those huts; a young man, a woman, making love. I no longer want any part of him, I want to be free, I want to be dead. Release me, gods! Rid me of this shame! My need is so desperate that the gods take mercy on me. I suddenly grow very small. I am almost gone, then I am expelled, with tremendous force, into a warm red darkness.

I slowly sink into the warm red darkness, and know no more.

*

Frau Doktor Blankert found me asleep when she opened the door, having started to worry about the old man in there alone, at the mercy of his visions.

"*Herr* Harinxma, are you all right?"

I woke up and saw her standing in the doorway, half in the shadows. Erasmus in drag.

"Yes," I said, "I'm all right."

I looked at the little statue in my hand. As I did so, I had a sense of incompleteness. Was there more?

"Did you find out anything worthwhile?"

She was looming over me with massive bosom; her eyes were concerned. "Yes," I said, "the whole thing. Almost, not quite."

"Would you like to tell me about it?"

"Maybe it would be best if I played back to you what I was given. I don't remember much of it, it was a strange experience. Very exhausting."

"It would be," she said. "All experimenters in psychometry agree that it is totally exhausting."

"Listen." I spun back the tape, turned it over, and switched on the machine.

I don't know who of us was the more surprised when I heard my voice trying to put into words what was given to me. It started haltingly, with obvious resistance on my part; but that did not last. I was embarrassed by what followed: cries, tears, moans, grunts. It became so theatrical that I was about to switch off the recorder, but she stopped me.

"No, no! Don't! This is very valuable! Please don't stop."

She had a right to know, embarrassing as it might be. I must confess that gradually the rambling story of the Roman officer and the little boy began to move me; toward the end it even acquired conviction. Why did I have that feeling of something missing? I switched off the recorder.

"Well," I said, "there it is. I must apologize."

"It is the fashion in certain circles, *Herr* Harinxma, to sneer at an experience like yours, but you must not. You may disavow any conclusions you arrive at, but not the experience itself."

I was in no condition to argue with her, I was washed out.

"Was this all?" she asked.

"There's nothing else on the tape, but I have the feeling there's more."

"To do with the punishment the officer received, perhaps?"

"You think he was punished? What for?"

"The army must have reacted forcefully to a commanding officer paying homage to the enemy. Losing his helmet in the process, enabling the barbarians to humiliate the army. They would not have left that unpunished."

"What form would the punishment have taken?"

"It's certain to have been severe. He may have been ordered to fall on his sword. Ask your pendulum."

I set my pendulum swinging over the little figure. "Was he ordered to fall on his sword?"

The pendulum went into a spin.

"See?" she said with satisfaction. Then, after a silence, "Is this all? Are you through with him?" She pointed at the little soldier.

"I think so."

She picked him up, put him back in his place, closed the sliding glass doors, and locked them. "All right," she said. "Let's go."

She went to the door. I put on my hat, collected my tape recorder and my pendulum, and tagged along behind as she marched down hallways with ringing steps, like a security guard. Outside, in the cold night, she locked the front door and held out her hand.

"It has been very interesting, *Herr* Harinxma. Would you mind sending me a transcript of that tape?"

"With pleasure, *Frau Doktor.* May I see you home?"

Thank God she said, "No, thank you. My car is just around the corner, and you look washed out. Go to bed, *Herr* Harinxma. You did well tonight. Good night."

"Good night, *Frau Doktor.*"

I watched her march down the street, bag swinging, until she vanished round the corner. Then I dragged myself to the guest house; the lady owner had given me the key.

On the river, in the misty darkness, a tugboat sounded a long-drawn-out, mournful blare. *Ultimum Vale.*

*

In the hallway the dog was waiting for me, sentimental, lonely, wagging his too-long tail. The lady had left a pot of tea under a cozy with a note: GUTE NACHT! I'LL BRING IN YOUR EARLY MORN-ING TEA AT THE USUAL HOUR UNLESS OTHERWISE INSTRUCTED. SCHLAFE WOHL!

I took the tray upstairs, followed by the dog. The room in front was quiet; the newlyweds must still be celebrating. The dog insisted on coming with me into the room; I tried closing the door on him, but he sniffed at the crack with such powerful suction that I let him in. He collapsed on the rug with a thud, keeled over, stretched his legs and tail, and heaved a sigh of bliss.

I started the bedtime dismantling process of the elderly. When I finally—sightless, toothless, and stone deaf—lay me down to sleep, I found myself wide awake. I turned on the light again, got up, rummaged in my suitcase, swallowed a sleeping pill, and took *The Faber Book of Modern Verse* with me to bed. The dog, who had been following me with his eyes, let his head thump on the floor again, satisfied that he was not about to be banished.

I opened the book at the marker and found myself reading T. S. Eliot's "East Coker." In Canada, after the day of the salmon, I had been captivated by its poetry, the mystical obscurity that carried an odd ring of truth.

"Old men ought to be explorers . . ."

I gazed at the ceiling, the book on my chest. After T. Gaius Mellarius had fallen on his sword, he must have expected the spirit of his father to welcome him. But the old centurion, who had loved him even in death, had not been there. He had been asleep, a seed in warm red darkness, to be born again, a new male infant squalling, another life of violence and blood, love and hate, passions, ecstasies, flashes of recognition. How many lives would it have taken for him to finally reach the point where—?

A curtain swept aside. The lifeboat, wallowing in a sea black with oil. The diving plane, my covering the body of the German boy with my own. All my life I had wondered why at that moment I had had a feeling of rightness, of total understanding, of having touched upon the meaning of life itself. I had relived that moment many times and never found the answer; was this it? Had the angry guardian angel, by turning away in disgust from his son for humiliating the army, condemned himself to a cycle of reincarnations until at last he reached the point where he could accept his son's deed and make one more step up the ladder to humanity? Had I reached that point when I sheltered the enemy the mate had tried to kill? Was that the elation I had felt as I lay waiting for death: the triumph of reaching, after sixteen hundred years, the same level of humaneness my son achieved by his act of folly?

The dog lifted its head, listening. I heard steps on the landing. A voice asked softly, *"Caesar? Wo bist du? Caesar?"*

I swung my legs out of bed, stepped over the animal to reach the wash basin, put my teeth back in, went to the door, and opened it at a crack.

"*Ah, guten abend, Herr Harinxma!* I haven't woken you, have I? I'm looking for my dog."

"He is with me, *gnädige Frau.* I think he'd like to stay here tonight."

"Ah, but that's not necessary! He has a basket, a blanket—"

"Both he and I would like it. All right?"

It was dark on the landing, but I could see she was baffled. I could hear it in her voice as she said, "If you wish. *Gute Nacht, Herr Harinxma.*"

I tried to exchange a look of conspiracy with Caesar but his head banged on the floor, he heaved a sigh, his tail gave one thud, and he was asleep again. I defanged myself, climbed back into bed, picked up my book, and opened it at the marker.

> As we grow older
> The world becomes stranger, the pattern more complicated
> Of dead and living. Not the intense moment
> Isolated, with no before and after,
> But a lifetime burning in every moment
> And not the lifetime of one man only
> But of old stones that cannot be deciphered . . .

C H A P T E R   T W E L V E

When, in early March, Sylvia and I arrived in Topsham for the birth of the baby, due any day, we found the house in an uproar. Helen and the children were in a frenzy which left Harry bewildered: never before had he experienced a mother and her children fired by a Cause.

They told us that this was the time of the toad migration: whole hordes of the beasts crossed the roads after dark and were massacred by passing cars. Some people were poisoning them because they did not want them in their gardens; others telephoned pet shops to ask if they sold toads, the gardener's best friends. Helen and a committee of tender fanatics had organized a group of volunteers who guarded the toad crossings with warning lights, buckets and shovels. She herself, heavy with child, was manning a Toad Hotline on the telephone, to put those who loved toads in touch with those who hated them and arrange a transfer.

"Dad!" she said, triumphant and fragile like Sally's blossom, "I *know* you want to be one of the guards! There's a Roman road a few miles north of here where there's a toad crossing. Would you guard it for three hours tonight? You'll be given a lantern, a bucket and a shovel to save the poor beasties from being slaughtered."

The night was dark and humid, warm for early March. I took over the watch from my predecessor, a young man with braids. He handed me a lantern, a shovel, a little bucket and said, "When you see a car coming, step into the road and swing the lantern. When the car stops, tell the driver you'll walk him through the zone, and shovel the toads into the bucket as you walk. You'll see them quite clearly in his headlights."

So here I stood, at the end of my great adventure: in the dark English countryside, surrounded by the soft applause of toads hopping across the road in the hundreds. Gazing at the stars, I suddenly felt the weight of the helmet on my head again, the

285

cloak around my shoulders, the sword at my side. I became aware of the majesty invested in me, the glory that was Rome; to be a centurion on duty meant to be entrusted with her immense, all-conquering power. At last, I felt not just who but what I had been.

Gazing at the stars, I wondered if my son would still be waiting for me across the river, hoping for a reunion, forgiveness, understanding, the return of the prodigal father. If so, he must be delighted that, after God knew how many reincarnations, the old man had finally gone soft himself.

A flash of light distracted me: the headlights of an approaching car. I stepped into the road and swung the lantern the way a Roman guard must have done two thousand years ago.

The car stopped, the driver wound down his window and asked, "What's going on?"

Instead of replying, *"Cave latronem barbaricum,"* I said, "You're approaching a toad crossing. If it's all right with you, I'll walk you through it at a slow pace while I shovel them out of the way. It's only a matter of a few yards."

The driver said, with the respect for the insane the British share with the red Indians, "Oh—right you are . . ."

In the beams of the headlights, throwing a gigantic shadow into infinity, I walked ahead in helmet, breastplate, sword and cloak, shoveling toads into my bucket, thinking *Sic transit gloria mundi.*

Old men ought to be explorers.

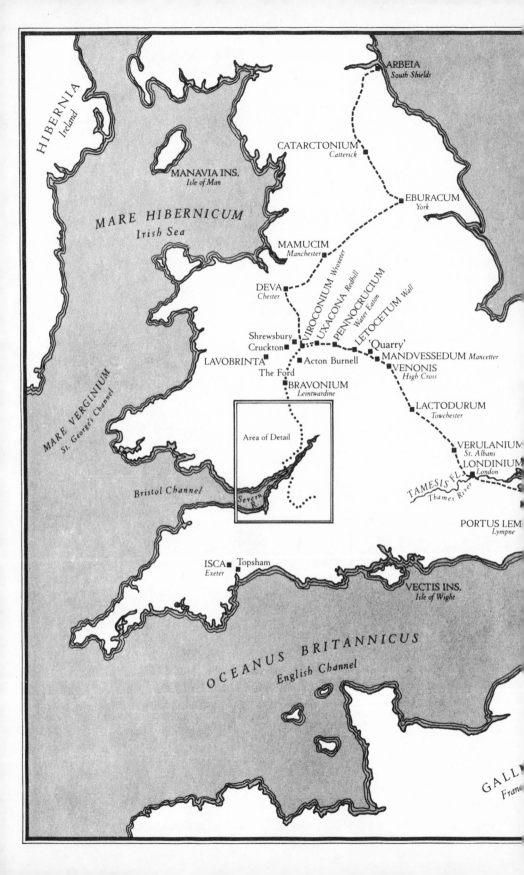

ROMAN BRITAIN
368 A.D.

MILES

0 10 20   40   60   80   100   120

- - - - - Route of the army under Field Marshal Theodosius
· · · · · Route of the detachment under Colonel Mellarius

MARE GERMANICUM
North Sea

FLEVO LACUS

RHENUS FLUVIUM

Rhein River

NOVAESIUM ■
Neuss

GALLICUM
Dover

BONONIA ■
Boulogne

GERMANIA
Germany

RHENUS FL.

Map inset:

MAGNIS *Kenchester*

MILES

0   10   20   30

ARICONIUM ■
Weston under Penyard

GLUUM ■
Gloucester

SILVA SILURUM
Forest of Dean

NEMETOBALA ■
Lydney Park

VENTA SILURUM *Caerwent* ■

PESCADORES ■

ABONA *Sea Mills* ■

COLLIS MORTIS ■
Cadbury Hill

AQUAE SULIS ■
Bath

SABRINA FLUVIUM
Severn River

ISCALIS ■
Charterhouse

Camerton ■

HORTUS ■

TRIBUNICIUS ■
Iford

Lullington

Glastonbury ■